Show Me the Way

fight for me

A.L. JACKSON

A.L. Jackson
www.aljacksonauthor.com
Cover Design by RBA Designs
Photo by **Predrag Popovski**
Editing by AW Editing
Formatting by Mesquite Business Services

The characters and events in this book are fictitious. Names, characters,
places, and plots are a product of the author's imagination. Any
similarity to real persons, living or dead, is coincidental and not
intended by the author.

Print ISBN: 978-1-946420-04-6
eBook ISBN: 978-1-946420-03-9

More From A.L. Jackson

Bleeding Stars
A Stone in the Sea
Drowning to Breathe
Where Lightning Strikes
Wait
Stay
Stand

The Regret Series
Lost to You
Take This Regret
If Forever Comes

The Closer to You Series
Come to Me Quietly
Come to Me Softly
Come to Me Recklessly

Stand-Alone Novels
Pulled
When We Collide

Coming Soon from A.L. Jackson
More sexy, heartwarming romance in the new Fight for Me series

Follow Me Back – Early 2018
Lead Me Home – Spring 2018

Hollywood Chronicles
A collaboration with USA Today Bestselling Author, Rebecca
Shea

prologue

Alabama – Eleven Years Ago

Rain pelted from the angry sky, and heavy gusts of wind howled through the trees, which thrashed in the blackened night. In agony, I ran, sure my heart had to be beating as loud as the thunder that cracked through the heavens above.

I gasped when my foot slipped on the slick, muddy ground, and I stumbled forward, landing hard on my hands and knees. I cried out, unsure where the pain was coming from—my mind or my heart or my torn flesh.

Why would they do this to me?

I wept toward the ground, stricken with grief, with betrayal, before I heaved myself back onto my feet, trying to find traction. I staggered toward the house, which was lit up like warmth and light just off the road. Clutching the wooden railing, I propelled myself forward and then flung open the door and fumbled inside.

I whimpered in misery when I paused to look around the room. Loss hit me as hard as the storm that raged outside.

Why would they do this to me? How could they be so cruel?

It took about all I had, but I forced myself to move, knowing

I couldn't stay. I had to leave. I had to get away. Choking back sobs, I clung to the banister and hauled myself upstairs and to my room. Knees caked in mud and blood, I dropped to the floor and dug out the suitcase from beneath the bed. I staggered to my feet and headed for the closet.

Tears clouding my vision, I tore clothes from their hangers and shoved them into the suitcase I'd tossed onto the bed, my movements becoming more frantic with each piece I ripped from its spot. The urge to escape only intensified when I moved to the dresser. Distraught, I ripped the drawers from their rails and tipped them upside down, dumping what would fit into the suitcase.

The whole time, I struggled to restrain the sobs bound in my throat. To keep them quiet. To pretend it hadn't happened. To pretend I didn't have to do *this*.

With shaking fingers, I tugged at the zipper.

"Rynna, what's going on?" The sleepy voice filled with concern hit me from behind.

Torment lashed like the crack of a whip. My eyes slammed closed, and the words trembled from my mouth. "I'm so sorry, Gramma, but I've got to go."

The floor creaked with my grandmother's footsteps. She sucked in a breath when she rounded me, shocked by my battered appearance. "Oh my lord, what happened to you?" Her voice quivered. "Who hurt you? Tell me, Rynna. Who hurt you? I won't stand for it."

Vigorously, I shook my head, finding the lie. "No one. I just . . . I can't stay in this stupid town for a second more. I'm going to find Mama."

I hated it. The way the mention of my mother contorted my gramma's face in agony.

"What are you sayin'?"

"I'm saying, I'm leaving."

A weathered hand reached out to grip my forearm. "But graduation is just next month. You've got to do your speech. Walk across the stage in your cap and gown. Never seen anyone so excited about somethin' in all my life. Now you're just gonna up and leave? If you can't trust me, then you can't trust anyone. Tell me what happened tonight. You left here just as happy as a bug in a rug, and now you aren't doing anything but runnin' scared."

Tears streaking down my dirty cheeks, I forced myself to look at the woman who meant everything to me. "You're the only person I can trust, Gramma. That's why I've got to go. Let's leave it at that."

Anguish creased my grandmother's aged face. "Rynna, I won't let you just walk out like this."

She reached out and brushed a tear from under my eye. Softly, she tilted her head to the side, that same tender smile she had watched me with at least a million times hinting at the corner of her mouth. "Don't you ever forget, *if you aren't laughing, you're crying*. Now, which would you rather be doin'?" She paused, and I couldn't bring myself to answer. "Wipe those tears, and let's figure something out. Just like we always do."

Sadness swelled like its own being in the tiny room. Loss. Regret. Like an echo of every breath of encouragement my grandmother had ever whispered in my ear. "I can't stay here, Gramma. Please don't ask me to."

With the plea, my grandmother winced. Quickly, I dipped down to place a lingering kiss to her cheek, breathing in the ever-present scent of vanilla and sugar, committing it to memory.

I tugged my suitcase from the bed and started for the door.

Gramma reached for me, fingertips brushing my arm, begging, "Rynna, don't go. Please, don't leave me like this. There's nothing that's so bad that I won't understand. That we can't fix."

I didn't slow. Didn't answer.

I ran.

And I didn't look back.

one

Rynna

Leafy shadows flashed across the windshield, interspersed by the blinding strikes of sunlight that burned from the sky as my car passed beneath the heavy canopy of trees where I traveled the winding two-lane road.

The closer I got, the harder my heart beat within the confines of my chest and the shallower my breaths grew. Cinching down on the steering wheel, I peered out at the worn sign on the side of the road.

Welcome to Gingham Lakes, Alabama, where the grass is actually greener and the people are sweeter.

Anxiety clawed through my nerves.

It'd been eleven years and what felt like a lifetime since I left the small city that could hardly be considered more than a town. I'd promised myself I'd never come back.

And there I was.

I just wished I had broken that promise sooner. Not when it already felt as if it were too late.

"Earth to Ryn."

I jumped when the voice boomed through the car speakers. I

was losing it. It seemed fitting. I'd been questioning my sanity ever since I'd signed on that dotted line.

"Are you there, or have I already lost you to the Deep South?" Macy asked. I could almost see her raising a dark brow at me.

"You really are dead set on breaking my fragile heart, aren't you?" she continued. "You left me here to fend for myself. Not a soul to go out with on Friday nights and no one to make me miracle hangover breakfasts on Saturday mornings. That's a travesty. Don't you dare shred it more by pretending I don't even exist. BFFs, remember? Don't forget it, or I'll show up with the sole purpose of kicking your skinny ass. Oh, and to get back those black jeans I know you stole. I've been looking for them for the last two days. I bet you have them hidden at the bottom of one of those boxes."

"I wouldn't dare," I barely managed to tease through the thickness that lined my throat. "Where those jeans probably are is under your bed in that disaster of a room. You're worse than a twelve-year-old boy."

I was doing my best to inject a smile into my voice, but there was no disguising the hitch in my words as I rounded the bend and the town came into view in the valley below.

Gingham Lakes.

God, it was beautiful.

The valley was a vast expanse of green. Flush with abundant, flourishing trees. The massive lake tucked at the base of the opposite mountain range appeared little more than a glittering mirage in the far distance, the river so serene and calm where it ran through the middle of the city and segmented it into the two mirrored-halves.

This place was filled with the best and the worst of memories.

With the best of people and the worst of enemies.

There was only one person who ever could have persuaded me to return.

Leave it to Gramma to do it in the sneakiest of ways.

"Tell me you aren't having second thoughts now that you've driven all the way across the country? By yourself, mind you, since you refused to let me come. You act as if I'd be a nuisance instead of a help. I can lift like . . . a thousand pounds. Pretty sure I'm the best mover in all the history of movers."

"Says the girl who thought it was a good idea to let a box filled with glasses tumble down a flight of stairs rather than carrying it down."

Macy chuckled. "Don't be jealous. Just add creative to my list of skills."

"Creator of disasters, you mean."

She feigned a gasp. "I take full offense to that. I even made pizza and didn't catch the apartment on fire."

"No," I ribbed.

"Truth."

Quiet laughter rolled free as that heaviness throbbed. "I'm going to miss you, Mace."

Right then, San Francisco felt a million miles away. An alternate galaxy. Really, it was just a different reality than the one I was headed toward.

Somber silence filled the space, and Macy lowered her voice. "Are you sure this is really what you want? You left the city you love and an incredible apartment downtown. You resigned from a job any one of us would kill to have. Hell, you were halfway up the corporate ladder. Worst, you left *me*."

My heart clutched while I fought with the urge to turn around and head back to San Francisco. I wasn't that broken girl who'd run from Gingham Lakes eleven years ago. I was strong, and I sure as hell wasn't a quitter. "You know why I have to do this."

"I do, and I know how hard it has to be for you."

Grief pressed at my spirit. The perfect complement to the determination that lined me like steel. "It is, but I need to do this for her almost as much as I need to do it for myself."

"This city won't be the same without you, Ryn." In all the years I'd lived with Macy, I'd only seen her cry once. I knew she was trying to hold it back. Still, the soft sounds seeped through the line, touching me from across the miles.

I pressed a hand over my mouth and tried to keep the jumble of emotions that quivered and shook inside me at bay. "You'll come visit."

She released a soggy laugh. "Hell no. There are, like, alligators down there. One look at all my lush, curvy deliciousness, and they'll be inviting their friends over for a feast."

I wanted to tell her I was plenty *lush* when I'd run from this place. The alligators were the least of her worries. I bit it back, keeping all those old insecurities buried where they belonged.

"You don't think I'm worth the risk?" I asked instead.

She sniffled, and I swore I could see her grin. "Yeah, Ryn, you're totally worth it."

I cleared the emotion from my throat, wondering how I was going to do this when the road took another sharp curve and the speed limit dropped. "I better go. I'm getting into town."

"Good luck, babe. You've got this. I want you to know I'm proud of you, even though I'm going to miss the hell out of you."

"Thank you, Mace," I told her.

I was definitely going to need it.

two

Rex

My eyes went round, and I came to an abrupt stop in her doorway.

"Are you sure that's what you want to wear?" Sweeping a hand through the long pieces of my damp hair, I gave it my all to keep the panic out of my voice.

Honestly wasn't sure if I wanted to bust out laughing or drop to my knees and cry.

Such was my life.

We were already ten minutes late, and there she was on her bedroom floor, wearing a hot pink tutu over a bathing suit.

"Uh-huh. We gots to look so pretty for dance. Annie said all the best dancers wear leg warmies, and her mama bought her all the pretty colors. Like a rainbow," she rambled as she tugged on the black high-top Converse she'd talked me into at the mall last weekend.

Right over a pair of old tube socks she must have found in one of my drawers.

The hideous kind with the two blue stripes at the top that should have been burned years ago.

"So I gots these." She rocked her heels on the ground as she sat back and admired her handiwork.

She suddenly looked over at me with that smile that melted a crater right through the stone that was my heart. Her single tooth missing on the bottom row and her attempt at a bun that looked like she'd just walked out of a windstorm were about the damned cutest things I'd ever seen.

"I'm the best dancer, right, Daddy?"

"You're the best, prettiest dancer in the whole world, Sweet Pea Frankie Leigh."

I just was betting that uptight bitch, Ms. Jezlyn, wouldn't agree. I'd already gotten one bullshit letter about "appropriate ballet attire," which was strictly a black leotard with *salmon* tights (what the fuck?) without any runs in them. Apparently, Frankie wasn't living up to those standards.

That was what I got for picking Frankie up late from Mom's and then coming home and telling her to get ready while I grabbed a quick shower. I'd been at the work site the entire day, had been drenched in sweat and grease and grime, and was trying to put my best foot forward.

Problem was, I was having a hard time figuring out how my best could ever be enough.

I pressed my palms together in some kind of twisted prayer. Then I dropped them and blew out a resigned breath. "All right, then. We need to get out of here before I get you in any more trouble."

Frankie hopped onto her feet and threw her hands in the air. "Ready!"

I chuckled beneath my breath, grabbed her dance bag from the pink bench right inside her room, slung it over my shoulder, and extended my hand. "Let's go, Tiny Dancer."

Giggling, she pranced over to me and let me take her miniature hand, so small and vulnerable in the massiveness of mine.

Following me out the door and down the hall, she skipped along at my side.

Innocently.

Joy lit up my insides. I swore all her sweetness held the power to blow back the thousand pounds of blackened bitterness built up around my heart. Like when this kid was around, it weighed nothing at all.

The day she was born, I'd sworn an oath to myself. I'd never allow her to be torn up by this vicious, cruel world. Refused to let it tarnish her the way it had me.

My entire life was protecting her from it.

I snagged my keys from the entryway table when I heard the sound of a door slamming somewhere outside. Frowning, I leaned back so I could get a glimpse out the window and across the street.

An older white Jeep Grand Cherokee was parked in the driveway of Mrs. Dayne's old house.

Guessed they had to finally be putting the place up for sale. Mrs. Dayne had lived there forever, long before we'd moved in across the street from her five years ago, but the place had been sitting empty for the last two months.

A fist tightened in my gut, grief I really shouldn't be allowing myself to feel. She'd just been so good to Frankie that it'd been impossible to keep her shut out. Hell, she'd barged right into our lives like she was supposed to be there, constantly bringing over dinner and those delicious pies from the diner-style restaurant she'd owned downtown.

Frankie rushed out the front door and onto the deck at the side of our house.

It was the way all the homes were situated in our neighborhood. The houses were elevated from the ground with the main doors located on the side rather than out front. Each had an open deck that extended out from the side of the house, giving a view of the street and neighbors' houses. The porch steps angled that direction and led down to the driveways that came up to the far side of the houses.

It probably would have looked strange if not for the big, leafy trees that outlined each of the lots.

They made everything feel cozy and secluded.

Just the way I liked it.

It was one of the main reasons I'd insisted on this place when I'd been looking for a fixer-upper to renovate.

Frankie released my hand and pointed across the street. "Hey, Daddy, look it. Someone's at Mrs. Dayne's house!"

Stepping out behind her, I closed the door before I attempted to tame a few pieces of hair that'd fallen from her bun and were now flying around her face in the hot breeze. I dropped a kiss to her forehead. "It's probably a realtor putting it up for sale, Frankie Leigh. Remember how we talked about that?"

With her head tipped back, she peered at me with confused but hopeful brown eyes. "She wents to heaven?"

"Yeah," I murmured softly.

The screen door at the side of Mrs. Dayne's house slammed, and I jerked my head up to find a woman crossing the small deck and jogging down the steps back toward the SUV.

Goddamn.

Maybe I was just caught off guard.

But just looking at her knocked the air from my lungs.

Let's just say I was unprepared for a woman that looked like that. Guess I'd been expecting someone dressed up. Older. And there was this girl, disheveled in a sexy, careless way. A massive mound of hair that was wilder than Frankie's was piled haphazardly on her head, wavy pieces falling out all around her. She wore a super tight white tank that disappeared beneath high-waisted jeans.

Those jeans should have made her look frumpy and unkempt, but instead, the whole package sent a skitter of lust racing through my veins and prodding at my dick.

She was the kind of woman who could make a grown man stumble on his feet.

Stunning.

Gorgeous.

Too sexy for her own damned good.

Or maybe mine.

I could call it a complication of abstaining for too long, but I was sure no woman had ever incited a reaction like this in me with just a glance.

She raked her arm over her sweat-drenched forehead as she headed straight for the cargo area of the SUV, which was crammed full of moving boxes. I wouldn't mind all that much if she were hauling stuff out of that house directly across the street, but it sure as shit looked like she was moving her things in.

Tell me this girl is not moving in next door.

I clenched my jaw and grabbed Frankie's hand, needing to get the hell out of there.

"Come on, Frankie Leigh, we've got to get a move on. You're already late."

But Frankie was already moving, bouncing down the stairs and along the walkway, waving her free hand in the air. The kid just adding to the stark sunshine that burned bright in the waning day. "Hi, hi, hi! I'm Frankie. Whose are you?" she shouted across the street.

Startled, the women's gaze darted our direction, and the determination in her step slowed when she caught sight of my daughter.

An amused smile grew on the rosy bud of her mouth when her gaze swept the ridiculous outfit Frankie was wearing. She seemed to hesitate for a second, eyes glancing around her like she was looking for something before she changed direction, heading our way. "Hey there, Frankie, I'm Corinne Dayne, but everyone calls me Rynna."

Rynna Dayne.

What the ever-lovin' hell?

Could damn near feel the bewildered excitement roll through my daughter while I stood there cursing the world that just fucking loved to curse me. "Your name's C'Rinne, too? That's Mrs. Dayne's name. She worked at the restaurant called Pepper's Pies and cooked all the pies, and my daddy ate them all, all, all the way gone. Sometimes we wents to go eat there, but mostly we ate at my house right here, but now she wents to heaven."

A bolt of sadness streaked through her expression, and fuck, if it didn't hit me, too. Still, the smile she wore only grew. "She made the best pies in the whole world, didn't she?"

Frankie's excitement only amplified. "Yes! You know Mrs.

Dayne, too?"

She started to cross the narrow street, all chestnut hair and java eyes and a body that was built for temptation.

Awareness ridged my spine like a steely stake of lightning, and I stepped back, my jaw tightening at the same time I protectively took hold of my daughter's hand.

That was all that women were.

Temptation.

Trouble.

Forbidden fucking fruit.

Because all they did was condemn you in the end. So, I stayed away. Kept my distance. If I didn't step into the fire, then I wouldn't get burned.

Kneeling in front of my daughter, she stuck out her hand. "It's so nice to meet you, Frankie. It sounds like you were a good friend of my grandma's."

So yeah.

I'd already figured it out.

It didn't stop me from flinching.

Frankie had stars in her eyes as she enthusiastically shook her hand. She might as well have been meeting Taylor Swift. "She told me I was her favorite, favorite friend, and sometimes she even let me go to her house and make some pies."

"Is that so?" Rynna said with a tease in her voice.

"Yep."

Rynna leaned in, and I caught a whiff of something sweet. "Want to know a secret?" she whispered.

Frankie bounced on her toes. "Oh, yes, yes please, I love secrets. I won't tell nobody."

Soft laughter floated out from Rynna's mouth, a mouth that was getting harder and harder not to stare at, all plush and pink and perfectly pouty. "Well, this is a secret I hope you tell everyone, because guess what? I have some of the recipes for those pies."

Frankie's mouth dropped open, and damn it if my stomach didn't fucking growl.

"You gonna make me some?" she gushed.

"Definitely," Rynna said, taking that moment to look at me with the threat of a smile on her pretty face, the angle of her jaw sharp while everything else about her was soft.

That sweet scent was back. Billowing in the breeze. This warmth surrounding her. Hot cherry pie.

My teeth ground together, and the smile slid from her face when she saw what must have been my irritated expression, and I swore I heard the slight catch of her breath when she met my glare. Could see a slight quiver in her throat when she straightened and took a step back.

Still, she stood her ground.

There was something unwavering about her. Like she had something to prove. To herself or me, I wasn't sure.

"Hi. I'm Rynna Dayne. Was named after my grandmother," she managed, though the words were rough as she stuck her hand out toward me like she'd done to my daughter.

I just stood there staring at it like it held the venom of a viper bite. Finally, I lifted my chin at her and gathered all the pleasantness I could summon. It wasn't much. "Rex Gunner. I'm sorry about your grandmother. And we're late . . . so if you could excuse us."

I gave Frankie a gentle tug of her hand. "Come on, Frankie Leigh. We've got to get you to dance."

Frankie trotted along at my side, looking back over her shoulder with what I knew had to be one of those adorable grins.

"What a jerk," I heard Rynna mumble behind my back when I turned and led my daughter to the passenger side of my truck.

Bitterness burned.

Yeah.

I was a jerk.

An asshole.

Whatever.

Better to burn bridges before anyone had a chance to cross them.

Shaking it off, I hoisted Frankie into the high cabin, making her squeal and pretend like she was flying. I strapped her in her car seat and jogged around to the front. I hopped into the driver's seat, wondering if it were possible for the roar of the engine to cover the hurt that sagged Rynna's shoulders as I took to the street.

Wondering why I felt like a complete piece of shit when I caught a glimpse of her in the rearview mirror. She just stood there in the twilight like she was caught in a dream.

Watching us go with disappointment on her face.

Befriending a sweet old lady was one thing.

Allowing a girl like Rynna Dayne into our lives—a girl that made my body react the way it did? Now that was pure stupidity.

three

Rynna

Why am I doing this?

Anxiety convulsed through my nerves as I waited for my computer to fire up. The truth was, I couldn't not know. I connected to my hotspot and logged on to Facebook. It felt like forever while I sat there, the screen churning, lighting up like a window to the past. I could almost feel it stretching its fingers out to touch me. To tease me with the control it'd held over me for so long.

For too long.

Fingers trembling, I managed to type the name into the search bar. A task I'd attempted at least twenty times before I'd set out on my journey back home. I had never found the courage to press enter.

Today, I did.

She was the third listing. A grainy picture. Almost indistinguishable. But I knew it was her.

Missouri.

She lived in Missouri.

I slammed the lid down.

That was all I needed to know.

As long as she wasn't here? I could totally manage staying in this town.

"Tell me you're miserable without me."

Laughing quietly, I flitted around the kitchen on my bare feet. My cell was pressed between my ear and shoulder as I slowly unpacked the few things I'd brought. I hadn't needed much since my grandmother had left everything she owned to me.

"Completely miserable," I told Macy, letting the tease wind into my tone as I hiked onto my toes to set my favorite Christmas mug on a high cupboard shelf.

"Huh. That's weird. I haven't even noticed you're gone," she deadpanned.

"Says the girl who's called me like ten times today," I ribbed.

She giggled. "Okay, okay, I might have kind of noticed." Her voice dropped to a whisper. "It's just that I think the apartment is haunted."

"The apartment is haunted? And this happened sometime in the last three days?" Skepticism rolled from my tongue.

"You know how these things work. Ghost girl has been stalking me, and the second she felt your absence, she slid right in to take your place."

"You know you're absolutely ridiculous, right?"

"Which is precisely why you love me."

Affection pulsed. How was I ever going to live without seeing her every day?

"Honestly, though, Ryn. How are you doing there by yourself? It must be weird to be alone in that old house. God knows it's weird around here without you."

I paused to look around at my dated surroundings—the floors linoleum, the cupboards hailing from the early eighties, the beige Formica countertops dingy and faded to a dreary yellow. The décor was mainly all the trinkets my grandmother had collected over the years, and the same two floral placemats I remembered from my childhood were still on the small round table.

It was as if she'd been waiting for me to return all this time. Next to nothing had changed since I left eleven years ago.

The house needed a full renovation. That was when, or if, I ever had the money to do it. Honestly, I still didn't know how I was going to manage to hold on to all these frayed threads, if I could come back here and take over where my grandmother had left off. If I had what it would take to breathe life back into everything she had built.

But when I inhaled? I could almost smell the lingering memory of sugar browning in the oven. When I focused hard enough, I could almost taste the tart cherries and sweet crust melting on my tongue. When I listened intently enough, I could almost hear the steadfast belief in her voice echoing from the walls.

"Honestly?"

"Yeah," she said.

An old warmth surrounded me, all mixed up with the reservations and fear that had kept me away for so many years. "It feels like home. Like I never left. Like I could walk through the door and my grandmother would be standing right in this kitchen, pulling a pot pie from the oven for dinner." I swallowed over the lump that grew heavy at the base of my throat, the loss that echoed back her presence. "I just wish I would have come back earlier. Before it was too late."

My heart clutched at the memory of the phone call I'd received two months before. A social worker had been on the other end of the line telling me my grandmother had suffered a massive heart attack while behind the wheel of her car, that though the responders had tried, there had been nothing they could do. She was pronounced dead upon arrival at the hospital.

Macy's voice dipped in sincerity. "You can't blame yourself, Ryn. Even if she didn't know the reason you left, I think she at least understood why."

"Then why does it feel like such a pathetic excuse now?"

"Maybe I was never lucky enough to meet your grandma in

person, but in all the time we lived together, I don't remember a day that passed without you talking to her. So maybe the circumstances sucked. But I promise you that she knew how much you loved her. And you want to know why it feels pathetic now? Because you've moved beyond it. Above it. You're not even close to being that timid, insecure girl who answered my ad for a roommate eleven years ago. You've grown, changed. Your grandma got it. That was one smart woman."

I exhaled slowly. "I know. I just . . . I wish I would have come back before it was too late."

Wished she had let me know she was in trouble. I wished we had more time.

But I guessed us Dayne women were stubborn that way.

"I'm betting your grandma didn't see it that way, which is the very reason you're back there now."

I gulped around the emotion, voice hushed. "Thanks, Mace. I needed to hear that."

She tsked softly. "Of course you did. This is why you have me."

From the other end of the line, I heard rustling, could feel her mood changing course as she settled back in the plush couch in the den. I could almost see the glass of red wine in her hand. "So, how is it being back in Gingham Lakes so far? Have you run into anyone you know?"

Her voice turned wry. "Tell me you found out bitch-face took a deep dive into the lake and never came back up for air. Or maybe she took a sharp curve driving a little too fast? Which would you prefer?"

A low chuckle rumbled free. "You're horrible, Mace."

"Psh. Don't tell me you haven't imagined it a thousand times."

"Okay, okay, maybe I imagined her demise a time or two."

Like every time I'd closed my eyes for two years after it happened. Wondering what it might have been like if I could have turned the tables on her and wishing all the same she could just take it back.

What had I ever done to warrant that level of cruelty? Could she possibly have known just how badly what she'd done had hurt?

Old memories twisted my stomach into knots. Traces of that evil, depraved laughter touched my ears, visions of her standing there like it'd meant nothing at all while she'd destroyed my entire world. It was as if crushing me had been nothing but entertainment.

"And no. I looked her up. She moved to Missouri."

"You looked her up?" Surprise coated Macy's tone.

"I just . . . had to."

Silence filled the space between us. "I get it," she finally said.

Bending down, I pulled my coffee pot from the box, puffing out a breath as I did. "To answer your question, no, I haven't seen anyone I know. My Gramma was right, the city has really grown since I left. It's not filled with the familiar faces like it used to be. I stopped by the grocery store this afternoon and didn't recognize a soul."

"Is that a good thing or a bad thing?"

I sighed. "I don't know . . . both, I guess. I used to love that I knew everyone. That I'd go into the restaurant and knew at least half the people there. It made it feel safe. But after everything? The rumors?" My lips pursed. "It's nice to be somewhere I love and have a clean slate. It feels like a second chance."

I just prayed it remained that way.

"Well, if there aren't any familiar faces, tell me there are at least some panty-melting ones you've run across. You know, some yummy to my tummy hotties hanging around, waiting to steal your heart? Knowing you're getting some will at least ease some of my worry for you."

A scoff scraped my throat. Leave it to Macy. "Oh, there's a hottie, all right, but he definitely isn't hanging around waiting to steal my heart."

It was that moment when I heard the low rumble of a powerful engine approaching in the distance.

Of course.

Gramma had always told me all you needed was to speak of the devil and he'd appear.

There'd been something about our encounter this morning that had left me unsettled. Something about that gorgeous stranger that had left me restless and curious.

Interest piqued.

The man was a paradox.

Hard and brittle and cold.

Yet so incredibly gentle with the little girl, who'd clung to his hand as if he were the center of her world.

There seemed to be nothing I could do but edge toward the window, stealing to the side to remain out of sight.

I pulled back the edge of the curtain and peeked out.

Headlights cut into the night, and my stupid heart kicked an erratic beat. That intrigue increased my pulse to a thunder. I was riddled with that same fierce attraction I'd felt when I'd looked up earlier today to find him towering over me, the way my stomach had twisted and the nervousness that had followed me back to Gingham Lakes took a new form.

The headlights grew brighter, illuminating the space between our houses before the monstrous truck slowed and turned into the driveway across the street.

"Oh, oh, oh, tell me all about it. Someone sounds pouty . . . and turned on."

"You know how my luck goes when it comes to men." The scales were always tipped to bad. "You shouldn't be surprised that my neighbor is like . . . gorgeous."

Macy squealed. "How gorgeous?"

I watched as Rex hopped out of his truck and went straight for the backseat.

All six feet three inches of mouthwatering deliciousness lit up by the moonlight.

"Like Greek God with a sledgehammer gorgeous."

I could hear her kicking her feet. "And how is this a bad thing?"

"I was pretty sure he would have preferred to drag me to the lake and drown me rather than tolerate my living across the street from them."

"Them?"

"I met his daughter, too. At least she was super excited to meet me."

I suppressed laughter as I thought of her rushing out of their house. The little girl had been a perfect kind of disaster in that hot pink tutu and those atrocious socks she had to have stolen from her dad.

She was a bluster of energy and innocence.

It was almost worry that entered Macy's playful tone. "Oh God, tell me you're not actually crushing on the married guy next door? That's just poor form, Ryn."

Through the milky, opalescent night, I watched as he pulled a sleeping Frankie from the backseat and shifted her so her head rested high up on his shoulder. He ran a hand over the back of her head and set a kiss to her temple.

The image was so at odds with the hostility he'd met me with earlier.

That intrigued attraction flared, my mouth dry as I watched him start up his walkway.

Maybe what struck me most was there was something sad about him, too. Something helpless and scared beneath all the harsh, hard dominance he wore so well. Something bitter and broken.

I found myself whispering when I came to the realization. "I'm thinking there's no wife."

"No wife . . . so . . . he's like . . . a single dad?"

"Maybe," I uttered so quietly as I peered through the night, drinking in the way his long legs took the steps, and then the way he angled through his front door with his sleeping little dancer girl. "I think so. I'm not sure."

Why did I want to know so desperately?

"Why are you whispering?" Macy whispered back.

I bit down on my bottom lip while guilty silence spun around the room.

Macy busted up laughing. "Oh my God, you are spying on him right now, aren't you?"

"Shut up," I told her, quick to let the curtain drop. I got straight back to work unpacking.

"Someone has a crush," she sing-songed.

"Stop it."

I was so not spying, and I so didn't have a crush.

I'd just met them, and the worst thing I could do was get mixed up with the angry guy across the street with his sweet, adorable little girl, who was a big fan of my grandmother. Apparently, she had really good taste.

But her dad? He obviously had some ginormous chip on his shoulder, and I had enough to worry about without giving thought to the flecks of sadness scored in the depths of his eyes.

Eyes the color of sage. Rimmed in the darkest gray.

No, I wasn't thinking about those soft, full lips barely hidden by the sexy scruff on his strong jaw. And I definitely hadn't noticed his big hands or the strength in his deeply tanned, muscled arms.

Nope.

Not at all.

A guy like that had heartache written all over him.

And I'd had enough of that to last me a lifetime.

The sound of a whisk clanging against metal echoed through the kitchen. With the bowl tucked under one arm, I cut butter into the flour in the other, giving myself over to the sense of deep peace that had taken me over.

The late night was like a warm blanket wrapped around the old house, holding me safe and secure, the vast silence a comfort as I slowly swayed in the kitchen.

I had the crumpled letter smoothed out on the counter beside me where I worked. Every so often, I would peek over at it, relishing in her presence. I had to have read it close to a million times since it'd slipped out with the file the attorney had given me two months ago. But I kept going back to it, wondering, why now?

Why hadn't she asked this of me before?

When you left, you told me I was the only one you could trust. Your broken heart had mine breaking that night. Isn't it funny how things come around? Because no matter how many years have passed, in the end, you are the only one I trust with this.

I know right now you're scared and questioning my intentions. But I'm asking you to trust me one last time. I made a life within those walls, gave it my whole heart. Maybe you never realized it, but all along, I was working so one day, I could give it to you. Now, it's yours. Give it life, Corinne Paisley. I'll be with you every step of the way.

My chest tightened as a wave of grief and love slammed into me.

I could feel the weight of her spirit dance around me. Soft, soft encouragement. The same as she'd always given me.

Belief. It was right there. Shining with all the questions that still remained.

"I am scared, Gramma. I'm not sure how I can do this without you. But I promise you that I'm going to try. I'm going to do whatever it takes to make you proud."

I jumped when the oven dinged, letting me know the temperature had reached three hundred and seventy-five degrees.

Maybe I really was letting this old house get to me.

I set the bowl aside and dug into the paper sack to find the almond extract.

Almond extract I was certain I'd purchased this afternoon at the store.

Almond extract that wasn't there.

With a frown, I sank back onto my heels. Frustration leaked into my veins.

Damn it.

My first pie, and I was already failing. It was one of those ingredients I could probably get away with not using, but it just wouldn't be the same. Looking around, my attention landed on the pantry.

"Let's see what you've got, Gramma," I mumbled, opening

the pantry door and rummaging through the few items that hadn't already been discarded.

"Aha." It was a cry of victory as I held the bottle of almond extract in the air.

Victory that was short-lived. It'd expired three years ago.

"Damn it," I muttered again. I tossed it into the garbage bin right before my eye caught on a white envelope tucked on a shelf at the side of the pantry wall. Like a forgotten partner to all the expired spices and extracts. A token of the past.

Apprehension swelled, anxious and uneasy, and I slowly moved forward.

It felt as if it were some kind of secret.

As if I were on some kind of forbidden mission.

Silly, I knew, but my fingers trembled when I reached in and tugged it free, the paper tacked to something sticky on the pantry wall.

That anxiousness thickened like molasses, my throat full and bobbing, my stomach twisted in a vice.

My name was written across the front, the familiar handwriting scratchy from an unsteady hand.

"Oh God." Grief came swooping back in, but I smiled through the tears that were suddenly clouding my eyes as I ripped into the letter.

There was so much comfort in knowing she felt confident that one day I would find what she'd left for me.

I tugged it out and quickly scanned the card.

All moments matter. We just rarely know how important they are until the chance to act on them has already passed.

My spirit flooded with love, and I clung tight to the reminder of this amazing woman who'd always viewed the world as if it were right on the cusp of something magical. The tough times nothing but a stepping-stone to propel us to where we were supposed to be.

I took a fumbling step back when I sensed the change outside my kitchen window. A light had flickered on across the street.

Drawn, I inched across the creaking floor, again keeping myself hidden as I crept toward the window. I pulled back the edge of the lacy drape and peered that direction, not sure if I felt guilty for doing it or if it was somehow my duty.

Because this time there was no question I was spying.

Unable to look away.

Somehow knowing I didn't want to.

The bulk of him took up the entirety of his kitchen window, his hair, which was a dark, golden blond and a little long on top, was in complete disarray and stuck up in all directions. As if he'd spent the night tossing in bed, waging a war I didn't understand. I couldn't make out his expression with the way he had his head dropped between his shoulders, his hands most likely propped on the counter to hold himself up. But that didn't mean I couldn't clearly see him fighting with whatever demons plagued him.

"Shit," I whispered, clutching the letter in my hand, waging my own war. The battles I'd once fought in this town had been lost. The memories of them stalled me with trepidation, the strength I'd found through the years away coming against them and instilling me with courage.

I glanced at the letter again.

And I chose to take a chance.

Before I could think better of it, I moved through the arch and out into the dated living room. I slipped on my sandals I'd left by the door.

Then I let myself out into the muggy, Alabama night, the air heady with wafts of honeysuckle and fresh-cut grass.

Moon, huge and high, cast the slumbering houses and trees in a silvery glow, and the steady trill of cicadas danced all around.

It felt like stepping straight back into my childhood. The memories of the nights I'd spent on the porch with my grandmother staring up at the stars seemed so close it felt as if I only had to reach out to go back to that time.

Inhaling the vestiges, I kept my footsteps as light as possible. Even still, they crunched against the gravel driveway, and I sucked in an emboldened breath when I stole through the night and across the street, silently making my way up his walkway.

Carefully, I climbed his steps, hand on the railing as if it offered moral support, and crossed his freshly stained deck. I stopped at his door, my heart the thunder that incited a storm within my chest.

What was I doing?

This was insane.

This guy hated me for no apparent reason at all.

Still, I found myself lifting my hand, my fist quietly knocking at his door.

I was shaking all over by the time the latch turned and the door flew open, and I was again met with the same unwarranted fury from earlier. Although this time it was harder.

All of it.

His scowl and his glare and every gloriously defined ridge of his body.

Oh. My. God.

There was nothing I could do to keep my eyes from dropping to explore the wide expanse of exposed flesh. His shirt was missing, and he was wearing nothing but boxer briefs.

I gulped. That foolish attraction drenched me through, wet and hot and sticky. Flaming free and leaving me weak in the knees.

My gaze latched on the tattoo that ran the entirety of his left upper arm. It was a landscape of a jagged cliff with a waterfall pouring over the side. The splashes rising up from the seething pool of water were bright, colorful feathers that floated and twisted as if blown by the breeze.

Sorrow and hope.

They were so clearly impressed into the depiction.

"What are you doing here?"

The severity in his voice cut through the night, impaling my stupor, jerking my attention up to his face.

Of course, it had to be equally as striking as the rest of him.

Powerful and dominant.

I shook as I took a fumbled step back.

Oh, wow, was this stupid. So damned stupid.

Still, I lifted my chin. "I was just . . ." I fumbled for an excuse to be standing at his door at one in the morning. "Wondering if you had any almond extract?"

His head cocked, and if it were possible, his eyes narrowed even more. "Do I look like I have almond extract?"

"Ummm . . ." I stammered.

Great.

I was a blubbering fool.

This man set me totally off balance. He was so different from the men I was used to back in San Francisco.

Rougher.

Unpolished and raw.

More dangerously beautiful than any man had the right to be.

Maybe it was because he reminded me a tiny bit of Aaron. The asshole back in high school who'd had a hand in the breaking of my heart.

But this was more.

Different.

Everything about Rex Gunner was unique.

Blinding in his darkness.

Warm in his coldness.

"I just—" I gestured back to my house across the street. "I was making my gramma's cherry pie and was missing almond extract when I saw a light on over here. I thought I would take a chance."

All moments matter. We just rarely know how important they are until the chance to act on them has already passed.

Was this one of those moments that mattered?

And why did I feel like I had to take this chance?

four

Rex

Lust sieged my body as I stared at her standing in the moonlight like some kind of vision.

Like some kind of wicked enchantress with the face of an angel.

Baking my fucking favorite pie, nonetheless.

Her scent was all around me. Cherries and sugar.

My mouth watered, and I clenched my fists in an effort to keep myself from reaching out and taking a taste for myself.

Maybe I was still back in bed and this was just a new element of the nightmares that haunted me night after night.

If this were a dream, I'd be inviting her in and sinking into that tight body. Fucking her hard and wild. Just the way I liked it. That would be right before she grew fangs and ripped me apart. Hell, with the way she was looking at me, it was clear she was already poised to tear me to shreds.

"Some chances aren't worth taking," I said, voice rough with warning. She needed to know she was crossing into territory where she wasn't welcome. Banging on my door in the middle of the night was completely off-limits. How could this girl possibly think this was okay?

I set my forearm high on the jamb, knowing every inch of me was bristling with the challenge.

All except for my dick. Apparently, that was the only part of me that didn't seem pissed off at the intrusion.

Her strong chin lifted in her own challenge. "No? Haven't you ever heard you never know if you don't try?"

"And how many doors have gotten slammed in your face because of that philosophy?"

"More than I could count. And why do I get the feeling you're about to add another to that number?"

A disbelieving chuckle rumbled in my chest. This girl was all kinds of grit and determination. "I'm easy to read, I guess."

A tiny snort huffed from her nose. "Hardly."

She angled her head, and those warm eyes turned almost pleading. "Listen, I'm going to be living right across the street . . ."

Just the thought of it left me antsy and agitated.

Her voice softened. "I don't know anyone around here anymore, and it'd be nice to have a friend. I thought maybe you and Frankie could use one, too."

Laughter ripped up my throat.

Cruel and low.

"Sorry, but I have all the friends I need, and I'd appreciate it if you stayed away from my daughter. She doesn't need anyone else making her promises they have no intention of keeping."

Before I could do something stupid, I slammed the door shut in her face. Exactly the way she'd been expecting me to do. I leaned my back against the wood, trying to catch my breath, to slow the raging in my spirit, that part of me that hated being such an asshole.

All the while trying to remind myself why it was necessary.

There was something about her that set me on edge. Left me feeling off-balance.

Self-control was not normally something I lacked, and fuck, it wasn't like she was out there offering herself up like a warm slice of pie.

But just looking at her had me itching for a taste.

I could feel her on the other side, her presence that swept the air unsettled and thick. Like I'd caused her physical pain with the rejection and she was projecting it right back to me.

Maybe she really was just trying to be nice.

Maybe she didn't have ulterior motives.

But that was a *chance* I just couldn't take.

Fear tumbled through his veins and clanged in the hollow of his chest. Frantic, he stumbled through the brushy undergrowth, the world buried by soaring trees. Branches lashed at the exposed skin of his arms and thorns latched onto the fabric of his shirt in an attempt to hold him back.

It propelled him harder.

Faster.

He screamed her name. "Sydney."

Sydney. Sydney. Sydney.

The howl of wind answered back.

Sydney.

I shot upright, chest heaving as I struggled to catch my breath. To orient myself to the movement that jostled me awake and pulled me from the dream.

"Daddy, Daddy, Daddy! Wakey, wakey, wakey. I made you breakfast."

Frankie was grinning at me as she jumped on my bed. Brown hair wild and free, just as wild and free as the way she looked at the world. At the way she loved. Wholly and without reservation.

I scrubbed both palms over my face, dropped them just as fast. It was not all that hard to return her grin.

Her expression alone was enough to chase away the exhaustion that constantly weighed me down. The few hours of sleep I managed were restless. Plagued with the curse that darkened my life.

I swallowed back the fear. The terror that one day it might steal her from me, too.

"You made me breakfast?" I asked, voice groggy, my touch tender as I brushed her too-long bangs back from her innocent face. "That's awful nice of you, thinking of your daddy first thing in the morning."

She giggled. "Of course I thinks about you, Daddy. And I made a whole big bowl, 'cause Grammy says you could eat a whole cow."

"Oh, she did, huh?"

She nodded emphatically, her eyes going wide when I hopped up and tossed her over my shoulder. Frankie roared with laughter, the kid dressed in shorts and a tee with that same damned hot pink tutu around her waist.

So fuckin' cute.

"That Grammy is going to be in big, big trouble when I see her today," I teased my daughter, who was bouncing on my shoulder as I started running with her down the hall.

She squealed, kicking her feet and holding on to me for dear life. "Oh, no, don't tell Grammy! It's our secret."

"I thought you said you were good at keeping secrets?"

Damn it.

The last thing I needed to do was bring up the conversation she'd had with Rynna yesterday. Just the mention of that woman had fantasies slamming me from all sides. Her face and her hair and that body.

Sweet, mouthwatering sugar.

I'd thought maybe the morning would have scraped the idea of her from my consciousness.

No such luck.

I shoved off the thoughts, refusing to give them voice. That was right when I came to an abrupt stop when I entered the kitchen I'd just finished remodeling.

Frankie scrambled upright, pushing those unruly locks from her face with both hands, a hopeful smile plastered on her face. "I mights have spilled a little milk, Daddy. Is that okay? I'm gonna clean it all gone, but I didn't want your cereal to get all gross and swoggy. Bleh."

Her nose scrunched, and her lips turned down as if she'd

tasted something sour.

I frowned when I saw a "little" milk was actually the entire gallon minus what she'd managed to pour into the cereal bowl. A pool of white swam between the small table set for two and the refrigerator against the far wall, the emptied plastic container floating in the middle of it.

Her shoulders went to her ears, her voice quieting. "Is you mad?"

Hugging her close, I pecked a kiss to her chubby cheek. "Of course, I'm not mad. We're just gonna have to get you to the gym with me so we can start building up these muscles." I lightly squeezed her tiny bicep. "How's that sound? You ready to start pumping some iron? Before you know it, you'll be as strong as The Hulk."

She giggled like it was the funniest thing she'd ever heard. "The Incwedible Hulk? You're crazy, Daddy. I'm gonna be Wonder Woman. Don't you know I'm a girl?"

She threw both her arms in the air before she started shimmying down my body, getting free of my hold, and heading straight for the drawer where we kept the dishtowels. She climbed up the step stool so she could reach it, that smile lighting up the whole room when she looked over at me. "Right, Daddy? Can I be the best dancer in the whole world and Wonder Woman?"

I crossed the kitchen to help her clean up the mess. "Yeah, Tiny Dancer, you can be whatever you want to be."

I'd make sure of it.

Because she was the single wonder of my life.

I'd do whatever it took to keep her that way.

five

Rynna

Sunlight poured in through the long row of dark tinted windows that overlooked the bustling street. It struck the murky space like a blazing orb of fire against the quiet darkness that held fast to the silenced space, the light still muted in the far reaches of the restaurant.

It left the space filled with a dim hue of warmth, the atmosphere an intricate dance of peace and regret and the remnants of my lingering fear.

Lovingly, I dragged my fingertips through the layer of dust that had gathered on the bar, exposing the shiny white counter hiding underneath.

Buried, but not forgotten.

Yearning pulsed through my being, my spirit full and my heart heavy, that lump at the base of my throat prominent as I slowly wandered through the old diner-style restaurant that for so long had been the center of my life.

How many days had I spent at this counter? A little girl coloring and painting who turned into a teenager studying for the SAT?

How many mornings had I been there before dawn, standing on the step stool so I could see over the counter back in the kitchen? I'd watch in awe as my grandmother would mix the ingredients, helping her pour them into the bowl, my arm straining as I'd followed her instructions and pressed the dough into pie crusts. The whole time I would quietly listen to her chatting about life, the woman so easily relating everything to the pies she made.

How much life had buzzed in the bustling diner, the families that had gathered in the booths and the old men who'd sat at the bar with their tall tales to tell?

That life had been silenced, but it wasn't gone. I could feel it. Bated, but simmering. Trembling all around where it was restrained, pressing and vying to be freed.

Waiting for someone to believe in it again.

For someone to breathe that life back into its walls.

And Gramma had somehow put her faith in me that I would be the one to do it.

Even after I'd run like a coward.

I just prayed I could live up to her belief.

I jumped when the old bell jingled above the door and someone called, "Knock, knock."

Heart leaping to my throat, I spun around. I did my best to beat down the jolt of fear that had taken hold. My eyes narrowed as I tried to make out the two figures in the doorway.

They stepped forward, coming into view in the dimmed light of the diner.

Two women.

Their faces unfamiliar, but both had to be around my age, maybe twenty-eight or thirty. One was dressed in something like I would have worn to the office back in San Francisco. A perfectly fitted pencil skirt, blouse, and heels, her black hair done up in an intricate twist. The other was more casually dressed in trendy jeans and a flowy tee, her hair cropped and messy.

Dusting off my hands on my jeans, I walked their direction. "Can I help you?"

"You must be Corrine Dayne's granddaughter."

I gave a slight nod.

"We heard you were coming into town," she said. "I hope we're not intruding, but we wanted to introduce ourselves. I'm Lillith Redd." The woman in heels stepped forward with a welcoming smile and pushed her hand out in front of her.

I rounded the corner and shook her hand. "It's nice to meet you, Lillith. I'm Rynna."

The other woman laughed. "Ah, forget that 'Lillith' nonsense." She hooked her thumb in her friend's direction. "This one right here goes by Lily Pad. Don't fall for that suit-wearing, straightlaced attorney vibe she's rockin'. She's actually kind of a wild child when you get to know her. And we finally get to meet *the* Rynna Dayne, not to be confused with Grandma Corinne. I pretty much feel like we're already best friends since your grandma never stopped talking about you. I'm Nikki Walters."

There was a kind, playful confidence about her, no hesitation when she reached out to take my hand.

Confidence.

Right then, I scrambled within myself to find it. To remember who I'd become in the years I'd been away. The strength and boldness I'd found. It was crazy how coming back to this town incited the instinct to cower and hide. "It's really nice to meet you, Nikki."

I glanced between the two of them. "So, you two knew my grandmother?"

It actually felt nice to find someone other than Frankie and her dad who remembered my grandmother. The fact I was there by myself and facing this alone was beginning to set in. That loneliness growing bigger with each second that passed.

It didn't help Rex Gunner had quite literally slammed a door in my face last night.

Standing on his porch like a fool as I'd offered myself up, only to have him so callously reject me, had stung. I wanted to hate him. To think him nothing but a jerk. But I couldn't.

Maybe it was the way my grandmother had raised me. To slow down and look deeper. Beyond the surface and the shallow to what was concealed underneath.

God knew I'd been judged enough as a child. I might as well have been on trial for my appearance alone, a thousand convictions made with each passing, sneering glance. And I had looked deeper at Rex. What I saw was pain and fear and a rickety defense lurking right under the hostility that seeped from his pores like poison. There was something so ferociously protective behind the shield of venom and animosity.

It filled me with the urge to break through it. To chip it away, piece by piece. To dig deeper until I'd discovered everything that was hiding underneath.

It didn't help that one look at him made my stomach shiver and shake.

I had no idea what it was about this guy, but every time I saw him, I was struck with an overpowering shock of attraction. The kind that spun my head and left my knees weak with the impulse to run my fingers over the hard planes of his body.

Which was crazy. I didn't know him. But I couldn't scrape the idea from my consciousness that I was supposed to.

Nikki's eyes widened as if my question had been absurd. "Of course we knew your grandma." With a moan, her eyes rolled back in her head as she tipped her face toward the ceiling. "She made the freaking best pies. Like, to die for."

Wistful laughter tumbled free. "Yeah, they kind of had that effect on people, didn't they? Now that woman could bake."

Her pot pies were almost as legendary as her sweet pies.

"Tell me you're actually reopening this place and you have all her secret recipes," Nikki pleaded as if my answer might save her life.

I glanced around the diner that had been shut down for the last two months, but with the poor shape it was in, you'd think it had been vacant for years. The entire place was covered in an inch of dust, the red pleather booths cracked, some torn. More concerning was the equipment in the kitchen that was old and in far worse shape.

Resolve set into my bones. "I'm going to try."

Lillith laughed a tinkling sound. "Oh, if you're anything like your grandma made you out to be, I think you'll fair just fine."

A sad smile emerged at just the edge of my mouth. "I think there's a chance my grandmother might have played me up to be something I'm not."

"Psh." Nikki waved a flippant hand. "As long as you have those recipes, you're golden."

"Well, following her recipes is the easy part. It's the two hundred thousand dollar loan I need to whip this place back into shape that I'm worried about," I returned, trying to make it a joke and not let the reality of it bring me down.

All the while, I wondered why these two set me so at ease that I felt comfortable sharing such personal details with them.

But I did.

Concern flitted across Lillith's face, her expression knowing. "I heard there was a tax lien?"

I sighed, but there was satisfaction behind it. "There was, but I was able to sell off some of my things back in California to pay the lien, as well as the back payments due on the house. That left me with the keys to both." A wry chuckle rumbled out. "And you know, about five dollars to my name." I wasn't quite that destitute, but it was close.

"Hey, a strong woman can work magic with five dollars," Nikki said, her grin wry.

"I just might need a little magic to come into play if I'm going to make this happen."

Sympathy lined Lillith's face. "I'm so sorry your return is under these circumstances. I hope you know your grandmother was a huge asset to this community and an even better friend. She is greatly missed. If there's anything we can do, don't hesitate to ask. I'm an attorney, and I'll do whatever I can to help you get this place reopened, whether you need me to file anything or need legal advice or even if you just need a friend to talk to."

Her words were carefully phrased, but there was a genuineness that seeped out with them.

"That's really nice of you. Thank you. I may need to take you up on that offer," I told her.

She smiled. "The entire town is really excited by the prospect of the diner reopening, especially with the hotel going in across the street. The whole intention of the Fairview Street Restoration Project is to mesh the old with the new. A cohesive fusion of the past and present, and I'd personally love to see this diner become a part of that."

Pride lifted in her expression when she looked over her shoulder and out the window at the construction taking place directly on the other side of the street.

Nikki almost rolled her eyes. She dropped her voice as if she were whispering conspiratorially, though not low enough that Lillith couldn't hear. "You'll have to excuse her. Her fiancé's company has the hotel going in, and this one right here is kind of pathetically in love."

Lillith swatted at her. "Shut it." She looked at me, grinning. "Nikki is the one who pretty much insisted I give him a chance, and now that we're together, she won't stop giving me crap about it. I think she might be jealous."

"Hey, don't act like you don't want to kiss my feet for bringing the two of you together. That was nothing but pure matchmaking skill. Think of all the orgasms I earned you."

"Nikki, what is wrong with you?" Lillith smacked her again.

Nikki set her hand over her heart. "I'm just a speaker of the truth. And yes, for the record, I am very, very jealous of all the orgasms. I mean, not that I want Broderick to be the one giving them to me. That would be kind of gross and wrong."

Nikki sent me a wink. "You know, considering we're best friends and all. I'm just envious of the sheer number of them."

She feigned a sad shake of her head. "It's a little greedy if you ask me. No one person needs that many orgasms."

"Oh, believe me, I need them all." Lillith was both fighting a grin and the redness on her cheeks when she said it, once again looking behind her to the construction site.

It was a large section of land cordoned off by a chain-link fence, the frame of a massive building just starting to take form.

I smiled at her dreamy look. It was impossible not to like them. They seemed polar opposites; yet, I was unable to imagine one without the other.

Lillith turned back to me almost reluctantly. "We'd better get out of your way so you can get back to work, but we wanted to stop in and introduce ourselves. Honestly, if you need anything, let us know."

"I'm glad you did, and I definitely will."

"Oh." Nikki's eyes lit up. "It's Friday!"

My brow rose in question.

She looked at me as if it should be obvious. "Um . . . hello? Friday Funday? That means you totally have to come out with us tonight."

"Really?"

Okay, maybe I was a little overenthusiastic. But I missed Macy like crazy and the truth was, I needed that—companionship and friendship. The true kind. The feeling of belonging when the last couple of days had made me feel as if I'd stepped out of bounds, directly into a place I knew so intimately but still so far removed.

Lillith nodded. "Oh, good idea."

"Of course it's a good idea," Nikki shot back.

Lillith widened her eyes at me. "For the record, if you say no, chances are Nikki will just come drag you out anyway. It's best to just concede and go along for the ride. God knows, I do." It was all soft, playful affection.

"At least you know what is good for you," Nikki tossed at her before she grabbed me by the wrist and shook my arm around. "Come with us. Please! I already feel like I know you, and . . . well, I think that you might be the missing *three* in our amigo. You complete us."

With both index fingers, she drew a heart in the air.

"See?" Lillith asked. "Just go with the crazy."

I grinned. I was totally going with the crazy. Forget the fears. It'd been eleven years. Who would even recognize me? And if they did, why would they even still care?

A shiver trembled through me.

What if they did?

Shaking it off, I smiled. I could do this. I *wanted* to do this. "That sounds like fun. Where should I meet you and at what time?"

Nikki slung her arm around my shoulder, and I walked with them toward the entrance. "Eight at Olive's. It's on the corner of Macaber and 5th."

"Why do I get the feeling you know this place well?"

Lillith widened telling eyes. "That's because Ollie owns it. This one can't stay away."

Nikki sighed dramatically. "Ollie. Hottest man in all the land. Friend-zoner extraordinaire. But one day, I will make him see what he's missing."

"Ah, things are beginning to make sense now," I said.

Nikki feigned sadness with the grim shake of her head. "No, Rynna, men make absolutely no sense whatsoever. There is no sense to be found."

I laughed. God, I really liked them.

"Isn't that the truth?" I said.

Lillith pushed open the glass door. It was smudged with its own layer of greasy dust, and the white logo on the front claiming Pepper's Pies was barely visible. Still, I could read it as if I'd drawn it myself. It was a shaker tipped on its side, flecks of pepper pouring over a tumble of pot pies and sweet pies and pizzas.

Gramma's offerings had always been unique and perfectly peculiar.

Just like the woman behind it.

I was washed with another wave of warmth, and I couldn't help but think I was supposed to return. That no matter what the past held, this was where I had always belonged.

We stepped out into the hot Alabama summer day, and I blinked against the sudden glare of sunlight and the rush of sticky humidity.

Clouds threatened in the distance, building in the sultry heat.

Lillith hummed with a near imperceptible bounce on her toes. Her attention locked on the small group of men across the street, who'd gathered in a circle just inside the chain-link fence.

Most of them were in work clothes: jeans and long-sleeved shirts and boots. Though a single man with his back to us wore a black suit and a yellow hard hat.

Nikki leaned in and mock-whispered in my ear, "Suit-guy would be the fiancé, Broderick Wolfe. You know, the one who constantly has this one's panties on fire. Look at her . . . she can hardly contain herself."

I bit back laughter, my whisper just as faked. "How long until she goes running over there?"

"Oh, I'd say about two point five seconds."

Lillith swatted at *my* arm, and God, for the first time since I'd returned, I felt truly, completely as if I were home.

"Stop it, you two. Like I don't hear you over there."

We both laughed. Nikki dropped her arm and moved to face me, pulling her cell phone from where it was tucked in her back pocket. "What's your number in case you get lost?" she said with a grin hugging her mouth as she dipped her head to look down. Her fingers were poised to input my number.

I almost got the entire thing out before my mouth went dry and the numbers came to a sluggish, sticky halt, my tongue unable to form a sound.

The man standing next to Broderick had turned around and was looking in our direction.

The smile slid right off his gorgeous face when he saw me staring at him. But somehow, the transformation into the hard scowl was just as mesmerizing.

Just as hypnotic.

Maybe more so.

Because I felt weightless beneath his glare.

Fluttery and uneasy.

Mesmerized.

Those sage eyes were so hard and intense. Capturing me. Holding me hostage. So dark they should have held the power to conceal the fire that raged in the depths, scored like markers in his spirit.

But I saw it. Felt it where it stuck in the heated, stagnant air.

The pain buried underneath.

Nikki lifted her head in question, her fingers ready for the last two numbers. "Hello?"

Snapping out of it, I cleared my throat. "Oh . . . um, sorry, six-two."

"Got it," she said before she gave me a salute and backed away. "Eight o'clock, my friend. Don't make me hunt you down. You know I will."

I tore my attention from the man pinning me to the spot from the other side of the street. His hold was just as heavy as if he were right in front of me, physically restraining me with those massive hands.

"I'll be there," I told her.

"You'd better be." She winked.

Lillith squeezed my hand gently before she backed away to cross the street. "It was great to finally meet you, Rynna. This is going to be good. I can just feel it. I'm so glad we took the chance and stopped in."

She said it without realizing the impact her words had on me. The way they flooded me with warmth and hope. The way they nudged the aspirations at the root of who I was, freeing them from where they'd been trapped deep inside.

My gaze roamed, drawn back to the man who hadn't moved an inch. Hostility rippled off him like heat waves.

I had no idea why I felt it. Compelled. Driven toward a man that seemed so rigid, so dangerous to my sanity.

But I felt it. He needed someone to revive his faith just as desperately as I did.

Because looking at him?

I suddenly knew he had none of it. That something had gone dim inside him.

That was the thing about chances.

We didn't know their outcomes.

If we'd succeed or if we'd fail.

It didn't matter.

I had to take a chance on him.

Six

Rex

"You sure you want to be here tonight?" I asked Ollie. Guilt was threatening to consume me. Suck me down. Take me under.

I fought it, trying to be strong, because it wasn't fucking right for me to be the one falling apart.

Ollie, Kale, and I were in the back office at Olive's where it was quiet. Private. The elevated voices from the throng of people out front were dulled, barely seeping through the walls, the evidence of the live band little more than a throb that vibrated the floors.

Ollie roughed a tattooed hand over his mouth like that single act might hold the power to erase the burden. A low, humorless chuckle rumbled from his chest. "Doesn't make much of a difference where we're at, now, does it? Fuckin' day will follow us, anyway."

"Yeah," I mumbled. Doubted there was a statement I agreed with more. This fucking date haunted us no matter where we went. No matter how much time had passed. There was no outrunning it.

Kale rocked back in the office chair where he sat at Ollie's desk. He had spun the chair around so he could face us, his long legs stretched out in front of him and his fingers threaded at the back of his head. "Twelve years. Twelve years, and it doesn't get any easier, does it?"

Ollie dropped his head back on the wall he rested against and squeezed his eyes closed. "Twelve years." Ollie's voice was nothing but a moan, close to tears. "Shut my eyes and, I swear to God, it feels like yesterday."

Ollie was a big, burly asshole, who was covered in tats, and if you didn't know him, he was intimidating as fuck. I'd seen grown men cross the street when he was heading their direction.

He'd bought Olive's back when it was little more than a dive, when the place was in shambles and going under. I'd come along beside him, doing the physical labor to restore the interior. But it was his vision that made it the most popular bar in Gingham Lakes.

"And a fucking century at the same damned time," I said, shifting on the file cabinet I was leaning on.

"I just . . ." Kale trailed off, unable to say the things every single one of us were thinking.

That it was too late.

That there was no chance.

There was no hope.

Even when it felt impossible to give it up.

Kale had always been the one who carried us through. He was an ER doctor over at the local hospital. He worked his ass off and usually did it with a smile on his face.

He was the kind of guy who would walk through hot coals for a friend. Hell, he'd stand right in the middle of the flames if it meant he could help a man out. Make your load lighter. The guy carried around the weight of the world, thinking it was his duty to offer relief.

Kale, Ollie, and I? We'd been through hell together. Each of us were so different, sometimes I wondered if we would have grown apart if it hadn't happened. Had to wonder if that fateful day had forged something indestructible between us. A bond and a burden that never should have been shaped.

A blessing given just the same as the curse.

Ollie groaned then fiercely shook his head, like he was shaking off the memories, the horror, before he strode across the small area and grabbed the bottle of whiskey. He poured it across the shot glasses and passed one to me and Kale.

He lifted his in the air. "To Sydney. We'll never forget."

I lifted mine, Kale did the same, the three glasses clinking in the middle. "We'll never forget."

I tossed back my shot, the burn of it sliding down my throat and filling my stomach with flames.

No.

There was no chance I would ever forget.

Ten minutes later, Kale and I had moved out into the front of the bar. I grabbed our regular table, which was tucked in the back, while Kale went to grab us drinks.

A blur of voices echoed off the red brick walls of the bottom floor. Olive's was all the rage in Gingham Lakes. Trendy and popular and packed.

A place I probably wouldn't step foot in if it weren't for the fact Ollie was the owner.

The din was a mind-numbing thrum that dulled the senses in the same way the dimmed, muted lights hanging from the ceiling somehow slowed the atmosphere, the band playing tonight super mellow and adding to the laid-back vibe.

Made me feel like I was right in the middle of everything without setting foot in the throng, this impression that the night might go on forever and it was all gonna end in the blink of an eye.

Raucous laughter and shouting seeped down from the upstairs area that housed a bunch of pool tables and led to the huge balcony that overlooked the river.

Tonight was no different than most nights at Olive's. The bar was packed, crawling with people out seeking a good time. A few minutes to cast aside their worries and cares.

I fought the urge brimming in my gut to pack it up and head home.

Truth was, I hated the idea of that, too. I knew my daughter was undoubtedly curled up on the couch next to my mom, who was all too happy to have her spend the night. Frankie Fridays, as she liked to call them, were their standing sleepover date.

If I showed up, Mom would shove me right back out her door. The woman was constantly nagging me to get out more. Insisting I needed time to "find myself" and figure out just how it was I was going to live my life.

She just had no clue I didn't need this bullshit. I had zero interest in the women who were watching the men who crawled the bar like hawks and the men who were watching them like prey.

That fucking game they always liked to play.

So, week after week, I sat back and pretended like I wasn't even there. Oblivious to it all.

I'd managed it for years. Until tonight. All that self-control fled the second the door swung open.

Twilight billowed in and the goddamned air was sucked from the room.

For fuck's sake.

Was she stalking me?

There had to be no other explanation. The woman kept popping up everywhere. Invading my space. Conjuring thoughts I couldn't entertain.

But there she was.

Again.

She walked right through the door of Olive's. Her presence stampeded out in front of her. Consuming everything.

Agitation lit me up, singeing my skin.

Tonight, she looked like she'd just stepped off the runway with those long, long legs encased in a tight pair of black pants and super high heels. Chestnut hair, which was normally all mussed and heaped on her head, swished around her like the silky calm of a midnight river.

Fuck. Me.

I didn't know if I liked her better like this or the total mess she normally was, the way she'd been earlier this afternoon when she'd stopped me in my tracks when I was in the middle of giving my crew instruction in front of Broderick Wolfe. No doubt, I looked like some kind of blundering idiot who couldn't find words.

Tongue-tied.

That was because I was too busy letting my dick do the talking, the traitor perking up at the sight of her standing outside her grandma's run-down, closed-up diner that had seen far better days.

Had taken Broderick calling me on it, all while wearing a knowing smirk on his face, before I'd snapped out of my stupor and had gotten back to the meeting.

Guessed I should have expected trouble the second I'd seen her outside Pepper's Pies with Nikki and Lillith.

I would have been right.

Her face split into a grin when her sight landed on the two of them. They were sitting at the bar, drinking their frilly drinks and chatting like they did just about every Friday night.

From behind me, a hand suddenly clamped down on my shoulder.

I jumped like some kind of pussy.

Just fucking awesome.

Kale laughed. "Dude, why so jumpy?" He set a fresh beer in front of me and pulled out a chair. By the time he sat, he was all grins and amusement.

That was just Kale's way. He had the ability to find the good in the moment, something light and easy and fun, even on a day like today.

"Did you start shit with one of those big fuckers and now you're scared?" He wasn't so discrete when he pointed at a couple of guys who looked like they'd probably rolled up on bikes and had rap sheets a few miles long. "Don't tell me I'm going to have to step in and protect you."

Leave it to Kale.

But that sure as hell wasn't what had me on edge.

I shifted a bit so Rynna was off to my side and not directly in front of me, situating myself in a way that let me pretend she wasn't there.

Pretended I couldn't feel the heat radiating from that tight body.

Pretended that feeling didn't exist. The one that left me restless.

Edgy.

Hungry for something I couldn't quite put my finger on.

I shot him a glare. "You wish, asshole. If anyone needs protecting, it's you, standing around looking like a pretty boy. You're just begging to get your ass kicked."

He cracked up.

"Hey, someone wants to kick my ass? It's only because they wish they were me. All the ladies love me."

He smirked, slinging back a gulp of the dark liquid dancing in the rocks glass he clutched in his hand. Kale was the cockiest asshole around. It was a total mindfuck he still managed to have the biggest heart of them all.

Sitting there, people had to think he'd stumbled to the wrong table. There I was, looking like I belonged with the guys he was just referring to while he was all sharp angles and crisp lines, clean-shaven, his blond hair slicked back, and his button-up and pants perfectly pressed.

"Take it you're not on call this weekend?"

He rocked back with a big, satisfied sigh. "Nope. I've got the whole weekend off. Don't have to be back until Sunday night. It's like a goddamned Christmas miracle right smack dab in the middle of summer." He hefted a shoulder. "Besides, figured Ollie might need me, too, so I asked for it off. Somehow it was approved."

I nodded, understanding, trying not to let myself get dragged right back into the somber mood from back in the office, knowing neither Ollie nor Kale needed that shit. Dwelling wasn't going to change a goddamned thing.

"So, how's my Frankie-girl?" Kale asked, quick to change the subject.

The smile on my face was instant. "Good. Started taking ballet. Cutest damned thing I've ever seen."

"No shit?" He shook his head. "She's getting so big. Time

flies, doesn't it? Seems like only yesterday she was learning to walk."

I roughed a hand through my hair. "Yeah. Goes by too damned fast. Blows my mind she only has another year before she starts kindergarten."

He pointed at me with the same hand wrapped around his rocks glass, laughter falling out around his words. "School . . . dude . . . you are so fucked. If I think you're overprotective now . . ."

I wiped the sweat that was suddenly beading on my brow. Honestly wasn't sure how I was going to handle that. Someone else being responsible for her care. The fact that I might not know exactly where she was at all times and who she was with.

I stomped down those thoughts, refusing to give them voice, and started to tell him about her bitch of an instructor, figuring he'd get a kick out of it.

That was right when I felt the air thicken.

I rubbed at the back of my neck, fighting it.

The shock of awareness that sliced through the darkened bar.

Tense and tight and hot.

It was a bitch knowing its origin and not being able to do a goddamned thing about it.

I barely cut my gaze to the side and peered through the dimmed lights. A smoky glow hugged the room, and my eyes climbed right back to the spot they shouldn't. I was nothing but a glutton for punishment, because there I was, desperate for a glimpse.

Still, I was unprepared. Unprepared for the way my skin itched when I caught her stealing a glance at me at the same time I was stealing one of her.

Quick and furtive.

Like she'd just realized I was there.

"Kid really is so damned adorable, don't know how you stand it." Kale was rambling, musing about the sweetness of my daughter and how my life had turned out totally different from what I'd ever expected it to. I sat there, shifting uneasily in my seat like a fool, letting myself feel something that had no reason to be there.

Lust for a woman I didn't even know.

Kale was bringing his glass to his lips when he suddenly let it drop a fraction, studying me from over the top. "What the hell is going on with you, man?"

"Nothin'."

"You seem . . . anxious." One quirk of a knowing brow. That was the pitfalls of having friends for life. Sometimes they knew you better than you wanted them to.

Because this was obviously not about the anniversary.

Still, I shrugged. "Nothing at all."

Doubt billowed through his expression, and another rush of disquiet had me shifting again. His eyes flicked off to my side before he looked back at me like he'd hit a bull's-eye. "Nothing, huh? Then why do you keep glaring at Lillith and Nikki like they've all of a sudden grown horns? I mean, it's no secret you've up and decided women are the devil, but those two you at least seem to tolerate. What happened?"

I pasted what I hoped appeared to be a look of indifference on my face. "Don't know what you're talking about. Nothing happened."

His brow drew tight, and he peered in their direction again, studying what had changed. Then he was cocking his head to the side with a knowing grin. "Who's the hot new chic? Doesn't look like she's from around here."

Another shrug. "Dunno."

Apparently, that shrug was the indicator of a lie, because Kale laughed. Far too loud and at my expense. "Oh, I see what's happening here. Seems someone actually is still in the possession of his dick."

"Don't." The warning came out hard. Nothing playful about it.

He knew better.

He shook his head. "That bitch sure as hell did a number on you, didn't she? You think it's a good thing for Frankie to grow up with you hating every woman who crosses your path? That shit's not healthy, man. You need to figure out your issues before you mess up your daughter's head with that chip you love to wear on your shoulder."

Yeah. That stung. My hand clenched around my beer bottle. "You're really going to sit over there and tell me I'm raising my kid wrong?"

He scowled. "Isn't that what friends are for? To call you out when you aren't seeing straight? Because it's time you realized your vision is completely skewed. It's been three years. And fuck, man, you know you're a great dad, but don't sit over there and act like there's not something missing."

He rocked back in his chair, arms going across his chest, like he was offering up a dare. "When's the last time you got laid?"

Ollie took that opportune time to show up at our table with a fresh round of drinks. He placed the rocks glass down in front of Kale before he slid an icy bottle my direction.

Ollie forced a smile, dude wearing his own special kind of veneer, shoving all the bullshit down, locked up and contained. "Pretty sure this one's cock has shriveled up and died. It's a sad, sad state of affairs."

My brow rose. "Thanks, man," I said, totally dry.

"Hey, just keeping it real," he said, giving me a clap to the back.

Taking a swig of my beer, I shook my head. "Why don't you keep it 'real' with someone else?"

A smirk pulled beneath his beard. "Now, what would be the fun in that?"

Kale leaned forward. "Seriously, man. Think about what you're doing. The vibe you're feeding and how that affects not just Frankie but you, too. You can sit there and pretend all you want, but I know you're lonely."

I swallowed around the lump, doing my best not to look Rynna's direction.

Call me a failure.

Because my gaze was slanting that way, drinking her in.

Fuck, I was a fool.

The way I welcomed the bolt of need that slammed me.

It was so goddamned wrong. But this unwanted feeling

bubbled up inside me, latching on to the sight of her laughing from across the room. The way her chin lifted and her mouth curved. Something so free.

A quality that didn't belong to me.

In discomfort, I looked back at Kale. "Believe me. Frankie's the only girl I need."

My everything.

The one I lived for.

The one I'd gladly die for.

And I'd never give anyone the chance to threaten that.

Seven

Rynna

"Who do you keep looking at?" Nikki swiveled on her stool, straining to look behind her. Muted light cast a shimmery drape of warmth over the bar, tossing it with shadows and mystery.

But one man stood out amid it all. And he was looking right back at us.

I smacked her leg, my voice a panicked whisper. "What are you doing?"

She had no shame.

She looked at me as if I were crazy. "Um . . . trying to figure out which lucky bastard has already snagged my new friend's eye. That's my job, you know. I'm head matchmaker, right, Lily Pad?"

She smirked in Lillith's direction.

Lillith just wagged her ring finger adorned with the huge rock as proof while she took a sip of her wine.

"No one's caught my eye," I said.

Honestly, it was a useless defense. Not with the way I couldn't stop from stealing another glance at the man who was beginning to consume my every thought. I wasn't one prone to obsessions. Or stalking. Or spying.

But there was something about him that wouldn't let me go.

Something that fascinated and enthralled.

Maybe it was his adorable daughter.

It had to be. It was the only explanation.

Nikki followed my gaze. She froze for a beat before her head whipped back in my direction. Her mouth hung open in blatant shock. "Oh my God! Tell me Rex Gunner isn't the one who has you all spun up over there?"

Before I could give her another futile excuse, awareness dawned on her face. "Holy shit. He lives right across from you." She rapidly snapped her fingers in front of my face as if she were on to something. "Oh, and his company has the contract for the hotel that's on Fairview . . . right across from Pepper's Pies."

My shoulder lifted as if I didn't care at all. As if he didn't actually have me so spun up I could feel the knots lining my stomach. "I went over and introduced myself to him the other day. That's it."

I conveniently left out the part where he'd slammed his door in my face. I figured guilt was found in the small details.

The ironic laughter dripping from Lillith's tongue sounded like a warning. "You should probably leave it at that. The only women Rex Gunner likes are his daughter and his momma. Otherwise, watch out. That boy is as cynical as they come."

I glanced his way again, snared by the way his throat was exposed when he tipped back his beer, the way the thick muscles rolled as he swallowed, that short, trimmed beard little more than a five o'clock shadow.

God, he was gorgeous in an earth-shattering way. As if I could feel the vibrations coming from him rippling under my feet.

I edged forward, my voice quieted to a whisper, way too eager for my own good. "What happened to him?"

Lillith and Nikki shared a look.

Nikki leaned forward, dropping her tone to match mine. "His wife just . . . disappeared. No one knows for sure what happened to her."

Was it fear that flashed through my blood? The man

screamed danger and peril and risk. But my heart told me for an entirely different reason than the flicker of morbid intrigue that tickled my consciousness. Still, my eyes were round as I leaned even closer to her. "Like . . . do people think she's . . . dead?"

Nikki howled with laughter and sat back, smacking her knee, obviously thrilled I'd followed her into that trap. "Ha! He probably wishes she was. My guess is she's just a selfish bitch who walked out when taking care of a baby became too much. Not that anyone knows since he doesn't talk about her, but I was never a fan."

She shrugged and took a sip of her cosmo.

Case closed.

"Not about her or about anything really," Lillith added, back to waving a caution flag. "I've known him since we were kids. We went to school together on the other side of town with Ollie and Kale. The three of them have had some horrible stuff happen in their lives. It affected them, shaped who they became. But Rex? He changed after his wife left. Don't get me wrong, he's a great guy. Honest. An incredibly hard worker. He grew his small construction company into the most successful contractor in the area. Loyal to the bone, and there's no doubt he loves that little girl. But I'm pretty sure his bitterness has seeped all the way to the marrow."

That sense I'd been feeling grew stronger. The need to look deeper inside the man who'd built a fortress around himself. Needing to protect himself from the pain so clearly etched in his eyes.

Mournful eyes I could feel continually flashing my direction.

Scorching me deeper with each hidden pass.

Nikki laughed. "You should see your face right now. Girl, you're in so much trouble. It looks to me like you're taking that warning as some kind of invitation. I told you I was the queen matchmaker, but I don't think even I'm that good."

Lillith almost rolled her eyes. "This from the girl who's been trying to get Ollie to look her way for the last five years."

"Hey! Sometimes these things take time. I'm a patient woman."

Her attention jerked toward a man who came out from the back of the bar.

"He's back. Look, there he is. That's who I was telling you about. That's my Ollie," Nikki raved not so quietly as she slapped my thigh a bunch of times to get my attention.

With the way she shivered at the sight of him, I would say her patience was wearing thin. I understood her fascination.

Ollie was rough and hard and incredibly good-looking. As good-looking as the other straightlaced guy who sat on the other side of the table from Rex.

There had to be something in the water, because both of them were almost as beautiful as the man who'd taken my thoughts hostage.

Almost.

But there was something about Rex that completely set him apart. Something that made him shine in all his surly darkness. Something that twisted my belly into a mess of anxiousness, attraction, and intrigue.

This prodding force that insisted I get to know someone who seemed desperate to remain unseen.

Nikki sighed when Ollie grabbed a couple drinks from behind the bar and carried them to Rex's table. "God, I love him."

With a sip of her wine, Lillith shook her head. "I'm beginning to think you're just infatuated with what you can't have."

Nikki blinked at her. "Isn't that the same thing?"

A tumble of laughter rolled from Lillith. "Not even close."

Nikki's gaze trailed back after Ollie. Not even trying to hide her stare when he rounded back behind the bar to help the other bartender. "For real . . . love or not, I would eat up that man."

I giggled quietly. On the drive over, I'd worried I had made the wrong choice. Worried I'd be continually looking over my shoulder. Wondering who might recognize me. If there would be rumbles and whispers and rumors.

But I hadn't felt it. Not for a second. I loved that these two had invited me out. That they were happy to make me feel a part of their tight-knit world. That they seemed to have no qualms about welcoming me into it.

I startled when a tall figure suddenly cast a shadow over us. I looked up to find a man towering at my side, his brown eyes raking me up and down, a grin riding his full lips.

I would have shrank away if I hadn't been one-hundred percent sure I'd never seen him before.

Apparently, there really was something in the water.

He was ridiculously attractive. Clearly, he'd discarded the jacket of his dark gray suit, the sleeves of his button-down rolled up his forearms. His stance was so casual and confident as he looked expectantly at me.

"I just noticed you sitting over here, and I thought I could buy you a drink," he said, his attention fully trained on me. "Name's Tim."

Nikki cleared her throat, the words ripe with mock offense. "I do hope that drink buying includes the rest of us."

He glanced at her. "If that's what it takes."

Tim was a little cocky for my taste.

And he wasn't Rex Gunner.

I lifted my margarita toward him, the green yummy goodness swishing in the salt-rimmed bowl. "I think I'm just fine. But thank you."

"You sure about that? You look awful lonely over here by yourself."

Irritation bristled beneath my skin. I was sitting there with my friends. How the hell could I appear lonely? But I was used to these kinds of pick-up lines in San Francisco when Macy dragged me out with her.

So I pasted on a fake smile and said, "I'm sure."

The guy shrugged. "Whatever. Your loss."

He turned on his heel and sauntered away.

"What an asshole," I mumbled under my breath, my eyes trailing him with a special kind of disgust.

Nikki jerked my attention back to her by swatting me on the knee and lifting her spent glass. "Speak for yourself, Ryn-Ryn. I totally could have used another drink."

I laughed. "At what expense?"

She widened her blue eyes. "Oh, come on. Take one for the

team."

Giggling, I dabbed at the trickle of margarita clinging to the edge of my lip. "He might not be bad to look at, but he was kind of a jerk. No thank you."

Nikki nudged Lillith with her elbow. "Yet, she likes Rex Gunner."

Lillith grinned before her expression shifted, swelling with soft affection. "I guess we like what we like. Broderick was definitely an asshole of the worst kind when I first met him."

I made the mistake of letting my attention wander back to Rex. Ollie was back at his table, and he and the other guy were engaged in their own conversation.

Rex seemed totally removed from it.

Just sitting there.

Glaring at me.

Unabashedly with intense, heated hatred.

"Maybe there's hope for everyone," I mumbled.

Tearing my gaze from him, I pushed to my feet, cleared my throat, and pasted a smile on my face. "I need to use the restroom."

Lillith gestured toward the hall to the right of the stairs. "Down the hall and on the left."

"Thanks."

I wound through the crowds huddled around the high-top tables. Voices were lifted to be heard above the hum of the band, laughter loud as people let go of the stresses of the week, embracing the chance they had to unwind.

I took the hall and ducked into the restroom, used it, and then washed my hands. I let a small smile lift the corner of my mouth.

Being there felt so right, even if Rex Gunner was messing with my head.

I dried my hands, swung open the door, and stepped out into the haze of the dimly lit hall. I gasped when the same guy who'd approached me at the bar stepped out in front of me, stopping me in my tracks.

"Hey," I said uneasily, peering behind him at the people

loitering at the far end of the hall. The noise level had escalated to a dull roar, the mood becoming rowdy, increasing with every second that passed.

I shifted anxiously on my feet, wondering if anyone would even hear me if I called for help.

Okay.

So maybe I was getting ahead of myself.

But getting backed into a corner by a guy I didn't know wasn't high on my list of safest situations. Not when a shiver of apprehension skated down my spine. A cold warning.

"Finally got you alone," he said.

I took a single step back and to the side, trying to put space between us. "If you'll excuse me, I was actually headed back to my friends."

He reached out, running the tip of his index finger down the side of my cheek. "You should ditch them and spend a little time with me."

Nausea turned my stomach. "I'm really not interested."

He inched forward. "No?"

"No." The word shot from my mouth.

I was so absolutely not interested. But this guy didn't seem to be able to take a hint.

"I think you're lying. I think you're really interested and you just don't want to look like a slut in front of your friends. Let's get out of here. I won't tell anyone."

What the fuck?

This guy was ridiculous. I took it all back. Any appeal he had was obliterated by his foul, offensive character.

I scoffed out a laugh. "And I think you're a total prick who can't seem to comprehend the fact I'd rather gouge my eye out with a fork than spend the night with you."

Anger flashed across his face, and he jolted forward, making me stumble back.

So maybe that was the wrong thing to do. Inciting this jerk. It was a risk. Some guys needed someone to knock them over the head before they got it and there were some who never understood the meaning of no. Apparently, he was the latter.

"Ah. Playing hard to get. I like it."

"I'm not playing, Tim." This time, the words trembled with a tiny spurt of fear. "I mean it. Just . . . leave me alone."

He slipped forward another inch, backing me the rest of the way into the wall. "See? You even remembered my name. Stop playing coy."

"She said she wasn't interested." The voice that rumbled in the hallway was rough. Low and dangerous.

My skin shivered for entirely different reasons.

Tim swung around to look over his shoulder, still keeping his body angled so I was backed against the wall but allowing me to see farther down the hall.

Rex was there. Fists clenched. Jaw rigid. Anger radiated from him in shocking waves. Those sage eyes glinted with hate as his lean, sinewy muscles twitched with restraint.

I just didn't know which of us he hated most.

It didn't matter.

I sucked in a breath of relief, succumbing to a feeling of safety so staggering it weakened my knees.

Tim clung to that sleazy cockiness. "Think you should turn around and mind your own fucking business."

"And I'd suggest you back the fuck away before you don't have the chance to walk out of here." It was nothing less than a growl.

Aggression ricocheted between the two of them. Growing and spinning and spiking.

Finally, Tim cracked a flippant, arrogant grin. Though, I could have sworn I saw his quake of fear. The realization that he didn't have a fighting chance.

Rex Gunner would beat him bloody.

He stepped away from me. "Whatever, man. You want her, have her. She's not worth the effort."

I sagged forward, dragging a bunch of cleansing breaths into my too-tight lungs.

Rex glowered at him, never breaking his menacing stare when Tim angled his shoulders to the side to slip past him, his pace increasing the second he was on the other side of Rex's raging hostility.

He disappeared at the end of the hall, and I pushed my bangs back from my forehead, which was sweaty and slick with the adrenaline.

"You okay?" Rex asked, voice still shaky and rough.

I nodded. "Yeah . . . he was . . ." I trailed off, forcing myself to stand straight. "Rex. Thank you. I—"

He cut me off with harsh, cold words. "You should go home before you get yourself into any more trouble."

Then he turned around and stalked away.

I stood there, staring after him, wondering what in the hell had just happened. Finally, I shook myself out of it, feet prodding down the hall. At the end of it, I searched the crowded room until my gaze latched on to the back of the man as he wound through the throng toward the bar.

For a beat, I contemplated, wondering if it was even worth it. Putting myself out there when he seemed to shut me down at every turn.

It didn't take long to come to the conclusion.

I followed the same path, angling through the bodies that seemed to grow thicker with each moment that passed.

I came to a stop behind him. He had gone straight for the bar, arms rested on top of it, gesturing with his chin to Ollie. Ollie only gestured back, as if they spoke some sort of secret language, a fresh beer gliding across the shiny dark mahogany and landing in Rex's grip.

He brought it to his lips and took a deep pull, that strong throat bobbing again. But there was a new kind of agitation that radiated from the movement.

As if he were upset.

I swallowed down my reservations and sidled up to him, wondering what had possessed me. What made it impossible to turn away from this man I barely even knew.

That intrigue grew greater and greater with each glimpse that took me a little deeper.

He exhaled heavily when he realized I was there, taking another sip without looking my way.

"I said thank you," I reiterated just loud enough to be heard over the din.

He sighed, rubbed his fingertips over those plush lips, and barely cut an eye my direction.

"You're welcome." It was gruff. Reluctant.

"Am I?" I challenged.

He coughed out a laugh with a quick shake of his head before he looked at me for a moment. Seriously. Genuinely. "Yeah, you are. Would have preferred to take the fucker out, honestly."

"Then why are you so pissed at me?"

He sighed again, this time as he scrubbed a hand over his face as he looked straight ahead. "It's just . . . let's just say today's not the best of days."

"What happened?"

He flinched, and his trembling hand ran over his short beard. "Some things are better left unsaid, Rynna Dayne. Only thing dragging history out into the open does is remind you just how fucking bad it sucks that there's not a damned thing in the world you can do to change it."

I studied him, trying to make sense of what he said, realizing it was a locked door I had no chance of getting through. Instead, I hiked myself up onto the stool.

Ollie's eyes went wide when he approached, his attention flicking between the two of us as if he were shocked Rex might actually be talking to me.

"What can I get you?" Ollie asked.

"A margarita would be nice."

Rex and I sat in silence for a few moments, saying nothing while Ollie mixed my drink and placed it in front of me. "Thank you," I said, taking a sip before I chanced a peek at Rex.

At his profile.

At his nose and his lips and his jaw.

Shivers rolled and those butterflies swarmed.

"Your daughter is adorable."

A smile flickered on his lush mouth. "Yeah . . . she's a handful."

His words were pure adoration, and for the first time, Rex

dropped his shield.

As if just the mention of her had the power to send it tumbling down.

So maybe I melted a little.

"I'd venture that kind of handful is the best kind."

His chuckle was slow. "Sometimes I wonder how I handle that little hurricane. Barely can keep up most days." Even though it came out playful, there was an undercurrent of sadness. A suggestion of fear.

I nodded before we both turned away, facing forward and sipping from our drinks. It was as if we both needed a breather, a moment to sort through whatever was happening between us.

It felt like maybe in the silence, we were calling a truce.

The band playing at the small stage behind us at the other end of the bar moved into another song. I'd barely been paying attention to them all night, the songs only a backdrop to the vibe, the band members just as trendy as the bar itself.

But this . . .

This was a song I knew so well.

They were singing a haunting cover of "Awake My Soul" by Mumford & Sons.

Slower and quieter than the original.

The lyrics were full of longing and heartache.

Mournful and somehow hopeful.

I sipped my drink, getting lost in the feel. In the comfort of the soft, scratchy voice of the singer, in the startling warmth that radiated from Rex.

My grandmother's face flitted through my eyes, her belief a whisper in my ear.

My teeth caught on my bottom lip when I turned to find him watching me.

Intently.

Something fervent rose between us. Alive and potent. It sent my nerves spiraling free.

He took a slow pull of his beer, his words measured. Careful. "I'm really sorry about your grandmother, Rynna. She was a really good woman." Sadness flashed through his expression.

"Don't know of anything worse than losing someone you love."

Emotion thickened my throat, stunned by his sudden care and swimming in the stark loss. "I feel like I lost her a long time ago."

The admission was strangled, ripped from my chest as if I couldn't keep it in for a second longer.

That stunning gaze searched my face through the shadows. "Had it been a long time since you saw her?"

There was no accusation behind it. Just honest curiosity.

"Yeah."

"Why'd you stay away so long?"

I choked out an uncertain laugh. "Because I wasn't brave enough."

He frowned. "You seem awful brave to me."

My head shook. "No. I'm not brave. Or maybe I just wasn't brave soon enough."

The lyrics lifted in the atmosphere, words about life and death and the impermanency of our bodies. I swore I saw Rex's spine go rigid.

I touched his arm, unable to stop myself. My skin lit up at the contact. He stared at it before he jerked away and pushed from the bar.

Shocked, I spun around.

His chest heaved and he looked . . . panicked.

"Rex—"

He roughed a hand over his face, cutting off whatever connection we'd shared. "I've got to get out of here."

Then he turned, stalked through the crowd, shoved open the door, and disappeared into the night.

Leaving me sitting there staring at the vacancy he'd left behind, wondering exactly what I'd done wrong.

eight
Rex

I was agitated.

Pissed and confused.

A disorder trembling me to the bone.

As hard as I tried, there was no corralling it. No shaking the bristling anger that had followed me through all of last night and into this morning.

It was a blinding fury that had taken to my veins when I'd found her backed into a corner by that piece of shit.

Hell. It'd been ignited the second I'd looked up from the table and saw him talking to her.

I didn't even know her, and she sure as hell wasn't mine, but I couldn't stomach the idea of her leaving with him. Of her going back to his place or maybe him going to hers.

The vision of him following her up her stairs had made me want to claw my eyes out. Two of them falling into her bed.

It was no surprise he turned out to be a pussy-bitch pretty boy who had the misconception he had the right to reach out and take whatever he wanted whether someone wanted to give it or not.

Would have relished in teaching him the lesson.

Enlightening the fucker on what it meant to show a little respect.

But that was the problem when someone affected you. The problem when someone got under your skin. When someone made you start entertaining all kinds of foolish ideas. Ideas of stepping up and getting involved in matters that were none of your concern.

Treading a line you had no business walking.

That fact had never been as striking as when she'd reached out and touched me at the bar. She was making me want things I couldn't want.

Things I had no fucking right to take.

But it didn't matter.

They'd been there, and I knew I had to get the fuck away before I did something I couldn't take back.

Before I crossed a line I couldn't cross.

I had one priority.

One focus.

A single reason to keep on the straight and narrow.

And that reason was currently hurtling down the walkway.

Brown hair flying and spirit soaring. Grin wide. As bright as the sun that blazed as it climbed the sky behind her.

The second I'd pulled my truck to the curb, she'd bolted out my mom's front door, arms lifted over her head and that sweet voice riding the wind.

"Daddy!"

I hopped out of my truck and went straight for her, scooped her up, and tossed her into the air.

Let her laughter rain down around me. A drenching reminder of what I was living for. I caught her, hugging her close while she tightened her chubby arms around my neck in a death grip. "Daddy! Guess what?"

I pulled back a fraction so I could see her face. "What?"

"Grammy gots me paints, and I painted a tree and a mountain and a squirrel, and now I'm gonna be an artist and take paintin' lessons and be the best dancer in the whole world and

Wonder Woman when I goes to the gym with you."

It was then that I spotted the thick smear of white paint across her cheek and the rainbow of splatters on her shirt.

I glanced at my mother, who was grinning like the Cheshire where she leaned against the doorjamb with her arms crossed over her chest.

"Now you're going to be an artist, too, huh?"

"Uh-huh. Grammy said my picture was so, so pretty. You think I could sell it and get so much money and then I can buy a dog? Oh, Daddy, please, I wants a puppy so bad."

I chuckled under my breath because it was the only thing I could do.

"I don't think a puppy is a good idea right now, Frankie Leigh."

"Oh, but, Daddy!" She stuck out her bottom lip before she grinned. "You wants to see my picture?"

I laughed. "Nothing I'd like better than to see that picture."

Wasn't lying last night. The child was a handful. A whirlwind that spun from one idea to the next without giving me time to process the first.

Sweet to the brim.

Most likely because all those dreams and ideas were gushing out from the inside.

I arched a brow at my mom as we approached. "So, we're painting again?"

Taking the single step up to the door, I dropped a kiss to Mom's cheek.

Her smile grew. "Oh, yes. We are definitely painting again. We had a blast, didn't we, Frankie Leigh?"

"So, so, SO much fun. Can I spend the night here every night?"

I feigned offense. "And you're going to leave your daddy all by his lonesome every night."

Frankie's horror was real. "Oh, no, Daddy. You can spends the night here, too. Right, Grammy?"

"Oh, Sweet Pea Frankie Leigh, I think your daddy might be too old for sleepovers. Unless he finally decides to start participating in the right kind. You know, of the *adult* variety."

The last she mumbled under her breath, and the woman had the nerve to shoot me a wink.

Mom had just turned fifty-two and was about as pretty as they came. The years had been good to her, and her spirit was as free as Frankie's.

"Sly, Ma. Real sly."

She laughed. "Oh, everyone needs a little push in the right direction every now and again. Speaking of, how was last night?"

I shrugged. "Uneventful."

That felt like a bold-faced lie.

But the last thing I needed to do was mention Rynna moving in across the street. Mom would hop on that so fast that I'd never hear the end of it.

I set Frankie back on her feet, scooting her in the direction of her room. "Go get your stuff, Sweet Pea."

She took off down the hall, and I straightened and looked at my mom. Obviously, she was dying for any juicy details she could get.

"Met Ollie and Kale for a couple of drinks then called it a night," I told her.

A long, restless night.

A pucker formed on Mom's lips. "You're no fun. Here I am, nice enough to have your daughter over for the entire night, and you don't even do me the service of having a wild night on the town. You know I'll be having one tonight."

Amusement shook my head. "You really are a terrible influence. I think I'm going to have to rethink these sleepovers."

She pressed a hand over her heart. "You wouldn't dare."

"Don't test me." It was purely a tease.

Everything about her softened. "How are my boys?"

A smile ticked up at the corner of my mouth. "Good. Kale has the weekend off, so I'm sure he's off making up for any fun I'm not having. Ollie is . . . it was twelve years yesterday."

A soft puff of air blew from her mouth. "Oh . . . I didn't even realize. How is he doing?"

"As well as can be expected, I guess."

Or maybe worse than could be expected. I didn't fucking know.

God knew that it still ate me alive.

A beat of silence hovered in the atmosphere, that same sadness that was always there, lurking in the background, before Frankie broke it. She came bursting back into the living room with her backpack bouncing on her shoulders, a poster board in one hand and her doll clutched to her chest with the other.

"Look it, Daddy."

Proudly, Frankie lifted her painting that was nothing but thick swashes of color.

"That's beautiful, Sweet Pea."

"What are we gonna do today?" she dove right in. "You wants to go swimming?"

I swung her into my arms. "Is that what you want to do? Go to the lake?"

She grinned that grin. The one that knocked all the foolishness free and the sense back into me. My heart heavy and full.

Devoted.

"Yes!"

I ruffled a hand through her rebellious hair. "Then, it sounds like we're going to the lake."

My headlights cut through the emerging night.

Twilight was at its deepest, the entire earth cast in that shadowy blue that stifled the air in the moments just before the night fully took hold of the day.

Frankie and I had spent the entire day at the lake, playing in the water, hiking, building a fire, and grilling the burgers I'd picked up before we'd taken the twenty-minute drive out to our favorite spot. The lake calm, the beach secluded, the sky cloudless.

It'd been the perfect kind of afternoon.

That same twenty-minute drive home had rocked Frankie to

sleep in the back of the truck, her little head bobbing to one side where she dozed in her car seat.

I pulled my truck into the driveway at the side of the house and killed the engine before going directly for Frankie, unbuckling her and then lifting her into my arms.

She felt so small and light like this, when all that energy had finally drained and she was just the tiny little thing that had been given into my care. The one who needed me to protect and shield her. Her shelter and her harbor.

I angled her to the side so I could slide the key into the lock and let us into the stillness of the small house that I did my very best to make a home. Half the time it felt like I didn't have a single clue what the fuck I was doing, but I got up every single morning and did it anyway.

Frankie barely stirred when I laid her on her twin bed and tugged the flip-flops from her feet, changed her into her pajamas, and tucked her under the cool sheet. Her head was on her pillow, those wild, tangled locks all around her. I brushed them back from her face, gazing down at her and wondering how something so good could come out of a situation that was so utterly fucked.

Wondering if she was my blessing.

My reprieve.

Or if the insane worry that constantly roiled inside me was another element of the curse that would haunt me for the rest of my days.

Pushing it down in the depths of my spirit, I leaned down and pressed a gentle kiss to her forehead, silently promising her it didn't make a difference either way.

That it didn't change my devotion to her.

This mad kind of love that took up every cell in my body. It came into existence the first time I'd held her in my arms.

Sparked to life that cold winter night.

A permanent flame.

One I'd thought had been forever dimmed.

On a sigh, I pushed to my feet and shuffled from her room, leaving the door open a crack and a light on in the hall in case she needed me. I headed into the kitchen, pulled a cold beer from the fridge, and popped the cap.

I took a swig as I peered out the kitchen window. It was the exact same picture that'd been there since the day I'd moved in. Though, I doubted I could ever consider the view the same.

nine

Rynna

The oven buzzed.

My nerves went haywire, shooting into overdrive as I grabbed the mitts and pulled the pie from the oven. The sweet, decadent scent spilled into the kitchen and basked it in a homey warmth.

"Perfect," I murmured beneath my breath, my chest filling with pride and something wistful as I took in the way the crust, which I had made from scratch, had baked to a golden brown. The sugar I'd sprinkled on top had caramelized to perfection, and piping hot cherries bubbled up through the hole in the middle.

I had the fleeting thought that this was the easy part. Baking something to perfection. It was the changing of minds that was difficult. Drawing people to what you had to offer and convincing them it was exactly what they needed.

So help me God, Rex Gunner was going to be my first customer.

And we weren't talking dollars and cents.

We were talking trust and camaraderie.

Friendship.

If I were being honest, I would admit I might envision more. Admit there was something about him and his little girl that called to me. Awakening that place in me that I'd shored away, a place that had always wanted the simple things in life.

Simple is better.

How many times had my grandmother told me that very thing as she worked her recipes that always related so easily to life?

At the very least, I was seeking a truce in this cold war Rex seemed intent to wage against me when I'd committed no offense or crime.

I let the pie cool for a few minutes before I gathered my courage and slipped on my shoes. I stepped out into the breaking night. Once again, I was struck with the overpowering sense of comfort.

The scent of the fragrant honeysuckle. The sound of the bugs that trilled in the bushes. The towering trees blowing in the whispering breeze.

Home.

That same small window that gave a direct view into Rex's house was lit. I could see him sitting by himself at a small table somewhere to the back of the kitchen area, continually raking a hand through his hair as he nursed at a beer.

He appeared so utterly alone even though I'd seen him return home with his daughter about forty-five minutes ago.

My spying no longer gave me the sense of violating his privacy.

It felt like a mission.

That it held a purpose for his greater good. Or maybe his little girl's. I didn't know.

I just knew there was absolutely nothing I could do but stand at his door with a peace offering.

A thank you.

Balancing the gooey pie in both hands, I nudged at the door with my elbow. My heart sped when I heard the scraping of chair legs against the floor and the rustling within the house, my blood becoming a thunder that rushed through my veins.

Then I sensed the pause. The presence that was so clearly right on the other side of the door, that severity hot as it blazed through the wood.

There might as well have been no separation between us.

Because I could feel him. The conflict and reluctance.

God, why did he have this kind of effect on me?

It only grew when I felt the resignation, heard the slow slide of metal and the creak of hinges as he barely cracked open the door, only a single wary eye visible. "What are you doing here, Rynna?"

I lifted my hands so he could see what I was holding. "I baked you a pie."

Exasperation bled into his tone as he opened the door a bit wider. "Why did you do that?"

"Because it's a neighborly thing to do." It almost came across as irritated. But then I was taken back to the way he'd stepped into the line of fire for me. The way he'd talked to me at the bar. Openly. As if he wanted to let me in but he didn't know how or if he could. The way he'd taken off as if I had suddenly become a danger to him.

My voice deepened with sincerity. "You saved me last night, Rex, I wanted to properly thank you."

"It's not necessary," he said, words gruff. If it weren't for that flash in the depths of those eyes, I would have bought the act.

"I just—"

"Please . . . leave us alone, Rynna." It was a plea.

He started to shut the door in my face again, but he winced, freezing when the sweet, excited voice broke through the aversion. "Ms. Dayne? What'cha doin' here?"

She rubbed her tiny fists in her bleary eyes. The little girl took the definition of bedhead to a whole new level.

Rex cringed, his lips pursing and that throat that kept making me lose my train of thought bobbing heavily. An edge of defensiveness threaded into his words. "We were at the lake all day . . . she didn't get her bath before she fell asleep."

"I not tired anymore, Daddy," she said, shaking her head as if she were shaking off even the idea of going back to bed.

"It's late, Frankie Leigh."

She totally ignored her dad, her smile so wide when she shot forward and wrapped her tiny arms around his thigh before gazing up at me. "What do you gots? Is that a Pepper Pie? Oh, yummy." She jumped in place and tugged at her dad's shirt. "Daddy, she gots a Pepper Pie! Is that for me?"

At least someone appreciated my efforts.

I smiled down at her. "It is for you. But it's super hot right now, so you'll have to wait until tomorrow to have a piece so you don't burn yourself. That's if your daddy says it's okay. And be sure to save a piece for him in case he wants one. Deal?"

"Deal!" She blinked at me. "I want a puppy!"

I subtly shifted the brunt of the weight of the pie from one hand to the other, the scalding temperature making its way into the mitts. "You do?"

"Uh-huh. But Daddy said it's not a good idea rights now. Do you gots any good ideas?"

"Um . . . I'm not sure." Light laughter slipped free, her sweetness tugging at my chest. Maybe there was such a thing as too adorable. Because right then, I'd probably give her anything she asked me for.

I shifted the mitts again, and Rex sighed.

"Is that hot?" His teeth gritted when he asked it. As if he were dreading my answer. As if he didn't want to be concerned but couldn't stop himself.

I shifted it again. "A little bit."

He looked to the ground, issuing a soft curse beneath his breath, the word only ringing in my ear because I was able to read it on the movement of his soft, full lips. On a resigned sigh, he stepped back and widened the door the rest of the way. "Come in . . . set it on the kitchen counter."

With the way he cringed, I'd have thought the invitation caused him physical pain.

I whispered, "Thank you," and slipped inside, my body grazing his when I passed.

A tiny gasped breached my lips. The heat on my hands was nothing compared to the heat that scorched my skin.

Attraction swept me head to toe.

It was possibly the most foolish emotion I'd ever felt.

Because it was unfathomable.

Overwhelming.

Too much.

Sucking in a breath, I forced myself to step the rest of the way inside.

My jaw dropped in awe. "Wow."

The interior of their house was totally not what I'd expected. I'd expected something closer to my grandmother's house. A quaint, comfortable home that could use a fresh coat of paint among a million other things.

Shabby and totally missing the chic.

Rex's place had been entirely renovated. The floors were a gorgeous, shiny wood, and the white crown molding lining the ceilings matched the mantel and hearth of the fireplace, which was the focal point of the living room. A big television hung on the wall above, and a brown leather sectional sat in the middle of the room.

And the kitchen.

Good God.

The kitchen.

It was a dream with its butcher block island, huge oven, and farm-style sink. That small table that was my vantage through the window was nestled in the middle of the two rooms.

"This is unbelievable."

Suddenly, I was remembering Lillith telling me how he'd grown a small construction company into the biggest contractor in the area.

I spun around. "You did this?"

Discomfort rippled across his gorgeous face, something humble and vulnerable showing through the rigid veneer. "It's kind of what I do."

"You definitely do a good job of it." I didn't mean to whisper it, didn't mean to get locked in his stare, didn't mean for my mouth to go dry, or my belly to tumble and twist and flip with the most foolish kind of butterflies.

Because his jaw clenched, and his spine went rigid with my compliment.

Swallowing down the lump in my throat, I forced myself to turn away and take a breath. To get myself together. I set the pie on the counter and turned back around. "I'm sorry to barge in the way I did. I just wanted to say thank you. I really hope you enjoy the pie. I know my grandma would have wanted you to have it."

I started to make my escape, when Frankie snagged my pinky finger in her tiny fist, her voice just as excited as ever. "You wants to see my room?"

My eyes darted to Rex.

That same anger from the first day, the anger I couldn't make sense of, the anger that seemed barely contained, flamed in his eyes. Glints of fire beneath the ornate pendant lights.

I could barely force out the words. "I'm not sure that's a good idea right now. I think it's past your bedtime."

"Oh, oh, I know. You can reads me my bedtime story. How's that sound? You wanna read with me? Can she, Daddy?" She was grinning at her dad, one hundred percent oblivious to the sudden rage I could see crawl just beneath the surface of his tanned skin, the muscles ticking as he stared me down.

"I—"

"Oh, please, please, please."

I looked at Rex for help, already knowing I was so far out of bounds. My mission taking me too deep into enemy territory, and I'd tripped a bomb.

But somehow, he softened when he looked down at her. As if the little hurricane was his calm. "Five minutes, Frankie Leigh, then lights out."

"All right, Daddy. Five minutes," she promised with a resolute nod. She turned and hauled me toward the hall that opened right between the living room and kitchen, just on the other side of the table.

I stumbled along behind her, chancing a glance over my shoulder to look at her father.

Fear.

It was so blatant beneath that hard, rigid, beautiful exterior that it clamped down on my chest, a fist on my heart.

The terror in his expression tore through me like a storm.

Whipping and rending.

I pried my gaze away and followed Frankie into her room, wondering what on earth I'd actually hoped I'd achieve when I'd decided to bake him a pie.

What I knew for sure was this wasn't it. Not that it mattered. That fist on my heart squeezed with soft affection when Frankie turned around and lifted her arms out to her sides.

Pure pride as she offered me all the pink.

"You likes it? My daddy let me helps him paint all the walls, and he took me to the store and let me picks my blankies and my drawers and ever'fing! Did you knows I been painting, and I'm gonna be a painter? My grammy says so."

My gaze traced the walls. Walls that were pink. More than pink. Wisped with the hints of fairy tales and happily ever afters, the faintest outlines of rainbows and unicorns and princesses lost in the strokes of color.

Delicately.

Carefully.

Beautifully.

At the bottom of one wall was a mess of color, choppy strokes and splotches so clearly added by a tiny hand.

Oh my God. Who was this man?

Frankie dropped to her knees in front of a bookcase and pulled free a thin, worn book, waving it in the air. "This one's my favorite."

"*Stellaluna*?" I asked, a small smile ticking up at the corner of my mouth when I saw the adorable bat on the cover, the story totally unfamiliar.

"Uh-huh."

She scrambled onto her bed. "You reads it."

I knelt by the edge of her bed. "Okay."

I opened it and began to read, that lump in my throat growing as I read each page. There was something about the way Frankie listened, quieted and subdued, glued to the words that tumbled from my tongue as I read about a baby bat that'd lost its mother and was raised by a mother bird, only to be reunited with its mother at the end, remaining friends with the birds who'd welcomed it to their nest.

Why did I feel like I might cry when I finished the last page? It was a happy ending, after all. But it was still there, heavy in the air when I looked back at Frankie. She had her sheet pulled up to her chin and was clutching the material. "Did you know I lost my mommy, too?"

She whispered it like a secret.

Like trust.

I guessed that was what I'd come seeking, but I was wholly unprepared for this kind of offering. My hand was trembling when I reached out and lovingly ran my knuckles down the side of her face. "I'm so sorry, Frankie. I lost my mommy when I was little, too."

Her eyes went wide. "You did?"

"Yeah."

Her voice dipped even lower. "Did you finds her?"

"No. I tried to, but I don't think she wanted to be found. But guess what? My grandma loved me so, so much, and she took such good care of me so I didn't have to be sad."

She smiled the sweetest smile, and that fist on my heart squeezed. Squeezed and squeezed so hard it made it difficult to breathe. "My daddy takes good care of me and loves me so, so much."

"He seems like a good daddy."

Vigorously, she nodded.

Leaning forward, I set a soft kiss on her forehead, knowing I had to get out of there before I lost myself any further. "I better go. Five minutes are up, and you need to get to sleep."

"Okay," she whispered, staring up at me, our noses two inches apart.

I smiled, getting drawn deeper into the heart of this little girl before I forced myself to stand. My footsteps slowed as I walked across her room. I flipped off the light and went to pull her door closed, but at the last second, I left it open a crack. Almost instinctively.

Quietly, I edged down the hall, slowed by the turbulent silence bound to the atmosphere.

I pressed my hands to my tremoring belly when I saw Rex standing in the middle of the kitchen. The expression he wore promised he'd overheard the conversation Frankie and I had shared.

Broken, splintered fury.

It poured from him in a torrent of agony.

"I'll just go," I mumbled.

Dropping my head, I started for the door, unsure if I was cowering or if I was just staggered by what I'd unwittingly forced my way into. I felt like a fool. Naïve and reckless. Because I'd come seeking something I hadn't understood.

And I'd just stumbled into the awareness that their lives were pieced together precariously.

Fragilely.

A tender, loving, imperfect balance.

It would only take one misstep to send everything toppling over.

I reached for the latch when I felt the flurry of intensity slide up behind me, the tension suffocating, the movement stealing the air from the room.

I spun around, my back plastered to the door as he approached.

Coming closer and closer.

He wasn't touching me.

But he might as well have been.

He rested a hand on the door above my head, his face dipping toward mine, his words a breathy grunt at my ear. "What the fuck do you think you're doing to me, Rynna?"

Lust and confusion trembled through my bones, this man pushing me away and then drawing me closer.

I thought maybe neither of us could ignore it.

The overpowering attraction.

Because the fever in my veins ignited a fire in my belly.

Torrid.

Blistering.

No words would form on my tongue.

"Tell me, Rynna. What do you want with us?" he murmured, low and rough. "Because I don't have anything to offer you, and I won't let you take anything else from us."

I attempted to process what he said, what he meant.

But I couldn't focus. Couldn't see. Could feel nothing but the heat radiating between us.

Wave after blinding wave.

I gasped a breath, and he inched closer, a single knee wedging between my legs. He planted both hands on the door above my head.

Caging me in.

I felt it when he gave, the strangled sound that left him on a groan when he pressed against me.

The man was so hard.

So big.

So overwhelming.

That bottled heat reached a boiling point. Desire throbbed, lighting up between my thighs.

"Oh . . . God." I whimpered when he rubbed his cock against my hip.

A desperate sound rumbled through the strength of his chest.

A hand was suddenly on my jaw, thumb under my chin, tipping my face up to meet the ferocity in his gaze.

Rage and restraint and desire. I couldn't decipher what was happening. The push and the pull. The hatred and the need.

I could barely speak. "I . . . I thought maybe you could use a friend."

"Told you I already have all the friends I need."

Frustration bled free, my words a quieted plea. "Fine, Rex. You don't need any more friends, but maybe I do. And maybe, just maybe, I don't want to ignore this."

My hand curled in his shirt. The beat of his heart was wild beneath my hold, the energy severe.

A brilliant, neon tether that burned between us.

A live wire.

Electric.

His jaw clenched, and he rocked against my thigh. His fingers sank into my sides, as if he didn't know whether to pull me closer or force me away. "This is wrong, Rynna. You can't do this to me."

"Do what?" I whispered.

"Make me want you."

"Why?"

Pain wrenched his face.

I struggled for the words, finally forcing them into the dense air. "The last thing I want to do is hurt you. You think I don't see it? That you've been hurt enough?"

His thick throat bobbed. "You don't know me, Rynna."

"And that's why I'm here. Because I want to."

Regret seized his expression, and he peeled himself away, putting space between us. "I can't."

My spirit coiled in rejection, and those old insecurities flared. Vying for dominance. I drove them back, refusing their chains. "Because you're afraid or because you don't want me?"

Releasing a jolt of bitter laughter, he raked both hands over his face. "It's a little more complicated than that."

"You can tell me, Rex."

He shook his head. "You should go home. It's getting late."

Disappointment gusted through me. Heavy and oppressive. "Maybe you're just a coward."

He flinched, and I turned away and pulled open the door. I started to step out when his voice hit me from behind.

"You know what it feels like to be left behind, Rynna?" There was a plea behind it.

I slowly turned back to look at him.

His hands were in his jean pockets, surrender on his face, begging me to grasp something he wouldn't allow me to see.

I swallowed down everything I wanted to say and instead gave a slow nod of understanding.

Then I stepped out and quietly latched the door shut behind me.

The second I stepped outside, I was swamped with the clear

memories of it. Because all too well, I knew the feeling of being left behind.

Rynna – Five Years Old

Cold gusts of wind whipped through the playground. Laughter floated on its wings from where groups of children ran through the fields, playing in their heavy winter coats.

My head was drooped between my shoulders, my hands close to freezing where I had then wrapped around the metal chains. The tips of my toes barely touched the scooped out dirt, and I dug them in, slowly rocking myself on the swing.

I glanced up as a group of girls raced by.

Laughing.

Giggling.

My chest felt funny and my tummy hurt.

I looked up when a shadow suddenly blocked the sun.

A smile wanted to climb to my mouth, but I didn't know how to make it shine.

"Corinne Paisley," my grandmother said so softly. She knelt down in front of me and covered my freezing hands.

"Gramma."

"Why aren't you playin', child?"

"They don't like me."

She frowned. "What do you mean, they don't like you? You got the invitation. That means the birthday girl wanted you here."

I quieted my voice. "They said I'm too slow."

My grandmother huffed. "Too slow? You're the fastest thing I've ever seen."

I shook my head and clung tighter to the chains. "No, Gramma."

My grandmother brushed her knuckles down my cheek, hooked her index finger under my chin, and forced me to look in her knowing eyes. "Why do you say that?"

That feeling in my tummy was back. It hurt and made me feel like I might throw up. "I couldn't catch her, Gramma. I couldn't catch Mama. I ran so fast . . . but I couldn't catch her."

My grandmother stood and stretched out her hand. "Come on, child. Let's go home."

ten

Rex

I jerked up to sitting. Darkness played against the walls, my bedroom lit with the faintest hue of the moon streaming in through the crack in the curtains. I blinked away the edge of sleep I'd been riding, shaking off the nightmare that drenched my skin with sweat, glancing at the clock that told me it was just passed three a.m. on Monday morning.

This time . . . this time, it wasn't the dream that'd pulled me from sleep.

I tilted my head and focused on the faint sound that seeped into my room.

Crying.

That was all it took for me to throw back my covers and jump to my feet. I flew out my door and through Frankie's, skidding to a stop at the side of her bed.

She wasn't fully awake, just tossing and whimpering in her shallow sleep.

"Shh . . . what's wrong, Sweet Pea?" I urged, voice a whisper as I was reaching for her, brushing back the hair matted to her forehead.

A flash of terror jolted up my spine.

She was hot.

I pressed my palm against her forehead.

Her skin was sticky with sweat.

Shit. She was burning up.

She blinked, her eyes searching for me in the shadows. "I don't feels good, Daddy."

I scooped her into my arms, pressing a bunch of kisses to her temple like the action alone had the power to soothe away any discomfort she might feel. Fighting the panic that churned within me, I carried her into my room, flipped on the light switch, and headed straight for the attached bathroom, flipping that light on, too.

Frankie blinked against the brightness.

"Sorry, Sweet Pea," I muttered, setting her on the counter but keeping one hand on her while I rifled through the medicine cabinet to find the thermometer. "What hurts?" I asked as I fumbled to get the plastic guard on the earpiece.

"Ev'ryfing."

My hands were shaking, and it took me for fucking ever to get the damned thing snapped in place. I forced myself to slow, to be careful as I slipped it into her ear, my heart thundering in my chest as I waited the five seconds for it to beep.

104.3

Fuck.

That panic surged.

That is bad, right?

Truth was, Frankie's health wasn't a gamble I'd ever take.

I gave her a dose of Tylenol then grabbed a washcloth from the linen closet, ran it under cool water, and pressed it to her forehead. I held it there as I picked her back up and carried her out to my bed, laying her on it. "Hang on one sec, Frankie. Daddy's going to make sure you get all better."

She just gave me a trusting nod and curled up on her side, clinging a little tighter to the doll she was always dragging around. I slipped into a tee, jeans, and a pair of shoes, before I had her back in my arms, grabbing my keys and wallet from the entryway table, and rushing her out into the night.

The hour was deep, moon hanging midway on the horizon, peeking out from behind a streak of wispy clouds stretched in front of it. I wrenched open the back door of my truck and got her into her booster seat, buckled her quickly, and jogged around to the front. I slid the key into the ignition and turned it.

The engine cranked but didn't turn over.

"Shit," I muttered under my breath. I pumped the accelerator and tried the ignition again.

A slow dread sank in with the realization.

Fuck.

The cabin lights hadn't illuminated when I'd opened the doors. I glanced up. The overhead light switch was still set to on.

Fuck.

Frankie had asked for the light so she could look at a book when we were driving back from the lake on Saturday night, and I'd forgotten to switch it off. Leave it to my old-as-shit truck. Or just to me.

The battery was dead.

"Shit." I drummed my thumbs on the wheel, calculating just how long it would take me to get the battery charger out of the shed to juice this thing up, when my attention snagged in the rearview mirror.

The sleeping house behind us was bathed in a shallow pool of moonlight, the windows darkened and encased in silence.

The woman probably hated me.

At least she should.

I still couldn't believe the dick move I'd pulled two nights ago, the way I couldn't stop from pressing myself against her, taking a little bit of what I couldn't have.

I knew better.

But I couldn't stop after I had heard what'd gone down in Frankie's room. That quiet understanding that had poured from Rynna, like she might actually have the ability to get what me and Frankie had been through. Like maybe she'd been through some of the same bullshit, too.

Goal had been nothing more than thanking her. But I'd gone

and gotten stupid. Had gotten too close. Had touched her because I couldn't stop myself.

Not when I was engulfed with her presence. Cherries and sugar. So goddamned sweet.

None of that mattered right then. The only thing that mattered was Frankie, who was moaning in the backseat, her head bobbing all over the place. Worst was I couldn't tell if she was nodding off to sleep or truly coming in and out of consciousness.

Any loyalty I had didn't come close to touching that.

I hopped out of the truck, wrenched open Frankie's door, and had her back in my arms in the next second. With one arm holding her against me, I grabbed her booster seat and then strode across the vacant street.

There was no hesitation when I bounded up the steps and pounded on Rynna's door.

I stood there, shifting my feet anxiously while I waited, that unease growing tenfold when I saw a light flicker on through an upstairs window. Thirty seconds later, footsteps were shuffling across the floor. I could almost feel her confusion when I sensed her peering out the peephole at us.

But the second she did, there was no delay, and she was tearing open the door.

Concern was written all over that face.

That goddamned striking face that made something inside me light up at the sight of her.

"Oh my God, Frankie Leigh." It was whispered panic pouring from her pretty mouth. "What happened?"

Those java eyes darted to my face.

Worry.

Fear.

I forced down every convoluted feeling I had about her. "She woke up with a fever. My battery's dead in my truck. Need to borrow your car so I can take her to the ER."

"I'll drive you," she said instead of agreeing. The girl was already sliding on a pair of flip-flops that had been sitting by the door.

"That's not—"

She held up a hand, cutting me off the way I had continually done to her. "She's sick, and you're obviously upset." Her tone softened. "I'll drive you. It's not a problem."

The part of me that always needed to prove that I could raise my daughter alone wanted to rear its head and fight her. I bit it back. Focused on the feeling of my daughter in my arms.

Frankie's well-being was my only concern.

"Thank you."

I should absolutely not be accepting this woman's generosity.

Every fucking one of the reasons why surged to the forefront of my mind. Screaming at me why this was wrong. To watch the line I was toeing.

Somehow, I couldn't bring myself to care.

Rynna grabbed her purse and stepped out, still wearing what she'd obviously gone to bed in—a pair of thin cotton striped pants and a black tank.

I dropped my gaze. At least I managed to find the self-control not to watch the sweet sway of her luscious ass.

Guessed it was the little wins.

I followed her to her SUV, situated Frankie into her booster seat in the backseat, and climbed in beside my daughter.

I pretended I couldn't feel the weight of Rynna's worry when she kept glancing through the rearview mirror at us, pretended her concern wasn't there, palpable in the air.

Pretended it didn't mean more to me than it should.

I brushed back Frankie's hair and pressed a kiss to her forehead, feeling the heat radiating off her, praying she was fine. I told myself every kid got sick. It was a part of life. But that didn't mean my guts weren't twisted. It didn't mean the fear wasn't there. It didn't mean that every day of my life I wouldn't be terrified of losing her, too.

eleven

Rynna

The big double doors Rex and Frankie had walked through three hours before swung open for what had to be the millionth time that night. I shot to my feet when this time it was finally Rex carrying out a sleeping Frankie in his arms.

The same blond-haired guy who'd been sitting with Rex at the bar on Friday night followed close behind them, and I had to do a double take when I saw he was wearing a pair of blue scrubs and a stethoscope around his neck.

Even though he still exuded that same uptight, rigid stance, Rex seemed relieved. The bounding tension that had orbited his being seemed to have dissipated.

And that relieved . . . me.

It was true.

Gone was the weight that had crushed like a pile of rubble and stone while I'd sat there alone, waiting for word. For anyone or anything to confirm that sweet little girl was fine. My rationale told me it was just a virus or a bug. Yet, this other part of me—the one that had panicked when I'd found the two of them standing outside my door in the middle of the night—had worried and fretted the entire time they'd been in the back.

God, it'd taken a matter of days for me to get in over my head.

But I'd barely been able to focus on anything else since I'd left Rex Gunner staring after me on Saturday night after I'd read Frankie that story. More confused than I'd ever been. His touch lingering on my skin and his words rambling through my head.

Honestly, I'd been shocked when he came to me for help.

But any reservations I'd wanted to hold had been wiped away by the sheer terror he'd attempted to keep veiled in the vast abyss of those stormy eyes. Eradicated by the fierce protectiveness that had radiated from him.

Most of all was this helplessness he couldn't seem to keep contained. It was in the way his chin had quivered as he'd stood on my porch with his daughter held in the safety of his arms.

"How is she?" I whispered, even though the waiting room was loud and bright. I couldn't do anything but reach out and thread my fingers through her brown hair. She was absolutely peaceful in his hold, and that simple touch sent a wave of affection bounding through my veins.

I sucked in a breath, surprised by the sudden, all-encompassing emotion.

Quickly, I turned my attention to search Rex's face.

His stunning, hard, brutal face.

Obviously, it was a more dangerous place to avert my attention. Because the emotion grew.

"It's just a virus." That rough, scruffy jaw was held tight, though there was a heavy solace that flooded out with the words.

The man who'd followed him out elbowed Rex in the ribs. "Rex here takes overprotectiveness to a whole new level. If he had let that Tylenol kick in, he would have known she was just fine."

Rex grunted. "Not a chance I was willing to take."

I wondered just what chances Rex was ever willing to take.

Though, I had to agree with him on this one. "It was good you brought her," I told him, hoping to encourage him. Hoping he'd get that I saw the kind of father he was.

The man next to him laughed a disbelieving sound, as if he took some kind of satisfaction in the situation. He shoved his hand toward me. "Dr. Kale Bryant, at your service."

I returned his shake. "Rynna Dayne."

A smug smile took to his handsome face, his eyes darting between Rex and me, his voice fueled by an undercurrent of laughter. "Oh, you have no idea just how nice it is to meet you, Ms. Dayne."

Rex almost rolled his eyes. "*Dr.* Kale Bryant. I remember the days when I used to let you cheat off my math tests, asshole. Take it down a notch."

Kale clapped him on the back. "Hey, don't go knocking that whole doctor bit. Your ass would still be sitting out here waiting to have your daughter seen if it weren't for me."

"I'm not knocking anything. You know I owe you."

Maybe I was surprised to hear the sincerity behind his admission. I guessed I shouldn't have been. Not with the way he clutched Frankie to him.

Guarding her.

Protecting her.

"We should get her home," I offered. Again, I glanced at his precious child. Her chubby cheek was pressed so perfectly to his chest and her fist was wound in the fabric of his shirt, as if the steady beat of his heart had lulled her into peace.

Rex lifted his chin to Kale. "Thanks, man. Honestly . . . don't think you know how much I appreciate you being there for her like this."

Waving him off, Kale let his gaze slide to the sweet child. "Anything for Sweet Pea Frankie Leigh. That's my godbaby, you know."

He looked at me when he said the last, and a smile was pulling through the exhaustion that threatened to drag me under. "No way."

Kale was all dimples as he raised his arms to the sides. "Don't let all these awesome good looks fool you. I'm totally capable of raising a kid." He threw a playful punch into Rex's shoulder. "Almost as good as this guy."

My smile grew as my eyes volleyed between the two of them, totally taken aback by the closeness Rex shared with Kale. But in a pleasant way. Maybe he didn't need any more friends, after all.

I looked back at him, and my stomach twisted.

But that didn't mean he didn't need something.

Someone to fill that glaring void that was so obviously radiating within him.

And with every layer that was exposed, more and more I wanted to be that person.

"I've got her," he grumbled barely above his breath when I attempted to help him get her out of the backseat of my car.

A calm stillness held fast to the cool air, daybreak just a hint of a blaze that lifted from the horizon. Glittering rays chased away the night and lit the sky in pinks and oranges and a welcoming blue.

The day brand new.

Bursting with possibilities.

"At least let me get the door open for you." I said it with zero frustration when I wrenched free the keys he had clutched in his hand and quietly climbed the porch steps.

Somehow, I'd come to understand this man felt he needed to do things on his own.

Or maybe he'd just been forced into that role, and he knew nothing else.

Behind me, I could feel them, this buzz of energy that emanated from their skin. It made me feel as if I stood at the very edge of something magnificent, a stranger peering in to witness something pure and absolute. Alive and profound. A thriving force that threatened to suck me into its depths.

Sliding the key into the lock, I turned the lever and opened the door, standing aside as he headed straight through, his long legs eating up the floor as he disappeared down the hallway.

I wavered there, my mind flashing back to two nights ago when he'd had me pinned just inside. The memory spun around me, that fury that had been so blatantly evident.

Almost as acute as the brokenness that had seeped from his flesh and poured into mine.

Nearly as intense as the desire that had lashed between us.

I didn't even know him, and the man was so mesmerizingly conflicted that he had me overwhelmed with the need to step closer. To dip my fingers in to explore and discover.

But it was more than that. There was something about him that made me ache. Something that made my chest and my spirit and my stomach revolt at the thought of walking away.

Sucking in a breath, I came to a quick decision. Stepping inside, I closed the door behind me and crept down the hall, unable or maybe unwilling to stop myself from peering through the doorway into Frankie's room.

My insides trembled as I watched them.

Rex carefully laid her in her bed. Gently, he brushed the chaotic tangle of hair from her forehead. His gaze was so tender when he stared down at her trusting face, his spirit so soft when he edged forward and brushed a kiss to one of her rosy, plump cheeks.

My throat thickened, and I clung to the jamb.

Enthralled and transfixed.

God.

This. Man.

He was undoing something inside me.

Uncovering something I'd never even realized I wanted.

Slowly, he stood. His body seemed so big in the emerging day, the raw strength of him wrapping me in chains. When he shifted, those eyes locked on me, his shadowy figure moving my direction.

I struggled to find air. Reason.

I fumbled a step back into the hallway, fortifying myself, never sure where his anger might take us or where this attraction might lead us.

He stopped in the doorway. His breaths short and heavy.

That same awareness flickered to life. Only this time, it seemed as if it'd gained power from the rising sun.

"Thank you." The words landed on me like a rough caress.

"Of course. When I told you I thought you might need a friend, I meant it. That means if you need me . . . I'm here."

He nodded, though it seemed reluctant. As if he were crossing an invisible line by agreeing. "Okay."

I nodded back, shocked that he'd yielded. "Okay. I'll . . . talk to you later. Just"—I fisted a hand over my heart—"please let me know if you or Frankie need anything at all. I'd really like to know how she's doing. I know I'll be thinking about her all day."

With that, I turned and headed for the door. I needed to get out of there.

Clear my head of the foolish ideas that had begun to spin. This foolish impulse to jump into torrid waters when I couldn't see the bottom. To sate the churning need that prodded at my consciousness.

Most of all, I wanted to respect him. The space he so clearly needed.

But I had no idea how that was going to work when it was starting to hurt when I walked away.

twelve

Rex

I watched her escaping down the hallway.

At least, that was what it felt like. Like she was fleeing. Putting as much space between us as possible.

She should.

Maybe she was smart enough to run from whatever steadily built in the atmosphere whenever we shared the same space.

Ominous and powerful and unrelenting.

Her footsteps were swift, that silky mound of chestnut a complete disaster where she had it twisted high on top of her head. It left the creamy, delicate flesh of her neck exposed.

I itched, fighting against every single emotion I couldn't allow myself to feel.

Fuck.

I needed her out.

Gone.

Away.

Where she couldn't confuse, corrupt, and confound.

Where she couldn't riddle my mind and tempt my hand.

Where she didn't hold the power to squeeze between the

cracks she continually chipped and etched into my spirit, like the exterior I'd built didn't even exist. The girl eased into those spaces that were meant to remain closed off and shut down.

Not that it seemed to matter.

The tension only amplified the farther she got. Her footsteps grew fainter, but the space between them ignited a new kind of gravity.

Everything grew taught and tight and rigid. The air. My chest. My thoughts.

Drawing me in a direction I knew I shouldn't go.

But standing there? I had no power. Because her scent still lingered around me, clouding my senses.

My mouth watered. Cherry and sugar. So goddamned sweet.

I was suddenly inundated with the way she'd felt against me two nights ago.

Her warmth and her comfort and that fucking insane body that made me lose my mind.

It'd been in that foolish moment when I'd given in to temptation when I should have been chasing her away. A single brush of her body had heated every inch of me. My cock harder than it'd ever been, desperate for a different kind of taste from the one she'd been offering. Fuck. How badly had I wanted to get lost in the slick heat of her tight body?

Every perfect curve seduction.

Every defined inch sin.

But it was the way she'd looked at Frankie when we'd rushed through the emergency room doors that had tipped me to uneven ground.

The floor crumbling from under me.

Logic shot. My feet were moving without my brain ever giving me time to calculate the consequences.

But right then?

I didn't fucking care.

Didn't care what this would cost.

I stalked down the hall and through the living room.

The air sparked with every determined step.

She was already down the porch steps by the time I caught

her by the wrist, and she gasped one of those throaty, sexy sounds that shot straight to my dick.

Fuck it all, if that simple contact point didn't ignite to an all-out boil. Heat streaked through my veins, eclipsing everything. Reason and sanity and judgment.

I whirled her around. In a second flat, I had her back pressed against the front of my truck where no one could see us. My fingers tangled in that mess of unruly hair, our faces a breadth apart. My heart stuttered when those innocent eyes latched on to mine, so wide and confused when she realized I had her pinned.

Just like me.

I crushed my mouth to hers, because I had no fuckin' time for hesitation. I just needed to feel something different from the constant turmoil that raged inside. For just a moment, touch on something that felt like hope.

Even when I knew it was so fucking wrong.

On a sigh, she opened for me. Her lips so damned soft when they began to move with mine.

Sweetly.

Tentatively.

I coaxed and prodded, needing more. My lips tugged and nipped at the soft plumpness, my mouth growing hungrier with each desperate pass. Begging for the kind of reprieve I was terrified only she could give.

She gave. Her breaths turned ragged when I swept my tongue into the well of her mouth for a taste.

God. I was right.

So damned sweet.

I deepened the kiss. Taking more with each lick of my tongue. Or maybe it was Rynna who was stealing bits of me with each nip and tug of those full, full lips.

Lust.

It consumed me.

Blinding.

Constricting my cells and straining my muscles.

I pressed every rigid, hard line of my body into all her soft curves. Overwhelmed. Aching in a way I hadn't in years. Like maybe if I got close enough things might not hurt so bad.

"Rex." It was all a whimper when she sank her fingers into my shoulders, and her touch became just as desperate as mine.

Her kiss just as mad.

Her hands coasted from my shoulders down my arms, hitting my biceps where we were skin on skin. The contact burned in the most blissful kind of way, and I sucked in a shattered breath when she was pushing up under the sleeves of my T-shirt, fingertips tracing across the tattoo etched on my arm.

I groaned.

In pleasure.

In agony.

I didn't know.

"Rynna," I grated at her mouth. I cupped that bewitching face in my hands before I glided my palms down her neck and tipped back her head. "I don't even fucking know you. How is it possible you have this kind of hold on me?"

The words were a jumble of incoherency. I moved my mouth down over her jaw. I was sure I was getting drunk on her breaths, getting lost in the crash of her heart that hammered with the thready beat of mine.

My hands trailed down that body. That body that had taunted me since the moment I'd seen her come barreling out of her grandmother's door. I traced her shoulders, moving across the hollow of her throat, trailing down her chest.

Maybe I'd known it then. That this girl would wreck me. Because I could feel myself coming apart. Piece by piece.

She sighed a barely audible, "Yes."

Fuck.

What was I doing?

But my dick was so on board, and all the reasons this was the damned worst idea I'd had in years went galloping into the distance.

I palmed one of those gorgeous tits, her nipple firm beneath the thin fabric of her tank.

She gasped and pushed harder into my touch.

"Shit," I muttered. Maybe it was that very second that

insanity took me over, because I didn't care that we were outside. That someone might hear us.

Instead, I edged back to look at her where she writhed against the grill of my truck, her chest arching with her need for me, her lips swollen and sweet.

Everything shook around me.

An earthquake.

Trembling and cracking and crumbling.

I yanked down the collar of her tank and exposed her.

She was braless. Her tits just shy of a handful, skin so smooth, nipples a dusky pink and pebbled tight.

"Gorgeous," I rumbled before I ducked down to lap at the peak, drawing her rosy nipple between my teeth.

She drove her fingers in my hair. Pulling. Begging. "Rex. Oh my God . . . please."

I growled, my mouth moving upward through the valley of her chest, my nose nudging beneath her chin to grant me access to the snowy skin of her neck.

Her pulse beat an erratic, unsteady thrum.

I latched on to it. Sucking her flesh into my mouth as I slipped my hand down her side, over her hip, and down to her knee. I hooked her leg around my waist, all too quick to press my eager dick to the overwhelming heat that blazed from her pussy.

Barely a hint of her through her sleep pants and underwear, but I nearly came right there.

It'd been so long. So fuckin' long, and I was losing my grip, sanity just slipping out of my reach.

I kept rocking my cock covered by my jeans against her clit, loving the way she moaned and whimpered my name, the girl struggling to stay quiet so her moans weren't carried on the wind.

Shit.

It was so sexy, the girl in the spotlight of the breaking day.

I wanted to tear every scrap of clothes from our bodies and sink all the way in.

Disappear in that tight heat of her body.

I bit down on her collarbone as I thrust against her like some teenaged kid who'd never gotten his dick wet.

But that was what it felt like.

Like I was coming up on something great.

Something bigger than I understood.

Every muscle in Rynna went tight, and she sucked a sharp breath into her lungs before she started quaking all around me.

She did her best to stifle a deep moan while she came right there against my truck.

Her knees went weak while I continued to work myself against her hot body, wondering just how far I was going to let this madness go.

It only took the weak cry floating from Frankie's room for me to find that answer.

For me to come tumbling back down to reality.

To the truth of who I was. To my responsibilities.

I edged back, fighting the dread that spiked like barbs at the base of my throat.

"Shit." I shook my head, trying to orient myself. To rip myself from her body. I stepped back, my body still raging, barely able to look at her after the shit I'd just pulled.

Rynna reached for me with a trembling hand. "Rex . . ."

How was it possible that I saw understanding flash through her expression?

"I'm so fucking sorry, Rynna. God, I don't know what the fuck I'm doing."

Rynna resituated her clothing, stepping back out onto the walkway, all lit up in the new day laying siege to the summer sky. For a moment, she just stared back at me. That energy flickered in the air. The softest smile rimmed her mouth. "You don't have to be."

Then she turned and crossed the street while I stood there like a fool, staring at the spot she'd just left vacant.

I guessed maybe that was what I'd always been.

A fool.

Shaking myself off, I rushed back up the steps and inside.

"Daddy." The tiny cry filtered down the hall, and I reined in all the emotions and locked them there where they belonged.

Because just like I'd told Kale, I only needed one girl in my life.

And right then?

My girl needed me.

The doorbell rang. The words to the book I'd been reading Frankie trailed off. Instantly, my breaths turned shallow, my heart skyrocketing with a boom.

God. I really had lost it, my mind and body still reeling from whatever the fuck it was I'd thought I was doing earlier this morning when I'd had Rynna up against my truck.

I'd resisted for years.

And it was the girl next door who'd become irresistible.

Guilt welled in the deepest parts of me. In those sacred places I'd just desecrated.

I shifted where I was propped up on the headboard of Frankie's bed with the book lifted out in front of us. My daughter was sprawled halfway across my chest, her head twisted to the side so she could see the pictures.

I'd basically been there all day, alternating between reading her stories, checking her temperature, and watching her sleep.

"Who's that?" she whispered. Those brown eyes lit with a flash of excitement, promising me whatever sickness she'd been suffering from had finally begun to run its course.

"Not sure. You expecting a party or something?" I teased, tapping my index finger against her button nose, trying to pretend like the mere idea of Rynna standing on the other side of the door didn't have me in knots.

She scrunched that nose with the cutest grin. "People aren't suppose to gets a party just for feelin' better, silly."

"No?" I feigned ignorance.

"No way! Only prize people gets for feelin' better is having to go backs to work."

Laughter shot from my mouth in the same second affection stabbed me in the chest, so deep I thought it might cut me in two. But that was the thing about loving Frankie Leigh.

I loved her so much it physically hurt.

I ruffled a playful hand through her hair. "Sounds to me like you've been spending too much time with your grammy."

Shock had her mouth dropping open. "There's no such thing as too much Grammy times, Daddy. Don't you knows that?"

I laughed again, almost deciding to ignore the door, but then Frankie hopped off the bed. She wrapped both her tiny hands around one of my wrists, yanking with all her might. Of course, the only nudge she gave was the one that shot through my heart. "Come on, Daddy. There's someone ats the door. We gots to see who it is."

"Okay, okay," I said, relenting, hating the way my nerves buzzed through my body when I did. The way those defenses wanted to go up.

All the while, I was wishing there was a way I could throw rescue ropes over the side.

That I could climb out of the bullshit mess I'd made of my life and jump into one where taking a girl like Rynna Dayne would be okay.

With Frankie's hand wrapped around my index finger, I stumbled along behind her. The kid was far too chipper as she bee-lined for the door. Maybe I had overreacted.

She popped up on her toes to peer out the side window and out on to the porch. She huffed when she dropped back onto her heels. "I finks we were too late. Nobody's there." I set a hand on her shoulder, guiding her behind me, that kick of protectiveness always at the ready to take hold. I twisted the lock so I could open the door and peer outside.

She was right.

No one was there.

But someone had been.

To my right, someone had left a tray on the short wooden table between the two rocking chairs. I'd made them what seemed a million years ago, back when I'd been nothing but a fool. We'd just been moving into this place, and I'd been thinking maybe I'd finally outrun that shadow.

The scar that forever eclipsed the true joy of my life.

I should've known better.

A large lidded bowl rested on the tray, and a tented card was propped to the side of it.

Squealing, Frankie flew out from behind me. "Oh, look it, Daddy. It gots my name on it. It *is* a present for me."

My gaze darted across the street. The old house sat silent and unmoving, just the branches of the big trees that fronted her yard waving their welcome.

Emotion slammed me. Unstoppable. Too much. Overwhelming.

Pushing out a sigh, I forced myself to walk all the way out.

My senses were punched again when I reached down and grabbed the handles of the tray. Only this time, it was the amazing aroma that lifted from the bowl, striking me like comfort and warmth.

Comfort and warmth that was intended for my daughter.

Thoughtful in a way I couldn't allow the woman to be.

My sweet girl trotted along beside me while I carried the offering inside and set in on the small dining table.

"What's it, Daddy?"

She peered up at me with that trusting grin, her fingers threaded together where she leaned against her elbows on the table to get a better look. She looked like she was already issuing up a prayer for the food she'd been given.

"Careful," I warned, lifting the lid.

It was a chicken pot pie. The kind Corinne Dayne had been famous for.

Homemade.

Handmade.

The aroma of it so overpowering, my mouth watered.

My damned hand was shaking when I reached down and snatched the note. Frankie's name was written across the front in the prettiest handwriting I'd ever seen.

I lifted the flap to find what was written inside.

> *Dear Frankie Leigh,*
> *Remember when I told you I had some of the recipes to my*

grandma's pies? I have a special secret just for you—I have the recipe for the pot pie she used to make me whenever I felt sick, too. It was always my favorite, and sometimes, I didn't even mind getting sick, because I knew she would make it and soon everything would be better. I remember being a little girl, just like you, eating this same pie at our kitchen table right across the street. With every bite I took, I knew that my grandma had to love me more than the whole wide world.

Last night, I wished with all of me that I could have taken your sickness away. But maybe there's a chance this pie might make you feel better the way it always did me. I sure hope so.

All my love,
Rynna

Damn her.

Damn her straight to hell for teasing me this way.

Damn her for weaseling her way in and making herself a place in a spot where she knew she would never stay.

Fuck me for wanting it.

"Read it to me! Oh, read it to me, Daddy! Wha's it say?"

"It's from Rynna next door," I told her, trying to keep the thick emotion from clotting my voice. "She said her grandma used to make her this same pot pie when she wasn't feeling well. She thought it might help you feel better, too, so she made you some."

Those big brown eyes went wide with hope, and her voice dropped like it might be a secret. "Do you think it mights be as good as cherry pie?"

My attention darted to the sweet pie still sitting on the countertop. The pie I'd dipped my finger into the second I'd gotten a chance this afternoon. Because shit. That little taste of her outside this morning had not been close to being enough.

"How about we test it out? You get some of this food into your belly, and I'll heat you up a small piece of cherry pie. How's that sound?"

"It sounds like you're the best daddy in the whole wide world . . . just like Rynna's grammy."

If only that were the truth.

thirteen

Rynna

I stepped out of my grandmother's diner and was smacked in the face by the Alabama heat. A sticky sheen of sweat slicked my skin, and my arm still burned from the exertion of scrubbing on at least thirty years of built-up lard and oils splattered on every surface in the old kitchen. I figured it wouldn't hurt to work on what little could be salvaged inside. It at least gave me something to keep my hands busy while I waited for my appointment with the bank so I could officially put in my application for a loan.

It was painful waiting. Not knowing. Wondering if I was going to have what it took to bring this dusty diner back to life. If anyone would believe in me. If they'd give me a chance to make this old dream a reality.

After today, I was bone tired. But there was an eager hum that whirred through my blood. A satisfaction that had been lacking in all the years I'd been away. While in San Francisco, I'd attempted to convince myself a life outside of Gingham Lakes was what I wanted.

Some part of me had always known it'd been a lie.

I could almost hear my grandmother whispering in my ear,

"Do what makes you happy, child. In my experience, joy is a choice. Life is rough. Don't expect it not to be. But if we aren't laughin', we're crying. Choose to laugh. Choose what brings you joy. And when you choose your path, it might not always be the easiest one, but it'll always be the right one."

I lifted my face to the blue sky, squeezed my eyes closed, and silently murmured, "I chose this path, Gramma. Even if it's not the easiest one, I know it's where my joy is waiting for me."

My eyes opened, my gaze landing on the construction site across the street. It was deserted, work done for the day, but that didn't stop my mind from wandering to Rex.

After I'd left his house yesterday morning, I'd gone home and crawled straight into bed. With being awake at the emergency room for most of the night, I'd anticipated I'd immediately fall asleep, but I'd tossed.

Exhausted but wired.

Drained but restored.

As if I'd been left spinning somewhere in limbo.

Lost in a blissful kind of purgatory where I'd stumbled upon a man with the skill to bring me to orgasm with a few mind-rending strokes of his body. But there had been so much pained remorse in his expression afterward that it'd sent me crashing to the ground.

No question, he'd needed to run to Frankie. It was exactly what he should do. His child should always be his first priority.

But what hurt was it was clear his regret went so much deeper than the simple fact we'd let ourselves lose control where we'd been hidden by his massive truck. Deeper than the fact he needed to pull away to return to her.

And with Rex?

I felt out of control.

Spinning from a thread and barely hanging on.

He knocked the ground out from under my feet.

Shaking myself out of it, I pushed from the door and locked up before stepping out onto the sidewalk.

The scene in front of me made me wonder how I'd ever left this place. The old buildings built up on each side, massive shade trees grown up through the planters and shading the store fronts that still boasted some of the old shops my grandmother had gone to when she'd been my age.

You'd think the restoration in progress would have stolen from the charm.

It didn't.

It only amplified.

The renovated buildings bore crisp new awnings and eaves, and the new brick structures climbed up between them to give the exact cohesive feel Lillith had been so proud of the day I'd first met her.

One day soon, Pepper's Pies would be a part of this rebirth.

I inhaled a satisfied breath and started for my SUV, glancing down to fiddle with my key ring to grab the right one.

Then I smacked right into a firm body.

"Oh goodness, I'm sorry, excuse me," I mumbled through my surprise.

Hands came out to steady me by the shoulders.

"Whoa, slow down." The man chuckled, and my attention shot up. My eyes grew round, and my mouth went dry, my heart bottoming out in my stomach.

He smiled at me.

Confused by my reaction.

His head angled to the side, tone filled with an easy chuckle. "Tiny thing like you should slow down before you fall and mess up that pretty face."

I took a staggering step backward. Still unable to say anything. Still unable to respond.

I couldn't breathe, my heart locked in the center of my chest.

A rush of dizziness swept through my head, my balance lost.

He didn't even recognize me.

The bastard didn't even recognize me.

I pressed a hand over my mouth, trying to keep back the cry that clamored up my throat, just standing there, staring at him.

Unable to move.

Paralyzed.

Frozen by shock.

By fear.

By hatred.

"You okay, beautiful?" he asked as if he had the capacity to care.

I wished with all of me I had the strength to slap him across the face. Or maybe spit in it. Scream at him to go to hell, right where he belonged.

Instead, I stood there staring at him in terrified disbelief.

He started to reach for me, and I finally snapped out of my stupor. I frantically smacked his hand away as I stumbled back. Fighting tears, I broke away and rushed for my Cherokee. I fumbled with the key, hands shaking so badly I could barely get it into the lock. Another rush of dizziness swept through me, a violent storm, taking me under.

I could barely haul myself into the driver's seat.

Nausea whirled.

I slammed the door and locked it, hands squeezing on the steering wheel. I fought the urge to shift my truck into drive, tuck tail, and run.

He was there.

He is here.

Bile climbed my throat when Aaron looked back over his shoulder at me. He shook his head as if I were insane then turned and continued down the sidewalk as if it meant nothing at all, as my mind was jerked back to the days I'd do anything to forget.

Rynna - Twelve Years Old

I grinned eagerly, excitement blazing through my nerves. I couldn't believe I'd been invited.

Something about this felt special. As if things were finally gonna change. I hated being left out. Gramma said it was just because I was too shy, but I wasn't so sure.

I threaded my fingers together and set them on my lap where I sat with my legs crisscrossed on Janel's bedroom floor.

We'd made a circle.

The circle.

My eyes made a pass over the faces: Kimberly, Sarah, Ben, Kerry, Janel, and Aaron.

Aaron.

Butterflies stormed my belly and sweat slicked my palms.

Aaron.

I kept glancing at him, wishing I was sitting right next to him, but I was too nervous to make the move.

But at least I was there. That was all that mattered.

A dim light glowed from a bedside lamp, but otherwise, the lights were off.

Janel set the bottle in the middle of the circle.

Kerry giggled. "This game is so stupid." But she was peeking at Ben when she said it, and I wondered if she was as nervous as I was. If everyone was.

Janel cleared her throat, and I thought no. Janel was never scared.

"Okay, these are the rules," Janel said. "When you spin the bottle, whoever it lands on, you have to kiss them for three seconds." Her voice dropped with the scandalous challenge. "On the lips."

"Even if it's a girl?" Kimberly asked.

Janel huffed. "Isn't that what I said?"

"Ewww." Sarah kicked her feet and violently shook her head.

"Stop being a baby," Janel said, eyeing her hard. "You said you wanted to come, so you have to play by my rules."

Janel was the leader. She'd always been. Me and Janel had known each other forever. Janel's momma worked at the diner with my gramma, so we were together a lot. Of course, that didn't mean I got invited to things like this.

Janel spun the bottle first. It landed on Sarah. Janel crawled over and kissed her on the lips. Everyone counted to three. Janel sat back. "See, that wasn't so bad, was it?"

Sarah pressed her hand over her mouth. "I don't think I want to kiss anyone."

Janel glanced at Kimberly with a roll of her eyes. "I told you she wasn't cool enough."

Janel set her gaze on me. "How about you?"

The nod of my head was emphatic, my nerves abuzz.

"Good. You're next."

Was it possible my belly could move all the way to my throat? Clumsily, I spun the bottle. It landed on Kimberly. I squeezed my eyes closed when I leaned across the circle and kissed her, a peck to the lips. It wasn't so bad. But that wasn't who I wanted to kiss.

And I felt so shaky, my heart fluttery and funny while we spun and spun, continually taking turns.

Aaron spun the bottle again. The bottle spun and wobbled until the top of the neck finally pointed at me. Those butterflies smacked their wings, my stomach wild.

Aaron started to lean across the circle. Janel set her arm out in front of him. "I think you two should do this in private. In the closet."

My eyes grew wide. "But—"

"My house, my rules, remember?"

I climbed to my feet, suddenly feeling sweaty as I glanced down at my body then at Aaron's when he reluctantly stood. Janel hopped to her feet. "This way."

I followed her across her room to the closet. Janel opened the door. "Get in."

It was dark inside, and for a second, I hesitated. Everything felt wrong and funny, the warnings my gramma had always given me about being smart and if something felt off, it probably was. To trust my gut.

I ignored it. I had finally been invited and I wasn't going to mess this up. I stepped inside, waiting for Aaron to step in with me, but then Janel laughed so loud a shudder rolled through me just as the door slammed shut in my face.

Laughter roared from the other side. Panic welled. I jerked at the handle, but it didn't budge. "Come on, Janel, it's not funny. Let me out."

More laughter. "Did you really think Aaron would want to kiss a fat cow? You're so stupid, Rynna Dayne. Like he would ever like you. Like any of us would like you."

Tears burned in my eyes. "Please."

"Twenty minutes time out for the cow," Janel sing-songed. Their laughter rang through the thin door, and I sank to the floor of the closet, hugging my knees to my chest, wondering if I would ever stop feeling so alone.

fourteen

Rex

"Open wide and say ah."

From her spot on the edge of the exam table, Frankie did as she was told, opening her mouth so wide I didn't know how he wasn't looking at the inside of her stomach. She gurgled an elongated *ahhhhh* that was mixed with a giggle and did her best not to fall into a fit of laughter when Kale put a depressor against her tongue and shined a light on her throat.

"Oh, no." If Kale weren't acting a fool, exaggerating his worry, I would have been on him in a flash, demanding to know which of the bajillion horrible illnesses could be the actual culprit for her symptoms.

So yeah.

I'd tumbled down the rabbit hole of internet searches on my phone while I'd been watching her sleep her fever away this last weekend.

Apparently, Google was the number you were actually supposed to multiply your worry by.

Because that shit was scary.

But Kale was being Kale.

Tossing out teases at Frankie like they were candy.

Frankie's eyes went wide. "What's it, Uncle Kale?"

He dropped his voice to a secretive whisper. "Don't tell anyone, but I think there are monsters living in your throat."

Frankie giggled harder and lifted her shoulders to her chubby cheeks. "Nu-uh. There no monsters livin' in my throat."

Kale huffed dramatically. "And how do you know that? I'm the doctor here."

"My daddy told me there's no such fing as monsters."

"And your daddy is smarter than I am?" With the way Kale cut me an evil eye, I wondered how much of his offense was feigned.

"Course he's smarter than you. He's the smartest daddy in the whole, whole, whole wide world." Her arms pumped up higher every time she repeated the word. She glanced over at me. "Right, Daddy?"

I shrugged from where I was leaned against the wall with my arms crossed over my chest. "My daughter is the smartest kid around. She knows her stuff."

He quirked a brow. "And that *stuff* is that you're actually smarter than I am?"

My lips twitched. "Guess so."

This time Frankie threw her arms all the way in the air. "I know all the stuffs."

"Is that so?" He poked her belly. Instantly, she was howling, grabbing at his hand.

"It's so! It's so! It's so, so, so." She kept chanting as he jumped into a full-fledged tickle attack, and my chest was doing that crazy thing where it felt too full and too proud and too content, which happened just about every damned time I looked my daughter's way.

I was telling no lies.

She was my light.

The life inside me.

She sobered about as quickly as she'd collapsed into laughter. "Am I alls better, Uncle Kale?"

He touched her chin with his knuckle. "All better, pumpkin

pie."

Her face scrunched. "I don't likes punkin' pie, Uncle. I likes cherry pie."

Of course she did.

Incredulous, his brow lifted. "You want me to call you cherry pie?"

He was holding back laughter, looking over at me like he was just waiting for me to bust up.

"Uh . . . can we not?" I said, pushing from the wall, irritated because I knew exactly where Kale's mind had gone traipsing. Right to that damned Warrant video Ollie had made us watch on repeat for the entire summer between third and fourth grade. Apparently, fourth grade was right about the time when Ollie had decided girls weren't exactly *gross*.

Or maybe I was irritated simply because the mention of cherry pie had my mind traipsing straight to thoughts of Rynna.

Neither of us could seem to resist whatever the fuck that insanity was that burned between us. No question, she was just as much a prisoner to the ruthless energy that thrived between us as I was. This violent need. Growing stronger every time it forced us together.

Irresistible.

Stupid.

Reckless.

God knew that was what touching her had been.

Reckless. Just because you knew something that didn't make you wise.

And I swore that touching her had scored the very depth of me.

It'd been too much. Too good. Too right when I knew every second of it was so goddamned wrong.

Most terrifying part was I wasn't sure I'd ever wanted a girl the way I wanted her.

Not in all my life.

Watching her walk away with all that understanding on her face? That had been a kick to the gut. Hurting her when it was the last thing I wanted to do. But the only thing I had to offer her was the fucking mess I'd made.

I shook myself from the thoughts. "Everything look okay?"

"All's good, my friend."

From under the arms, Kale lifted Frankie, hoisting her into the air and making her squeal and flap her arms like she was flying, before he set her on her feet. He patted the top of her head. "Good as new, right, Frankie Leigh, Cherry Pie?"

He winked at me, and I elbowed him in the side. "Don't even, man."

Gasping through a laugh, he clutched his ribs. "Dude, not cool. Not cool. I'm just messing with you. Why so serious all the time?"

Frankie started skipping around the small examination room. "Rynna makes the bestest cherry pies ever, ever. Daddy even said they mights be better than her grammy's."

Kale looked down at her before looking at me with something gleaming in his eye. "Rynna, huh?"

"Yep," Frankie answered, not having a clue that Kale's question was actually directed at me. "She bringed me one when I had the sicks and her pots pie made me all better. Oh, Uncle Kale, it was soes good!"

"This Rynna sounds really nice," Kale said. Again, eyeing me like the bastard he was.

"Mm-huh! She's so, so nice. She even wrotes me a letter." Frankie rambled off all the details I sure as hell didn't want Kale to have as he opened the door. She kept at it as she capered down the hall, alternating between skipping and twirling and leaping, which she'd learned at ballet yesterday.

When we hit the waiting room, she darted for the children's play area set up in the corner. The small space was packed with a ton of kids, their parents, most of them their moms, sitting around in the bright plastic chairs waiting for their names to be called.

I turned to Kale. "Thanks for doing this, man. Know it's not standard for you to do follow-ups in here like this."

Blowing out a long breath, he glanced over at Frankie, who had already struck a conversation with a little boy about her age.

Swore the kid didn't have a shy bone in her body. Always making friends wherever she went. Social in a way that made me itch. I always had to watch her like a hawk. Not that I wouldn't anyway.

"I was happy to, Rex." He shifted back to look at me, the amusement he'd been wearing since the moment we'd stepped through the clinic doors replaced by his worry. "It's time you stop thinking you have to go this alone all the time. I'm here for her, too. I love that kid. You have to get that."

On a sigh, I roughed a hand through my hair, my attention moving back to my daughter, who had climbed the steps to the short plastic slide and was propelling herself down. "I know, man. It's just—"

"It's just that you think you're supposed to," he cut in, his arms going across his chest. "You think if you give up even a second of the responsibility, a second of the worry, you're betraying your daughter in some way."

"That's not true."

"Isn't it? Hell, I'm surprised you even let your mom take care of her in the afternoons when she gets out of preschool."

I let a smirk climb to my mouth. "I'm kind of questioning that, actually. She'd look pretty dammed cute with a hard hat on the job, don't you think?"

His eyes narrowed. "I'd be laughing right now if I didn't think you might actually be serious."

I chuckled, head shaking with a bit of amusement before I dropped my gaze toward my booted feet. "Nah, man. I . . ."

Kale set his hand on my shoulder. "You're a disaster, man. Know you don't want to hear it, but you have issues, and I'm worried about you."

"It's just . . . it's so goddamned hard to let her out of my sight. Feel like I'm always scrambling to stay in front of everything, trying to stay one step ahead to make sure she's safe."

His voice softened. "You know that's not always going to be possible."

Dread curled in my stomach. That same old misery that stalked me in the day and hunted me in the night. The helplessness and fear and agony that had scraped and scraped at my spirit.

Perpetual torture.

I wondered how there was anything left of me.

"You've got to understand, Kale."

"Of course, I understand. I was there, man. I went through it, too. But you can't spend the rest of your life a prisoner to that time."

How the fuck were we supposed to move on from it when that time was unending?

"I'm trying."

"Are you? Then why don't you come clean about what's going on with this Rynna girl? The smoking hot chick who just so happened to be at the emergency room—at two-thirty in the morning—with the guy who refuses to accept help from anyone other than me, Ollie, and his mom, and barely even then."

Unease stirred through me. That same feeling that had been nagging at me for days. The dread and the need and confusion. "Battery was dead in the truck."

"Hmm."

"Hmm, what?"

"You're an awful handy dude for having to ask a woman for help in the middle of the night."

"Frankie was sick. Didn't have time to spare."

"You needed someone, and you went to her."

Fuck.

He was right.

I needed someone. And I went to her.

I went to her.

Agitation had me shifting on my feet.

He squeezed my shoulder a little tighter. "Tell me what's going on with you two."

My attention was locked on Frankie as I rubbed a hand over my mouth, trying not to think about the way I'd felt pressed against Rynna. The way her heart had beaten and mine had come alive for the first time in years. "Only thing that's going on is shit that can't be."

"And why's that?"

My chest tightened, and I looked to the ground, voice dropping so low I wasn't sure he could hear my confession. "It feels like cheating."

I could feel Kale's sympathy all mixed with a bolt of exasperation. "And who exactly are you cheating on? Because that bitch left you and Sydney is gone. They are both gone, man, and they aren't coming back."

My entire being flinched. Anguish and this blinding guilt that ate me up from the inside.

Kale's voice dropped to match mine. "You need to tell Ollie, Rex. Fucking get this off your chest once and for all so you can finally move on."

"I'm not sure how to do that."

Question was, did I really want to?

Rynna's face spun through my mind. I swore I could feel that place that had ached forever transform. Grasping for something different. Something better.

And that scared the shit out of me.

I glanced over at Kale. When I caught his expression, my irritation came back full force. "Why the fuck are you grinning?"

"Oh, you know . . . because it's super entertaining to watch you realize you just might want something but the thought of it makes you want to crawl right out of your skin."

"Always such an asshole," I mumbled.

"Who doesn't hesitate to say it straight. Admit it. You like her."

"I don't like her. I don't even know her."

"But you want to." The jackass had the audacity to sing it as he twirled his finger in a circle in front of my face.

I smacked it away.

He was worse than a thirteen-year-old girl.

"Come on, man. Admit it. You want to." He flashed me one of those ridiculous smiles that had every girl in town dying to lock that shit down. All fucking dimples and bright white teeth. "Tell me about that pie." He waggled his brows, keeping right on with the ribbing, having no idea the knives he was driving into raw flesh. "Tell me how badly you want her to eat yours."

My throat bobbed, that guilt rising around me like jagged cliffs. Guilt for giving in. I had already made more mistakes with her than I could make excuses for. Had already gotten deep enough that I wasn't sure I was ever going to climb out.

"Oh shit," Kale muttered under his breath. "You lucky bastard, you already did. And you're over there pouting about it."

I shifted away, not needing to pretend I was keeping a close eye on Frankie. "Not like that . . . we just . . ."

Visions assaulted me. The ecstasy on her face when she'd come with the sun shining on her gorgeous face. How good she'd tasted. How right she'd felt in my arms.

"Just what?" he pressed.

I blew out a frustrated breath, voice barely a gritted whisper. "It was just a kiss."

Kale laughed. "Just a kiss, huh? Considering you haven't touched a girl in years, I'd bet the pink slip to my car, which you know is my baby, that it meant a whole lot more to you than it just being a kiss. You have some kind of superhuman strength or balls of steal or some shit, because those fuckers should be so blue they'd have fallen off by now." The guy knew me better than anyone, and he didn't hesitate to pull punches.

"You think you regret whatever you're feeling now? Just wait to see how much regret you feel when you don't do anything about it." He sighed. "It doesn't have to be a big thing, Rex. Test it out. Hang out with her as a friend. See how it goes. It's not like you're asking her to marry you."

I flinched with that, and he snorted, shaking his head before he spun all the way around and waltzed over to the reception desk. Two nurses behind it immediately tuned in to whatever the flirty bastard had to say as he rested his forearms on the counter and leaned toward them.

And I wondered how he'd done it.

Managed it.

Overcome it.

Or maybe I was the one who'd really been at fault all along.

fifteen

Rex

Hand rubbing over the tense muscles at the back of my neck, I paced, boots crunching on the gravel in front of her house.

Back and forth.

Back and forth.

Shit.

Shit. Shit. Shit. Get it together, man.

Friends.

That was what Kale had said.

I could do that.

I forced my feet to carry me up the steps and across her porch, and I gave a good pound to her front door. It took all of thirty seconds and what felt like an eternity for the door to crack open. I almost backed the fuck out because all I saw was hesitation in her movements before something like relief took to her features.

"Rex," she whispered, opening the door wider.

"Hey."

A small smile graced that gorgeous mouth. "How is Frankie?"

Something about that calmed the erratic racing of my heart,

and I felt myself smiling in return. "As good as new. It might have had something to do with a pot pie that mysteriously showed up at our door."

A flush touched her cheeks, and she bit her bottom lip, everything about her completely genuine. "I hope she liked it."

"Oh, there's no question of that."

That redness deepened. "I'm so glad she's feeling better."

"Me, too. Can't thank you enough for helping me out that night."

"I meant it, Rex. I'm here."

I nodded, rushed my fingers through my hair, the air growing thick around us. A swirl of that potency.

"So . . ." I trailed off like the pathetic fucker I was.

"So . . ." she prodded, those dark eyes going warm and soft.

I sucked in a breath, fingers going back to nervously thread through my hair. "There's this thing Broderick Wolfe invited me to tomorrow night at Olive's. Just a small party to celebrate the progress that's been made on the Fairmont Hotel. I know Lillith and Nikki will be there. Thought it'd be cool if you came. You know, as friends," I added way too quickly.

Smooth.

So goddamned smooth.

I had to stop from rolling my eyes at myself.

"Friends?" she asked, a brow lifting, the word nothing but a doubtful tease. Couldn't blame her, especially considering the last time I'd seen her, she was coming against my truck.

"Yeah," I said, shoving my hands into my pockets. My tone turned deep with honesty. "Not sure I have a whole lot more to offer right now, Rynna."

Silence pulsed around us. Thick with implication. With our reservations and all the things I didn't know how to say.

She blinked back at me then finally spoke. "That sounds great. I'd love to go."

I breathed out in relief. "Good." I backed away, letting a huge smile climb to my face. "That's really good. I'll pick you up at eight."

She smiled the softest smile with another short nod then

closed the door.

And I felt good. Really fucking good. I could do this.

sixteen

Rynna

*R*ex held open the door. "Ladies first," he said with a tiny smirk lifting on the corner of his sexy mouth.

Nerves tumbled through my body, and my teeth caught on my bottom lip. "Thank you," I murmured, ducking my head and stepping inside the packed bar.

A warm dimness held fast to the trendy space, the dull roar of voices an easy drone in the air. Edison bulbs hung from the ceilings and flickered against the red brick walls like flames.

People were everywhere, vying to get a stool at the bar or snag one of the high-top tables situated throughout, totally lost in their own worlds as they cast their troubles aside and stepped into the carelessness of the weekend.

That didn't change the fact I felt as if I were in a spotlight.

I didn't know if it were the fact I stood beside who had to be the most beautiful man I'd ever seen. Or maybe it was because I was still reeling from running into Aaron outside Pepper's Pies four days ago.

When Rex had asked me to come to this party, my first instinct had been to tell him no.

Both because just looking at the man had me fearing for my heart and because the impact of him merely standing at my door leapt to my throat and spread beneath my skin like a slow burn.

The other had been nothing but straight fear.

Pure, petrified fear.

But I refused to allow history to chase me away. Not from the place I loved. Not from where I belonged. Not ever again.

So, I'd stepped out of my comfort zone and said yes. This man was worth the risk I knew I was taking.

He lifted his chin, and I followed his line of sight to the bar. Ollie was behind it, giving him the same gesture of welcome. Turning that potent attention on me, Rex angled his head to the side. "This way."

He ushered me ahead of him and toward the stairs. A sign was set up beside it stating the second level was closed for a private party.

Warily, I glanced over at him. "I thought you said this was a small party."

He released a low chuckle. "Broderick Wolfe doesn't exactly do anything small. Big seems to be his middle name."

My brow arched with the tease. "Ah, I see how it is. You actually invited me along to protect you."

His gaze flicked down my body.

Hot.

Needy.

Those magnetic eyes skated across my bare shoulders and dipped to the valley between my breasts. I released a shaky breath as his gaze drifted over the soft peach dress I wore. The thin straps were satin and crisscrossed over the open back, and the front of the fitted bodice dipped into a shallow V. The skirt was flowy and soft and landed just above my knees.

Those eyes slowly trailed up to meet mine. "I think it's safe to say there won't be a soul looking at me. Not with you looking like that."

A shiver raced down my spine.

Friends. Friends. Friends.

I chanted his defense in my head, as if I might hold the power to claim it and make it real when standing next to Rex Gunner felt nothing like being friends.

It felt like sex and need and desperate hearts.

It felt like hope and healing.

There was no question we'd both been hurt. Beaten down and broken in life's own cruel ways.

I wanted to reach out and discover his wounds. Maybe let him discover mine.

"You aren't looking so bad yourself," I managed, choking over the words like a fool. Uttering them aloud seemed foolish. Not when he was dressed in fitted jeans and a light pink button-up, the sleeves rolled up his forearms. High enough to reveal a few of the colorful feathers inked on the top of his forearm.

I'd nearly stumbled over myself when I'd opened my door to find him that way. So ridiculously sexy, his scruff trimmed, his hair that perfectly imperfect mess.

The tension on the ride over in his truck had nearly been more than I could bear. I'd been hyper-aware of every movement, from the flex of his lean muscles as he'd shifted into gear to the clench of that chiseled, stoic jaw. He'd seemed to have to hold himself rigid in restraint, barely offering a word because one more stimulus might have been the one to tip us over the edge. The detonator to a bomb. The one to shatter our shaky, flimsy ground.

He seemed to war with what to say before he shook his head and pasted on a thin grin. "Come on, let's get up there before Brody thinks I bailed on him."

I started up the steps. Rex placed his hand at the small of my back. I bit back a gasp. It was almost impossible. Not with the way electricity raced through me like a shot of adrenaline.

He groaned the smallest sound. But I felt it, the rumble he emitted. I wasn't alone in this.

We managed to make the climb to the top, and I was sucking in another breath when we stepped out onto the second floor. It was magnificent.

Just . . . jaw-dropping beauty.

The interior matched downstairs, the walls red brick and

warm with age. Rows of pool tables lined the far back of the massive room and another elegant bar ran the adjoining wall. Linens, floral arrangements, and formal place settings adorned the tables set up in the middle of the room, all of it obviously brought in exclusively for tonight's party.

What really captured my attention was what faced out front. An accordion wall of glass and rustic wood had been completely opened to the balcony. Planters filled with trees were strategically placed around the area, and strands of Edison bulbs that matched downstairs were strung up between them, covering the outdoor space like a sparkly, glittering ceiling.

It was hard to tell where one space ended and the other began.

But it was the view of the river winding through the city I loved that sent a tumble of nostalgia battering my senses.

"It's beautiful, isn't it?"

I jerked with the rough voice beside me.

I shook myself out of the stupor and offered Rex a small smile. "I almost forgot how beautiful Gingham Lakes is."

A frown pulled at his brows, and he searched my face. "Is that what you wanted? To forget?"

My laughter was tremulous. "It's easier that way, isn't it? Forgetting? Forgetting means things don't hurt so bad."

Pain gusted through his striking features. "And sometimes pain is better than forgetting."

My stomach twisted, and I fumbled for something to say, wanting to reach in and discover exactly what it was he was clinging to. He stopped me by speaking first with an easy diversion. "I'm going to head to the bar. What can I get you to drink?"

"Chardonnay would be nice."

He dipped his head before he headed that direction, winding through the small groups of people who were gathered around. Their conversations were quiet, and the band playing on a small elevated stage in the corner were hardly more than an accent to the vibe.

"Oh my God!"

I spun on my heel at the screech that came from behind me. Nikki was coming right for me, dressed in a flaming red dress, eyes wide with excitement. She hugged me as if she hadn't seen me in years. "Oh my God," she said again, holding me by the outside of my upper arms. "What are you doing here?" Her eyes looked me up and down. "And holy shit, you look fabulous. Are you trying to make us all look bad?"

I felt the heat rush to my face. "Thank you."

Compliments from friends used to be difficult for me to take. Macy had thought it her God-given duty to wipe that idea from my existence, and she'd done a good job of it. She'd nearly scraped all the old insecurities away, and I refused to let them settle back into my skin.

I took her by both hands, squeezing as I smiled. "And are you serious right now? You look like a freaking goddess."

She hiked a shoulder. "What can I say? If given the opportunity to dress up for my Ollie, I'd be a fool not to take it."

I chuckled. God, I really loved her. "Well, he'd be a fool not to notice."

It was almost hurt that flashed in her eyes, but she shook it off. "So, what are you doing here? Did Lillith invite you?"

Again, she was looking around. It was right when Rex broke the crowd, the man so ridiculously gorgeous my breaths turned shallow and my heart took off at a sprint as he strode our way. All lean strength and powerful presence.

"Oh wow." Nikki whipped her attention back to me, mouth dropping open in disbelief.

"It's nothing," I whispered. "We're just friends."

"Really?" Her voice was a wry, scandalous accusation.

"Really," I promised, even though it somehow felt like a lie.

"Nikki," Rex said a little hard with a slight dip of his head.

"Rex," she returned, laughter in her voice.

He handed me the glass of wine. "Here you go."

"Thank you."

I took a sip when I caught sight of Lillith moving our direction. Her hand was wrapped up in the man I knew to be her fiancé.

Broderick Wolfe.

He was tall and wide and impeccably dressed in a suit that had clearly been tailored to perfectly fit his muscular body.

"Rynna. You're here. I love it. All my favorite people in one room." Lillith walked up to me and hugged me before she stepped back and angled her head. "Rex, how are you? It's so nice to see you."

There was a bit of worry in her voice when she asked it. As if she might be protective of me.

"Good," he said in that rough voice. He turned and shook Broderick's hand. "Thanks for the invitation. The place looks great."

Broderick shook his head. "I'm glad you're here. None of this could happen without RG Construction. You're company is the backbone of the operation."

Wow.

That was some kind of praise.

I glanced at Rex. His expression was rimmed with satisfaction as he returned Broderick's handshake. "My men are incredibly skilled. I couldn't be prouder of them."

Broderick laughed, this loud, boisterous laugh as he set a hand on Rex's shoulder. "Always so humble." Broderick looked around the group. "This man right here is the driving force behind an incredible team. He literally has saved my ass at least a thousand times during this project."

He returned his attention to Rex. "You didn't earn your reputation for nothing. I sought you out because *you* are the best. In three short years, you brought RG Construction back from what could have been its demise. That is no easy feat."

Rex flinched.

It was subtle.

But I saw it. Felt it.

His voice was hoarser when he spoke. "If we're looking for someone to give credit to, let's give it to my mother. She was the one who taught me there is nothing hard work won't achieve."

God, this man was an enigma. Hard and soft. Modest and proud. Layers and threads and dimensions of mystery.

Broderick just shook his head as if he couldn't believe Rex, either, before he turned a charismatic smile on me. "And who do we have here?" He reached for me, taking my hand between both of his.

Lillith had her hand tucked under his arm, her smile so free. "This is my friend Rynna I was telling you about. She's the one who inherited Pepper's Pies across the street from the new hotel."

Broderick's face lit. "It's so nice to finally meet you. I was hoping you would choose to reopen rather than selling. Pepper's Pies has an important history in Gingham Lakes, and I know it'll remain the same in the future. If there's anything you need to help with the process, please, don't hesitate to let me know." Even though his words could have been used in a boardroom to sell his next biggest idea, there was a distinct tone of sincerity woven into them.

"It's nice to meet you, as well. And I will definitely keep that in mind. Thank you for the offer."

Broderick looked around the room. "I'm a firm believer Gingham Lakes's revitalization belongs to all of us. We're all responsible for coming together to make it a better place for all residents."

Lillith pushed her cheek into his arm, as if she were overcome by her love for him, and he pressed the softest kiss to the top of her head.

My heart throbbed, and I couldn't help but glance at Rex, drawn to this man who stood stoically at my side.

Broderick gestured to the room. "Dinner should be served in a few minutes. Why don't we all find a place to sit so we can enjoy ourselves?"

As he led us over to a large round table where we all took seats together, Broderick worked the room, welcoming the rest of his guests and inviting them to take a seat. Dinner was served, and we ate and drank and laughed. Lillith and Nikki made it easy to fit in, and it even seemed as if Rex might. Even though there was some part of him that remained reserved.

Afterward, Broderick stood and asked if he could have a

word with Rex.

"Excuse me for a minute?" he asked.

"Of course," I told him.

Lillith was in deep conversation with a couple at the next table, and Nikki made an excuse to head downstairs, undoubtedly to find Ollie.

I went to the bar and ordered another glass of wine then wandered out onto the balcony, drawn to the view.

It was quiet, the air still warm, though it'd cooled with the night, and a slight breeze added to the peace in the air. A blanket of stars opened up the vast canopy that stretched on forever above, and I inhaled the scents of the city, the honeysuckle and the river and old buildings.

Home.

I got lost in it, in the soft music that fell on my ears and the peace that radiated back from the city I'd tried to forget I loved.

I jumped when the breath landed on my bare shoulder. "I'm sorry I ditched you."

A small smile tugged at my mouth, and I glanced over my shoulder at the gorgeous man standing right behind me. "I understand. It's a work party."

"I'd rather be hanging out with you."

Butterflies.

Was that normal? It didn't matter. They were there, fluttering at my insides, whipping and stirring and inciting. I slowly turned to face him. "I'd rather be hanging out with you, too."

A soft gust of wind blew through, soft lashes at the longer pieces of his hair, those hypnotizing eyes filled with so much turmoil and questions. He reached up and touched my cheek. "Rynna."

Chills skated my spine.

The band had shifted songs, and strains of an acoustic guitar filled the air. The scruffy voice of the same singer who'd played the last time I was there rode on the breeze. He was singing "Collide" by Howie Day. The lyrics grazed across my skin, eliciting a rash of goose bumps, the same as the callused fingertips that trailed down my arm.

The words spun around us, and slowly, Rex edged forward. His arm slid around my waist and pulled me against him.

His palm went to the small of my back, his thumb just brushing against the bare skin exposed by my dress, the other hand landing on my neck.

My entire world shook.

Slowly, we began to rock in the slowest kind of dance. Both mesmerized by the song and the feel and the overwhelming vibe, his heart thrumming in sync with mine. We were caught up in it, as if time had stopped, the two of us giving ourselves over to the moments that passed. I would have been content for it to go on forever.

He drew me closer, his nose running along the back of my ear. "You are so beautiful, Rynna," he murmured. "So beautiful it fucking hurts to look at you."

"Rex," I whispered, my fingers curling in the fabric of his shirt.

He suddenly stepped back, leaving me gasping as he roughed a frustrated hand over his face. "Think we should get out of here."

Slowly, I nodded and followed him back inside.

seventeen

Rex

What the fuck was I thinking? Inviting her there? Thinking I could handle this?

Friends.

I bit back bitter laughter and led her inside, trying to keep some distance between us when the only thing I wanted was to strip her from that dress and sink inside. We said our goodbyes, thanking Broderick. Lillith gave me a look that promised she would cut off my dick if I did wrong by her friend.

But that was the fucking problem.

I didn't know how to do her right.

Had no idea how to give her what was so clearly building up between us.

A savage storm.

Brutal.

We stepped outside and into the night. Our footsteps echoed on the sidewalk. All the things we wanted to say roiled in the silence between us. I unlocked my truck and helped her into the front seat. My entire body went rigid when I was struck with another wave of that sweetness, the girl inundating me with every tempting, delicious part of her.

Sugar and spice.

Cherry fucking pie.

She was goddamned stunning.

I rounded the front of my trunk and hopped into the front seat. But I didn't start the engine. I just held onto the steering wheel, peering out front and letting her confused silence impale me.

"I'm sorry," I finally said.

She smiled a tentative smile, graced with all that understanding. "For what?"

I scoffed out a laugh as I shifted into gear and pulled onto the road. "For always being such a dick."

She laughed the faintest sound. "You're not always a dick, Rex. I know there's more to you."

"How's that?" I asked. The words flinging between us were almost playful.

"There's no mistaking it when you're with your daughter."

Gruff affection rumbled in my chest. "That's 'cause she's the best part of me."

"She's amazing," Rynna mused, staring out the windshield, her striking face filling up my periphery.

"Yeah. She's all I've got."

I could feel her gaze land on me. Hot and heavy. Demanding in her stare. "Is that the way you want it?"

Unease itched beneath my skin. "That's just the way life goes for me, Rynna. It feels like most days I'm barely hanging on. Barely getting by. She's my life. My heart. Don't think I have room for anything else."

"Because you lost the other half of it?"

Pain lanced through me, cutting me in two. "Lost myself a long fucking time ago. Not sure I'm ever going to get it back."

Her gaze returned out front, her voice growing so soft as she murmured her confession. "You know . . . when I came back here, I was terrified of what might be waiting for me." I could feel her turmoil, the grief this gorgeous girl had kept inside. "Terrified of what had chased me away in the first place. But I knew that what I'd left behind, what was waiting for me, was worth the risk. I didn't want to be afraid anymore."

A frown pulled at my brow. "What were you running from?"

Her laughter was hollow. "Shame. Embarrassment. When I look back, I think maybe I was running from myself." Her chuckle seemed to be completely at her own expense, and her attention dropped to her fingers, which she wrung on her lap. Locks of that chestnut cascaded around her delicate neck. "When I was younger, I was the chubby girl. Awkward. Uncomfortable in my skin."

My eyes lifted, dragging down her body in a sweeping pass. She was lush and curved and fucking perfect, and I hated the idea that she'd once felt anything less.

Her voice softened in wonder. "It feels so ridiculous now, the way I'd let the teasing affect me. I don't know if it was really my size or if I just was insecure and everyone knew it and they took advantage of it. When my momma left, she left a vacancy I didn't understand at the time. I was so lonely, and I think the lonelier I got, the hungrier I got for interaction, but I seemed to always get excluded. I think somehow the kids fed on that. It got worse as I got older."

She glanced at me. Helplessness struck on her features. "It got to the point where I couldn't take it anymore, so I ran."

A shot of rage tumbled through my veins. For her as a little girl. Couldn't imagine it. What if someone treated Frankie like that? "I'm so sorry, Rynna."

She shrugged. "Maybe it made me stronger. For years, I was too afraid to return. But after my grandmother passed, it finally set in. I lost all those years with her, and I didn't want to run anymore. I was tired of running from who I am. Even if I still find myself looking over my shoulder, I won't allow anyone to chase me from my home."

"You belong here," I managed.

I could feel her eyes flicker over to me. "I don't think it's any mistake you and Frankie were the first people I met."

Hesitation brimmed around me. I knew what she was saying. What she was asking for. Never had I felt more at war with what

I wanted and what I knew was right. I turned right onto our street, the words grating from my tongue. "My life's a train wreck. One that just seems to go on forever. Every fucking time I think I'm doing something right, it goes to shit."

"What happened with your company three years ago?" she suddenly asked. Peering over at me, she fiddled with the silky strap on that lust-inducing dress. Like she knew asking it was crossing a line. Pushing me further and willing to do it, anyway. "What Broderick mentioned?"

"Just another time life stabbed me in the back. This time it was my business partner. Asshole nearly destroyed me. He made me look like I was a part of his shady practices, stealing from clients, falsifying documents. I very well might have ended up in jail like he did. I managed to prove I had no clue what kind of bullshit he was pulling back at the office while I was out working my fingers to the bone with the crew. Still nearly lost the company because of it, but somehow I managed to hold it together."

Hatred pulsed through my veins. Still couldn't believe the bastard had pulled that shit. It'd nearly knocked me on my ass. The blow was almost as harsh as coming home and finding my wife had left me.

"That's horrible."

Nodding, I pulled into her drive. "It was. Pisses me off the fucker just got released. Takes about all I have not to hunt him down."

She laughed this incredulous sound, honesty gliding onto her face. "You want to hunt yours down and the weak part of me wants to run the other direction."

"Don't ever let anyone chase you from what belongs to you, Rynna Dayne."

eighteen

Rynna

Tension roiled between us. That tether pulled taut. Drawing us closer. I swallowed around it and reached for the latch. He was quick to open his door, jumping out and rounding to my side before I had time to step out of his massive truck. He helped me down, and his hand scorched where he aided me by holding on to my elbow.

"Let me walk you to the door. Last thing I need to be worried about is you here by yourself and some asshole taking advantage of you."

He quirked this belly-flopping grin that pierced me like an arrow. "Unless of course that asshole is me."

He barely angled his head to the side. There was something so endearing and self-deprecating about it. Everything about him right then was at odds with the surly, bear of a man I'd met weeks ago, the man exposing himself, layer by layer.

I lifted my chin, both in strength and vulnerability, tossing all the uncertainties and questions out into the open. "Should I be afraid?"

"Yeah, you should be." His response was hard, but there was

no missing the fact his irritation was aimed at himself. He set his palm on the small of my back, helping me through the gravel drive in my heels, an inch behind as we ascended the porch steps.

We crossed the planks. That tension wound higher with each step until we were nothing but needy pants at my door. Slowly, I turned around to face him.

His presence sent a ripple of energy vibrating across the floorboards, the overwhelming sight of him the owner of my breath.

He stood beneath the faint glow of the hurricane lamp that hung outside the door. A sculpture of sinewy muscle and raw strength, forged through years of obvious physical labor. Every inch of him was rugged, from those roughened, callused hands to the crinkles set deep at the edges of his eyes.

The man was a carving of pure, daunting beauty.

"What exactly am I supposed to be afraid of, Rex?" My brow twisted, and my voice quieted with the admission. "Because when I'm around you, the last thing I feel is afraid."

"I fuck everything up, Rynna, and the only thing I've got to offer you is my mess. I *can't* do this."

Restraint rumbled in his chest, the sound so deep I felt it shake the ground beneath my feet.

I gently cupped one side of his rugged face. "I'm not afraid."

It was a promise.

An appeal.

"You should be," he grated. "Warned you, my shit doesn't ever end well."

"Maybe that's a chance I'm willing to take."

He groaned and he planted his hands high above my head. The man panted above me, torn, desperate, his nose just brushing mine. "God damn it, Rynna. God damn it."

I felt the moment he broke. When the thread pulled too tight and this mesmerizing man snapped. His mouth descended on mine.

Overpowering.

Overwhelming.

Dizzying.

Lips and tongue and nips of teeth.

And those hands. They were on my face. My neck. My waist. Somehow, I managed to hold on to him and spin away as I fumbled with the lock. He pressed against my backside, his cock against my bottom, and his mouth leaving a trail of fire at the side of my neck. We stumbled into the darkness of my house, breaking apart as I turned to face him.

The only light trickled down from the lamp I'd left on upstairs.

Slowly, he clicked the door shut behind him. We stood there, two feet away from each other, staring.

Chests heaving.

Before we collided.

A tangle of tongues and bodies.

The man frantic, trying to touch me everywhere.

"What am I doing? Fuck, what am I doing?" he muttered incoherently, kissing me deeper. Madder. Wilder.

I pushed up on my toes and tore my mouth from his so I could kiss down the strong column of his throat. His head thudded back against the door, his entire body pressing against it as if he needed it to keep him standing.

He grated my name, and I kept kissing at his throat while I worked free the button on his jeans, hands shaking.

Every reservation spun out of control.

Out of reach.

It was only spurred further when the defined muscles of his abdomen jumped and twitched beneath my touch, when he mumbled, "You're killing me, Rynna. Fucking killing me."

Desire rippled from him in heady waves.

And I felt so brave and bold, my kisses brazen as I nipped at the hollow of his throat, my fingers sure as I inched down his zipper.

Before I could consider it—the ramifications and the repercussions and the distinct threat to my heart—I dropped to my knees and pulled his jeans and underwear down to the middle of his thighs.

I refused to think of anything but setting him free.

Hoping he'd find a little of that freedom in me.

Even if it was only for a few stolen moments.

But God, I was unprepared. Just an unsuspecting, naïve fool when his thick cock bobbed out in front of me, level with my eyes.

Engorged and hard.

As big and ruggedly beautiful as the rest of him, the fat head already dripping with his need.

A flood of desire rushed me, and my stomach twisted into a thousand knots. It incited an ache in the deepest part of me. My core was a ball of fire. Heat spreading fast and throbbing between my thighs.

I pressed them together as if it might offer relief, my mouth dry, my heart thrashing against its boundaries.

Racing ahead of me as if it already knew our destination.

Those big hands were suddenly on the sides of my head. He forced me to look up at him. Hunger glinted in his eyes, a dangerous cocktail of sorrow and need and restraint.

That mesmerizing sage deepened to steel. It was when I knew he'd taken another turn.

All needy, dominant man.

"Is this what you really want? You want me to fuck that sweet mouth?"

I shivered with the promise of his words. Again caught off guard by this man who'd left me on unstable ground.

"I just want to make you feel good," I whispered.

He was so hard. Every inch of him. From the clench of his jaw to the ripple of his stomach to his length that protruded and dipped and bounced in front of me.

The tip barely grazed my lips. My tongue flicked out and swept across the velvet flesh.

Rex hissed. "Fuck . . . Rynna. I can't fucking do this. This is wrong. So fucking wrong."

But instead of pushing me away, he tugged me closer. A raw groan escaped him when I wrapped both my hands around him at the base and sucked his crown into my mouth.

He rasped a curse and rocked forward. Control slipping. Control I somehow knew he used as a defense. As a way to keep everyone at arm's length.

My tongue pressed at the underside of his cock, and I pulled him deeper.

Drawing him in.

Slowly.

Just as slowly as I began to work him with my hands.

And maybe I should have known I was in trouble when I began to shake. When the entire room spun at the feel of him. At the impact of him.

At the way I completely succumbed when he muttered, "That mouth," as he hooked his fingertips below my jaw, drawing my eyes up to meet his.

His thumbs brushed the curve of my cheeks before he moved them to the edge of my lips. His eyes flashed with something tender. Soft and gentle.

Before something else entirely took them over. Something raw. Possessive. Intense.

His hips began to snap, jutting forward. He pressed himself deeper into my mouth. Filling me so full I struggled not to gag. So turned on I writhed where I knelt on the floor. The man so powerful I had to surrender.

"God . . . Ryn . . . Ryn . . . feels so good. Fuck . . . so good. That mouth."

A flood of words poured from his mouth as he fucked mine.

Wildly.

Madly.

Greedily.

And God. I liked it. I liked it that he'd taken control. Liked that he stood over me, taking what I wanted to give. Liked that I held the power to make him moan.

I liked *him*.

I liked him so much. More than I should. In a way that was getting messy. In a way that was soft and fragile, breakable, as it spun the most complex web inside me. Strands of want and ribbons of need.

"Rynna . . ." He grunted my name, a deep, reverberating utterance that echoed the walls. I swallowed around him, taking him as deep as I possibly could. Every part of me ached. My jaw and my heart and that needy throb at begged at the juncture of my thighs.

His thrusts turned rough. Hard and demanding. "Harder . . . please . . . take it."

I pumped him savagely, just as ruthlessly as he took my mouth, my hands picking up the same frantic rhythm as his assault.

And I could feel it. His balls tighten and lift. The ripple of his abdomen, those powerful thighs straining.

That electricity licked and lapped.

Striking.

"God damn it, Rynna. God damn it."

His hips snapped twice more.

Frantic and frenzied.

Before every glorious inch of him went rigid. A tightly keening bow.

He pulsed with his orgasm, and his head kicked back on a guttural roar as he let himself go.

It was exactly what I'd wanted.

To see this man undone.

To get a glimpse of him with his walls toppled.

And the sight of it . . . the sight of it was magnificent.

His cock throbbed and jerked as he spilled into my mouth, and I gulped him down as I stared up at the ecstasy on his face.

Slowly he opened his eyes, but the same frenzy remained in them. Fire. He quickly lifted me from the floor. Before I could make sense of it, my bottom was balanced on the back of the sofa, my dress around my waist, his fingers spreading me.

Filling me.

His eyes were desperate as he stroked me deep. I moaned as he fucked me with his fingers, his thumb bringing me to ecstasy.

So fast.

So fast I was shocked by the bliss that exploded in my body. A flashflood that came out of nowhere.

Laying me to waste.

My fingers dug into his shoulders as I came. Wave after wave.

He slowed, panting, eyes wild. He stepped back as if he couldn't make sense of what had just happened between us, slowly lowering my feet to the ground.

"God damn it." His words cracked.

I sagged, holding onto the back of the couch for support. Spent. Drained. Confused.

He was quick to tuck himself back into his jeans. Looking everywhere but at me, he roughed agitated hands through his hair. "God damn it. *God damn it*. Friends. Friends. What bullshit."

He started to frantically pace.

"Rex," I whispered, trying to break through whatever freak out he was having.

"I can't ... I can't believe I just—fuck!" he shouted and threw an aimless punch into the air. "I can't do this."

My knees were shaky, and my heart was erratic. I stretched a hand out toward him. "Why can't you? Why can't you do this?"

I'd never been a beggar. I'd never chased a man except for the one who'd broken my heart the day I'd turned eighteen. I was a quick learner. If a man didn't want what I had to offer, then he didn't deserve me.

Yet, there was something about Rex Gunner that made me want to shout and plead and pound on his chest. Demand he open up. Show me everything he kept shored up inside.

That same something told me he *needed* what I had to give. That whatever I'd been lacking, he'd found in me, too.

"I have to get out of here," he said, stalking for the door.

Shocked and confused, I watched, hurt bubbling up and coating my tongue with disbelief.

He was just going to leave? After what we'd just done?

I pressed my lips together, my chin trembling as I fought tears. Tears bred of hope and frustration. "I told you I'm not afraid. Why are you? All I'm asking is that you take a chance on me. Life's not worth living without taking them."

He froze at the door, and he laughed this horrible, cutting sound. He shifted to look at me from over his shoulder. "You want to know why I'm afraid, Rynna?"

His head angled to the side, and his eyes brimmed with a kind of hatred I knew wasn't directed at me. "I'm afraid because I fuck everything up. I'm afraid because everything I touch? Everything I love? Eventually, I taint it. Ruin it. And then there's nothing left but misery and suffering and fear. And my daughter . . . my Frankie? She's all I've got left. She's the one good thing that remains unblemished. And the few bits remaining of me? They belong to her, because I've already given everything else. I told you, I don't have anything to offer you. I'm sorry. I'm so fucking sorry, but I refuse to do anything selfish or stupid that would put her happiness at risk."

He opened the door, but he paused, wavering before he peered back at me again. Surrender carved into every line on his gorgeous face. "I don't have any chances left to take, Rynna Dayne. I've already used up all the ones I've been given, and if I take anything else? I'd be nothing but a thief."

Without another word, he strode out, letting the door drop closed behind him.

It was that moment when the man officially twisted me in two.

Because when he walked out that door? He took a part of me I had no chance of ever getting back.

nineteen

Rynna

I was going to be late.

Shit.

I was going to be really, really late.

And I couldn't be late.

Everything was riding on this meeting.

In one heel and wearing a fitted skirt, I stumbled out of the walk-in closet, which was filled with a bunch of boxes my grandmother had left behind.

I stumbled, my hand darting out to the wall for support, and paused for a beat in an attempt to shimmy on the other heel. Once I was at least the same height on both sides, I tried again.

Two steps away from the small dressing table on the far side of the room, my ankle rolled.

All the way to the side.

Pain splintered up the outside of my leg.

"Shit," I yelped as I tried to rebound and stop my fall. The only thing I managed to do was to propel myself forward. Falling fast. My hands shot out, and my fingertips just snagged the edge of the stool a split second before my face slammed against the floor.

My knees weren't so lucky.

They dug into the worn carpet, pantyhose shredded.

Awesome.

My head dropped between my shoulders, and I fought the sting of tears that rushed to my eyes.

Tears of frustration. Tears of worry. Tears of this heartache that had grown every day since Rex Gunner had walked out my door two weeks ago without another word.

I'd told myself I was just being stupid. Foolish. Chasing a man who obviously wanted nothing to do with me. Just because I told myself those things didn't mean I could so easily convince myself of them. Not when they felt like a lie.

God. Why did life have to be so complicated? I had enough to worry about without the gorgeous man and his adorable daughter who lived across the street. And somehow, they had become the center of every thought.

Laughter jutted from my mouth.

The maniacal kind.

The kind that could have been sobbing. It all depended on how you heard it. Or maybe on the way you looked at it.

If you aren't laughing, you're crying. Now, which would you rather be doing?

My grandmother's soft encouragement prodded at my consciousness, and I could almost feel the pad of her thumb brushing across my cheek.

I drew in a deep breath, hoping it might give me clarity, guidance, the words a chorus of convoluted whispers that tumbled from my tongue. "I don't know if I know the difference anymore, Gramma. Things are getting complicated. So complicated, and I don't know how to handle them all. I don't know if I can do this. It feels like I'm going to fail."

God. What if I failed?

The thought made that gulp of air in my lungs throb and threaten to burst. It was a complete rejection of the idea.

Needing to pull myself together, I lifted my head and started to climb to my feet. A frown pulled across my brow when my sight latched on an envelope I'd never noticed before. It was tucked in a small cubby on the dressing table.

"Oh, Gramma."

I sat up on my knees, fingers trembling with affection and grief. I reached out and pulled the envelope free. I was quick to turn it over, rip open the flap, and tear out the card.

I devoured the words.

Obstacles are everywhere. They often feel insurmountable. Impossible. Sometimes they are nothing but stepping-stones. Other times, they are a diversion. A distraction. More often than not, they are there with the simple purpose of showing you that you *can*.

But every now and again, they are a redirection. A deviation. A repurposing. And this detour? It will guide you to a destination you never imagined you'd go but where you belonged the whole time.

"What are you trying to tell me, Gramma?" I whispered into the nothingness. That nothingness echoed back. Crushing me with affection. With loss. With the memories of her voice and her reason and everything she'd given up for me.

I clutched the letter to my chest. Cherishing her words. It didn't matter that I couldn't decipher them. All that mattered was that they were meant for me. Given in a moment I needed them most.

My grandmother always had that way about her. Insight. The uncanny ability to know when I needed a kind word or a soft prod.

Resolved, I pushed to my feet, tore off the ruined pantyhose, and shoved my feet back into the shoes. I dusted a little powder on my nose and ran some shimmery nude gloss across my lips.

I looked at myself in the mirror. "You can do this, Rynna Dayne. You wanted this. Now, go and get it."

I rushed downstairs and through the living room, grabbing my leather bag and the portfolio I'd prepared that waited inside. Silently, I went through the details in my head. The things I would say, employing some of the strategy tools I'd learned back in San Francisco.

Maybe I was supposed to have gone there. Maybe that experience had been preparing me for this day all along.

I didn't mean to falter a step when I strode outside and into the morning light.

But I did.

Because Rex Gunner was there, just backing out of the backseat of his truck where I knew he had just gotten done strapping his daughter into her booster seat. His care for her was nearly as breathtaking as his presence.

Regretful eyes moved my direction. I thought maybe he didn't have the power to stop them. Just the same way as I couldn't stop my own. My gaze drank him in as if he were forbidden fruit. Something—*someone*—I wanted so desperately I was willing to try to pluck him free from all the thorny barbs and spindly spines that kept him bound.

That *destination* perilous.

Hazardous to my health.

Sucking in a stealing breath, I shook off the reaction and forced myself to walk down the steps and to my SUV, barely glancing back when I pulled out of my drive and headed down the road.

But in that barest glimpse I saw him.

I saw his pain. I saw his fear. I saw his regret. And I swore I saw him standing there, held back by that gnarl of branches, wishing I could reach him, too.

But sometimes we have to admit when those obstacles just run too deep.

Spine stiff and straight, I shifted anxiously in the hard plastic chair. My legs were perfectly pressed together, from my thighs to my knees to my ankles, the portfolio neatly placed on my lap as I waited.

Each second that passed was excruciating, my heart

thundering so loud I kept expecting someone to lean my direction and shush me. To tell me to rein in the riot of nerves that stampeded out ahead of me, only to do laps around the small waiting room of the bank.

My gaze darted everywhere, to the tellers, then to the few clerks who were opening and managing accounts in the grouping of cubicle offices that took up the right front side of the bank.

Who would these people be rooting for in this race?

For me?

For my grandmother?

For the vacant, deserted diner that sat only three miles away, begging for someone to take mercy on its desolation?

Scrubbing away the grime would only get me so far.

If I were going to get any farther, I needed money. God knew that *five dollars* I'd had left to work magic with hadn't gotten me very far.

A woman appeared at the end of a hall. "Ms. Dayne?"

"Yes?"

She cast me a generous smile. "Mr. Roth will see you now. Right this way."

Trembling, I stood, fingers shaking as I straightened my skirt. "Thank you."

I attempted to gather my wits, to put on a brave face, to wear resolve and confidence. I knew I would be riding the fine line of approval since my loan was high risk, and I could only hope my belief in the business would throw it over the edge in my favor.

I followed her down the short hall to where the private loan offices were located. My heels clicked on the tile floor, in tune with the hammer of my heart. It drummed harder and harder with each step.

She gestured with her arm into an office, murmuring, "Good luck," as she turned to walk back the direction we'd come.

Swallowing hard, I lifted my chin, painting on that firm confidence and forcing myself to wear a smile as I turned the corner of the doorway and stepped into the office.

I faltered to a standstill.

My breath gone.

Stolen.

Stopped by an obstacle I wasn't sure I could overcome.

Timothy Roth.

Tim.

Handsy asshole from the bar.

Doesn't understand the word no.

He cracked an arrogant smile. "Well, well, well, if it isn't the lovely . . ." He paused to inspect the name on the application that sat open on his desk. The pre-approval application I'd dropped off three days ago before my scheduled appointment with the head loan officer.

Timothy Roth.

"Corinne Dayne." He rocked back in his big leather office chair, looking as if he'd just won the lottery. Or more like he was just holding hostage the numbers to my winning lottery ticket.

That sounded about right.

Dread slithered up my throat, like the slow, slimy slide of a snake. Constricting from the outside. Suffocating from the inside.

"Mr. Roth." It was a breath of uncertainty. Of indecision and doubt.

Why? First Aaron, and then this asshole? What was I going to do?

He gestured a little too eagerly to the chair that sat across from his desk. "Please, shut the door and take a seat."

My body quaked, but I did what I was told, the door snapping shut behind me, my feet unsteady as I took the three steps to stand in front of his desk. In discomfort, I eased down onto the chair.

Get it together, Rynna. This is too important for you to mess up now. Don't let either of these jerks hold you back.

I wasn't fool enough to think all things didn't come at a cost. And sometimes that cost was your pride.

"Thank you for meeting with me," I managed.

He had his elbow propped on the armrest of his chair, his index finger at his temple and his thumb under his jaw. Blatantly, he looked me up and down. His eager smile curved into a smirk.

"The pleasure's all mine."

I ignored the lump that thickened in my throat. "I hope you've had the chance to look at my application."

"Yes, I have, and we appreciate you looking to our establishment for your needs."

Okay. This was good. We could totally ignore our previous awkward situation.

I nodded, continued. "As you read, I inherited Pepper's Pies from my grandmother when she passed away several months ago." God, I hated the way it came out, as if she were nothing but a distant memory. Not when her loss was a fresh wound that ached inside of me. I forced a small smile. "The location is on Fairview, a prime location, especially with all the renovations currently happening in the area."

He thumbed through the paperwork. I eased a little, my rigid spine softening when he turned his attention from me and to the reason I was here.

"And you're asking for two-hundred-thousand dollars?" he asked, still perusing the sheets. "How did you come to this number?"

"Yes. I had an estimator come in before I took over holdings on the building. It should be sufficient to get us up and running again."

He nodded. "That's good."

Hope blazed to life.

I shifted to the edge of the chair. "You can see we have the profit and loss estimates on page thirteen. With the reputation of the diner, I was told I could expect profits to exceed the loss within a year. It will give me plenty for the upkeep of the diner, a modest salary for myself, and the ability to pay the loan each month."

Okay, maybe it was a bit of a stretch. I'd be riding a fine line. But I was willing to put in the extra work.

Studying that page, he rubbed his chin. "Estimates are estimates, Ms. Dayne. There's no guarantee customers will be rushing back to the diner."

That hope fizzled a little, but I pulled it together, prepared for this type of resistance. "I wouldn't consider my situation atypical. Most small businesses begin with a loan, just the same as I'm seeking from this bank. And most start-ups don't already have a name behind them. We have a built-in customer base, and with the hotel going in across the street, there will be hundreds of hungry people in front of my restaurant every single day."

A smile twitched at the corner of his mouth, and I smiled back eagerly. He flipped the folder closed and rocked back in his seat, threading his fingers together. "I'll tell you what . . ."

"Yes?" I edged forward more just as he leaned over his desk, unable to stop myself from mimicking his posture, those dreams I'd once held now dangling right out in front of me like a carrot.

His voice lowered as he leaned even closer. "We discuss this over dinner and you can show me just how badly you want this loan."

Something sinister had infiltrated those words.

Something dark and vulgar.

The hairs at my nape prickled in a sickening kind of awareness.

"Excuse me?" I asked, barely able to speak.

"You look like a smart woman, Ms. Dayne. I think you're playing coy again."

Every sleazy memory of him came rushing back, the arrogant man who didn't know how to take no for an answer and thought women should bow at his feet. But this was his job. Was he really going there?

"I think you need to *demonstrate* just how good you are." Every word was packed with innuendo. "Show me why I should recommend this loan for approval."

He cocked his head. The man with all the power. My dreams held hostage in his filthy paws.

Nausea turned my insides.

"So you're saying I have to go out with you in order for you to recommend my application be approved?"

He glanced over my shoulder toward the closed door before his seedy gaze returned to me. "Call it a business exchange."

"You can't . . . that isn't legal." I was floundering, looking behind me to the closed door. Praying by some miracle someone was standing there and could vouch for this insanity.

Because he was out of his mind.

"I'm merely asking for a meeting, Ms. Dayne." His intentions were so much more than a meeting.

And I wondered how many *meetings* this vile man had held over his client's heads. No doubt, I wasn't the first.

Stunned, I climbed to my feet. Memories of Aaron ripped through my head. The manipulation. I would never allow it again. "You are unbelievable. I would rather work every hour for the rest of my life to save the money to reopen my grandmother's restaurant than degrade myself with you."

He rocked back in that massive chair that was almost as big as his head. "All I asked for was proof of how much you wanted this loan, Ms. Dayne. I have no idea what you're insinuating."

I sneered. "And you are nothing but a liar. For the record, I want that loan more than anything. I'd just rather die than let you touch me."

Wrenching open the door, I flew out into the hall. Fury rose to the top of the tangle of emotions he had me in, my instincts kicking in.

Timothy Roth had messed with the wrong girl.

I was going right around this obstacle. Deviating course. Going straight to the top and reporting him.

I would see to it that Timothy Roth would never manipulate another woman sitting in his office again.

It was late Friday afternoon when there was a knock at my door. A shiver of nerves rocked through me, but I forced them down, refusing the insecurities that kept trying to creep back into my consciousness.

I crossed the living room and peered into the peephole, frowning when I could only make out the arm of a man wearing a dress shirt.

Warily, I unlocked the door and cracked it open, a crest of

unease washing over me.

Unease that hadn't been in vain.

I should have listened to my gut.

Just like my gramma had always told me.

I tried to slam the door shut when I saw the angry, twisted features of the man looming on the other side.

It was the same second I hit a wall of fear.

Or maybe I toppled headfirst into a vat of it.

Because it swallowed me. Saturating every inch. Every cell. Every fiber.

Screaming, I turned my back to the door and planted my feet against the floor. I pushed back as hard as I could.

"I already called the police. They're on their way."

Lies. Lies I prayed would break through his derangement. Because I'd been right. Timothy Roth was insane. Just in an entirely different way than I'd ever imagined.

Blood sloshed in my ears and terror slogged through my veins.

A steady *thwump, thwump, thwump*.

Liquid metal.

Heavy.

Too much.

Panic and fear.

No. No. No.

The threat did nothing to deter him. The door banged open an inch before I was bearing down again. With all my might. With all the fight I had in me. The latch so close to catching.

His voice seeped like venom through the crack he made. "You fucking bitch. You fucking bitch whore. I'll kill you for what you did. I know it was you. You ruined my life, you stupid bitch, and you are going to pay."

Fingers were in the frame, forcing it open.

Adrenaline and anguish. I screamed with them as I shifted a fraction. I rammed into the door with my shoulder.

I gave it everything I had.

The pain of it nearly split me in two.

But sometimes wills and physical strength were two different things.

Because he kicked the door, sending it crashing against the interior wall.

I flew to the floor.

Tim pushed his way inside, a menace that cast a shadow on my grandmother's house as he stepped toward me. I slid back across the floor, the bare skin of my thigh chaffing against the carpet.

Sobbing.

Hating that I couldn't stop the terror from taking hold.

Hating the words that fumbled from my mouth.

That I pled.

That I begged.

"Please. No. Oh, God, please, I'll do anything."

Anything.

Because it was the brutal truth of the horrible matter.

I *wouldn't* rather die than let Timothy Roth touch me.

twenty

Rex

I was going to lose my fuckin' head. I stormed through my kitchen, raking my fingers through my hair like it might stand the chance of calming me down.

Frankie was having her usual Friday night sleepover at my mom's, and I was supposed to be heading out to meet up with Kale to grab a bite to eat, after which no doubt we'd end up at the bar so we could hang out with Ollie for a few hours.

But there I was.

Fuming.

I had no claim. No right to think of that girl as mine. That didn't mean my heart and body and mind weren't screaming it when the piece of shit who'd been giving her a hard time at Olive's a few weeks back pulled into her driveway. When he stumbled out of his shiny silver Mercedes and staggered up the inclined bank toward the deck steps.

What the hell was she thinking? Messing around with that scumbag?

My brain spun with a shit-ton of possibilities I didn't want to entertain.

Had she gone back to the bar on a night I hadn't been there and run into this douche and decided to give it a go? Had she given him her number that night? Had something been going on all along?

No. I knew better than that. There was no chance she'd been fucking around with him before I'd been a complete bastard and pushed her away.

My thoughts headed south.

Right to that mouth.

That fucking mouth that had been wrapped around me two weeks ago.

Warm and wet and sucking me deep, the girl on her knees like some kind of offering.

A sacrifice.

Somehow, I'd gotten that was what it'd been. That she'd been cutting herself wide open. Letting me take and use and exploit.

And I'd wanted it. Wanted it so badly. Wanted *her* so badly. But how the fuck could I do that to her? Not when I still couldn't make sense of the disaster zone that was my heart. Not when I was locked up in bullshit chains that she didn't need to be tied to. The last two weeks had been torture, pretending she wasn't right there, across the street. That I didn't care when there was a fucking uproar demolishing my insides.

I made another pass through my kitchen, peering out the window like some deranged ex-boyfriend.

Did I actually think that asshat was any worse than I was?

Shit.

Maybe I did. Because I was back to glaring out my kitchen window with my fingertips digging into the granite countertop. Hoping they might sink in and permanently embed themselves. Anchor me so I couldn't do something supremely stupid.

Like run out the door and start making demands I had no right to make.

Why the hell was the fool hesitating at the base of her steps? Why were his shoulders and back heaving, hands in fists?

This guy . . . it was like . . .

Like he was pissed.

Not pissed.

Enraged.

My heart did something funny when he finally snapped into action. It was a slow, unfurling of awareness that pushed around the periphery of my consciousness as I watched him climb the steps. An overwhelming sense that slicked like ice down my spine, forcing me to stand and take note.

My eyes narrowed, scrutinizing his every move.

I didn't have a direct view of the door since it was on the side of the house, only the deck where the douchebag stood fully in my line of sight. He pounded on her door with the back of his fist.

There was movement. I couldn't actually see her door, but somehow, I knew she'd cracked it open. It was a shift in the atmosphere. I *knew* she opened it just as assuredly as I knew that she tried to force it closed.

Then the piece of shit was trying to shove it open. He reeled back, lifted a foot, and kicked it in.

Rynna.

Rynna.

Every fear I'd ever had tumbled free and lit my veins.

Gasoline and flames.

My soul screamed.

I wouldn't fucking let this happen.

Not again. I flew out my door, down the steps, and across the street before I was barreling up hers.

My heart was in my fucking throat, stomach twisted in a single knot of dread. Dread that raged. A steely demand that I protect her.

Save her. Defend her. Keep her. It chanted through that hollow space.

Would have run out to protect anyone. I knew I would. Still, there was no questioning the driving force was completely different when I came up behind the bastard and saw Rynna sobbing on the ground.

Fear consumed her, her expression full of horror and pleas as she scooted back across the floor.

He loomed over her, encroaching, filled with that rage I'd sworn I'd witnessed from the window. He was spewing a verbal attack I knew was mere seconds from becoming physical. "You fucking bitch. You ruined my life."

He was so consumed with debasing her that he hadn't noticed I was there. That I was inching forward, trying to quiet my breaths that were jolting from my lungs in spastic quakes.

A chill climbed to the air. Freezing. Clotting the tension. Every second stretched out. Dense and dark and deep.

A whimper from the ground, and my heart nearly fucking left my chest when those java eyes flashed my direction.

It only lasted for one of those extended seconds, but there was more communication in that brief exchange than in any conversation I'd ever had in my life.

Relief.

Deliverance.

Trust.

She poured it into me. Filling me full.

And this girl . . . this girl looked right back at him, continuing to beg like I wasn't even there.

So fucking smart and aware.

It would make taking out this piece of shit a whole ton easier than it would have been if he knew I was coming.

He didn't.

I rushed, and from behind, I hooked my arm around his neck. I cinched down against his throat, my other hand held around my wrist to keep my hold locked tight, my mouth at his ear. "Hey, fucker, remember me? Warned you last time if you didn't leave the girl alone, you wouldn't be able to walk away. You think I was joking?"

For a blink, he went slack, a huge breath sucked into his lungs at his surprise, his own awareness seeping through his rage and into his consciousness. That was all it took for every muscle in his body to tighten before the bastard started fighting back. His fingers sank into the flesh of my forearm, nails digging in like a bitch, the pussy battling to break free.

I tightened my hold, teeth gritted as I struggled to keep him restrained. "Rynna, call the police so we can send this dick where he belongs."

She was already on her knees, pushing to stand, her limbs shaking uncontrollably as she tried to find balance. Her eyes darted to the spot behind me where I remembered she'd stowed her purse the night I'd shown up here with Frankie.

No doubt, that was where her cell phone was.

I met those eyes again, not needing to say a word.

Go. I've got you. I won't let anything happen to you.

She bolted that direction.

The bastard thrashed, throwing an elbow into my ribs at the same time as he threw back his head. His skull cracking against my nose almost sent me to my knees. Pain exploded across my face. Blinding. Splitting. Enough that I momentarily lost my hold.

It gave him enough time to kick out a leg, tripping Rynna as she was rushing around us to make it to her purse.

She flew forward, slamming her head against the corner of the entryway table that was set against the wall next to the door as she fell face-first to the ground.

Rage.

This time it was my own.

"You asshole. You think I'm gonna stand here and let you hurt her?"

Never.

Fuck.

Never.

Once again, he was going her direction. I lunged for him, plowing into his side and catching him off guard. He stumbled and lost his footing. The two of us toppled to the floor where we were a tangle of limbs and punches and splattering blood.

His.

Mine.

I straddled his chest. Pounding my fist into his face. Blow after blow.

But the fucker fought. Fought and fought and fought.

Clipping me on the chin, he sent me sailing back, and he

scrambled to get on top of me. He was on me, pinning me down. He smashed his elbow into my cheek.

"You piece of shit . . . is that all you got? Only way you can get a woman is by forcing her? Huh? Is that how the game is played by pussies with nonexistent dicks? Or is it just so small no one knows it's there?"

I knew I was taunting him. Enraging him more. Inciting him to keep pounding on me.

But that was just fine.

Only thing I was doing was buying time.

Because the girl had already dialed 9-1-1, shouted out her address, had given the vile piece of shit's name.

She'd be safe.

That was all that fucking mattered.

I tried not to wince when I saw him cock back his fist, his knuckles going straight for my temple. This shit was gonna hurt. Probably knock me out flat.

She was worth it. She was worth it. She was worth it.

Sirens whirled in the distance, coming closer and closer.

She would be safe. She would be safe.

But that fist never met its mark. The asshole howled in agony. He flew off me, catching air, tumbling across the floor before he was bent over on his knees, clutching the side of his head. Blood poured out from between his fingers and dripped to the carpet.

I squinted, wondering if I was having some kind of hallucination. The perfect kind. The one where the most gorgeous girl I'd ever seen was standing above me. That chestnut hair matted, mangled with blood. Chest heaving. A huge glass vase gripped in both her hands, an enormous crack zigzagging down the middle of it, and a river of fractures splintering out.

Outside, engines roared. By the sound of it, at least three cruisers came to a screeching stop in front of Rynna's house. Feet pounded and voices shouted.

Seconds later, they were piling into her house, shouting for everyone to freeze.

Rynna dropped the vase. It finally gave up its fight with the impact, shattering into a thousand pieces when it hit the floor.

Just as Rynna was doing the same. Dropping to her knees and hitting the floor.

Sobs wracked her body when she realized it was over.

That she was safe.

Right then? It was the absolute only thing that mattered.

twenty-one

Rynna

"Thanks again, man," Rex said to Seth, the last officer at my house. He was a guy Rex had apparently known since high school, someone Rex considered a friend.

"Just, stay safe," Seth said, glancing between the two of us before he ambled down my porch steps and slipped into the driver's seat of his Ford sedan and pulled away.

Timothy Roth had been fired this afternoon. Apparently, my complaint of sexual harassment hadn't been the first he'd received. Apparently, when his wife found out the reason for his termination, she'd kicked him out.

His wife.

I trembled at the thought of it, at the arrogance and stupidity of the man and how much worse it could have been.

The taillights of Seth's patrol car splashed another dose of red into the blaze of reds and oranges and purpled blues that twisted into the sunset as he accelerated down the narrow neighborhood road.

Then it was as if the dial had been turned up on the silence.

So loud it was profound.

As loud as Rex Gunner's presence that eclipsed all.

A thunder.

A thriving, living being.

His gruff voice cut into the tension. "Don't like that you refused treatment. You sure you don't want me to give Kale a call?"

I chanced looking over at him where he stood behind me on the far side of the deck.

My savage savior.

Streaks of blood were dried on his face, and a small gash oozed from the corner of his eye. His clothes were tattered, soiled with sweat and blood, his hair a mess, body still bristling with remnants of pent-up rage.

My lungs inflated at the mesmerizing sight of him. Every part of me expanded. Reaching toward him.

"You're worried about me?" I managed. "You're the one who came to my rescue. The one who put himself on the line. Again. I can't . . . what if . . ."

His head angled and his shoulders rolled back, and the man took a powerful step forward.

The energy spiked.

"You think I'm not worried about you?" It almost sounded like an accusation. He took another step forward, the man a raging tower of protection. "You think I wouldn't do it all over again? You think I would have let him hurt you?"

He was suddenly in front of me. My breath gone when he stood over me.

An imposing, conquering shadow.

Eclipsing the fear that had taken me hostage. If it weren't for Rex, today would have ended in an entirely different way.

He lifted his fingers and brushed back a chunk of hair stuck to my cheek. His words rumbled like a threat. "I wanted to kill him, Rynna. He was going to hurt you, and I wanted to kill him. I would have. Second I saw you were in trouble, my heart was screaming out to protect you. To protect what *belonged* to me. To shelter what was *mine*."

Mine.

The word trembled around us.

"Thank you," I whispered. A tear slipped free, and my body began to shake with the aftermath. With the reality of it all.

A gasp ripped from my chest when I was suddenly swept off my feet and into the strength and security of Rex's arms. He had one arm under my back and the other beneath my knees, my body held possessively against the strength of his chest.

"Won't let anyone hurt you," he murmured against my forehead. Carrying me, he angled through the door. "I'm gonna take care of you."

"Rex." It was a whimper.

"Shh. I know, baby. I know."

I clung to his neck as he carried me upstairs. At the landing, he took a left and headed into my bedroom, pushing right past my unmade bed and through the cutout arch that led to the bathroom.

As if this man already knew the way.

He set me on unsteady feet and turned me to face the counter. My eyes met his in the mirror. A low growl climbed his throat, and he leaned around me to turn on the faucet.

The air constricted.

Charged.

I swore, our slowed, measured movements attracted every molecule within five miles. He wrapped his arms around me from behind, taking my hands in his and placing them beneath the fall of warm water. He gently rubbed our hands together, the basin filling with pink-tinged water as he scrubbed the blood free from our dirtied hands.

"Two weeks, Rynna. Two weeks I've been dying, hating the way I left things between us. Hating that I hurt you."

His words brushed my cheek, and his presence filled my senses.

Overwhelming.

He squirted soap onto our hands, continuing to wash away this afternoon, as if he wanted to erase the possibility of what could have happened.

Carefully.

Meticulously.

His voice was a soft scrape at the shell of my ear, sending shivers down my neck, turning my heart into a thundering orb at the center of my chest. "All that time, I was wishing with every part of me I could change my circumstances. That I could be right for you. Then *this*, Rynna. Then this happened and I don't fucking care, anymore. Don't fucking care that this is wrong."

His eyes captured mine through the mirror. They flashed with a warning. An omen. A prediction.

"I'm not afraid," I whispered, my promise striking the throbbing air. He gathered my hair in his hand, shifting it all to one side, exposing my neck. He pressed his lips there in the barest kiss. "That's funny, because I'm fucking terrified of you." His nose ran up to the back of my ear. "Terrified of this."

A shiver rolled down my spine, and Rex eased back a fraction, taking the hem of my shirt and drawing it slowly up my body.

That shiver shifted. An avalanche of chills. He peeled it over my head before he did the same to his own, scrubbing at his face before he tossed his shirt to his feet.

My gaze traced him through the mirror, and I swallowed around the emotion that grew thick at the base of my throat.

This complicated, amazing man drove me crazy with desire. Crazy with need. Crazy with this want that had become its own entity inside of me.

He reached up and let his fingertips flutter across my exposed shoulder and down my arm. Tingles spread in a slow slide. All the fear I'd felt earlier transformed into this emotion I wasn't sure I'd ever felt before.

Something so real it staggered my senses.

He reached back and unfastened my bra, drawing the straps down my arms.

My nipples pebbled as my breasts were exposed, and his chest heaved with a grunt. "So beautiful. So goddamned beautiful," he murmured.

His fingers pressed under the waistband of my shorts.

"You want this, Rynna? You want me?" There was a tremor

in his words. That same warning that flamed in his eyes. "Because I'm done running from you."

"I want you so badly it hurts."

He heaved a breath before he dipped down and kissed a path down my spine as he dragged my shorts and underwear down my legs.

"Oh God," I whimpered, hit by an onslaught of sensations.

Need and want and desire.

But it was that emotion that pulsed in the depths of me that nearly sent me to my knees. Wave after wave. Seeping and saturating. Trembling in my throat and tightening in my stomach.

"Rynna." It was a groan as he kissed down the cleft of my bottom and unwound my clothing from my feet, the sound so guttural it rumbled against the walls.

Then I was back in his arms and he was carrying me to my bed, lying me in the middle.

He stood with his chest heaving. So much stunning strength. The man so gorgeous and darkly appealing my mouth went dry.

Every thought and reservation fled from my mind. Every pep talk I'd given myself over the last two weeks about forgetting him and moving on scattered in the wind.

Because when it was just him and me?

There was nothing but the beat of our hearts.

Nothing but the call of our spirits. It was something louder than all the questions. Something bigger than his past. Something higher than our obstacles.

Something fierce rippled as he looked down at me completely naked on my bed.

"Are you sure?" he grated.

My hands fisted in my sheets, my body arching toward him. Needing him in a way I'd never needed anyone before. "I already told you I'm not afraid. You, Rex Gunner, are a chance I'm willing to take."

"You shouldn't be real." It was rough. Just like the man.

I bit my bottom lip, loving when he let me glimpse under all that hardness. "Yet, here I am."

"And what happens when you're gone?" There was

something so sorrowful in it, a stab right to the center of my chest.

Slowly, I climbed up onto my knees and stretched out my hand. I brushed my fingertips down the side of his rugged face. "And what happens if I stay?"

For a beat, his eyes dropped closed, and he leaned into my touch before he snatched me by the wrist and pressed my palm to his mouth. "And what if I don't let you leave?"

God, this man. He pushed and pulled. Taunted and tugged.

Slowly he edged back, eying me with those mesmerizing eyes as he kicked off his boots. Without freeing me of his gaze, he unfastened his belt. His abdomen flexed and bowed as he tugged on his fly and lowered the zipper.

Desire swept through my body.

A battering storm.

Anticipation and need.

He nudged the jeans down his legs and took his underwear with them.

He stood there in the shadows that fell into my room.

Completely naked.

Bare.

So beautiful a downpour of desire soaked me through.

I hadn't been lying to Macy. This man was what gods were made of. Sleek and defined. Carved in hard, indestructible perfection.

All except for the broken pieces I knew he tried to keep concealed, buried deep inside. I saw them so clearly. Held in the depths of those eyes. Those eyes that were looking at me as if maybe I should run if I didn't want to be devoured.

But I did.

I so desperately did.

He edged forward an inch, big hand splayed across my chest, nudging me down onto the mattress. I was spread across its width, the man towering over me from the side.

I writhed, hips jutting into the air, not caring for a second that I was desperate.

That I needed him.

His touch and his body and that spirit that had already taken me whole. He ran a fingertip down the inside of my thigh. "Last two times I touched you nearly ruined me. Seeing you like this? Don't think I'm ever going to be the same. Stealing my sleep. Stealing my breath. Stealing my sanity. Little thief."

Chills flew. A chaos of sensation.

His hands were on my knees, pulling them apart.

I'd never felt so exposed, and I gasped out a shocked breath when he leaned down and gave one long lick up my slit.

He pulled back, and it was almost a smirk that was riding his sexy mouth as he stared down at me, as if he were looking at the sunrise for the very first time. Shifting his attention to my face, he grazed just the tips of his fingers through my folds. "Stunning. Fucking stunning. Feel like I'm in a dream when I'm touching you this way. Like I'm lost in some kind of fantasy and I don't ever want to wake up."

Redness flushed across the surface of my skin

"And you . . . you make me feel like I've finally found my reality. Like I finally figured out exactly where I'm supposed to be." A million emotions flashed across his mesmerizing face. Regret and lust and this consuming affection he couldn't keep contained.

He crawled over me.

Slowly.

Carefully.

I sucked in a staggered breath when the man was suddenly caging me, hands planted on either side of my head, those powerful thighs wedged between mine.

His cock bobbed against my belly, and a shudder ripped through my body.

He sank down onto his elbows, hot hands framing my face. "I don't understand this, Rynna. The hold you have on me. But when I look at you? Get this feeling that I'm looking at everything right."

"Rex." His name was a tremor.

A plea.

He leaned down and kissed me.

He kissed me carefully.

Gently.

Tenderly.

That energy lapped through the air. A slow, steady built. A current stoked by each pass of his tongue, by the heat that sizzled across our flesh, by our hands that explored. I ran my palms across his chest and over his wide shoulders, down the sinewy muscle of his back to his narrow hips.

I wrapped my hand around him, stroking him slow from the base of him to the tip.

He pulled his mouth away from mine. Head tilting back, he released a long groan. "Rynna . . . fuck . . . Rynna."

He pressed back up onto one hand, touching my face, a hand on my cheek before he edged back even more. He grasped me by the back of my knee and spread me wide. Jagged pants ripped from his lungs as he took himself in his hand and rubbed just the head of his cock through my center.

Flames.

I swore that single touch set me on fire.

"Rynna . . . fuck . . . you are gonna destroy me."

I whimpered, "Please."

Jaw clenched, he began to work himself inside me, tiny thrusts as he spread me, as he stole my breaths and seared himself into my body.

He was so big, so big that my nails sank into his shoulders. I knew he was holding himself back, forcing himself to remain in control.

He slowly worked himself farther.

Deeper.

Until he was seated fully.

Owning me.

His cock throbbed in the tight clutch of my walls.

The hand that had been on my thigh skimmed over my hip and up my side, cupping my breast, gliding to my jaw. "Fuck, Rynna . . . you feel so right. So fucking right."

"We are right," I murmured toward his face.

He groaned again before he pulled almost all the way out and paused, that mesmerizing stare held fast on my face. As if he held the power to see straight inside me.

Or maybe he was just begging me to look to the depths of him.

In that moment, everything went electric, that current lashing and zapping in the air.

Then he consumed me with one dominating thrust.

A thrust that shocked the air from my lungs and sent it scattering somewhere in the vicinity of my heart. My heart I could feel shattering. Shattering with emotion.

With need and affection and this feeling that was rising to obliterate all else.

The same annihilated heart that struggled to keep up with the battering crash of his.

He went back to holding me behind the knee.

He watched down on me while he dominated my body.

Eyes raking my flesh. My face. My breasts. Where we were joined.

Again and again.

As if he couldn't get enough. As if he never wanted it to end.

His body glistened with sweat as he worked over me. Muscles bowing.

His fucks deep.

Passionate.

Whole.

Pleasure glowed. Bright white flames.

He was looking at me as if I weren't real.

As if I were a fantasy.

Something he could never deserve or hold or keep.

When he'd already won every part of me.

Body and mind and quivering soul.

He shuddered through a frantic swallow, barely hanging on. "Fuck . . . baby . . . Ryn. Baby. You are a fucking miracle. No woman should feel this good. Fuck . . . I don't know if I can hold back."

"Then don't."

"Shit. You are so fuckin' sweet. So goddamned sweet." And I

loved the grin that quirked at the side of that mouth. That mouth that was descending on mine, his hand on my neck. He kissed me until my head spun then he edged all the way back onto his knees and grabbed me by the waist.

He lifted my hips in the air.

My body arched.

All spread out.

My hands fisted in the sheets. I held on while Rex Gunner let go.

His control gone. The man driving to the depths of me. Where bliss spun and tightened and burned.

Gasps shocked from my mouth.

His fucks so desperate they were almost sweet.

He hissed through the wild rocks of his hips. "You are a miracle. Look at you. So damned sexy. So gorgeous and you don't even know."

He drove harder.

Faster.

His frenzied pants lifted into the air.

He tightened his hold with one hand, the other grazing over my trembling belly, and his thumb found my clit.

"Oh God," I cried out.

And I could feel my own reality slipping away. The burn of pleasure he incited with every thrust of his cock.

The man fucked like a barbarian that had perfected his art. Rough and grueling and driving me mad.

Higher and higher toward where day and night spun.

"Rex—"

Everything burst.

Strobes of light that flashed behind my eyes and the pleasure that exploded in my body.

Fracturing.

Scattering wide. Bliss.

It rode every nerve and obliterated every cell.

A sound tore from my throat, given voice where it came to life from somewhere in my spirit.

Because just like Rex had said, this shouldn't have been real.

It was too good. Too much. Too overwhelming.

Pleasure rushed.

A landslide.

So intense I thought it might go on forever.

Rex drove deeper and harder and wilder. His fingers sank into my hips, and he jerked my body to meet each dominating thrust. The man coming unhinged. Every breath a grunt. He gripped me as if he were clinging to safety, afraid he would be swept away, too. His head kicked back, and he roared toward the ceiling.

And I floated on his ecstasy. My walls clutching him tight. My heart holding on tighter.

For a few moments, we remained there, his shoulders and chest heaving as he panted for air. He slowly lowered my hips to the bed, wincing as he pulled out before he slumped down on top of me.

Threading his fingers through my hair, he rolled us to our sides. He stared at me, blinking in wonder as he brushed his thumb over the curve of my cheek. "That was . . ."

"Incredible," I whispered, almost shy.

"Incredible might be an insult. Feeling this way should be impossible, Rynna Dayne. Not sure how I'm going to walk out of this house and ever be the same."

"What if I don't want you to walk out of here ever feeling the same?"

"Don't think there's any worry about that." He studied me, hesitating, before he spoke, his admission scratchy. "I haven't been with anyone since Frankie's mom."

Shock burned through my mind and jolted my spirit, questions tumbling through my head, this man who was such a mystery.

I shifted onto my elbow, causing Rex to roll onto his back. I searched him in the shadows. "What? Why now? Why me?"

"Because you change everything, Rynna. You walk in a room, it's better. And when you walk away, everything grows dimmer. Colder. And I'm tired of living in the dark." He brushed back the hair that fell against my cheek. "But that doesn't mean I'm not terrified. That I'm not scared I'm doing something wrong.

Making bad choices, the way I have all along. Last thing I want to do is hurt you."

I dipped down and placed a soft kiss to his chin, rising back up to meet the intensity of his stare. "The only thing that would hurt me is you walking away."

"My daughter . . ." I watched the heavy bob of this thick throat, the fierce protectiveness seeping through his pores.

I pressed my palm over the erratic thunder of his heart. "I know. Your daughter . . . your beautiful Frankie. I promise you I would rather die than hurt her, just like I know you'd rather die than see her hurt."

His heart pounded harder, and a dent pulled between his eyes. "How's it you just get it?"

"There are some things that just aren't that hard to understand. Like loving a child. It's complete. Absolute. There's no middle ground. So yeah, I get it."

"She's gonna fall for you, Rynna."

A soft smile pulled at my mouth, and I scratched my fingertips through the scruff on his jaw. "That's good, because I'm already falling for her."

Falling for you.

I didn't say it. Because I had my own fears. That he might not be ready. That the words might push him away. I figured when he looked at me, it was blatant, anyway.

Tentatively, I reached down to run my fingers through the soft locks of his hair. "What happened with Frankie's mom?"

He flinched. "I don't fucking know, Rynna. I came home one day, and she was . . . driving away. She didn't even stop when she saw me pass her on the road." His eyes squeezed shut. "Thought everything was fine. Left for work that morning, and then boom . . . gone. Some bullshit letter left behind about me working too much and she couldn't take it anymore."

Nikki was right. What a selfish bitch.

"What was she like?"

Emotion flashed through his eyes. Hurt and hatred.

"Last thing I want to be talking about is her when I'm lying here with you. Because right here? With you? That's where I want to be, and the last thing I need is her here in the middle of it."

"You don't need to tell me anything, Rex," I whispered, just as softly as my fingers that trailed across his jaw. "But when you want to? When you're ready? I'll be right here, ready to listen. I promise you there isn't anything you could say that would turn me off or send me in the other direction. Because this is where I want to be, too."

He nodded, his hand on my neck. "You know . . . your grandma . . . she was there with Frankie when I got home that night. Watching over her. Caring for her. She helped to get me through that time."

At the thought of my grandmother with Frankie, warmth spread beneath my skin. She truly had been a part of their lives. I guessed I'd only related it to the pies. But she'd meant something to them.

Without a doubt, they'd meant something to her.

"I'm so glad she was there for you."

"She was amazing."

"Yeah," I whispered.

Contentment rolled through my being as a slow, slow caress, and I snuggled closer, laying my head on his chest, my ear against the steady thrum of his heart.

"Can't believe what nearly went down this afternoon," he muttered, lightly gliding his fingertips along my bare back.

Fear flickered in my spirit. "Me, either. But it's over. I don't want to dwell on what might have been or could have happened. I just want to be thankful for what did."

"But the loan you were after that set that bastard off? What now?"

I kept drawing patterns on the rippling muscles of his pecs, words subdued. "I wait, I guess. Pray that they approve it and this whole mess doesn't affect it in any way."

"You mind me asking how much you were asking for?"

"No, I don't mind. Two hundred thousand. When I found out my grandmother left everything to me, the attorney had an estimator go in to give me and idea of what repairs would be needed to reopen. He wanted to give me the option to cut my losses and sell it off for what it was worth."

"And that's what you wanted? To come back here and take all that on?"

Soft affection slipped from my mouth. "When I was growing up, running that restaurant was the only thing I wanted. I couldn't imagine anything but being there at my grandmother's side."

"Why'd you leave, Rynna?"

Sadness wove into the fibers of my being and I tilted my face so I could see him. "Because I thought I was in love and it turned out it was nothing but a joke. I couldn't be the joke anymore, Rex. It hurt too bad."

"Fuck . . . I hate him."

"It wasn't just him. It was everything. Everyone. The school. This town. I knew if I stayed, everyone would be laughing at me."

I could still see Janel, that evil, depraved laugh, no care as she crushed my soul and destroyed my world.

"I was humiliated. Betrayed. At the time, I saw no other option than running, thinking I couldn't stay here and face the people I thought cared about me. I was so young. Looking back now? It seems ridiculous that I let them affect me so much."

He tightened his hold. "It's amazing how much power the ones we care about most hold. Especially when they're hurting us."

"Yeah," I whispered. "I just wish I hadn't stayed away so long. I wish had come back when she was still alive. She wanted so badly for me to come home, even though she paid for my college, encouraged me to find what I loved. What made me happy. And I was fine in San Francisco, satisfied on some level, but it never brought me the true kind of joy I knew she wanted for me. And then . . . she was gone . . . and I was too late."

He shifted a fraction, staring at me intently, almost cautiously. "Did you come back for her, or for you?"

"At first? I—" I blinked, wandering through the emotions I'd felt at the news.

Agony.

Grief.

Guilt.

The fear that had stumbled my feet and the hope that had pushed me forward.

"I was terrified to come back, but I did it because there was a part of me that had never let this place go. It didn't take more than my walking through the doors of that restaurant for me to realize this was where I belonged. All the years I spent working in a corporate office and, it turns out, I just want my fingers buried in dough."

Warm laughter floated out. "And here you are . . . home . . . right where you're supposed to be."

"Yeah."

"Making pies." A tease slipped into his tone.

A grin pulled at the corner of my mouth, and I edged back onto both hands, grinning down at him. "Oh, you like those pies, huh?"

He leaned up, kissing the tip of my nose, the caress of his lips chained to my heart. "Mm-hmm . . . I definitely like those pies."

I could feel the heat flush my body, my voice growing quiet when I asked, "Did you eat the one I made you?"

He rumbled a greedy sound. "Every single bit. All except for the piece Frankie had to have. And fuck me, if I didn't want that piece, too."

"Stingy."

"You can't blame a man who knows what is his." He was all smirks, this easy cockiness where he lay in the middle of my bed.

God. He was beautiful and I still couldn't believe he was there. That this was real.

A rush of joy took me over. This happiness that spread far and fast. I fell into his playfulness, the ease I had no idea this man could show. "Is that what won you over? My pies?"

"Maybe . . . a little."

I swatted his chest. "No more pies for you."

A shock of surprise jutted from my lungs when he suddenly flipped me, straddling me from above. His fingers dove into my sides, this hard, callused man, laughing as he tickled me. "Those are just wicked words, woman. Don't you dare tease me like that."

"Oh my God . . . Rex, stop! Stop! I'm so ticklish," I squealed, struggling to break free and never wanting to go anywhere.

"Not until you make me all the pies."

I tried to catch my breath and fight him off and hold him all at the same time. "No. No more pies for you."

"Tell me, Little Thief. Tell me you're going to make me all the pies." He kept on with his sweet, sublime attack until we were a laughing mess of prodding, tingling fingers, hysterical, shrieking laughter, and wild, pounding hearts.

It tapered off when he pinned my hands to the bed above me, those piercing sage eyes holding me firmer than the hold he had on my wrists.

That awareness spun. Fierce and intense.

"You belong here, Rynna. You'll make it work. I have faith in you."

And then he was kissing me as if he didn't ever want to stop.

twenty-two

Rex

Fear tumbled through his veins and clanged in the hollow of his chest. Frantic, he stumbled through the brushy undergrowth, the world buried by soaring trees. Branches lashed at the exposed skin of his arms and thorns latched onto the fabric of his shirt in an attempt to hold him back.

It propelled him harder.

Faster.

He screamed her name. "Sydney."

Sydney. Sydney. Sydney.

The howl of wind answered back.

Sydney.

I panted and thrashed. My head spun, fumbling through my thoughts to make sense of where I was. Warmth surged through my body when hands smoothed across my face, the softest voice cutting through the darkness. "Shh . . . I'm right here, Rex. I'm right here."

Relief gushed out on a shattered breath, and I grabbed her and pulled her against my body.

I buried my face in her hair.

"Are you okay?" she whispered.

"I am now," I told her. Because it was the truth.

Rynna.

Fucking Rynna.

Little Thief.

She was making me pie.

Fuck, she was making me pie.

She fluttered around her kitchen, this amazing girl spinning me up more with every swish and sway of her hips.

She had pulled on a pair of lace underwear and had slipped on a long-sleeved, red-and-black plaid button down that she'd rolled up her forearms. The bottom hem of the shirt just barely covered that glorious, round ass, and those sexy legs were bare. Long and sleek and driving me wild.

Obviously, she was right when she said this was exactly where she belonged.

I wasn't talking some bullshit chauvinist crap like that fucker who'd thought he could take whatever he wanted from her, either. Her body. His vengeance.

I was talking about her ease and grace. The joy that was so apparent in her eyes, and the pride that poured from her every time she glanced at the recipe she'd clearly memorized. But still, she kept peeking at it with an outpouring of love. Like she felt her grandma right there with every step.

I shifted on the wooden chair, trying to rein it in. Ideas barreled out ahead of me. Everything I was so fucking stupid for wanting calling out for me like it just might be within my grasp. Of course, all the reasons I couldn't have them taunted me just in the periphery. Threatening to reach in and pluck me straight out of this moment.

Problem was, that asshole piece of shit who had shown up at her door earlier this evening had stolen something from me, too.

My damned sanity. After what went down, there wasn't a

whole lot of it left anymore.

Proof of it? I was sitting at the small table beneath the kitchen window that faced my house.

At two in the morning.

After I'd woken from that same fucked-up nightmare. After I'd let this amazing girl see that part of me.

She'd comforted me, whispered her belief when she had no idea where my panic was bred. When she had no clue there was a part of me that was screaming out in grief. Terrified. Feeling guilty for letting her soothe me when that part of me was condemned to agony for all my life.

I'd rolled over her, taken her, soft and slow while she'd gazed up at me through the shadows of the night.

We'd showered and then fallen back into her bed where we'd slept for a few hours. I woke to her sweet body wrapped around me, and we were right back at it again.

It seemed once we got started, neither of us could get enough. Afterward, she'd tugged at my hand and hauled me downstairs. There was a knowing grin on her stunning face, turning me inside out when she'd plopped me right here and told me to stay.

Like I was going anywhere.

I'd already had her three times tonight. It shouldn't have been possible, but there it was.

Lust. Curling in my guts. My dick way too eager for another round as I watched her light footsteps as she crossed the floor, the way her hair fell across the silky skin of her neck as she leaned over to pull the piping hot cherry pie from the oven.

A pie that smelled like its own kind of miracle.

Night pressed against the drawn drapes, and the simple globe light on the ceiling cast a pool of golden warmth over her. While she'd worked for the last forty minutes, we'd been chatting

About anything and everything.

Two of us completely at ease. I'd asked her about her time in San Francisco and what it was like to work for a corporate accountant. She'd told me all about her best friend, Macy, that sweet softness in her expression when she'd talked about the girl who'd helped her out of her shell.

Of course, she'd been all too eager to know how Kale, Ollie, and I had first met, the girl laughing as I told her about the trouble we'd constantly gotten into as kids.

I'd wanted to tell her. Just lay it all out. But how could I expect to rein her with something that was so complicated when I still couldn't figure out how I was feeling myself? When I still didn't know how much I could give her when there was this antsy part of me that wanted to give her everything?

"Just a couple more minutes," she told me with a smile from over her shoulder.

"You really are trying to ruin me, aren't you, woman?"

She giggled. Fuck, that was cute, too. "How's that?"

"I think you know exactly what you're doing."

"And what would that be?" Playing along, each of her words dripped with the sexy tease.

"Charming me with those pies and bewitching me with that body."

"If that's all it takes," she said, tossing me a grin as she cut into the pie.

"You got more ammunition in your arsenal? Because you come at me any harder, I'm done for."

She laughed, shaking her head as she slipped an angled spatula into the pie and pulled out a steaming sliver, quick to set it on a plate. She padded over to the freezer, grabbed a gallon of vanilla ice cream, and scooped a heaping pile of that on, too.

I could see it almost sizzle when it hit the pie, melting fast. My stomach growled in anticipation.

"Since you're so impatient, this is still super hot, so it's going to be more like cobbler."

I grunted. "You can't expect me to wait with something that smells that good."

Redness heated her cheeks, this humble sweetness taking hold.

Damn, I really liked that. I liked that she was proud and brave and didn't hesitate to say what was on her mind. Her pride came with this modesty that made me want to wrap her up and sing her every praise that could ever fall from my lips.

I was starting to believe she deserved every single one of them.

She was still smiling when she moved my direction. My mouth watered. Wasn't sure if it was because I wanted to devour that pie or sink my teeth into those hips that swished back and forth.

Hypnotizing.

Stirring.

Inciting.

Fuck. This woman.

I leaned back in the chair when she came to stop at my side. Setting the plate down in front of me, she leaned close to my ear, her voice soft. "At least somebody appreciates my pie."

My hand went out, palming one of those hips, voice turning sincere. "I won't be the last. I promise you that. People are gonna flock to that diner in droves as soon as the word gets out."

She cupped the side of my face, and my heart was doing that crazy thing again, speeding and knocking and thrumming.

"How do you make me feel like I can do anything?" she whispered.

"Know you can." The words were gruff as my hand slid from her hip to her waist.

She let out a little yelp when I hoisted her onto the edge of the table, then she was giggling as she grabbed the fork and scooped up a bite, holding it up in front of my mouth. "What, you need me to feed you, too?"

For an answer, I cinched down on the outside of her thigh and tugged her closer. "Apparently, I'll take whatever you're willing to give me."

"How about this?" She waved the fork in front of my face, teasing me, taunting me. I reached out and grabbed her by the wrist, opening wide and pulling it inside.

On all things holy.

It melted on my tongue, an explosion of tart and sweet.

"Good?" she asked. A sudden dash of insecurity threaded its

way into her tone.

My approval rumbled around the fork as she slowly pulled it free. I chewed and swallowed, watching her face the whole time, her expression nervous as she waited for my reaction. "It's perfect, Rynna. Perfect like I'm starting to believe you might be."

Her delicate throat bobbed, her expression wistful when she glanced at the pie. "I'm not close to being perfect, Rex. I just want to do it justice. Make my gramma proud and find joy in it at the same time."

A soft puff of laughter jetted from her lungs. "And sometimes it seems silly . . . how badly I want it. How much it means to me."

I brushed my thumb across the top of her thigh, hand still clinging to the side of her, needing that connection. "You want all the good things, Rynna. There isn't any shame in that."

I took the fork from her and scooped some onto it. "Here. Taste."

Nearly died when she moaned around the fork, the way her eyelids drifted closed.

Savoring.

"See. You've got nothing to worry about, baby."

Her eyes fluttered open, and her lips parted. A fleck of sugar was stuck to the corner of her bottom lip. Edging forward, I licked it clean.

"Delicious," I murmured at her mouth, and she was moaning again, her fingers locking themselves in the skin of my shoulders. I kissed her a little deeper, and that sweet tongue slid against mine. Slowly this time. Like she was savoring me just the same as she was savoring the pie.

Pulling back, I dug the fork back into the pie and slipped another bite into her mouth.

She chewed slowly, watching me.

The air shifted between us.

Charged.

That current coming alive.

I swore that this girl emitted her own kind of gravity.

I dove back in.

Tasting her mouth.

Her tongue.

Her lips.

Relishing.

Wondering how a single moment could feel this good.

She took a fistful of my hair, nudging me back so she could take the fork and feed me another bite. She watched me chewing while my fingers tapped across the top of her thigh and to the inside. I brushed my fingertips along the edge of the lace that covered her.

A whimper, and she was feeding me more, just as I was pushing those panties aside, exposing her pussy, which was just as delicious as the rest of her. Wet and throbbing. I slicked my fingers through her slit, circling them around her engorged clit, my eyes never leaving her face while I rolled that pie around on my tongue.

"Rex."

"Yeah?" I rumbled, not minding a bit when she was feeding me another bite. With my free hand, I gripped her knee and hooked her heel on the edge of the table, teasing her the whole time, before two of my fingers were pressing inside the warm well of her body. Her walls clamped down, throbbing and needy. I began to drive them in and out, the girl all spread out on the table, as delectable as her dessert.

She cried out when I pulled my fingers free, and then I watched her eyes glaze over when I dipped those fingers in the pie and lifted it to her mouth.

"Oh . . . God . . . what . . ." It was all a strangle of words as I pressed my fingers between those lush, full lips.

The girl sucked them clean.

"A little dirty and a whole lot sweet. Just the way I thought you'd be," I said, gruff and hard.

She moaned. The sound vibrated around my fingers, and I ripped them free. In the same second, I was grasping the back of her neck and jerking her forward. I kissed her mad while my fingers went back to work, sliding deep and sure, because shit, I wasn't leaving this house without driving this girl just as wild as she was driving me.

She gasped when I suddenly had her by the outside of both thighs, spreading her wide. I licked her up and down. Her clit. Her ass. Everywhere in between.

Hands fisted in my hair, and I couldn't help but smile. She was guiding me to her clit. "Please. I can't . . . I need you."

I lapped and sucked as she continued to whisper incoherent words.

Her own kind of praise.

The girl nothing but the tease of perfection that I held in the grasp of my hands.

I pulsed my fingers into her, letting my other hand wander along the crease of her ass, the girl releasing all these shocked sounds of pleasure into the air.

Feeding that gravity.

Making it feel like it just might be impossible for either of us to walk away. She came with a cry. With her fingers curling in my hair. With her heart manic and her breaths harsh.

And mine. Mine ached and wished this chance were one I should actually take.

She slumped forward.

Shaking.

Boneless.

Standing, I slid an arm under her legs and the other under her back, and carried her back upstairs to her room.

The whole way, I prayed I wasn't making the biggest fucking mistake I'd ever made.

twenty-three

Rynna

$\int$hooting upright, I clutched the sheet to my bare chest and struggled to pull in a breath. A deep sense of dread echoed from my bedroom walls. This unsettled feeling that something was off. I squinted through the play of shadows outside my window where daylight slowly breached the sky.

It took me all of two seconds to realize what was amiss.

I was alone.

After what had happened between Rex and I last night, I'd hoped to wake up in the safety of his arms, praying he'd found some of that same security in mine, too. I wasn't sure I'd ever felt so helpless than when I'd woken to find him flailing and jerking in my bed, lost to some kind of torment I couldn't understand.

I'd wanted to.

To understand it.

To understand him.

I hungered for him to embrace the feelings that grew between us.

Steadily.

Greedily.

I'd seen it last night, emerging through the storm in his eyes, scaling those fortress walls he built around himself and tumbling free to the other side.

He kept allowing me deeper and deeper, below those layers that fought to remain concealed. Just the same as I allowed him into mine, giving him bits of the horror that had sent me running.

Sliding from my bed, I stood. My attention caught on the small piece of folded paper that had dropped to the floor. It must have been tangled in the sheet. For a moment, I blinked at it, both terrified and eager to read what it might say, before I reached down and tentatively picked it up.

Slowly, I unfolded it, my eyes quick to scan the choppy scratch of handwriting dented on the page.

You are more beautiful than the sun breaking the day. Believe me. This morning, I had the privilege of watching them both, and I didn't want to stop. Little Thief, what am I going to do with you?

My heavy heart gave, fluttering and flapping, so insanely light. I pressed the letter over the manic thrum, not even attempting to hold back the grin that took hold of my face.

Rynna - Sixteen Years Old

"What are you doing?" Worried confusion streaked through my mind when I entered the back office to clock out. Pepper's Pies was getting ready to close. The day had been busy, and I was tired and hungry. I'd spent the last six hours rushing around the dining room, taking care of customers, along with Janel and her mother, while Gramma had been in the back with the cook baking.

The aroma of chicken pot pie still wafted through the diner, the flaky crust and seasoned vegetables and savory chicken teasing my nose with the thought of finally sitting down to eat.

But it was the sight in front of me the clenched my chest.

Janel was lingering at the far wall where we hung our personal items, tucking a stack of cash held together by a money wrapper into her apron pocket. Shock had widened her eyes when she whipped around to face me where I stood in the doorway.

She wouldn't.

Janel's surprise shifted into a smirk. "Don't be jealous I got great tips today and you made next to nothing. If you didn't spend so much time eating the pies, you might actually make some money around here."

Her jibes sank into me like darts, making me bow back, hit with physical pain. "I had more tables than you," *I said, forcing off the hurt, because that was just Janel's way. I had learned to live with it. It was the only way I could remain friends with her, if that's what I even wanted to call it.*

Janel swept a long lock of blonde hair over her shoulder. "Well, tips have more to do with how you look and make a customer feel that putting their stupid food in front of them so they can stuff their faces. But I know you can't relate to that."

Anger slithered beneath my skin. I stilled when I heard my grandmother grumbling from out front. "What on earth . . . till is short a full hundred dollars."

My mouth dropped open again, my head slowly shaking when I looked back at Janel. Guilt flashed through her pale blue eyes, and she rushed across the tiny room and grabbed my arm by both hands. "Rynna, please don't say nothin'. My momma has been real short this month. Don't think we're gonna make rent. I'm so sorry. I just . . . I'm so ashamed. I didn't want you to know."

My head shook again, torn, my voice dropping to match Janel's. "Why didn't you just tell Gramma? You know she'd understand. Front you the money."

"You know Momma's pride," *she begged.*

I swallowed around the jagged rock that cut up the base of my throat. This felt all wrong. So wrong.

I hesitated, and Janel squeezed my arm. "Please."

I barely nodded and shifted to call down the hall, "Oh, Gramma, I'm so sorry I forgot to tell you. I needed it for new gym shoes."

Gramma rounded the corner. "Corinne Paisley, you need to remember these things. Here I was, getting all worked up over nothing."

189

"It slipped my mind. I'm really sorry," I promised, glancing over my shoulder at Janel who'd turned away and was changing her shirt.

"Just glad it's accounted for. Why don't you get yourself some dinner, and I'll sit down with you in a minute."

"That sounds great."

"How about you, Janel? You and your momma want to sit with us?"

Janel grabbed her purse from the hook. "Have plans, Mrs. Dayne. But thank you."

Janel blew by both of us, and I headed out to the kitchen to grab a plate, hating the way regret had gathered in the pit of my stomach. The way everything felt wrong. Off. Like I was an accomplice of something I didn't want partner to.

Filling a plate with dinner, I wound out front, stopping at the soda machine to grab a Coke. Laughter rang out behind me, and I swiveled to peek at one of the few tables still occupied in the diner.

It was filled by four boys.

Boys who were getting close to being men.

Aaron was at the window, his brown hair buzzed, so handsome that achy spot inside me flared.

I startled when I heard the giggle behind me. Janel was shaking her head as if she felt sorry for me. "Oh, Rynna, don't do that to yourself. You know he's so far out of your league. That crush you've had for all these years just makes you look pathetic."

Discomfort climbed my throat, a sticky hurt that slicked my skin. I wanted to tell her to shut her stupid mouth. That I was so tired of her mind games. Of her manipulating every situation.

It wasn't the first time I'd covered for Janel.

Not by far.

But I didn't say anything. I just dropped my head and walked to the other side of the diner and sat down in the booth I always shared with my grandmother.

twenty-four
Rex

"Daddy!" Frankie came barreling out my mom's door, brown hair a disaster and flying all around her. The kid was sporting that smile that melted me into a puddle of goo. Nothing but sticky sap right at her feet.

She had on a tank top and shorts. Since it was Frankie Leigh, she wasn't about to stop there. She was also wearing an old pair of suspenders, which she'd gotten God knows where, and sky-high heels she'd pilfered from my mom's closet that were ten sizes too big.

And surprise, surprise, that damned hot pink tutu.

Couldn't help but grin.

Guess I really was a sucker for all that Frankie flare.

"There's my girl." The second she reached me, I swooped her into my arms and tossed her into the air. Exactly the way I knew she liked. My heart gave an extra boom at the sound of her laughter that rang through the morning. That sound alone had to be my single greatest joy.

I caught her, hugging her to my chest, pushing my nose into her hair, breathing in my little girl.

"I missed you," I whispered into the mess of hair on her head. I held her to me a little closer, and Frankie wrapped those tiny arms around my neck, the force of her smile touching me even when I couldn't see her face.

"I misses you, too, Daddy! But mes and Grammy had so much fun. She lets me do my very own *skupture*, right, Grammy?" She wiggled out of my tight hold, shifting in my arms to look back at my mom, who was standing at her usual place in the threshold and grinning back at us.

"A sculpture?" I clarified as I carried Frankie up the sidewalk.

"Uh-huh."

"And what did you sculpt?" I asked.

Those brown eyes widened like I was clueless. "A puppy, silly. I told you I wants a puppy so, so bad. Oh, Daddy, can I? Can I have a puppy? I'll be the best puppy mommy ever!"

A pang hit me hard.

Cutting me deep.

I fought against it, the memories threatening just at the cusp of my consciousness. Since Rynna had come into my life, it felt like everything was right there, trembling beneath my nose, begging to be exposed.

The thought of Missy still killed me, finding my girl dead at the side of the road on the same damned day my wife had left me. I'd had that dog since before I'd lost Sydney, and she'd been my solace, a reason to live when I hadn't wanted to go on.

But life was brutal that way.

Threatening to take everything in one fell swoop.

If what happened with Sydney hadn't been enough to make me ridiculously overprotective of Frankie, desperate to keep her safe, the cruelty of that day had solidified it.

I shoved the thoughts down and softened my voice. "Still don't think that's the best idea right now, Frankie."

"When's a good time?"

"Now we're sculpting?" I asked when I got within a couple feet of my mom, praying it'd distract Frankie from demanding an answer to that question.

"We dabble in all the art forms, don't we, Sweet Pea Frankie

Leigh? Call us multitalented. Just like your daddy." Mom ruffled her fingers through my daughter's hair. There was so much affection in her gaze when she looked at us both, I couldn't help the surge of love that went crashing through my senses. It was like something inside me had been unlocked, and every sort of emotion I'd tried to keep repressed billowed out without my permission.

The love.

The longing.

The fear.

The regret.

Rynna's face glided through my consciousness, her touch a faint whisper across my skin, breathing all that beauty and life.

Stirrings of hope shook through me like tremors of warning. Like quivers that staked deeper, demanding more. The ground shifted between the two extremes. Tossing me back and forth with no idea which was going to send me stumbling straight into a free fall.

Guilt throbbed, urging me to take heed of that distorted sense of loyalty. Thing was, I was having a harder and harder time remembering just what I was supposed to be loyal to.

Mom's head tilted as she studied my face. Saw the second she came to a conclusion, because her brow lifted in a slow, knowing arch. "You have a good time last night?"

I tried to form a quick lie, but it wouldn't come fast enough. Not before my mom latched on to something in my expression that sent her mouth curling into satisfaction.

"Ahh, I see," she said. "Looks like you had a *really* good time last night."

How the woman still had the power to send a rush of embarrassment flooding my face, I didn't know. But there I stood like a twelve-year-old kid who was trying to come up with an excuse for his mom finding his dirty magazine stash under his bed.

"Ma," I said with a huff of a breath as I set my daughter on her feet. The kid wobbled in those ridiculous shoes.

Shit. I felt guilty for even holding her when I was suddenly belted with a thousand memories from last night.

Rynna.

Fucking Rynna.

Little Thief.

Guessed the woman conquering my body wasn't all that unexpected. But it was the way she'd taken hostage of my mind that was close to sending me into a tailspin. The way she'd stolen a place for herself inside me. A place I didn't think it was possible for her to keep.

For years, I'd never been tempted. Had never given in, because I knew what I was living for. The reason for every beat of my heart. My gaze dipped to that reason. To the tiny thing that swayed clumsily in her tutu and those heels, her hands over her head as she attempted a spin she wasn't even close to being capable of pulling off.

My perfect Tiny Dancer.

"Go get your stuff, Sweet Pea." My voice was quieted, muted to the point where the only sound was my devotion flooding the room.

"'kay." Frankie scooted across the room, heels catching on the carpet, the little thing disappearing at the head of the hallway.

I jerked with the soft hand that suddenly landed on my forearm. "Hey," Mom said. Her voice was the same gentle command as the one she'd raised me with. All the innuendo she'd been teasing me with had vanished. "What's going on with you, Rex?"

Looking at my boots, I roughed a palm over my mouth, like it might have the power to seal in all the things I was itching to confess. "Nothin'," I said.

"Don't *nothin'* me. You think I don't know you? My boy? My son? My kid, who's worn that same expression since he was seventeen? You think I don't know when you're terrified? And that's something that just about never leaves those eyes, Rex. But today? It's different, and I know you know it, just as well as I do."

I forced myself to meet her knowing gaze.

"When are you going to realize you deserve to be happy?" she prodded.

My head shook. "I'm trying, Ma. But I'm terrified of doing something stupid. Making a wrong choice, the way I always do. Of doing something that jeopardizes Frankie."

"And you finding happiness again threatens that? That just sounds foolish to me. The way I look at it? The happier you are, the happier she's gonna be."

Guilt flamed all around me, worry closing my throat. "You think she's unhappy?"

Her brow creased into the few lines that showed her age. "God, no. Not at all. That's not what I'm saying. What I'm saying is that child adores you. Thinks you walk on water. Thinks you can do no wrong. But there's gonna come a day when she's old enough to see the shadows in your eyes. The ones that are chased away just by looking at her. She's your life, Rex. We all know that. Finding happiness again won't mean that you love her any less."

She moved to stand closer to me. She set her hand over my heart. "This? It's missing something. It's been for a long, long time. Long before that bitch ever up and left you two. Maybe it's time you find it. You can't move forward without moving on."

Emotion ran my throat. Stinging and burning. I attempted to swallow it down, but the words were scratchy when I released them. "But what if being with her is wrong? What if I fuck up again and chase her away? What if Frankie falls for her?"

What if I do?

Couldn't even bring myself to state the last because I already knew I was well on my way.

Glee flashed in Mom's eyes, her grin victorious. "So you're saying there is a girl?"

"Ma." Affectionate frustration. She knew exactly how to goad me.

She softened again, her smile going gentle, understanding brimming in the warmth of her eyes. "There are no certainties in this life, Rex. We fail, we win, and we straight up lose. You know that first hand. But what you haven't accepted is that the only security we have is how we use the moments we're given. We waste them or embrace them. We cherish them or we let fear taint them. And yeah, some chances are higher risk. Of course they are, and I'm not saying to run out and be reckless. You don't have to rush in or make any big decisions. You can protect your daughter while you test the waters. But you aren't ever gonna know unless you *try*. You just have to decide if this girl's worth giving her that chance."

Chances.

I almost smirked. Almost wanted to tell her she sounded just like Rynna.

Rynna.

Fucking beautiful Rynna.

"I don't even know where to start," I admitted through a sigh. "Been keeping people at arm's length for so long, don't have the first clue about how to get back in the dating game."

But there was something about me and Rynna that felt like we'd already surpassed all of that. Our connection went deeper than testing the waters. Bigger than dating or seeing how it went.

Something strong blazed between us. A connection that shackled us together.

Unavoidable.

Irresistible.

Truth was that last night I'd felt closer to her than I'd felt to anyone in so damned long, and I wasn't talking Frankie or my mom or the guys.

This was about being united with someone. Bonded. Tied.

That connection had lit into a frenzy when I'd sat in the darkness of her room and watched her sleep.

Fuck.

She was gorgeous.

The kind of gorgeous that wasn't just skin deep, even though that body made me crazy with need.

I was talking about the goodness that poured from her.

Sunshine and sweet.

I'd watched her until the sun started to show, like it was drawn to her the same as I was to this girl. Finally, I'd forced myself from her bed so I could clear my head.

Thing was, the confusion had only grown the more distance I put between us. That gravity calling me back to her while all my resolutions and dedications had warned I was making mistake after mistake.

"You could start by doing something nice for her," Mom said.

"Nice?"

She laughed. "Don't tell me you're so far gone you don't know what nice is? There's gotta be something you could do for this girl to let her know you care. That you're interested. Doesn't have to be extravagant. Just show her you aren't the uptight, grumpy pants this whole town thinks you are." A smile slipped into the words.

My brow rose. "Grumpy pants?"

Frankie was suddenly right at my side, dancing around, singing, "Grumpy pants, grumpy pants, my daddy is a grumpy pants," over and over again.

Maybe Frankie could see it better than I'd thought.

And maybe it was fucking time I did something about it.

twenty-five

Rynna

*P*anic had me sailing out from the back of the kitchen and rushing through the dining room of Pepper's Pies.

But this was a different kind of panic.

Not the kind incited by Timothy Roth.

This was a huge banging on the other side of the wall, the floors shaking and the fixtures trembling, so fierce I was terrified my grandmother's restaurant was about to come crumbling down.

Confusion jolting me back, I skidded to a stop at the end of the hall that led to the restrooms.

My eyes narrowed as I attempted to make sense of the scene.

"What in the world are you doing?" I finally managed. Dust billowed in the enclosed area, and three strange men were in the midst of it, tearing out the plasterboard of the wall that blocked off the restrooms.

One stocky guy barely grunted an answer. "It's demo day."

Demo day?

"What are you talking about?" Exasperated, it tumbled out as I took a lurching step forward.

Another guy, dressed in a paint-stained tee, jeans, and work boots, tossed the piece of plywood he'd pried free into a small pile, which was growing quickly. "Boss sent us over. Told us this needed to get done and fast."

"Boss?"

"Gunner," the other guy huffed as he ripped free a huge piece of plywood that sent another plume of white dust billowing in the air.

Gunner.

Gunner. Gunner. Gunner.

The name spun through that haze before realization broke through the fog.

Oh God, what did he do?

I stepped back, trembling, the emotions tumbling through me too convoluted they were too much to fully understand. So, I latched on to one. That one that was frustrated and shocked, unable to process the actions of this unexpected man.

I rushed back into the kitchen and grabbed my purse and keys before flying out the door and hitting the road, my destination clear.

RG Construction.

I haphazardly parked and then flew through the entrance of the building. The interior space small enough that I didn't need to do anything but round the secretary, who jumped to his feet.

"Excuse me, ma'am."

I didn't slow, I just thrust open Rex's office door. I barged right in, the door banging against the inner wall when I did. I was flustered and angered and awed all at the same time. "You'd better have a good explanation."

Surprised, his attention jerked up from the papers he was pouring over. "Rynna."

God. He knocked the breath right out of me. I stood in the doorway, trying to brace myself, to remember why I was upset in the first place. Oh, yeah. "Why are there three men at my restaurant tearing it apart?"

Slowly, he stood, stealing a little more of the air. The man so powerful . . . so beautiful that I couldn't think.

"You needed a job done, and I had the resources to do it," he said.

Shaking myself out of the stupor, my eyes narrowed. "So, you just . . . sent them over? Without consulting with me? I . . . I . . . I . . ."

I had absolutely no idea what to say to him. When I finally figured it out, it came rushing on a screech of frustration. "I don't have any money to pay you."

"You don't need to pay me."

"What?" Another screech. This time with a foot stomp. He was insane. We'd spent one night together. Okay. The most extraordinary kind of night. One that had altered my world. That and about two magical hours making out on his porch like teenagers in the middle of the night last night—but that was totally beside the point.

"I care about this community, Rynna." There was almost a smirk hiding behind the staunch somberness of his expression and ridiculousness of his words.

"Are you kidding me?"

"Gingham Lakes is flourishing, and re-opening Pepper's Pies is only going to be an asset to it." I saw him rubbing his thumb and forefinger together. As if he'd been practicing the speech and he was making sure he was keeping time.

"You can't just—" I threw my hands in the air. "You can't just go into my restaurant and have your way with it. I have plans. I want . . . I *need* to do this. To figure it out myself. Not have some guy come in and do the job for me because I'm not capable."

Pricks of tears burned at my eyes. Maybe I was revealing too much. Getting to the heart of the matter that came flooding out without my permission. The fear I didn't have what it took to make it. That I was going to fail before I even had the chance to get started.

But shock dammed them when Rex flew around his desk and backed me against the wall. "Some guy?" he demanded.

All the aloofness he'd attempted to wear was gone. In its place was the same compelling, confusing man who'd pushed and pulled and taunted me since the day I'd met him. "That's all I am to you? Some guy?"

I stared up at him, trying to decipher what was in his eyes.

Hurt.

It was hurt and fear and there was so much of it that it made my heart wobble. Thrown off. The man always managed to catch me off guard. "You know what I meant," I said softly.

He blinked at me, his words nothing but honest. "No, I don't."

I reached up and touched the thunder at his chest. With trembling fingers, I let them tap across the vibrating strength. "What I meant is it's not fair for you to come in and take over for me. Not when you didn't even ask me. That's my grandmother's restaurant. She gave it to me. Trusted me with it. And for you to go in and take over without consulting me? It makes me feel as if you think I can't do this. As if you think you need to rescue me. You're not just some guy, Rex. You mean so much to me. More than you know."

My voice dipped at the confession, and he sighed this strained sound, both hands planting above my head. He inched closer, pinning me to the wall. It spun my mind, the heat of him trembling all the way to my soul. God. He was too much. Devastating and overwhelming and irresistible.

When he spoke, his voice was raw. "And what if you're doing a little of that rescuing yourself? You think I don't believe in you? Fuck, Rynna . . . I'm doing it because I believe in you so much, I want to be a part of making it happen. I just . . . wanted to surprise you."

Shivers tumbled down my spine, landing in a pool of emotion that just kept getting deeper and deeper. Pretty soon, this man was going to drown me. Take me all the way under.

Emotion clotted my throat, and I forced the shaky words out around it, fiddling with his shirt and barely peeking up at him when I spoke. "Rex, I am so grateful. *So grateful.* But this is one of those things you should have asked me about. It's a big deal, and it's a lot of money, and if you do believe in me? Then you need to respect me enough to talk to me about something that is going to affect my life this much. I can't take that kind of money from you. I can't because it's not right. I want to work for this. Earn it. Breathe life back into Pepper's Pies because *I can*."

"I just wanted to do something nice for you."

I laughed softly, letting my touch glide up against the hot flesh of his neck. "Nice? Your idea of nice is a little extravagant, don't you think?"

A light chuckle rumbled in his chest. "Maybe. I warned you I'm not so good at this."

He edged back and set a hand on my cheek, stark sincerity climbing into his expression, that sincerity a revelation of his fear. "I told you I didn't have anything left to give you. And now, I want to give you everything."

Every part of me softened. "Rex . . ."

And, God, I wanted it, everything he was willing to give.

"Too much, too fast?" he asked, a self-deprecating grin rimming his mouth, so sexy and sweet.

"I'm not sure there's ever going to be too much when it comes to you. I'm just asking you to talk to me."

His thumb brushed the angle of my cheekbone, and my mouth dropped open a fraction, relishing in the feel of his simple touch. "Warned you I have no goddamned clue what I'm doing. That I always manage to fuck up."

"You're not fucking up. We're just . . . learning each other."

He pressed against me, his voice growing rough. "Like all the ways I'm learning you."

I clung to his shirt, flooded by warmth.

He edged back. "How about I make you a deal?"

"What kind of deal?" Cautious. Careful.

"You need a loan."

"Rex," I warned, already knowing what he was getting ready to say.

"Just hear me out." He paused, waiting for me to give him a tiny nod before he continued. "You figure out how to get all the equipment for the restaurant, but we do all the installation and renovation."

"Rex—"

He pushed a finger against my lips. "And you pay me back. Consider it a loan for something I believe in."

My heart thundered, and my breaths became shallow. He pressed the gentlest kiss to my forehead, the word a vibration against my skin. "Please."

Setting my hands on his waist, I chewed at my bottom lip as I shifted to look up at him. "What does this mean?"

What do we mean?

I wanted to ask him, but the tensing of his body cut me off. As if he didn't want me to say it. To bring it out into the open. The fact that neither of us seemed to truly know where we stood. If we were coming or if we were going.

He pulled me against him. "I need to figure out some shit in my life, Rynna. I warned you, it's a mess. But I'm going to fucking try. There's a lot I can't make sense of, but it's time I do. Figure out who I am and who I'm supposed to be. Take care of some shit I should have a long time ago. But the one thing I do know? The one thing I know is I want you in my life. And if I can at least give you this? Then please . . . let me. Let me take this chance."

twenty-six
Rex

Rain battered the roof and lightning lit up against the darkened windows. Thunder a constant rumble in the toiling sky.

I was already rushing for the door after I'd heard the bell ring.

My jaw dropped a bit when I flung it open and found her standing there. Drenched. Chestnut darkened to mahogany.

Standing there in the rain looking like a second chance. A better day.

Four soaked paper bags were wrapped in her arms, precariously clutched to her chest like she could keep them from ripping apart and sending all the items contained inside from toppling to the ground.

"Rynna," I finally managed when I processed she was really there, standing on my stoop. I widened the door. "Come inside before you get struck by lightning."

She ducked past me, filling my senses with all that sweet, intensified with the soak of the rain.

Fuck. She was undoing me. Minute by minute. I let the door fall shut behind her. "Here, let me help you with that." I took two bags from her.

"Thank you."

"What are you doing here?" I finally asked, feeling the satisfied grin slide to my face, because I sure as shit wasn't gonna complain.

She cast me a cautious smile. One that slammed me right in the center of the chest. Kind of the way Frankie annihilated me every time she looked at me a certain way. Though, this was different. Obviously. This was lust and want and confusion and every-fucking-thing I wanted more and more.

She hefted a shoulder. "I just thought I would do something nice for you."

Nice.

My chuckle rumbled like a partner to the sky. "Nice, huh?"

She bit her bottom lip with a nod. "Yeah. It seems my neighbor is a little on the *thoughtful* side. I figured I'd return the favor. How does dinner sound? Of course, I might owe you dinner for the rest of my life."

I dipped my head her direction, whispered at her ear, "Why's that sound like the best damned payback I've ever been offered?"

She giggled and headed for my kitchen. "I see how it is. You want me when I'm baking for you."

A growl slipped free, my eyes honing in on the slow sway of her delicious ass as I followed her. Voice lowered to keep my next words from little ears. "Oh, believe me, baby, I want you all the time. But you don't actually think I'm going to refuse you cooking for me, do you? Especially considering I was just about to take out a frozen pizza to toss into the oven."

Setting the bags on the counter, she looked back at me with a feigned gasp. "Blasphemy."

I set the bags I was carrying beside them. "A man's got to do what a man's got to do."

Her expression went tender, and she reached up, cupping my cheek in one of those soft, soft hands. "And you should know I would consider it an honor that I get to help with that now."

She peeked in the direction of the hall where we could hear Frankie playing, talking and squealing, living in her own blissful little world. "Is this okay? That I'm here? I don't want to confuse her or rush you. I just . . . I wanted to spend the evening with you. With her," she added quickly, like it might scare me away.

And fuck. Yeah. It scared me, just not the way she was probably thinking. I wanted it, I was just too scared to hope for it. But it didn't matter, that anticipation was right there, strumming an escalating beat inside of me.

Savage and fierce. As fierce as the storm that rattled the windowpanes and drummed on the roof.

I threaded my fingers through hers, brought her knuckles to my lips. "What do you say we take it slow in front of her? Get her used to the two of us. She's gonna have questions, and when she does, we answer them."

She worried her lip, peeking up at me. "And what's the right answer, Rex?"

Releasing her hand, I let my fingers glide into those silky locks of damp hair. That was all the contact I needed for my chest to tighten, for the things held within to go haywire. A disorder that was shifting into something new. I pulled her closer and set a kiss to her forehead, murmured against it, "We tell her we care about each other. Simple as that."

Did she know that's how I was feeling? Did she know every time I looked at her, another piece crumbled out from under me, my footing no longer my own?

I leaned down, my mouth barely brushing the edge of hers. "I want you here." I inched even closer, the heat of her body lighting me up. "Really fucking want you here. In the end, I think that's all that matters."

I moved to grip her by the waist, and her breath caught as my fingers cinched around her, everything growing thick when I let my nose trace up the column of her neck.

That overpowering scent was back. Radiating from her skin. Sweet, sweet bliss. Cherry pie.

I groaned, and she exhaled, then we both froze when we heard the pound of little feet thunder down the hall.

I stepped back, putting space between us, and a rush of redness bloomed on Rynna's neck.

Like she'd been caught.

It was so fucking cute.

Frankie skidded to a stop at the end of the hall when she saw Rynna in the kitchen. "Rynna! What's you doin' here?"

My daughter kicked right back into action, flying across the floor, jumping around in front of Rynna to grab her attention.

As if she didn't already have it. Because Rynna smiled when she saw my kid. Smiled like it meant something.

A bolt of old fear struck somewhere deep in my chest. A warning that I'd crossed a line when I'd let Rynna into our lives. That I'd been begging for trouble. Taunting me with a reminder of that penalty I'd forever serve. Punishment for what I'd done. Did I think I was exempt?

Rynna knelt in front of my daughter, her expression soft, almost as soft as the way she brushed her fingers through Frankie's wild mane of hair.

"I thought maybe you could help me make dinner. What do you think about that?"

Frankie's eyes went wide with excitement. "Really? I gets to make dinner? Oh yes! Are we gonna make a Pepper Pie?" She threaded those tiny fists together, pressing her hands up under her chin in a plea. "Oh, please, let's make a Pepper Pie!"

Light laughter fluttered from between Rynna's lips. Those goddamned lust-inciting lips. I tried not to think about them wrapped around me when she tugged one of Frankie's hands free and hooked her pinkie finger with Frankie's tiny one. A team. "Did you think we'd make anything else? How about a shepherd's pie and then a cherry pie?"

With that, Rynna peeked up at me. Searching for my reaction. My reaction that felt like I'd just had a fucking metal arrow speared straight in to my heart. It attached to something unseen, something buried, once thought dead, and plucked it out.

"That sounds like the best deal in the whole wide world!"

"Come on, let's get your hands washed. We have a lot of work to do."

Rynna sent me a wink when she picked Frankie up from under the arms, turning her attention fully on my daughter when she did. Carefully, Rynna squirted Frankie's hands with soap and held them under warm water, rubbing and rinsing her hands together, two of them giggling at something silly Frankie said.

"Here we go . . . you sit right there." Rynna hoisted her so she was sitting on the edge of the counter, steadying her with a hand against the belly. "Be careful, okay?"

"'kay," Frankie promised, and Rynna went to work, pulling ingredients from the bags, talking to Frankie the whole time. "My grandma used to sit me right up on the counter when I was a little girl like you. Right up close where I could see and help."

"Dids you like cookin' with C'rinne?"

"I loved cooking with Corinne." Something wistful seeped into Rynna's tone. "I miss it so much. But it makes me happy that I get to teach you the same as she did me."

"I likes you teachin' me. Did you know I'm gonna be a painter? My grammy says I'm such a super good painter, like my daddy."

Rynna glanced at me with a small smile. No doubt, my daughter was getting ready to spin into one of those conversations that jumped from topic to topic faster than a person could keep up.

"Is that so?"

"Oh yes! And I'm gonna get a puppy. I wants a puppy so bad."

This time Rynna's glance back at me was curious, searching, before she slowly turned back to the green beans she was running under the faucet. "You want a puppy, huh?"

"Oh yes. Oh yes, yes, yes."

I sighed, trying not to show any frustration that was focused solely on myself. "Told you it's not a good idea right now, Frankie Leigh."

She started to pout, and Rynna was quick to hand her a bottle of cream and a measuring cup. "Do you think you could fill that up to that line for me?" she asked, running her finger along the one-cup indicator. She purposely redirected my kid like a pro.

"There you go," she encouraged as Frankie carefully poured the cream into the bowl, and Rynna placed the bowl on Frankie's lap. She took her hand and showed her how to whip up the mixture before she was back to rinsing something else. It was kind of amazing how the girl juggled three different recipes at the same time. Second nature. Right back to that graceful ease she'd shown me back at her place five nights ago.

I leaned against the far counter with my arms crossed over my chest.

Watching them.

Trying to keep that feeling reined. Trying not to get too far ahead of myself.

But I could feel it. Everything barreling that direction when I listened to the way Rynna spoke softly with my daughter. She gave her instructions, let her help, laughed as Frankie made mess after mess. The entire time, she was completely patient with a child I was well aware required a lot of patience. Rynna's tolerance never slipped, and I swore, it wasn't faked.

Swore she wasn't putting on a show.

Swore this wasn't some kind of pretense.

And fuck, it was terrifying.

As terrifying as it was perfect.

Because I wanted it.

I wanted her.

An hour later, the three of us were sitting around the table, sharing dinner, the best fucking shepherd's pie I'd ever eaten.

I told both of them, too.

Frankie grinned, gave Rynna a high five.

"We dids it, Rynna," she said, my kid so damned happy.

Maybe as happy as I was.

Maybe, just maybe, this was where we were meant to be.

That for once in my life, I'd been granted reprieve.

She slipped out the door with a peck and a reluctant goodbye.

I couldn't stop myself, I bolted right after her, snatching her around the wrist, unable to let her go. My kiss a demand as I pushed her against the outside wall. She whimpered, hands on my face, mine on her hips.

"I really should go," she whispered.

"I know . . . but I don't know how to let you." I hoisted her up, those legs around my waist. She rubbed against my jeans, her pussy a tease. My dick pressed at the fabric, desperate for release. "Fuck, Rynna. What are you doing to me? Making me lose my mind. Have no control when you get in the room."

She nipped at my mouth, kissing me, rocking against my cock. "The only thing I know is how desperately I want you. How desperately I want *this*."

"What is it you want?" I barely managed. Groaning deep, I strained harder against her, wondering just how horrible of a parent I'd be if I stripped her right there and fucked her against the wall.

"This. You. Us. Frankie."

At her confession, I froze, my heart going stone in the center of my chest before it started thudding. Thudding with possibility.

I pulled back to search her eyes through the darkness. The air was bogged down with humidity, the residual of the storm a wet mist coating our heated skin.

She stared back.

No reservations.

No fear.

Just blatant, unblemished hope. A beacon calling me out of the storm.

"I . . ." All the bullshit that still haunted my life stalled my words, the promise I wanted to give her freezing on my tongue. Because the last thing I wanted was to do her wrong.

Hurt flashed through her expression before it filled with soft understanding. Because that was just the way this girl was—flush with grace. Too good to be real. She edged back a fraction to search my face. Reluctantly, I released her, helping her slide down onto her feet.

I stood there, a shadow blocking all that light.

She tilted her head, her hand on the side of my face. "Do you still love her?"

My chest grew so damned tight I was sure it was going to

explode.

"Your ex-wife?" she pressed.

That was the problem. Her hunch was off base. Thrown in the wrong direction. But when it came down to it, Frankie's mother was the problem. That stupid fucking loyalty I'd clung to for far too long.

It lashed at me, a scourge of regret.

"Fuck, Rynna," I whispered harshly, the ground swept right out from under me. "I—" I averted my gaze to the wooden planks, struggling to find the correct answer to her question. Because she deserved to know, and still, I didn't know how to tell her.

Warily, I shifted my attention back to her and plucked out the only honesty I could find. "When it comes to Frankie's mom? The only emotion I can process is hate." I blinked, swallowing hard. My insides burned. Flames. Unrelenting hell. "But then I wonder if I have the right to hate her. Not when I was the one who drove her away."

"She left you. She left Frankie. I don't know the circumstances. But for that alone? I hate her. I hate her for the simple fact that she could possibly walk away from you two. If I had been given a gift like that, I wouldn't ever have let it go."

A soft puff of air escaped my throat, and I wound an arm around her waist and pulled her against me. I pressed a kiss to the top of her head. "Rynna."

Rynna.

Fucking Rynna.

Little Thief.

Trying to steal my heart.

Frankie squealed, clapping her hands as she dropped to her knees on our front porch. The tiny puppy scuttled toward her, jumping up on her chest, licking her face. "Daddy! Daddy! It's a puppy. Look. It's a puppy. It's the cutest puppy in the whole wide world."

She hugged the wiggling body against her probably a little too tightly, but the little ball of fur just went wilder, clawing up her chest to get closer to her face so he could lick her like he'd found his long lost best friend.

Unfortunately, Frankie was under the impression she'd found hers.

Shrieks of laughter rang in the air. "Daddy! He's kissin' me. He's kissin' me. I fink he loves me."

The sight of it sent a rock sinking straight to the pit of my stomach.

My gaze cut to Rynna, who was standing there watching the two of them with an affected smile on her face. Her eyes were full of an emotion I wasn't sure I was ready to recognize.

A lump formed in my throat. Heavy. As heavy as that rock that sat in the pit of my stomach. It only grew when Rynna edged forward and knelt in front of Frankie. Then she reached out and gently ran her hand over the puppy's head, her gaze growing even softer as she looked at my daughter.

"He's a golden retriever. What do you think we should name him?" she asked.

"How's about Milo? Milo's my friend at school who's a boy and he's so nice and this puppy is a boy so I finks we should name him Milo because he's nice, too."

Rynna didn't even skip a beat at the ramble that fell from Frankie's mouth. She just let her smile grow, glancing down at the puppy. He was currently on his hind legs thinking he could jump his way onto Rynna's lap. "He is a nice boy, isn't he?" she cooed, letting the puppy lick her face. "Milo it is, then."

"Milo! I love Milo! I love Milo. Can I take him for a walk? Do you gots a leash?"

And the two of them? They disappeared, trotted alongside the road, Frankie screeching her joy, Rynna right there in case the puppy tugged hard enough to get loose.

Thirty minutes later, I watched as Frankie ran with the puppy nipping along at her heels through Rynna's front door. Rynna stood on the same deck that had changed everything, hugging her arms across her chest and biting at her lip as she watched the two of them bound inside.

I'd held back, standing against the railing, unable to process what was going on inside me.

I edged up behind her. I could feel it. The chill that skated her spine, the way she shook as I released a breath against her ear. A few strands of chestnut rustled with the air and tickled my lips. "A dog, huh?" I whispered.

There was a swift intake of breath before she cautiously turned around to face me. "I . . ." She glanced back at the house. "I'm living here alone, and I thought I could use a friend. It gets lonely at night."

She turned around to face me fully. Bewilderment twitched along her brow. "Do you not like dogs?"

A vice of grief wrenched up my insides. I was right. Ever since Rynna Dayne had come into my life, every old wound had been unbound, released from its confines, spinning and taunting me where they danced right under my nose.

"Of course I like dogs." Could barely force it out through the hardness that ridged my lips.

Longing twisted through her features when she glanced back at the door, looking back at me like she was begging for me to understand. "I know you and I are new. But Frankie . . . I saw that puppy and the only thing I could think about was her. About how excited she would be. I . . . I wanted to give her something she didn't have." Rapidly she blinked, and tears threatened at her eyes. "I wanted her to love something that's a part of me. Are you mad?"

I couldn't hold back anymore. I jerked her against me. "Fuck, Rynna. Of course I'm not mad."

I hugged her tight. Kissed the crown of her head. Wishing I could explain how it brought back memories I didn't know how to deal with.

I was numb as I stood by the side of the road, staring blankly as the taillights disappeared in the distance. I tried to blink through the squiggle of red, neon lines that lit up against my bleary vision. It was like looking at the sun and then closing your eyes. Or maybe I just wished they were closed. But they were open wide, my gaze sucked down.

Down.

Down.

Missy dead at my feet.

I gulped around the vision, bile in my throat, agony in my chest.

Mrs. Dayne was there, her hand on my forearm. "Don't worry. I've got her. You do what you've got to do."

She picked up Frankie where she was laying on the gravel, face-down, barely able to process what was happening through the daze that clouded my mind. My daughter's cries. Taillights.

What had I done?

What had I done?

A shovel.

Dirt.

Sweat on my nape.

I struggled for a breath, that numbness fracturing when I picked Missy up and carried her to the hole. I laid her in it.

I squinted, trying to see through the haze.

A shovelful of dirt.

Another.

A mound of nothing.

My girl. My wife. Gone.

They always were.

"You wants to be my bestest friend?" Frankie's small voice slipped through the thin wall, muted just the same as the light. Rynna's echoed back, so goddamned soft it penetrated to the depths of me.

"You want me to be your best friend?"

There was no answer, but my mind was conjuring a clear picture of Frankie vigorously nodding her head against her pillow. Could picture Rynna where she knelt on the ground beside her bed where she'd been reading my daughter her bedtime story.

Of course, because Frankie had again insisted.

"I'd like that," Rynna murmured, and there was shuffling,

what I knew was a tender kiss.

My heart fisted. There was a special kind of terror when things felt too right. Too good. That lulling calm before your life was demolished by a devastating storm.

"Good night, Sweet Pea," Rynna said.

My ear was tuned to the movement in Frankie's room as Rynna stood and flipped off the light. Her presence grew denser with each step. Could feel it swallow me from behind when she emerged at the end of the hall.

An avalanche of need.

A landslide of desire.

She edged around the couch. Since Frankie was safely tucked away in bed, Rynna curled up at my side. We were still being careful, easing Frankie into the idea of Rynna and me.

I wound an arm around her, pressed a kiss to her temple.

Milo yipped, and Rynna cooed, pulling him into her arms. She settled back into my chest and released a contented breath.

A breath that filtered through me like peace.

Like warmth and light.

Milo nudged my hand, and a restless sigh pressed between my lips when I looked down to find those huge brown puppy eyes staring up at me. He whimpered again, his snout damp, prodding at me. Relenting, I ran my hand over the soft, soft fur of his head.

My chest tightened and I felt another piece of me break.

God damn it.

Rynna snuggled closer. God damn it straight to hell.

Rynna.

Fucking Rynna.

Little Thief.

twenty-seven
Rynna

"No." Nikki sat forward as if the tiny bit of information I'd let slip was the most scandalous thing she'd ever heard.

I glanced around the quaint city sidewalk where Nikki, Lillith, and I sat out front of a small café under an umbrella sipping our coffees. People meandered, peering into the large storefront windows, enjoying their Saturday morning. Lush trees grew up from planters, strategically placed along the walk, their bright green leaves and thick branches shade for the old two- and three-story buildings that had been renovated as part of a restoration project over the last ten years.

Macaber Street was much like what was happening on Fairview where the diner was located and the new hotel was going up. I could only pray Pepper's Pies would see this same kind of revitalization. That it would flourish and mobs of people would move in and out of its doors. It was the life I was looking for right there. Within my reach.

Which was what had Nikki in a stir.

I lifted a shoulder and took a sip of my ice-cold Frappuccino. "What?"

She gave me a look that told me I was insane. "Um . . . you did just say RG Construction had taken over the renovation on Pepper's?"

"So?"

She laughed and glanced at Lillith, who was burying her smile in the plastic lid of her coffee. Disbelief filled Nikki's tone when she aimed her inquisition back on me. "RG. As in Rex Gunner. Asshole extraordinaire, who just so happens to be your neighbor and you have so clearly been crushing on since the day we met you."

I would have bristled at the insinuation of Rex being an asshole if it weren't for the heat that rushed to my cheeks, beating any other emotion to the punch. There was no stopping it. Not when I was immediately assaulted with the memories of last night.

Frankie had been at her grandma's, which meant Rex had me all night. Again and again. The man hard and commanding and rough. Demanding my pleasure just as sure as he'd demanded his. My body his claim. I'd never had sex like that. Not in all my life.

I shifted in the metal chair.

Nikki's mouth dropped open. "Oh. My. God."

My eyes widened in as much feigned innocence as I could muster. "What are you talking about?"

Yeah. I was brilliant when I was put on the spot. I wasn't much of a player of games. But I honestly didn't think Rex would appreciate me gossiping about how freaking fantastic he was in bed to my friends.

"Don't you 'what' me, young lady. I know there's a story behind all of that." She circled her finger around my face, as if in my expression was a written confession. "And a good one, too. Fess up. There's no way you two are just doing *business* together." She air-quoted the business part.

Lillith swatted Nikki's arm. "If she doesn't want to talk about it, don't force her." Lillith looked back at me with an apologetic grin. "I swear that she chases all the good ones away because she thinks she needs to know every detail about everything."

"That's what friends are for. The details. I want all the details." She looked to the sky as if she were casting up a petition. Her attention dropped right back to me with a plea on her face. "Come on, Rynna. Tell me. I can't stand it. I want to know how you convinced Rex to work for you. I mean, not that you're not all kinds of gorgeous, because we all know you are, and I'm pretty sure you could enchant just about any man with your sexual wiles, but we're talking Rex Gunner here. "

Leaning forward, I rested my forearms on the table as I fiddled with a paper napkin. "He's not an asshole."

Not even close.

"He just . . . doesn't normally let people get to know him."

Nikki's brows rose. "And you know him?"

"We're . . ."

"You're what?" This from Lillith. She shifted forward. "Are you and Rex seeing each other?" Shock lined every syllable of the question.

Uneasily, I glanced down the street, not sure how to describe what Rex and I were. What we had.

Not when it felt like everything but still lacked a name. "We've been spending time together," I settled on.

Nikki smacked the table then pointed at me. "I knew it!"

"You're dating Rex Gunner?" Lillith drew in a sharp breath, totally taken aback.

"Is that such a surprise?" I didn't mean for it to come across as defensive. But it did. I was feeling protective of Rex and the misguided reputation he had. As if he wasn't deserving of love. Or maybe there were those distorted doubts that I wasn't good enough.

Not to mention those specks of insecurity I felt at the mystery that remained hidden in his eyes, this needle of discomfort that poked and prodded and warned there was something he was keeping from me.

I was right there and he was terrified to let me the rest of the way in.

Lillith softened. "I am surprised, but not in a bad way. Rex deserves to find happiness. He's had it rough. I couldn't imagine a better person for him and that little girl than you."

My lips pursed, and I decided to go with blatant honesty. Because Lillith and Nikki made me feel that I could. "I'm sorry. Sometimes . . . there are times when an old defensiveness appears out of nowhere. High school wasn't exactly easy for me, and trust comes hard sometimes."

Lillith glanced at Nikki. "I don't think it was easy for any of us."

"Oh, Lillith and I are no strangers to the high school bitches, are we Lily Pad? Believe me, we get it, and I promise you, our circle is safe. We invited you into it because we *like* you. That's it."

Gratitude throbbed, and a soft smile pulled to my mouth. "That really means a lot to me. I hope you know that."

"Of course we know it. We're awesome." Nikki capped it off with a wink.

I laughed lightly. Truly loving that they had welcomed me into their circle.

My phone buzzed on the table. Excitement pulled across my ribs. I was biting at my bottom lip as I grabbed it from where I'd placed it face down, beating back a smile when I saw the text from Rex on the screen.

Rex: You still hanging out with your girls?

He'd teased me this morning when I'd tried to leave my bed, which he'd been gloriously stretched out in the middle of. The best kind of topping for twisted sheets. Naked and perfect and turning my world upside down. He'd told me he could think of much better ways to keep me entertained. It'd taken about all I had to rip myself away and force myself into the shower.

He'd just followed me in there.

I tapped out a quick reply.

Me: Finishing up soon. Will I see you later?

I set it back down. Obviously, I hadn't done that great of a job containing my grin.

Nikki and Lillith stared back at me. Then Nikki howled. "Oh girl . . . you have it bad," she drew out. "You should see your face right now. You are in so much trouble. Put a fork in that pie because you are done."

"Stop it," I whispered, laughing at her reference to pie and trying to hide the emotion that pressed in. This shimmery pulse that throbbed and vibrated, stretching out spindly fingers to find purchase in those secret places. Those places that were reserved for when it was right.

For when you just knew.

"So are you two like, together, together?" Lillith asked.

"Yeah." As soon as I said it, those questions brimmed. Ones that hovered around the darkness that would dim his eyes.

"What?" she pressed.

Uneasy, I hesitated, hoping I wasn't sharing something with them that would upset Rex. But I didn't know who else to turn to. Because when I truly thought about it, it scared me.

"His ex-wife . . ." I blinked, choked around the words. "I don't know if he's over her."

Just the thought gutted me.

A hollow, vacant space that radiated pain. He said he hated her. But there was so much pain around it, it made me itch.

"That bitch didn't deserve either of them." Nearly every word that came from Nikki's mouth was light, filled with a tease and the easy way she looked at life. Not this. It was hard. A little bit bitter.

I hated the idea of crossing a line. Invading his privacy by asking for details he hadn't offered.

But there was an ugly part of me that was shrouded in doubt. Turned out, old insecurities were hard to ditch. "What was she like?" I'd barely managed the choppy question when my attention caught on a big white truck that passed us, did a U-Turn, and pulled to a rumbling stop at the curb beside us.

"Holy shit," Nikki mouthed, laughing under her breath. "Is that actually Rex Gunner? Looks like you're not the only one who's done for."

My heart surged to my throat when both passenger side windows glided down. Rex slanted me an almost shy smile that was every kind of sexy from the driver's seat, that expression alone seeping into my spirit and finding a home.

From the backseat, Frankie waved frantically. Milo on her lap, yipping as he tried to paw his way out the window to get to me.

"We's goin' on a picnic, Rynna! You wants to come?" Frankie shouted.

Rex had offered to keep an eye on Milo for me when I was getting ready to leave this morning, claiming Frankie would love to see him when he picked her up this morning from her grandma's.

Wasn't that a sign? It had to be. I soared on it.

"It was all Frankie's idea," Rex said, voice gruff. The sound raked my skin and brought up chills. "She wants to spend the day at the lake, and we thought maybe you and Milo might want to join us."

"We gots all the food, Rynna, but we ain't gots no Pepper Pies. Is that okay?"

Oh my heart. That little girl was undoing me. Just as quickly as her dad. Affection thrummed, fluttery and thick and somehow light.

"That's just fine, Sweet Pea," I told her.

"Hey there, Rex," Nikki sang, grinning as she rocked back in her chair. Leave it to Nikki to put him in the hot seat. "Tell Ollie hi for me."

An exasperated, "Nikki," was the only response she got.

His gaze shifted to Lillith for the flash of a second, his chin lifting in a subdued hello, discomfort ridging the lines of his expression.

But still, there was something significant about him sitting there, all rough and burly in his huge truck.

Something sweet in his offer.

Because this?

This was an offering.

"I would love to go." I glanced back at Lillith and Nikki. "You don't mind me cutting this a little short, do you?"

Nikki waved me off. "Get out of here. The lake sounds way more fun. Besides, Lily Pad over there is getting antsy to get back to Brody. It's totally fine. You know, just leave me here all by myself. I don't mind. Not at all."

Lillith laughed. "So dramatic."

Nikki's eyes widened. "And how else would I get any attention around here? Seems everyone has all their attention trained somewhere else." Her widened eyes slid back to me, all a meaningful tease.

I dropped the peck of a kiss to her cheek. "Thank you. Next time we get together, I'll make you dinner. How's that sound? I need all the practice I can get if I'm going to make the restaurant a success."

Her eyes rolled back in her head. "Girl, don't tease me. Tomorrow? I'll be at your house at seven."

I chuckled. "It's a date." I shifted my gaze to Lillith. "Are you in?"

"Wouldn't miss it. Have fun."

I hopped into the front seat of Rex's truck.

He threaded our fingers together, clutched them tight on the seat between us.

It felt like a claim.

A statement.

I peeked back at Frankie and down to our hands, before I looked up at his gorgeous face, mouthing the words, "Is this fine?"

He squeezed my hand tighter. Like I was his and he was mine.

"This is more than fine, Rynna."

Joy.

I'd never known the full truth of it.

Not until then.

We'd swung by my house, and I'd pulled on a swimsuit, sliding on a pair of shorts and a tank over it, and changed into more appropriate shoes.

Twenty-minutes later, Rex's truck jostled on the dirt road that was nothing more than a worn path carved by the vehicles that traveled the winding road. It curved as it climbed deeper into the forest that lined the lake, which was tucked at the base of the mountain on the outskirts of town.

I'd thought I was prepared. That it didn't matter anymore. That I could keep them at bay. But memories kept breaking loose the deeper we trekked into the forest. The closer we got, the harder the betrayal churned my stomach.

The louder the phantom laughter became. Even eleven years later, I could hear Janel's words floating through the forest.

"You're such a fool. Did you really think he wanted you?"

I swallowed back the tingle of tears that burned my throat and threatened my eyes. It was a long time ago, and I wasn't that same girl who'd run barefoot through these trees. Sobbing. Hurting in a way she'd never known existed until she'd been taught the harsh realities of this world in the cruelest of ways.

None of that mattered.

Not now.

Not with Rex running his thumb over the back of my hand, Frankie belting out the silliest song I'd ever heard from the backseat, and my little puppy secure on my lap.

"Sorry this is so far off the beaten path. Frankie and I kind of like the place to ourselves when we come to the lake, don't we, Frankie Leigh?"

"Yup! We gots our own secret spot that no one knows about. Juss for us."

Rex tossed me a small wink.

My heart, already filled too full, gave an extra wayward beat.

God, he was gorgeous with the sun shining through his opened window. Rays of light speared through the leaves of the trees, sending bright flashes of light against his face as we wound through the thicket. The longer pieces of his dark blond hair were lit up like a blaze of white fire, the hard curve of his jaw and scruff defined by the glowing outline, those earthy eyes a perfect match to the trees.

"Here we go," he said. He pulled to a stop where the path came to a dead end. We climbed out, and I helped Frankie down while Rex grabbed the cooler from the bed of the truck. I kept ahold of Milo's leash and Frankie's hand as we followed him down a narrow trail.

Lush bushes and towering trees lined the twisty path. A gentle breeze rustled through, dragging with it a fragrant bough of wildflowers and leaves and earth.

In the distance, a trickle from a stream cascading down from the mountain could be heard, and birds chirped overhead.

Tranquility and peace.

I inhaled, breathing all of it in, struck with the memory of why I'd always loved this place so much.

Two minutes later, the trees opened up in front of us, revealing the lake.

A glassy expanse of blue.

Calm.

Craggy rocks made up the low cliffs the area was well known for, and the trail weaved down around them, guiding us to a secluded cove and beach.

Awe stoked that fire that continued to grow in my spirit.

"This is gorgeous."

I'd almost forgotten the draw of this place. The stark beauty that gave Gingham Lakes its name.

Frankie jumped up and down at my side, yanking at my hand to lead me closer to the water. "It's our super special secret place. And nows you know! You can't tell any ones! Promise?"

Releasing her hand, I ruffled my fingers through the unruly mess of hair on her head. "I wouldn't dream of telling anyone you and your daddy's secret."

She grinned up at me, flashing me a row of tiny teeth and so much belief. "It's your secret now, too, silly. Right, Daddy?"

She looked to Rex for confirmation. He was setting the cooler down beside the small ring of rocks that had been made for a fire.

He looked over at me.

Meaningfully.

Powerfully.

"Yeah, Frankie Leigh. Now it's Rynna's secret, too."

A shiver rocked me. A different kind than the flood of old memories that had threatened to dim this day.

This was a river of hope.

He was letting me in. Letting me be a part of them.

I looked down at Frankie, who was still grinning at me. "This is exactly the kind of secret I like to keep." I said it to her, but I think I was making that promise to Rex. A promise that I wanted more. That like I'd told him outside their house the other night, I wanted this.

Them.

Us.

That I would protect it just as fiercely as he protected Frankie.

Milo barked his tiny bark, jumping all around, chasing after a butterfly that flitted by.

"Can we go swimmin'?" Frankie asked. She pranced over to her dad, wearing that hot pink tutu over a one-piece bathing suit. The little girl so adorable she caused that secret place to ache.

I guessed maybe I held secrets close, too.

"What do you say we eat first, and then we'll go? Rynna might like to take a hike to our super, super special place."

"Our secret, secret place?" she whispered through barely contained excitement.

He nodded.

Her attention whipped over to me, the child dancing back my direction. "You wanna, Rynna? You wanna go to the super, super special place? Daddy said we could!"

His expression was tender when he tore his gaze from me and turned it on his daughter, a smile fluttering around his full, full lips.

I wondered if he had the first clue the kind of father he was. Amazing, wonderful, and kind.

"I'd be honored to go to your super, super special place," I told her, and Frankie did a twirl, spinning me up tighter. My heart winding up in the fibers of this sweet child. Knitting and weaving and uniting.

I could feel it.

The impact of Rex's daughter becoming a permanent part of me. "Let's go!"

"Give me just a second to get things organized, Sweet Pea," Rex said, tossing a few sticks into the ring of rocks.

I walked over and knelt down beside him. "Anything I can do to help?"

A smirk pulled at the corner of his sexy mouth, voice a rough, muted whisper. "Could you do me a favor and lean in closer?"

I was confused before I followed his line of sight to where my shirt was drooped open, cleavage on full display.

I smacked his shoulder. "Rex." I chuckled beneath my breath.

He laughed from his belly and into the air. It bounded against the cliffs.

Ricocheting back.

Boom after boom that rocked my heart.

"This way." Frankie raced ahead of me, hauling me along, her excitement infectious. There was no stopping the permanent smile on my face.

We followed an even narrower, isolated trail than the one we'd taken to get to their picnic spot. Sunlight poured in through the super high trees that towered over us, their trunks slender and their bark gray. Dense branches covered us overhead and soft dirt padded our feet.

We hiked higher, my legs burning from the exertion as we climbed. Five minutes later, we shifted course, the trail guiding us back around to where there was a break in the forest.

My breath caught.

A thundering roar filled my ears, and a cooling spray brushed my skin. We stood on an overhang of rocks that jutted over the lake. Just to the right of us was a rushing waterfall fed from a stream running from the mountain.

It poured over the cliffs and pounded into the lake twenty

feet below. Farther away, the cliffs rose in height, fifty or sixty feet high, three more rivulets cascading over the side.

"Whats you fink?" Hope framed Frankie's features when she grinned up at me.

"I think this might be the most beautiful spot I've ever seen."

"Me, too! You fink Milo likes it? I fink he does. Look at him sniffin'."

I laughed. "I'm sure Milo loves it. How could he not?"

She tugged at his leash, taking him from my hold. She took off with him down another trail that wound down closer to the lake.

"Be careful, Frankie Leigh," Rex warned, that voice hitting me from behind. "Stay up here away from the water."

"'kay, Daddy. I knows all the rules. You don't have to keep tellin' me. Sheesh."

I laughed again. But the sound was stolen when I shifted to look over my shoulder to where Rex stood.

He was watching me.

That gaze piercing.

Penetrating.

Hungry.

He slowly edged forward, shards of loosened rock crunching beneath his boots. Power radiated from each predatory step.

Chills flashed across my flesh when he edged up behind me, erupting like a storm, a current of electricity. His callused palms just grazed the surface of my arms from the caps of my shoulders gliding all the way down to my hands.

He laced our fingers together, wound his arms around my waist, and pulled my back against his chest. His hold possessive where he had our hands fisted at my shaking belly.

Leaning down, he planted a soft kiss at the side of my jaw, right over my pulse point that thrummed like the wild, before he released a contented breath and hooked his chin over my shoulder.

Bliss.

It was the first time he'd pulled me into a full embrace out in the open.

Where Frankie could see.

Frankie blushed through a giggle. "You two a huggin'? Grammy said Daddy gots it bad. You gots it bad, Daddy?"

He told his mom about me?

"Guess I do, Frankie Leigh." His voice was gruff when he inclined his mouth to my ear. "Daddy gots it so bad."

Shivers rolled.

Wave after wave.

"Come here," he said. He guided me down to sit on the rocks and situated me between his legs so we could still keep an eye on Frankie. Then his arms were back around me, his nose in my hair. Frankie and Milo played, running around, darting from each other, tumbling on the soft earth beneath the trees.

"Thank you for asking me to come with you two. It means a lot to me."

I chanced peeking back at him, my head rocking against the thunder beating from his chest.

"Don't think you have the first idea what it means to me that you're here, Rynna."

He pressed a kiss to my forehead.

Tender.

So tender it sent a tumble of emotion spiraling through my body. They crashed through me like the river that rushed just in the distance.

"I've never done this before," he admitted.

"Bring someone out here with you and Frankie?"

One small nod, but it seemed a lifetime's admission. "Yeah. Not even my mom."

"Because it's your secret." It was almost a tease. All except for the affection packed in it.

Those eyes slid to Frankie, who tossed a stick for Milo, before he returned his attention to me. "Yeah, it's our secret. Something shared just between Frankie and me. Because she's my life." He hesitated. "Want you to be a part of that now, Rynna."

My life.

Everything pressed down. So much joy. "I want that, too," I

barely forced out around the emotion that clogged my lungs.

He threaded our fingers together on both hands, hugging me closer, our fists solid where my heart hammered at the confines of my chest. I could feel him gulp for air, the heavy bob of his thick, strong throat. His words were gravel. "Did you ever dream of it? Want it? Being a mother? Because it's a lot, Rynna, what I'm asking of you. I understand that, and I don't want to push you into something you're not ready for."

I slowly shifted, the hard rocks cutting into my knees, his piercing eyes spearing the rest of the way into me.

Hope and fear radiated back.

"Always, Rex. I always wanted to be a mother. To have a family. And it might have looked different in my mind. But this . . ." I glanced back at Frankie. "You and Frankie are the most wonderful things to ever come into my life. No. I didn't expect you. Not at all. But now that I have you? I'm not letting either of you go."

Almost frantic, Rex pulled me into his arms, his face pressed to my neck. "Fuck, Rynna. How's it possible you make me feel this way?"

A scream jolted us out of our bubble. Our heads whipped around to see the last second of Frankie tripping, her toe caught on an exposed root. She flew forward, her little body tumbling down a rocky incline that sloped down on the far side of where she'd been playing.

Dust flew. Before it'd even settled, Rex was on his feet, sprinting that direction, and I was right on his heels.

"Frankie," he shouted, voice panicked.

Anxious energy stirred the air.

He bolted for her, taking the fastest route, straight over a slippery ridge of wet rocks. Water splashed beneath his shoes as he jumped from one large boulder to another then down to the dirt trail, at her side faster than I could process the entire scene.

"Frankie," he shouted.

Two seconds later, I was there. My heart pitched and churned. Terrified, I peered over his shoulder where he dropped to his knees at her side.

Frankie was sprawled face down in the dirt, head just barely missing a sharp rock where she skidded to a stop.

"Oh God," I whimpered.

And Rex.

Rex was shaking everywhere. Shock slammed his body. These visible, palpable ripples of horror that seized his body. He kept screaming, "Frankie!"

Agony.

It blistered from him, impaling me with each harsh breath he heaved from his lungs.

Uncontrollably, he shook, his hands a mess when he cautiously set them on her back. "Frankie Leigh, Oh God. Baby girl, are you okay? Tell me you're okay."

Frankie moaned, and my breath caught when she flopped over to stare up at the sky. My eyes rushed over her, searching for injuries, while Rex sat up on his knees with his hands rushing over her without touching, as if he were searching her for those same wounds but scared he might make it worse.

Frankie blinked toward the heavens, her voice raspy when she spoke. "Whoa. You see that, Daddy? That was the biggest fwip I ever did."

Relief heaved from my lungs in an audible gush, adrenaline draining fast. I dropped to my knees just as Rex was gathering her in his arms.

Where I felt relief, Rex seemed to be in . . . shock.

Frenzied, he pulled her against him, hugging her tight, refusing to let her go.

I inched closer to them. Dread sank into my spirit when I glanced at Rex again. When I glimpsed his eyes.

Turmoil and fear and desperation.

I wanted to reach out and touch him. Tell him it was okay. Promise him that Frankie was fine. Erase whatever had condemned him to this kind of torture. But he was hugging her to his chest, his jaw clenched so tightly I was sure he was fighting tears. Fighting whatever chaos raged inside him.

So instead, I turned my attention on Frankie. Gently, I reached out and brushed back the tangle of hair that had fallen across her eyes. A slick of mud covered her from her chin up the side of her face, but I didn't see any blood.

"Are you hurt anywhere, Frankie?" My words were scratchy.

Frankie crooked her arm, showing off the flaming-red scrape on her elbow. The shallow wound was quickly filling with blood. "I fink a need a Band-Aid."

Rex winced.

I looked back up the trail, realizing she couldn't have rolled more than four feet. That she'd just tripped. Something little kids did all the time.

Taking a chance, I set a hand on Rex's arm, hoping it would break through the terror that tremored through his body. Muscles twitching. Jaw clenching. "Hey . . . she's okay. She's okay. She didn't fall far. It was just an accident. She's okay. It's okay."

He didn't respond. He just shifted and climbed to standing, keeping her cradled in his arms. His cautious movements seemed at complete odds with the intimidating power of his stance, with the almost vicious steps he took when he headed straight for the trail.

Unsure of what to do, I rushed and grabbed Milo's leash where he'd scampered just off the trail. I followed close behind, surprised when Rex headed directly for his truck instead of going back to the picnic spot.

He loaded Frankie in her booster seat, peppering a bunch of kisses on her forehead and murmuring, "We're going to get you checked out, baby girl. You're fine. I promise, you're fine."

He said it as if he were trying to convince himself.

Still, he said absolutely nothing to me when I slid into the cab.

He turned over the engine. It roared to life. We rode in silence back in to town, tension wound tight as the truck jostled back over the crude path. He drove straight to the emergency room where we'd taken Frankie that night weeks ago.

Somehow, it felt as if years had passed since that night.

So much had changed in such a short amount of time.

Rex killed the engine. Silence descended, so thick it stole the air. I could almost feel the magnitude of the breath Rex inhaled as he stared through the windshield at the ER sliding doors. His gaze remained trained on that spot when he finally spoke. "Told you before I don't take chances."

I reached out, hand trembling as I set it on his forearm. Corded, sinewy muscle flexed, bunching and straining beneath the tanned skin and tattoos that wound down his arm.

"It's about taking the right ones, Rex."

He swallowed. My eyes traced the tremor of his throat, my gaze going soft when he looked over at me.

There was something there.

A plea.

The man begging me for understanding.

To *get* it.

I thought maybe he was waiting on me to run. To spook. To leave him like the woman who was supposed to be Frankie's mother.

In that second, I hated her a little more.

I nuzzled the top of Milo's head. "Take her inside. I'm going to call Nikki and see if she can pick up Milo, then I'll be in."

I'm not going anywhere.

A reluctant, disbelieving smile pull to one side of his mouth. The man so brilliant and good it wasn't fair that all that life was hidden behind whatever had beaten him down.

"Okay," he said.

He hopped out and unbuckled Frankie, and when I looked back at them from over my shoulder, Rex was pulling his daughter into his arms, her head on his shoulder.

She stretched her little fingers toward me.

I did the same.

Our fingertips met.

A flash of energy.

That connection profound.

"I'll be right in, Sweet Pea," I promised through a murmur.

"Hurry . . . I needs you."

"I need you, too," I whispered.

I'd never been playing games.

But now I was playing for keeps.

Rynna – Seventeen Years Old

"You bitch," Janel whispered her hatred from behind me, and I jerked to look over my shoulder. Janel stood in the doorway, seething mad with tears in her eyes. Janel's momma had just rushed out, pressing a hand over her mouth, as if she were either trying to accept what I had just told her or was wanting to reject it.

"I'm sorry, Janel. But I . . . I can't continue keeping these secrets for you. Lying for you. You need help."

"I need help? You don't know anything."

"I know you've been stealing from my gramma, I know you stole from the dance fund at the school, and I know I've been covering for you, and I'm not willing to do it anymore. Your momma needed to know."

Janel scoffed out a hard laugh. "You just want to make yourself look good, same way as you always do." Her voice sing-songed with bitterness. "Rynna Dayne, angel of Gingham Lakes. Holier than thou when she's nothing but a self-righteous bitch." She sank back, shaking her head. "You're gonna pay for this, Rynna Dayne."

twenty-eight

Rex

Dusk hovered in the atmosphere, and the sky had dimmed from pink to gray. I sat on my front porch on the rocker watching this clusterfuck of a day slip away. Bugs droned from the stilled trees, the air calm while my heart still banged around, lashing with unstable beats.

I looked up when the front door slowly creaked open. Rynna's footsteps were quiet as she stepped outside into the encroaching night. "I just checked in on Frankie. She's asleep."

I nodded at her, and she stepped all the way out, Milo trotting out beside her. She drew the door closed, all but an inch so we could hear if Frankie needed us.

She'd been fine. Of course, she was fine. My freak out uncalled for, which was something Kale had been all too eager to tease me about. I'd demanded he check her for any unseen injuries that we could have missed just by looking at her. He'd shot off some statistic on the average number of falls a kid Frankie's age had a day, pointing out that it wasn't like she'd taken a tumble over the cliff.

I didn't care. When it came to Frankie, I didn't take chances.

Rynna handed me a fresh beer. "Thought you could use this."

My laughter was soft. Incredulous. Disbelief that this girl could come battering into my life and the only thing it took for her to knock down my walls was all that kindness and faith. "Thanks," I muttered.

After twisting off the cap, I took a long pull.

Ice-cold amber glided down my throat.

Rynna eased out onto the porch and sat on the steps. Her back was to me, her arms wrapped around her knees as she stared out at the peace that hummed around us.

Lost in thought.

Contemplation.

The girl was so damned gorgeous I was having a hard time differentiating the emotions that thrummed and danced and glowed. It was a war against the ones that screamed and warned and howled. The chaos in my heart and mind made me want to rip the hair from my head.

Crazy how everything I'd lived my life on suddenly felt like a lie.

With Rynna, I knew it was all or nothing. I couldn't keep shutting her down and shutting her out. Couldn't keep giving her these warnings without giving her a reason.

It was time I gave her all of me.

I needed to fess up the bullshit that haunted my life. Tell her everything. I just didn't fucking know how to drag it all out into the open. If she would run. Hate me like I deserved for her to.

Agony cinched down on my chest, and my mouth flopped open and closed. The words too thick on my tongue. Finally, I forced them out into the stilled, deepening night. "Warned you that you don't want my mess." It came out hoarse. Choked.

Rynna didn't look back at me. She just sent all that belief floating out to the stars that were beginning to blink in the sky. "And I told you I wasn't afraid."

I sat forward on the rocker, elbows on my thighs as I rolled the beer bottle between my palms. "Lost the first girl I loved when I was seventeen."

Fuck.

A lid had been ripped off, and all the torment that'd boiled inside, contained and hidden, escaped.

Bubbling out and spilling over the sides.

Overflowing.

Burning and singeing and scalding.

Pain shocked through me. As shocked as the breath that left Rynna on a gush of air.

Waiting patiently. So goddamned kind and understanding.

A soft puff of laughter rippled out. Dubious and low. "I loved her, Rynna. I fucking did. Can still feel exactly the way my stomach would feel any time I thought of her. The way I felt when I touched her."

She glanced back at me. I worried I was giving her too much. Being too honest. Maybe I couldn't burden her with everything. Not yet. But she needed to know *this*.

Of course, because it was Rynna, sympathy lined her striking features, her mouth and those eyes that always seemed to see so much deeper than I wanted them to.

My chin fucking trembled. "Ollie's younger sister, Sydney." It left me like the whisper of a confession. "She was a year younger than us."

Surprise flashed before she tamped it down. She just sat there. Twisting her fingers. Listening.

"He would have killed me if he knew." My voice drew tight. "That I'd been living in his little sister for the past six months. Sneaking off with her every chance I got. Two of us lying through our teeth about where we'd been when we'd been in each other."

Pain slithered up and down my throat.

Constricting.

Suffocating.

Could almost feel the ghost of her. The faint brush of her hand. Couldn't tell if I welcomed it or hated it.

"We were all out at the lake. We were drinking, sitting in the bed and on the tail of my truck. Kale was off doing God knows what with his girlfriend, and Ollie had invited a few other girls out. One of them was coming onto me. Sydney—"

Her name hitched on my tongue.

My stomach coiled in knots.

White-hot agony.

"Sydney was there. Watching. Hating it. Hating that I couldn't say a damned thing and that girl was straddling my waist. I laughed it off like it wasn't a big deal while Ollie goaded me. Telling me I was nothing but a pussy and it was about time I saw some action. About time that I got my dick wet."

"Rex," Rynna whispered. Pain radiating from her. Or maybe it was just mine echoing back.

I blinked against the memory.

"She jumped out of the bed and stood next to my truck, demanding I take her home. She was so mad, Rynna. So fucking hurt. And I laughed at her and kissed that girl because that was what I thought Ollie expected me to do."

My eyes squeezed closed.

It didn't matter.

That same fucking vision flashed.

The last time I saw her.

The words dripped. Soured. Old decayed wounds. "I won't ever forget her face, Rynna. I'd broken her right there, and I didn't even mean it. Ollie shouted at her to just go home, telling her she didn't belong there, anyway. She looked at me one last time . . . torment in her eyes. Then she turned and started down the dirt road. And I let her go."

I let her go.

Fuck.

I let her go.

"No one ever saw her again." Guilt stampeded through me. Over me. Trampling me into the ground.

Rynna gasped. "Oh God, Rex,"

"I just watched her storm off into the night, Rynna. I fucking watched her go. I didn't chase after her. Had no fucking clue she was even missing until the next day."

She shifted onto her hands and knees and crawled the short distance across the boards of the porch until she was at my feet.

Tears shined in her eyes.

"What happened?"

A tremor rolled my throat. Horror. Hate. Fear. I'd carried it for twelve fucking years. That girl chasing me through the days and haunting me in the night.

"We searched. Searched and searched and searched for what felt like forever. I hunted through that forest every day. Months. A year. Maybe more. Screaming her name. Begging her to come back. She was gone, Rynna. Fucking gone. No trace. No suspects. No clues."

In agony, I looked at her, fighting the moisture that had gathered in my eyes. "Now I do it in my dreams. I hunt for her. Scream her name. Desperate to find her when I know with every part of me she's gone." My teeth ground. "Buried in some shallow grave."

Tears streaked her cheeks. "Oh God, Rex. I'm so sorry. I'm so sorry. I can't . . ."

She gulped around the tragedy. Like maybe the magnitude of it was slowly sinking in. Her arms wound around her stomach like she might be sick. "Oh God. Oh My God . . . Ollie. Oh God," she whimpered. Looking up at me, she set one of those tender hands on my jaw, her face pinched in anguish.

How was it even possible she was looking at me that way? Grief striking her cheeks and sympathy in the warmth of those eyes?

"Did you ever tell Ollie? Does he know you loved her?" she almost begged.

My head shook. "He'd kill me, Rynna. He'd fucking kill me. I just let her walk away. She's gone *because of me*. I was responsible, Rynna."

"No."

"There's no lie you could tell me, no lie I could tell myself, that would convince me otherwise. I know it, Rynna. I know if I hadn't have done what I did, she would still be here."

It sliced through us. A double-edged sword. Piercing through the atmosphere.

My gaze traveled out into the night, to the duskiness that held to the sky, trees gusting in the wind.

Swore I heard Sydney's spirit howling back.

"You'd think what happened would have driven the three of us apart. But it tied us together some way. Ollie's been . . ." I gulped around the barbs spiked in my throat. "He was a goddamned mess, Rynna. Blaming himself for that night when the blame has always been on me, and I'm the bastard who can't bring myself to tell him. He tries to pretend he's okay, but he's not. None of us are."

Tenderly, Rynna touched my chin. Her lips trembled and her tears wouldn't stop falling.

I almost managed a grin. "Kale is like a rock. Think he's the one who held Ollie and me together when we were falling apart."

"Does he know?"

I gave a regretful nod. "Yeah. He called it the second things started up with Sydney and me. Think the asshole manages to see everything before it even goes down."

Rynna gave me the softest smile before she laid her cheek on my knee, watching me, holding on to my leg like she could keep me from splitting apart. The girl my strength when that was all I'd ever wanted to be.

"Tell me how you met Frankie's mom," she whispered, encouraging me to go on.

"Was lost for a lot of years, Rynna. Fucking *lost*. But the wilderness gets lonely, you know? So, I fucked around. And that was messed up, too, because any time I touched another girl, when I closed my eyes, only thing I saw was Sydney's face."

Rynna flinched, but I continued, unable to stop the train wreck from tumbling from my mouth. "Then Frankie's mom . . ."

Rynna's spine went rigid.

"It was just the same as always. Met her at a bar on the other side of town. Went back to her place. Whole time, that same guilt ate me up because the only thing I could think was I wished she was Sydney. Then one day, she showed up at my house, telling me she was pregnant."

My voice dropped low, and my mouth angled at Rynna like I were offering her a dirty secret. "I freaked out. Accused her of lying. Claimed it wasn't mine . . . because fuck, I couldn't have a kid. Not with her."

Rynna tried to subdue a sob. But it tore free. A partner to the ripping wind. "She'd told me fine. She'd get rid of it. No problem. She took off down my driveway. Next thing I know, I was chasing her, pleading with her to come back, promising her we'd figure it out. She told me the only way she was going to keep it was if I married her."

The words deepened like a plea. "My mom always taught me to do the right thing, Rynna. So, I did. I married her. I didn't even know her, didn't even like her, and I fucking married her."

"Rex," she whispered.

My gaze turned to where she was still on her knees, staring up at me. Emotion throbbed all around. Circling us. Drawing us in.

My body shook, every part of me overcome. Overwhelmed. "And then . . . I'm holding this baby girl in my arms . . ." I held out my hands, palms up, like somehow Rynna might get it. Like she could see me holding Frankie Leigh for the very first time. Like she could experience what that felt like. "And suddenly, it's not just the right thing. It's the *very best thing*."

More tears streaked from the warm well of those shimmering eyes.

My voice was gravel. "Never thought I could love like that. Not after Sydney. And I thought I'd gotten lucky. That maybe I'd been given another chance. So, I let myself love them both. Let them become the center of my world, just like they should be. I had my dog, Missy, and my girls, and we got this house and everything was fucking perfect."

I blinked around the confusion. Around my mistakes. "Don't even know where I went wrong. Working too long. Too many hours. Thinking I was doing what was right for them. And Frankie's mom . . . she was suffering, and I didn't even know it. I came home just as the sun was going down one night—"

I was numb as I stood by the side of the road, staring blankly as the taillights disappeared in the distance. I tried to blink through the squiggle of red, neon lines that lit up against my bleary vision. It was like looking at the sun and then closing your eyes. Or maybe I just wished they were closed. But they were open wide, my gaze sucked down.

Down.

Down.

Missy dead at my feet.

The words wouldn't even form on my tongue, wounds ripped open wide. Gaping and bleeding. Garbling the confession because I just didn't know what the fuck I'd done wrong.

Just didn't understand.

Still didn't.

And her hands. Rynna's hands were on my face, and she was leaning on both her knees, wedged between mine, forcing me to meet her eyes. "She abandoned you and Frankie. That's not your fault."

"It doesn't matter, Rynna. I still lost her. Every girl I've ever loved has left me. After Sydney disappearing? Anytime something happens to Frankie . . ." I fisted my hand, pressed it against the raging of my heart. "I'm terrified, Rynna. Terrified of her slipping away, too. Terrified of something horrible happening to her. If I lost her . . . fuck . . . I can't. I won't. I'll die first before I let something happen to her. Do you get it now? Why I'm terrified of you? Why I'm terrified of the way you make me feel? This afternoon, I—"

Her words were muted but desperate. "I need you to listen to me. What happened this afternoon with Frankie wasn't your fault. It wasn't neglect. She was playing, loving the amazing life you've given her. Experiencing it the way she should. Living it to its fullest because that's what she is. She's life. She's joy. She's rambunctious and curious and perfect, and the last thing you want to do is limit that. You can't keep her from falling, Rex, but you can be there to pick her up when she does. That's what matters the most."

My forehead dropped against hers, and I whispered into the darkness. "After Frankie's mom left, I waited for her, Rynna. Waited because I thought that was what I was supposed to do."

Loyalty.

Distorted and confused.

It spun around me like a bad fucking dream.

"Truth is, I didn't want anyone, anyway. Didn't want to repeat it. Refused to ever fall into that trap again."

I gathered that gorgeous face between my hands. "And then there was you. There was beautiful you standing across the street, and every promise I'd made myself suddenly felt like a lie. You make me feel again, Rynna. You make me feel like every chance is one worth taking. Like you're leading me out of the darkness that's ruled my life. When I close my eyes, who I see is *you*. Show me the way, Rynna. Show me the way out of it. Fuck. Please, show me the way."

She pressed her mouth to mine.

Hard.

"Rynna," I moaned.

Fucking Rynna.

Little Thief.

twenty-nine

Rynna

Strong arms wrapped around my waist, and the rocker groaned when Rex pushed to standing, taking me with him. He hiked me up into the strength of his arms, my legs immediately cinching around his narrow waist.

With one arm locked around my waist, he gripped me by the jaw with the other hand, controlling our kiss, ruling my mind where I disappeared into the abyss of this complicated man.

My spirit roared.

A thunder of grief and torrent of love.

I wanted to sing it. Sing it for him. For this man who'd lost so much and deserved every good thing the world had to give. Instead, I poured it into him. Into our kiss and into every desperate touch.

He gripped me tighter, wedging open the door, carrying me inside. With his foot, he held the door open, breaking away for the briefest flash when he called, "Milo, come," his voice gruff.

My tiny puppy scampered past his feet, trotting right over to the bed Rex had set up for him in the corner of the living room, already knowing his place.

Then Rex got right back to kissing me. A hand wound up in my hair and the other locked around my waist.

I ached for him in a way that was only possible when someone's joy mattered more to you than anything else. When you'd give up yours to see them smile. When you'd sacrifice to make them happy.

When you were so far gone the only thing that mattered was them.

My gramma had told me I'd just know.

That it'd be magic.

And that was what this felt like.

Magic. Magic composed of so many threads. Layers of wounds and grief and tragedy. All of it bound by a seed of hope that had been planted somewhere along the way.

It bloomed.

Bloomed so big and bright that this man was the only thing I could see.

It felt too powerful to be one-sided. Too vast to be warped.

Lives pieced together precariously. Fragilely. A tender, loving, imperfect balance.

He carried me down the hall, only pausing for a moment to look in at Frankie, who was fast asleep. The man smiled up at me when he partially drew her door back shut, his expression so profound as he swept his hand back into my hair, his words a grumbled rasp. A root that had blossomed from that hopeful seed. "Want to do this every night, Rynna. Want to tuck my baby girl in bed then take my other girl to mine."

He walked us the rest of the way into his room. He kicked the door shut and tossed me onto his bed. I bounced on the mattress, a wave of need capturing me. Chasing away the fears and the questions that had plagued us since we'd met.

Nothing left to stand in our way.

He reached back and clicked the lock before reaching down and peeling his shirt over his head, revealing the overwhelming strength of his chest and the ripple of his abs glowing in the wispy tendrils of moonlight that flooded his room.

I heaved out a breath.

"Every night, Rynna. I want to take you. Fuck you. Love you. Keep you."

My entire body shook, the impact of his words tearing through me like an earthquake.

I pushed up onto my palms, squirming on his bed. "I'm not going anywhere."

He flicked the button of his jeans and shoved out of them.

Baring all.

Oh God.

He was magnificent, his cock jutting free, pointing to the sky. Needy for me.

Me.

"Gonna make you a moaning, sweaty mess, Rynna Dayne, then I'm going to do it all over again."

"I'm yours."

The air crackled.

Alive.

Fire and heat and flames.

I writhed as I stared up at him.

Muscle and strength and that amazing heart underneath.

He inched forward, making me insane when he reached over from the side of the bed and dragged my shorts and the bathing suit bottom off. He dropped them to the floor, ran his fingers between my thighs. "So fucking sweet."

"Rex, I need you."

"You have me, baby. Anytime. Anywhere. Always."

He climbed onto his knees on the bed, slowly dragging up my tank and setting it free, quick to do the same with my bikini top.

He tossed it over his shoulder, a wicked gleam lighting in his eye. He leaned closer, framing me in with his big body, mouth blowing across my breasts.

Instantly, my nipples budded into tight, pebbled peaks.

My hips jerked. "Rex. Please."

I needed him more than I'd ever needed him before. I felt closer to him than I ever had. All his exteriors ripped away, shields down. It was just him and me.

I set my palms flat against the hard, defined ridges of his

abdomen, and he rubbed his cock against my center.

A slow, sensual tease.

A shiver slipped down my spine. It dove straight into the pool of desire that grew to a boil in my belly.

My hands slid up his smooth skin.

Greedy as they explored. Savoring every inch. "You're so beautiful, Rex Gunner. Inside and out. Thank you for letting me see it. For trusting me with it. With who you are."

I let my fingers trace across the tattoo on his arm that so clearly wept.

Finally understanding what it meant. The kind of loss that would go on forever.

He cupped my face in the palm of his hand, something so serious blanketing his expression. "Who I am is yours, Rynna. I'm going to fix the bullshit in my life I should have fixed a long time ago."

My mouth dropped open to ask him what that meant, but he took it as an opportunity to delve his tongue between my lips in a kiss that seared my soul.

All thoughts evaporated.

"Rynna." My name was a plea. A prayer. I don't think either of us could tell the difference anymore.

He wedged deeper between my thighs. His cock so big, trapped between us, begging for release.

Need throbbed, and he suddenly grasped me by the knees, spreading me wide as he edged back onto his. He dove in, licking through my folds.

I moaned, writhed, fisted my hands in his hair. "Rex."

His only answer was to devour me. Fucking me with his tongue. Long laps and sweet, dizzying sucks.

Pleasure wound. So fast that I restrained a scream. That I writhed and moaned and whimpered his name.

It built to a pinpoint. Ready to burst.

The second before I did, he was over me. One hand planted next to my head as he hooked his other arm under my right knee.

He pinned my leg up high on his arm, pressing our chests together.

I could feel the beat of his heart where it raged against mine.

Wild. Wild and free.

He slowly pressed himself into my body. Never looking away.

Taking.

Owning.

Obliterating.

My mouth dropped open while his jaw clenched.

He began to move. His thrusts slow. Each rock of his hips deliberate. A slow, steady conquering. Winding me right back up.

He teased me with the most exquisite kind of torture. Passion stretched taut. Palpable and alive.

It was too much and too little and I begged him for more.

The physical and emotional that had waited anxiously on opposite sides suddenly charged toward the other.

The two crashed in the middle.

Sublime devastation.

Body and soul.

Tears pricked at my eyes and streaked down my face.

Because I was again overcome.

Overwhelmed by this man. I inhaled and filled my lungs with the magnitude of him.

Lake and earth and the clearest sky.

He moved in me in barely contained thrusts, slow and hard in his claiming command while I spun through the brightest kind of bliss.

Blinding.

Where I basked in this unfathomable beauty.

In that place that had become us.

Real and whole.

His mouth brushed against mine. "You changed everything, Rynna. Where I found an end, you saw a beginning. You saved me. Called me from the shadows. You changed everything the day you walked into my life. You are my heart's second chance."

I floated on the ecstasy of that chance.

Elevated.

Tossed into our perfect harmony.

Where I'd fall forever.

Weightless.

Rex clutched me by the shoulders, his rocks turning frenzied as he clutched me against him, as he burrowed his face into my hair, as he whispered my name.

"Rynna."

And Rex.

He fell with me.

Exactly where he'd always belonged.

thirty

Rynna

*P*eace swam through his room, a dusky quiet broken by the milky moonlight streaming in from the window. I didn't think there could be anything more perfect than being nestled in the crook of his arm with my head resting on his chest.

Tangled together.

Basking in the afterglow.

He gently brushed his fingers through my hair, and I sighed, so content, and I could only pray this incredible man felt the same. I rolled a fraction so I could place a kiss over the thrum of his heart. "You're my heart's second chance, too," I told him through a murmur.

He shifted me to lay on top of him. Nudging me back, he peered up at me. "How's that?"

I played with one of the longer locks of his hair. "The entire time I was in San Francisco, I felt as if I was missing something. When I left . . ." I blinked through the memories, searching for what to say, wondering if I should even bring it up.

The past was the past.

But he'd shared his, and I needed him to know mine.

"I won't pretend what happened to me comes anywhere close to what you went through. To what you and Ollie and Kale lost that day. But I lost a piece of myself when I left. More than one piece," I admitted in a hurried whisper. "I left behind my dreams and my innocence and my hopes. I left behind my grandmother. My only family."

The loss of her drummed through me. A woeful ache.

He threaded his fingers through my hair and cupped the side of my head. "You don't have to minimize what you went through, Rynna. Yeah, what happened with Sydney was brutal. So goddamned brutal. But I know I'm not the only person in this world who's suffered."

Rex wavered for a moment, before his words dropped low. "What happened, Rynna? What sent you running?"

Blinking into the distance, I let my thoughts slip back to that time. "There was this girl . . . we were friends." I shook my head, my voice going even quieter. "But really, we weren't. I told you before how I never quite fit in. I was always on the outside. Lonely. Looking back now, I see how she took advantage of that. That I was willing to take any abuse if it meant I had friends."

I could feel the flinch of his fingers he held against the side of my head. "It got worse as I got older. Much worse. I found out she'd been stealing, and maybe it was stupid, but I was actually worried about her." Regretfully, I looked at him. "So I told her mom."

My head shook. "She was so angry. So angry. I should have known when she warned me I was going to pay for it that she meant it. But I was naïve that way. I never suspected cruelty because it was so far out of the realm of anything I'd ever wish against someone."

"What happened?" His voice was a low rumble, and I could feel his unease. I could feel anger sifting through him, shaking out and taking hold.

I eased down onto his chest and laid my ear against the soothing thrum of his heart. I wasn't sure I could look him in the eyes when I made this confession. Distractedly, I traced over the tattoo on his arm and shoulder, whispering the words into the dense air.

"I'd had a crush on this boy for as long as I could remember . . . middle school at least." It was almost sorrow that formed on my mouth, though it was brittle with hurt. "I never thought he'd look my way, then one day . . . one day he asked me out."

"You want to grab a bite Friday night?"

I stood behind the long counter at my gramma's diner, looking behind me, around me. Was Aaron really talking to me? Every one of the butterflies in my stomach held their breath. My heart shook so hard I was sure everyone in the diner could hear it.

"Rynna?" he prodded.

Mouth dropping open, I stared blankly at him, my tongue not cooperating. "You . . . you want to go out with . . . me?" I finally managed to stutter around the shock.

"Yeah. Why wouldn't I?" He shrugged a muscular shoulder, and my wide-eyed gaze got transfixed on the motion. This had to be a dream, right?

"So what do you think?" He angled his face down to capture my attention. "Don't break my heart, Rynna."

Don't break his heart? Oh God. Oh God. This was really happening. "Um . . . yeah . . . yes. Definitely. I definitely want to go out with you." I nodded frantically.

He grinned and those butterflies scattered, a frenzy in my belly. He smacked the counter before pointing at me. "Pick you up at seven."

I tried to keep the tears out of my voice while I let the story bleed free. "God, I was so excited, Rex, that this boy actually liked me."

A growl stalked his throat. I could feel it, hear it all the way to my soul. He tightened his hold on me. As if he didn't want to hear it but needed to, the same way I needed to tell him.

"I was on cloud nine. He picked me up and took me out. He kissed me right across the street in front of my gramma's door. It went on like that for three weeks. The two of us together. Kissing and touching and me feeling like I finally was important." A sob threatened at the base of my throat, words hitching as I forced the last out. "That I wasn't invisible."

"Rynna." It was a shaky breath that blew between Rex's lips.

I angled up so I could look down at his face. "I was so tired of being invisible, Rex. Of feeling stupid and unattractive and unlovable. So tired of being alone. But I should have known. God, I should have seen it coming a mile away."

I stood at my full-length mirror, twisting this way and that, looking at myself from every angle, trying to convince myself that the dress I wore looked good. That my rolls didn't show. That Aaron liked what I looked like, and it didn't matter if they showed, anyway.

It was my birthday.

My eighteenth birthday, and I was so finished being scared. Finished with all the doubts and insecurities that threatened to explode and send me cowering under the covers of my bed. I was going to live this life, and live it to its fullest.

That was what Gramma had always taught me to do.

It was time to start embracing it.

Hurrying out of my room and downstairs, I bounced into the kitchen.

Gramma turned away from the new recipe she was testing by the stove. "My, my, look at you, child. All grown up."

In the center of the old kitchen, I spun around in my dress. "Thank you for buying it for me, Gramma."

"Of course. Every girl needs a dress to celebrate their eighteenth birthday. You're a woman now, and as gorgeous as ever, if I say so myself."

I felt the blush climb to my cheeks. Because after tonight, I really would be a woman. In every sense of the word. "Thank you, Gramma, so much."

She looked at me softly, and I gazed back. Love spun through me with the intensity of the sun. "I hope you know everything you mean to me, Gramma. I hope you know I appreciate every single thing you've done for me. Everything you sacrificed. That you raised me. That you've loved me the way you have. I know you always worried it wasn't enough, but I could never ask for anything more than you."

Moisture shined in her grayed eyes, and she smiled. Smiled a smile that encompassed the meaning of both of our worlds. She reached out a weathered hand and twisted one of the curls I'd ironed into my hair. "We've made quite the team, haven't we?"

"The best team," I said, reaching out to wrap my arms around her. "Thank you, Gramma. Thank you so much," I murmured at her ear, inhaling the sweet scent of vanilla and sugar that somewhere along the way

had become a permanent part of her.

She hugged me tight, so thin and frail yet so incredibly strong. "I love you more than you'll ever know, Corinne Paisley. You have been the greatest light of my life. It has been the greatest honor raising you into the woman you are."

Tears slipped free, and I sniffled.

She pulled back and wiped them away. "Stop that, now, or you're gonna mess up that makeup you spent the last two hours perfecting." She nudged me toward the door. "Go on, have fun."

I stepped back and squeezed both her hands in mine. "Thank you. I love you so much."

Sight bleary with tears, I swallowed around the knot of hurt wedged at the base of my throat. "I left the house so happy that night."

"Fuck, Rynna. I can't . . ." Rex itched beneath me, muscles straining, as if he had to stop himself from jumping up and going back to that day to stop it from happening. But that was the thing about the past. It was over. All except for the scars it left behind.

"He picked me up at the end of the street. I hopped in his truck. I can still remember how he squeezed my hand, told me that tonight was just him and me." Agony wheezed from my throat. "And for a moment, I felt beautiful."

"Fuck, Rynna." It was grit from Rex's mouth. Hate bound with the protectiveness he so clearly felt for me.

"He took me to the lake. I was nervous and excited. There was this . . ." My brow pinched at the memory of it. "Old shack. Barely standing. So secluded I don't know how he ever found it. There was a fire already burning in a pit near the shore. He said he'd come out and set it up for me. It was the first time I felt uneasy about everything. Something about it felt off. I should have listened to that flicker of intuition."

I turned my stare down to Rex, who was grinding his teeth, hands tightening, holding on to me.

"I should have listened." It left me a on a grated rasp.

Aaron led me into the shack. Immediately, his mouth covered mine. I kissed him back, fighting the quiver of fear that slicked beneath the surface of my skin.

I liked him.

I liked him so much.

I was just nervous. It was my first time. Everyone was nervous when they left themselves vulnerable to someone else. When you gave them this kind of trust.

I'd been enamored with him for all of forever. I finally had this chance, and I'd be an absolute fool if I let anxiety and insecurity get in the way.

Not again.

I'd been doing it for too long.

But when he led me to the small cot backed against the far wall and started to undress me, I couldn't stop shaking. Shaking and shaking and shaking. Nerves skittered free and fast. Naked, my stomach tightened, and I couldn't relax. I pressed my knees together, suddenly wanting to cover myself. It didn't let up when Aaron undressed in the muted darkness.

I should have been watching his muscular body in the shadows. Instead, I squeezed my eyes closed and fought tears.

"Shh," was all he said when he climbed over me and wedged between my thighs. My legs shook. I squeezed them against him, because something about this felt all wrong. My fingers dug into his shoulders and a whimper escaped my lips.

A sharp pain stole my breath when he thrust into me. I tried to hold it back, but a small cry escaped.

And those cries—they wouldn't stop coming, though, I bit them back, keeping them subdued as he kept driving into me, his head shifted to the side, away, never looking at my face

Tears flowed, almost silent as I stared at the ceiling, wondering how his kisses had felt so good when this felt so . . . wrong.

I knew it.

My gut told me.

Wrong. Wrong. Wrong.

Something was so unbearably wrong.

I just didn't know the extent of it until he groaned and pulsed before he quickly pushed off me and climbed to his feet. His naked body was lit up in oranges and reds against the lapping flames reflected in from outside.

Then Aaron, he smirked.

I blinked down at this amazing man who lay completely still, listening, knowing he wouldn't judge me. But that didn't mean my voice didn't quiver with shame and agony. "He gave me this look before he ducked down and grabbed my clothes from the floor. He balled them against his chest and just . . . walked out with them. I couldn't stop crying, Rex. Couldn't stop crying. I kept calling for him. Screaming for him to come back. Not to leave me. Never in my life had I felt more alone than the moment when he walked out on me after he'd taken my innocence. After I thought I meant something to him."

"That piece of shit." His words barely made it between his clenched teeth.

My tongue darted out to wet my lips. "I stayed in there for so long. It was horrible. It was dark, and I was naked and alone. Finally . . . finally, I stumbled out to find him, trying to cover myself when I did."

Grief clamped down on my heart. "I stumbled out and . . . there was . . . there was a bunch of kids from school," I finally managed. Every word was filled with the disgrace I'd felt that day. "They were waiting for me to come out. They all just started laughing, like my standing there naked . . . hurt . . . terrified . . . was the funniest thing they'd ever seen."

The group of about eight laughed. Laughed as I stumbled on my feet. My body sore. The trickle of something foreign ran down my leg.

My head dropped, not wanting to meet their eyes.

Oh God.

Help.

I twisted awkwardly, bending over and pressing my thighs and knees together, my arms crossed over my chest.

As if it might shield me.

Shield me from the insults.

From the jeers.

From the laughter.

I barely peeked up, gasping when I saw Janel at the center of it. With Aaron. One of his arms was wrapped around her waist, her body plastered to his side, her hands on his chest. He'd pulled on underwear and was casually draining a beer as if he hadn't just degraded me in the worst way.

Oh God. No. My head spun with dizziness. Nausea churned in my stomach. I was going to be sick.

I stumbled a step backward, trying to quiet the cries that were tearing from my aching throat. Raking from me like broken glass. "Aaron," *I mumbled the plea.*

"Oh, Rynna." *Janel took a step toward me, her blonde hair lit up light a ring of flames from the fire behind her.* "You poor, pathetic thing. Did you really think he'd actually go out with you? Did you actually think he wanted you?"

"Oh my God . . . look at all that fat. Dude, did you really just put your dick in that? Not sure how you stomached it." *I didn't want to acknowledge it, but I couldn't help but look at Remi, Aaron's best friend, who was laughing hysterically where he stood by the bonfire.*

Aaron looked at him with a grin before he planted a kiss on Janel's temple. "Like I wouldn't do anything for my girl. And it was dark." *He hefted a shoulder.* "Didn't make it all that bad."

Janel smirked at me.

Horror.

It spun around me in whipping, rending lights. The world canting.

Oh God.

Oh God.

"Ah, poor, Rynna Dayne, always such a good girl. But look at her now, nothing but a filthy, fat slut."

Another string of lights. Flashes from a camera.

Picture after picture.

"Janel," *I begged.*

No.

I tried to cover myself, wrenched over as I sobbed.

Janel just sneered. "You should have known better than to fuck with me."

Then it hit me. A pie. Splattering. Blueberries in my hair, streaking down my chest, dripping on my belly.

Howls of laughter.

"Happy birthday, Rynna," *Janel mocked. She tossed me my dress.*

I gasped out in relief, scrambling to gather the fabric that landed two feet in front of me and hugged it against my body.

Jeers and abuse struck me from all sides, and I clutched the material to my chest, as if it might stand the chance to shield me from the torment.

Take it away.

Hide me.

The confession tumbled from me on a downpour of tears. Rex clung to me, horror in his posture as he held me as close as he possibly could.

"I ran home. Mortified. Knowing those pictures were going to be plastered all over the school the next day. Knowing my gramma would see them and know what I'd done. So I ran. I ran and ran and ran and I never stopped running, Rex. Not until I came back here."

Not until I'd collided with this mesmerizing man.

"Rynna, what's going on?" The sleepy voice filled with concern hit me from behind.

Torment lashed like the crack of a whip. My eyes slammed closed, and the words trembled from my mouth. "I'm so sorry, Gramma, but I've got to go."

The floor creaked with my grandmother's footsteps. She sucked in a breath when she rounded me, shocked by my battered appearance. "Oh my lord, what happened to you?" Her voice quivered. "Who hurt you? Tell me, Rynna. Who hurt you? I won't stand for it."

Vigorously, I shook my head, finding the lie. "No one. I just . . . I can't stay in this stupid town for a second more. I'm going to find Mama."

I hated it. The way the mention of my mother contorted my gramma's face in agony.

"What are you sayin'?"

"I'm saying, I'm leaving."

A weathered hand reached out to grip my forearm. "But graduation is just next month. You've got to do your speech. Walk across the stage in your cap and gown. Never seen anyone so excited about somethin' in all my life. Now you're just gonna up and leave? If you can't trust me, then you can't trust anyone. Tell me what happened tonight. You left here just as happy as a bug in a rug, and now you aren't doing anything but runnin' scared."

Tears streaking down my dirty cheeks, I forced myself to look at the woman who meant everything to me. "You're the only person I can trust, Gramma. That's why I've got to go. Let's leave it at that."

Anguish creased my grandmother's aged face. "Rynna, I won't let you just walk out like this."

She reached out and brushed a tear from under my eye. Softly, she tilted her head to the side, that same tender smile she had watched me with at least a million times hinting at the corner of her mouth. "Don't you ever forget, if you aren't laughing, you're crying. Now, which would you rather be doin'?" She paused, and I couldn't bring myself to answer. "Wipe those tears, and let's figure something out. Just like we always do."

Sadness swelled like its own being in the tiny room. Loss. Regret. Like an echo of every breath of encouragement my grandmother had ever whispered in my ear. "I can't stay here, Gramma. Please don't ask me to."

With the plea, my grandmother winced. Quickly, I dipped down to place a lingering kiss to her cheek, breathing in the ever-present scent of vanilla and sugar, committing it to memory.

Then I tugged my suitcase from the bed and started for the door.

Gramma reached for me, fingertips brushing my arm, begging, "Rynna, don't go. Please, don't leave me like this. There's nothing that's so bad that I won't understand. That we can't fix."

I didn't slow. Didn't answer.

I ran.

And I didn't look back.☐

"I just . . ." The words whispered from me on a regretful plea. "I just wish I would have come back sooner. I just wish I would have realized it didn't matter what they'd done to me. My gramma would have never looked at me differently. She loved me, no matter what, and I let them steal eleven years of that."

Fingers sank into my flesh, rage barely contained. "I want to hunt that little fucker down and kill him, Rynna. Who the fuck would do that to you? And that bitch? Fuck. I can't even fathom it."

Aaron's name threatened on my tongue, the fact that I'd seen him on the sidewalk in front of the restaurant a couple weeks before. But there was no use in saying names. On laying blame. I just wanted to let Rex in, let him see me, understand me, the same way as he'd allowed me to understand him.

"It was a long time ago, Rex."

"But it doesn't take away what they did."

"No." My head shook, a tweak of hope lifting the corner of

my trembling lip. "And you're right. I spent a long time being terrified of them. Just the idea of ever seeing them again had kept me chained to San Francisco. But maybe they regret it now. Maybe the years passed, and they recognized the depravity of what they had done. Maybe they look back, and they're struck with shame and remorse and would take it all back if they could."

Rex touched the side of my face. "You are nothin' but grace and good, Rynna Dayne. Forgiving them that way."

"Holding on to hate would only hurt me more."

It was almost a grin that lit on his face. "Am I allowed to hate them for you?"

I bit my bottom lip, fighting a smile. Again, overcome by him. By that beautiful exterior and the amazing heart beating its own kind of grace underneath. "If it makes you feel better."

He clutched me to him, burrowing his face into my neck, pressing his lips against my skin. "Yeah, it makes me feel so much better."

Then he nipped at me, and a giggle slipped out.

Because Rex Gunner made me feel completely free.

I moved to stare down at him, and I swore his eyes saw all the way to the depths of me.

The air shifted.

Hit with that charge.

A bolt of electricity.

I sucked in a breath, and he placed his palm at the center of my chest, nudging me back until I was sitting up, straddling him.

He gripped his length in his hand.

Already ready. Wanting more.

Which was just fine, because everything I had belonged to this man.

thirty-one

Rynna

Morning light flooded through the window. Bright, white, and glowing.

I thought maybe I was, too.

I watched Rex, the man lost to sleep. Peace floated around him like a full-body halo where he lay face down on his bed. Twisted in his sheets. A hint of his perfect, round ass peeked out from above the satiny material, the ridges of his muscular back on display, his shoulders so deliciously wide.

My gaze traced every inch of exposed skin.

Even though he'd been so lost, he'd opened up, willing to be found.

Redness rushed across my chest and up to my face, this feeling that was so heavy and warm and light fluttering through my senses. Everything so incredibly right.

Not even trying to stop my smile, I quietly dressed and slipped out of his room.

I peeked in at Frankie. I had to stifle a laugh when I found her facing the opposite end of her bed, sprawled out across it. She had one arm thrown over the side and a leg bent at an odd angle so her foot rested against the wall.

Not even sleep could keep that rambunctious child tamed.

My heart thrummed.

Love. Love. Love.

Pulling her door closed a fraction, I continued to edge down the hall, eager to start the day. Milo would need to be taken out.

On top of that? I figured Rex would love to have a fresh pot of coffee waiting for him when he woke.

Or maybe . . .

Maybe I would have one of Pepper's breakfast pies ready. The kind my gramma had been known for most. It was close to a quiche, but the entire thing was topped with a flaky, delicious crust. People had come for miles to have it start their days.

A grin gripped my entire face when I thought of Rex's reaction. The way he'd look at me when he stood all rumpled and sleepy at the end of the hall, finding me in his kitchen.

That man and his pie.

When he heard me approaching, Milo scrambled to his feet. Nails scratching at the wood floor, he scampered over to me. His tail and hind-end wagged all over the place, his whole body shaking.

"Morning, sweet boy," I said. I scooped him into my arms. "I bet you need to go potty, don't you?" I cooed, nuzzling my nose against the top of his head. He licked my chin.

I slipped on the flip-flops I'd left by the couch and grabbed his leash.

Right as I was reaching for the knob, light knocking sounded against the wood. It stopped me short. Ears perking up, Milo twisted in my arms, his attention trained that direction. I fumbled my fingers through his soft fur. "It's okay, sweet boy. Let's see who it is so they don't wake up the whole house."

I glanced at the clock. It wasn't even seven in the morning. Frowning, I quickly and quietly twisted the lock, careful as I eased it open.

Confused, I blinked, trying to see through the bright sunlight that poured in from behind the figure on the porch.

A blazing silhouette just on the other side of Rex's door.

I attempted to shake myself from the hallucination. To focus clearly. Desperate to find who was really there and not what my mind was taunting me into believing.

Bewilderment stirred through my brain, nudging at the recesses of my mind, prodding at every hurt I'd triumphed. Every fear that had attempted to hold me back. I could feel the trigger being squeezed. Shooting me straight into the worst kind of dream.

No.

I blinked at her.

No.

Movement at the end of the hall tore my attention from the figure standing on the porch. My mouth flapped open, questions wanting to pour out when I found Rex standing there, wearing only his jeans.

But I couldn't say anything.

His own shock had frozen him in place, those sage eyes wider than I'd ever seen.

"Janel," he finally rasped. Her name was barely audible, but it struck my world like an atomic bomb.

Detonating.

Exploding.

Destroying.

Slowly, I looked back at her. My knees went weak.

And the entire world dropped out from under me.

thirty-two

Rex

I could barely see through the fog. Through the haze of my mind.

Clouded.

Confused.

Hurt and hate. They spun through my spirit, a goddamned cyclone that blistered my blood.

I stood at the end of my hall staring at the woman who couldn't be anything more than an apparition.

A fucking ghost. A demon cast from hell to torment the living.

Or maybe that was just where I'd been condemned.

Hell.

Punishment for giving up and giving in.

Because Rynna stood there, as shocked as I was, her knees going weak when Janel's name finally tore through my lips like lead.

It might as well have been a bullet.

Rynna fumbled back a step. Her hand shot out to the wall to keep her from falling. Janel stared at her. Shocked. Angry.

Jealous. I didn't fucking know. All I knew was she finally said her name.

"Rynna?"

She said it like she knew her.

"What are you doing here?" Janel all of a sudden demanded, words a harsh breath.

Guessed that was what finally knocked me from the trance. The fact she had the audacity to come into my house and make any kind of claim. I angled forward, head cocked to the side as I stalked across the floor of my home.

My home.

Frankie's home.

The home I had every intention of becoming Rynna's, too.

"You really gonna fucking stand there and demand to know who's in my house? Are you fuckin' kiddin' me?"

"Rex." Janel's blue eyes found mine. Wide and innocent. The way she'd always looked at me when she wanted something most. Which was usually about all the time. Maybe I didn't recognize it until then. But there it was, the truth of it glaring back at me.

Three fucking years, and she was going to stand there looking at me like that?

"Get the fuck out." My voice was grit.

Rynna reeled at my side. Gasping over a breath. She barely caught herself before she fell to her knees, clutching Milo to her chest.

"No." It was a whimper from her mouth.

Grief.

"Rynna," I whispered, arm going out to gather her up. To steady her. To let her know it didn't matter this fucking bitch was standing at my door.

Panic surged through me when she dodged my touch and lurched forward, grabbing her purse from where she'd set it on the floor the night before, and then bolted out my door.

Janel stumbled out of her way as Rynna blew by.

No fucking way was I letting this happen.

I darted after her. "Rynna. Stop. Don't leave. Don't . . . fuck, don't leave."

Don't leave.

She didn't seem to be able to focus when she looked back at me. She kept moving, stumbling down the steps of my front porch and clinging to the railing with one hand and Milo with the other, her eyes glazed over with confusion.

With horror.

With disbelief.

Like she was running from her own ghosts.

"Rynna," I begged it again, desperate where I stood at the edge of my porch. Right where I'd confessed to her all my secrets last night.

"Please . . . just . . . don't," she pleaded. Her eyes flashed to Janel for a beat before she had a hand up to stop me. Frantic, she swallowed. "I have to . . . I have to get out of here."

"Rynna."

With a sharp, erratic shake of her head, she turned, fumbling as she shot forward.

Every part of me wanted to chase after her. Last thing I wanted was to be standing there, helpless, watching her flee across the road and disappear inside her house.

But I had an issue I needed to manage.

Hands clenched, I slowly turned to look at where Janel stood at the far end of the porch. She was twisting her fingers, throat wobbling, just as sure as her bottom lip. "I'm so sorry. I didn't mean to just show up—"

My head cocked, words nothing but fiery darts that cut her off. "You're sorry?" I took a menacing step forward. "Three fucking years, and you're sorry?"

"Rex . . . I . . . I can explain."

"I don't want to hear anything you have to say."

My heart dropped to the fucking floor when Frankie was suddenly there in the doorway, tiny fists rubbing at her sleepy eyes. "Daddy? Who's is here?"

"Baby," Janel suddenly said. She lunged forward, going right for her.

Anger.

Disgust.

Disbelief.

They roiled.

I reached out and gripped her by the upper arm, probably harder than I should have. "Don't you dare."

She looked at me as if she couldn't believe I would stop her. As if she had any right. I pushed her behind me and dropped to my knees in front of my daughter. Almost frantic, I brushed back that unruly disaster of hair from her face while I felt everything inside me bust apart. "Need you to do Daddy a big, huge favor."

She grinned, and I fucking cringed when she glanced over my shoulder.

And I fucking saw it.

The recognition. The goddamned pictures I used to show her, thinking her seeing her mother's face might comfort her. Back when I promised my daughter that her mother would be coming back. That everything would be all right. Knowing someday Janel would come to her senses and return.

When I'd remained devoted.

I'd prayed for it.

Begged for it.

Motherfucking loyalty.

"Is that's my mommy?" She seemed confused by it, not exactly excited.

Wary.

That panic lit in an all-out frenzy.

"Yes, baby. Yes. I'm your mommy."

Every muscle in my body seized, and I wanted to lash out. Shout at Janel. Tell her to go right back to hell where she'd come from.

I shifted so Frankie could only look at me, and I begged her with my eyes. "Daddy needs you to do me that favor, Sweet Pea."

She nodded at me. Like she'd just caught on to my turmoil.

I squeezed her by the hips. "Need you to go into your room and shut your door. Don't come out until I come get you, okay? Can you do that for me?"

She nodded with all that trust. "Course, I can."

"Good girl," I told her, hoping my words didn't shake.

I didn't rise until she turned the corner at the end of the hall, only pausing to peer back at us once, curiosity and a shot of fear in the wells of her brown eyes.

Like she could feel mine.

Years of suppressed, barely checked hate.

It was all there in the clench of my fists when I finally pushed to my feet. My teeth ground so hard I was sure they were grating to dust. And Janel? She just stood there with a pleading expression on her face. A face I'd once thought pretty.

Gorgeous even.

This woman, who I'd allowed to twist me up and tie me, left me hanging out to dry.

Tears sprang to her eyes and raced down her face. "She's so big." Her words hitched.

"It's been three years. What did you think?" Mine were nothing but spite.

Her head shook, and she looked away, dropping her gaze. "I don't know. It feels like it's been forever and like it was only yesterday."

A huff scraped my throat. "Yesterday? She was barely walking when you left. She starts school next year. You don't get to come here and pretend like you didn't miss anything when you missed *everything*."

My head shook. Harsh. A jolt to clear the chaos. The disorder that tumbled and shook.

I angled back on her, bitterness bleeding out. "What do you want?" This woman could come in and rip apart our unstable world.

Standing there, wearing all that bullshit innocence written in her features. Holding all the power in the palm of her seedy hand.

"You're my husband."

She might as well have punched me in the face. Kicked me in the gut. Her statement blew through me like a grenade. "Don't fucking call me that." It dropped out in a low, slow threat.

"It's the truth."

Hostility shook my head. "You haven't belonged to me in a long time."

"I never stopped belonging to you. You didn't sign the papers, remember? That was your choice. A choice I let go."

Fuck.

Mother. Fuck.

"Doesn't mean anything," I grated.

She took a pleading step forward. "It means everything. I—"

Hopeless, she looked to the house that was supposed to be our home. The one she'd set afire. Burned it straight into the ground, leaving that bullshit note about how it was all my fault before she just fucking took off and left us behind.

Right then, I might as well have been back there. A prisoner to that day. Missy lying dead at my feet and my wife driving away.

Leaving me.

My attention moved across the street, to the impenetrable silence that hovered like stone around Rynna's house.

Don't leave me.

A sob erupted in the air, stealing my focus, my purpose. I jerked my head back to Janel, who pressed her hands over her heart. Like she was trying to keep it inside. "You're with her? With Rynna?"

"How do you know her?" I demanded.

Apparently, last night I'd ripped off the lid to Pandora's box. Every demon in my past flying out. Guess it only seemed fitting one stood on my front porch. Seeking a way in when I'd been so diligent at keeping everything out.

Rynna.

Fucking Rynna.

Little Thief.

The second she'd stepped into my life, she'd turned everything upside down.

A frown crossed Janel's brow, hesitation thick, before she quietly spoke, "I didn't know her well, but I knew her well enough to know she's Corinne Dayne's granddaughter. We didn't run in the same circle, though. It just . . . caught me off guard that she's here. I'm . . . I know I don't have any right to be jealous, but I can't help it. I thought when I came back we . . ." She trailed off, her intentions hanging in the air like a thick shroud of dread.

"Well, you thought wrong. You left us. You can't come back and expect anything to be waiting for you."

"You know I couldn't stay any longer. I was dying inside. You—"

"Then what are you doing here?" My biting words cut her off.

"I . . . I got help. A counselor who helped me see we just needed to work through our troubles. Courage to fight for it. For my family."

Fight for us?

Mocking laughter rocked from my lungs. "You're here to fight for us? To win me back?"

"Yes." She said it so simply. So easily. Like I should just let go of three years of hurt. Like I should just let go of Rynna.

"It's a little late for that."

"It's never too late." She reached out. Both hands circled around my wrist. "At least I need to see Frankie Leigh. I can't go on without her, Rex. I have never been the same since I walked away from my child. Never have known a torture like the one I've been livin'. Please, I need to try to make it up to her. She needs to know her momma."

Agony crawled over my body.

A devouring beast.

Fangs sinking all the way to bone.

How long did I pray for that? Beg and plead and cry out to the emptiness of the night? Nothing but a beggar on his knees, willing to give up anything for his daughter's life to be whole. Fulfilled. For her to never feel an ounce of the betrayal that I'd worn around like a second skin.

And there was her mom. Without my permission, my gaze moved back to the open door. To my kid. I'd always done what was best for her. Problem was, right then I had no clue what that

269

was. What was right.

"Not sure I can give you that kind of chance, Janel."

"She's my daughter."

"Who you abandoned," I bit out, voice muted so Frankie couldn't hear.

A sob tore from her. A loud, guttural moan. "I'm so sorry," she whimpered. "So sorry. I'll do anything to make it up to her. Anything. Please give me a chance. I just need to see my daughter."

thirty-three

Rynna

I stumbled into my house, drawing in big, sucking breaths. Trying to keep it together when I already knew that was impossible.

Janel.

Janel.

Rex.

Frankie.

Oh God.

Agony sliced through my being, cutting me in two. Clutching Milo to my chest, I tipped my head back toward the ceiling. Tears slicked down my face and dripped into my hair.

Why?

Why did life have to be so cruel? Fate twisted. Warped and perverted.

I set Milo on his feet and frantically dug in my bag to find my phone. Uncontrollably, my hands shook when I tried to find Macy's contact. Finally, I managed to push send. It rang twice before her groggy voice came onto the line. "Hello?"

It was three hours earlier there. No doubt, I'd pulled her from sleep. But I needed her. Had no one else to turn to. Sorrow wrenched from me on panted, shattered cries. No words but the tumble of frenzied, horrified confusion that gripped my mind.

"Ryn . . . is that you?" I could picture her shaking herself out of the haze of sleep. Panic surged into her voice. "Ryn, what's wrong? Tell me what happened."

"She's here." It was a whimper.

"Who?" she demanded before she caught on. Silence eclipsed the flood of worry that had been rolling from her mouth. "Shit," she muttered. "Where'd you run into her?"

"She's . . ." I struggled to find the explanation, choking over the revulsion at even having to say it. "She's Frankie's mom."

A moan slipped from my tongue.

"Oh God, Rynna . . . sweetheart . . . shit. I'm so sorry."

"I can't believe it," I whispered.

Rex. The man I'd lost myself to.

She'd belonged to him. I couldn't stomach it. The picture of her touching him. Of him touching her.

Sickness spun.

Spun and spun and spun.

Riding an agitator that fully wrung me out.

"Does he know?"

Grief constricted my chest. "No." It was a wheeze. "I finally told him last night what'd happened. But he has no idea it was her."

That was when I hadn't thought it would matter. When the name and face meant absolutely nothing because the only thing remaining had been the scars.

Those scars had been ripped wide open.

"What are you going to do?"

"I don't know. She's . . . she's over there now, and I don't have a fucking clue what I'm supposed to do. She's her mother."

It dropped from me like a stone.

Sorrow.

Dejection.

Regret.

Janel was Frankie Leigh's mother. That was a fact I couldn't change. One I couldn't stand in the way of, no matter how much I loved that little girl.

"Ryn, I'm so sorry. Tell me what to do. How can I make this better?"

"I don't think there's anything you can do."

"I can't stand the idea of you clear across the country hurting and no one there to feed you gallons of ice cream."

I choked out a soggy laugh. "I wish you were here, too."

"If you need me, you know I'm on the first plane. You say the word, and I'm there."

"I know, thank you."

"Just . . . hold tight, Ryn. He's probably as shocked as you are. See what comes of it. What he has to say."

I nodded. It was the only rational thing I could do.

Wait.

And I thought the waiting just might kill me.

Three hours later, I was at the diner. It turned out I couldn't wait. Couldn't sit idle while Janel was directly across the street with Rex and Frankie. Not when I couldn't see through the walls or hear what they were saying.

Torture. I couldn't find another word to describe the turmoil that seethed within. Pulling and ripping and grinding. It felt as if I were being torn apart, rended by white-hot agony.

So, I went to the one place I would find solace. I stood holding a sledgehammer in my hands, blinking into the dimness of the old restaurant as if I had any clue what to do with it.

As if I could make a difference.

A thick coat of dust had settled on the floor, and plastic sheets covered the booths that had been moved against one wall, waiting for the contractor who'd been hired to reupholster them. The old tabletops ripped out, the empty spaces waiting for new tables to be delivered.

It was amazing what Rex's men had already accomplished.

It seemed almost a dream now. The excitement and hope I'd

felt the last time I'd been in this very spot just a couple of days ago, envisioning its completion. The day I would finally be able to turn on the neon open sign I'd ordered. When customers would begin to pile in, eager for a taste of my grandmother's legacy that would become my own.

It shivered around me, a haunting reminder that these walls still held their secrets. My past an echo that had hit its end and came bounding right back.

I turned toward the old counter, hands fisting around the wooden handle. At least it gave me something to hold on to.

I froze when awareness struck me from behind.

The door slowly creaked open. It was instant, the way the air thickened and the tension pulsed.

It slammed the walls. Amplifying. Lifting. Increasing. Pulling and pulling and pulling.

Gravity.

I swore I could feel his wary footsteps tremor across the floor and climb my legs. That connection streaking free. Though this time in a frenzy.

Slowly, I released the sledgehammer to the ground, turned around. The man had the power to reach right out and pluck the breath from me. My lungs heaved at the sight of him, and I whispered, "Rex."

"Rynna." He shifted on his feet, an agitated hand jerking at the longer pieces of his hair. He looked at the floor as if it might hold an answer, his tone low, laden with guilt. "God, Rynna . . . never in a million years would I have expected what we woke up to this morning. I'm so fucking sorry."

Lightheadedness spun, and I gulped for air, trying to focus. To see straight. To focus on what was most important. "Where's Frankie?"

He swallowed when he met my eye. "Took her to my mom's. Didn't want her in the middle of this. Not when I don't have the first clue what the fuck I'm supposed to do."

"What does she want?" The question broke in desperation. *What do you want?*

I wanted to ask it, but I was terrified. Terrified of the answer.

Terrified of how this man made me feel. How he'd consumed me entirely. Everything that was mine, his.

My body.

My heart.

My mind.

Mouth trembling, he stared at me, expression distant, the man shaken from his own axis. "Frankie. Me. Fuck, I don't know."

A strangled sob sprang from the depths of me, and I clutched my stomach. "And what do you want?"

In a second flat, Rex rushed me. Those big hands were on my face, forcing me to look at him. "I want you. God, Rynna, I want you."

The relief was almost as fierce as the pain. As fierce as the stark grief that passed through his eyes. Eyes that swam with the deepest guilt. "Need to tell you something, Rynna."

I blinked at him. Strung up. My world hinging on what he might say.

He squeezed his eyes closed, his expression pinching in regret. "I . . ."

"What?" I begged.

Shaking his head, he slightly angled it to the side and pulled me closer, as if he were pleading with me to understand. "She's still my wife, Rynna."

My heart froze.

Froze in horror. In disbelief.

"What?" I begged again, but this time because I didn't want the answer he'd given. I wanted him to tell me I'd misunderstood. That he didn't mean what I'd heard.

I struggled to break out of his hold, and he held me tighter. "I never signed the papers, Rynna. I'm so sorry. I should have told you. God, I should have told you."

Another rush of dizziness swept through me. This time it was so intense, it nearly knocked me from my feet. "You're . . . still . . . married to her?" The last came off as an accusation.

After everything we'd shared? After everything I'd told him and he'd told me? And he'd failed to mention this?

My mind flashed through a barrage of memories. The things

Rex had eluded to. The way he'd first reacted when we'd met. The fact he'd never been with another woman after Janel left. Not until me. He'd kept warning me and warning me he didn't have anything to give.

Horror flooded the words. "You were waiting for her. The whole time, you've been *waiting* for her to come back."

Tears streaked free, and I struggled to break out of his hold. "We never even had a chance, did we?" It barely made it out over the sobs that clogged my throat. The grief that clenched my chest, making it hard to breathe. "You were always waiting for her."

Now she was here.

Janel.

Oh God.

I pressed my hand over my mouth, trying to keep it all in. To keep from spewing the hatred that had blazed back to life the moment I'd seen her standing in his door. Tell him who she really was. What she'd done.

But she was Frankie's mother. How could I do that? I couldn't be that person. One who maligned Janel's name because she had what I wanted. Who was I to know if she'd changed? Like I'd told Rex, it'd been more than ten years.

My spirit thrashed, rejecting that notion, convinced I knew exactly who she was. But was that because of my jealousy? Was it because she was Frankie's mother? Because she was Rex's wife?

Wife.

Nausea crawled through my senses, a sickening poison injected straight into my veins.

Rex fumbled to get his hands back on my face, eyes so intense, his presence powering straight through my body. It only ruined me all the more. "No, Rynna. No. Fuck. Of course, we have a chance. You and me? We're supposed to be." His tone was despairing.

I blinked at him, trying to make sense of the situation. To sift through every horrible emotion. My anger. My hurt. The love that shined far too bright. Trying to look inside myself and find what was right.

But the betrayal glared, blinding. Both Janel's and Rex's. How could I make sense of the two? "You lied to me."

"No, Rynna. I was going to tell you. I promise, I was going to tell you."

"You had plenty of time to tell me last night. You're married, Rex. *Married*, because you chose to be. Because you were waiting for her to come back to you. Oh God." A whimper burst from between my lips.

"I swear, Rynna, swear to you."

Frantically, my head shook. "You need to figure out what you want from your life, Rex, because I can't be with you. Not when you're with her."

"No," Rex grated, shaking his head. "There's no chance of me bein' with her, Rynna. Not when it's you I want."

"I can't—" He cut me off with a kiss. A kiss so desperate I nearly got lost in it. I wanted to let go. Let him take me and love me and capture me. Pretend it was real. Pretend this man wasn't married and his wife wasn't waiting for him back at his house.

Hands still on my face, he pulled back. "Please."

I gripped him around both wrists, staring at him through bleary eyes. Hot tears streaked down my face and into the webs of his fingers.

This beautiful, intricate man who wasn't mine.

Misery.

Agony.

So much hurt.

It whirled around us. A tornado that screamed.

"I can't keep you when you never really belonged to me."

A moan pulled from his throat, and he gripped me. His voice was a rasp. "Don't do this, Rynna. You promised me you wouldn't run. That you wouldn't leave. *You promised.*"

Janel's face taunted me. The idea of her touching him. Of him touching her.

"I can't," I whispered my heartbreak against the top of his head.

He made a choking sound, as if I were causing him physical pain, before he turned and walked away. He pulled open the door, paused to look back at me, grief scored across every line in his face. "You promised you'd stay."

My head shook. "And I trusted you not to lie to me."

His throat bobbed as if he were swallowing the reality down.

He was married, and he'd never thought it important enough to tell me.

What did that make us?

Then he turned and was gone.

Rex

I had to pry myself from her, force myself to walk out her diner door when it was the last thing I wanted to do, fucking agony clamoring along behind me the whole way.

She'd promised me.

I stalked out into the blazing day, squeezing my eyes against the harsh reality, wondering if this was what it felt like to be eaten alive. If you could feel every part of yourself being devoured and destroyed, helpless to do anything but accept that you were getting ready to die a slow, painful death.

Bit by bit.

Because I was. I was fucking dying inside, all those pieces I'd offered into Rynna's hands shriveling into nothing.

It just left more room for the bitterness.

More room for the anger and hate and questions to flood and inundate.

In a daze, I climbed into the cab of my truck, slammed the door, and turned over the ignition. The engine roared. I pulled out onto the road.

Torn.

Wanting to turn right back around and beg Rynna, when instead I headed in the direction of my house.

I still couldn't believe my wife had shown up at my door.

Fuck.

My wife.

I scrubbed a hand over my face like it might give me some kind of clarity when nothing had ever looked hazier.

She was back and she wanted Frankie and me and I had no idea what to do with that.

Reject it was what I wanted to do. Send her fucking packing so Rynna and I could get right back to where we'd been last night. Tangled and bound. Perfectly tied.

Memories of the pledge I'd made pressed in, taunting me in the periphery of my mind, that vow I'd stood and taken.

Could I just disregard it? Shun it? The commitment I'd made? And why did I feel even an ounce of it when she'd been the one to up and disappear?

Motherfucking loyalty.

She was the one who'd broken the vows we'd made. Betrayed and abandoned and deceived. I mean, fuck, I had no clue where she'd even been for the last three years. What she'd been doing. Most sickening was realizing I really didn't care.

But it didn't matter anyway, did it? Rynna had made her decision. Pushed me aside just like I deserved for her to.

God. What had I been thinking would happen when I didn't tell her? Those words locked on my tongue like some dirty secret. Rynna had been right. I'd waited. I'd waited for years for Janel to come back. But the part Rynna was missing was she'd changed everything. Once she'd shown up, the hole Janel had left behind was no longer vacant. Not when Rynna had inhabited every inch.

Now that space was a pit again—deeper, darker, suffocating. Nothing but a hollow chasm, sucking me down where I'd be forever falling in an endless black hole.

I made a left onto my street. I drove passed the rows of happy houses shaded by towering trees, the perfect family neighborhood.

Slowing, I eased into my drive, flinching at the sight of the same beat-up car Janel had taken off in three years before still sitting there. Grim and foreboding beneath the cheerful rays of summer light.

Everything that should have been right was nothing but a contradiction.

Because Janel returning was a prayer I wished would have remained unanswered.

Dropping my forehead to the steering wheel, I exhaled a heavy breath before I forced myself to man up and climb out. That didn't mean I didn't hate every step that brought me closer, my footfalls slackened with dread.

I slid the key in the lock and cracked open the door. There wasn't a whole lot left but resignation when I stepped inside.

Janel was in the kitchen, and she whirled around, wringing her hands together and looking at me expectantly.

I tossed my keys to the small table by the door. "You can stay," I told her, voice hard.

She exhaled a relieved breath and started for me. Repulsed, I gave a harsh shake of my head and took a step back. She stumbled to a quick stop. Was she actually so clueless she didn't get why I'd push her away? Did she not grasp what she'd done?

"You can sleep in my room, and I'll sleep on the couch." Might as well have spit the words at her. But I couldn't help it. That anger was slipping and sliding, sinking in deeper, the freedom I'd found in Rynna binding me in chains.

Disappointment flashed across her face, and she went back to twisting her fingers. I kept on, giving her what I could, feeling like I didn't have another choice. "I don't want you alone with Frankie."

"But—"

"You don't get a say in this, Janel. You left, and if you want to see Frankie, then it's gonna be on my terms. Or else you can walk right back out that door." I pointed at it, hoping she'd take it as an invitation.

She gulped, nodding for me to continue. "Okay. I told you I'd do anything."

"She's going to be confused, so you need to be respectful of that. Let her get used to you. And you're going to have to prove to me that you actually want to be here. That you've changed before I can trust you with her."

Her blue eyes widened in sincerity, her blonde ponytail swishing as she took a surging step forward. "I will. I'll do whatever it takes. Maybe . . . maybe I can go to work for you in the office. Do something with my hands. Show you I'm responsible. I've changed, Rex. I've changed."

Mine widened in disbelief. "I think you're getting ahead of yourself, don't you?"

"I just want to make things right. What . . . what about us?"

"There's no us, Janel."

She stumbled over a whimper. "Because of Rynna?"

Pain pierced me, a straight shot right through the center of my heart. I tried to hide it, but I knew Janel saw it. "It's none of your business what I've got going on with Rynna."

"You're my husband, Rex."

I stalked passed her and into the kitchen. I grabbed a beer from the refrigerator, doing everything I could to keep myself in check. "Who you left."

"And now I'm back. I came back to you because I missed you so much. Every single day," she begged.

I cringed. Didn't want to hear it. It didn't matter what she had to say. "It's too late."

Her voice was a plea behind me. "It's never too late."

thirty-five

Rynna

I'd thought I'd timed it right. I'd mastered peeking out the window to make sure the coast was clear before I raced from my door to my car. Making sure our paths didn't cross.

But there they were, Rex stepping outside and turning around to lock his door, Frankie bounding down the steps, calling my name. "Rynna, Rynna! What's you doing? We's goin' to the lake. You wants to come?"

Janel was between them, at the top of the steps. Arms crossed over her chest. A sneer on her face when she met my eyes.

I gulped around the agony. Fumbling, I tried to hurry and unlock my SUV. I had to get away. Escape. Instead, my hands were shaking so badly I dropped my keys. They clattered to the ground. The only thing I managed was to draw more attention to myself.

I snatched the key ring up, trying to steady myself, my heart and my hands and my voice. "I don't think that's a good idea, Frankie."

"Ah, man. But I misses you."

I miss you. I miss you. I miss you.

The world spun around me. A circuit of torment. I inhaled, blinked, my words barely a whisper. "I miss you, too."

So much.

"Does Milo wants to come and play?"

Behind Janel, Rex slowly turned around. His entire being flinched when he saw me, and instantly, he cast his eyes to the floorboards of his porch. As if I'd broken him every bit as much as he'd broken me.

The hate in Janel's expression shifted, and she looked up at him, beaming, before she set her hand on Frankie's shoulder. "Come on, sweetheart. We'd better go before it gets too late."

I floundered to get into the driver's seat before slamming the door shut. I choked back tears as I pulled out of my drive, refusing to let her see me fall apart, my teeth clenched as I took the three quick turns to get out onto the main road.

I lost it just down the street, my eyes blurring over. I pulled into a convenience store parking lot, whipped into a parking spot, gripped the steering wheel in both hands. Head dropped. Gasping.

He lied to me.

Maybe this was the way it was supposed to end, anyway.

Maybe Janel had changed. What if she was exactly what they needed? The one who would make them whole again? Who would chase away the darkness that lingered in the depths of Rex's eyes?

Every part of me rejected it. The fact she was Rex's wife. That he belonged to her. Not when my heart screamed he was mine.

I jerked when the diner door swung open. But I wasn't struck with the presence I'd been aching for over the last five days. Instead, I was slammed with a stark, radiating anger.

I'd been sweeping up some of the mess left behind by the resanding of the long countertop, again looking for something to keep my idle hands busy.

Knowing if I kept still for too long I might go insane.

My mouth dropped open when a woman stormed into my restaurant. All bristling fire and animosity.

She wore jeans, boots, and a flowy, whimsical blouse. Her blonde hair had been darkened underneath and curled into long waves, the woman beautiful in an earthy, natural way, aged by the faint traces of smile wrinkles at the edges of her mouth.

But her eyes.

Her eyes were warm and sincere, even though they were raging mad.

Sage.

My heart clutched.

This was Rex's mother.

She crossed her arms over her chest and looked me up and down. "Well, you must be Rynna Dayne."

I set the broom and pan aside. I tried to straighten myself out, to keep myself from falling apart, my voice shaking when I finally spoke. "I am. You must be Jenny Gunner."

Still, her name tripped on my tongue.

Standing there, she seemed to war with something, and she blew out a strained breath from her nose and lifted her chin when she came to whatever conclusion she'd been looking for. Some of that anger slipped away. "I wish we were meetin' under different circumstances," she said. "Honestly, I came over here thinking I was gonna knock a little sense into you for breaking my boy's heart, but from where I'm standing, looks to me like you're suffering from that breaking, too."

I choked out a laugh. Wow. She was . . . something. Confident and brazen and sweet. Country to the bone. So much like the women I'd been surrounded with all my years growing up.

I forced myself to smile, though it came out weak. "Yeah . . . I think I'm dealing with a bit of a heart breaking."

A bit.

My stomach tumbled with the shards of jagged, broken glass that coated my insides, gouging into my flesh. Deeper and deeper with each breath.

It was a constant, excruciating pain.

She cocked her head. "So, what's the problem then?"

That choked laugh turned into a cry. "What's the problem?" My head shook, and I blinked at her through the motes that floated through the haze of light streaming in through the windows. "Rex is married. His wife is at his house right now. What kind of person would I be if I stood in the way of that?"

I went back to the same justification I'd been trying to feed myself, the rationale that they might be better with Janel. All week, I'd been trying to persuade myself maybe it was meant to be. That it was best if I walked away.

But I was beginning to wonder if I wasn't trying to cover the hurt, the fear of finding her there, and what that would mean for Rex and me. If I could ever rid her face from my mind if I ever allowed him to touch me again. Or maybe I was just afraid of facing that same kind of rejection that had chased me away in the first place.

Jenny Gunner didn't even hesitate. "Just the fact you'd even consider it proves to me that you are the exact kind of person he deserves."

For a beat, I turned away, gathering myself, before I turned back to her. "She's Frankie's mother, Jenny. I—"

"You love them." It wasn't a question. It was a solution.

My hands pressed against my chest. "So much. Which is why I'm willing to let them go."

She turned away from me and began to wander around my restaurant, her fingers tracing across the new tables that had been installed this week. Her voice dropped into a slow musing, "You know, I raised my son to be good. To respect whoever crossed his path. To honor his promises. Maybe it was because his father up and left me the second I told him Rex was on his way, but I drilled that loyalty into him so deep. And I won't ever regret that. The man he became."

She turned to gaze at me from over her shoulder. "He's a good, good man. Honorable and noble. And when he loves, he loves with all he's got. And that love has come back to bite him in the ass time and time again."

She looked toward the ceiling. She inhaled deeply and a tremor slid down her spine. "When Sydney disappeared, I was terrified I wouldn't ever see my son again. Physically, sure, he was there. But the rest of him? His amazing spirit? His smile so wide and his belief so big? It was gone. And then there was Frankie . . . Frankie Leigh. She rekindled a part of him that'd gone dim. Lit him up. He'd sacrifice anything for her."

She glanced back at me. "And Janel? She's always been a sacrifice. He chose to love her because he should. And I won't diminish that. Say it was wrong. Not when my son was tryin' to do what was right. But the bad seed in that equation was Janel. She's always been nothing but a leech." She looked around the restaurant, shaking her head. "Honestly, can't believe your grandma tolerated her so long."

Strangled confusion fell from my tongue. "What did you say?"

She turned back to me. "Your grandmother . . ."

My brow pinched. "I know you said my grandmother . . . but Janel . . . she worked here? When she was with Rex?"

Her eyes narrowed in confusion. "Don't really know a time she lived in this town when she didn't work for your grandma. From what I know, she started out when she was in high school."

Oh God.

My arm went around my belly. I had no idea why I'd assumed Janel no longer worked at Pepper's. That once I left, my grandmother would have let her go.

Regret churned.

Once I'd gotten to California and called Gramma to let her know where I was, I'd told her I didn't want to hear a thing about what was happening in Gingham Lakes or its people. I'd told her the only person I cared about was her.

I'd wanted to shun it and hide it and pretend the rest never existed.

Of course, life here had just gone on.

Gramma had no idea what Janel had done to me. There'd been no reason for her to cut her loose.

"What's wrong?" Jenny asked, taking a cautious step my direction.

"I . . . I didn't know she was still working for my gramma. That she was here. It feels . . . wrong."

So wrong.

So off.

Awareness pressed in. A thread tickling my consciousness, vying to make itself known.

"You knew her?" Jenny asked.

I barely nodded. "I lived with my gramma growing up."

Jenny huffed. "Everything about Janel is wrong, Rynna. Make no mistake about that."

She approached me, touched my cheek. Her expression turned pleading. "My son deserves to be happy. And my grandbaby? She deserves to be safe. Both of them deserve to be loved. The right way. And I know I don't know you all that well, but I've always considered myself a good judge of character, and I'm betting you deserve it, too."

I felt jarred when she suddenly stepped back and began to walk away. Just as she pulled the door open, she looked back at me. "I don't trust her, Rynna. And you and my boy . . . your hearts are in the right places. But any sacrifice you and Rex are trying to make are only opening the door for her to hurt them all over again."

My head was still spinning when I left the diner. Streetlamps shined down, twilight the deepest blue where it took to the sky, the Alabama air cooled by the shallow gusts of wind that blew through the quieted corridor, the shops lining the street shut down for the night.

I'd spent the entire day inside.

Working and cleaning and trying to process what Jenny Gunner had been trying to say. It'd felt like a warning. I'd pondered it until the windows had dimmed and darkness had begun to take hold.

I stumbled toward my Jeep parked at the street, my mind five miles away on that little house across from mine. I jerked back when I saw the man at Pepper's windows, hands cupping around his eyes as if he were trying to get a better view inside through the tinted windows.

Slowly, he peeled himself back, ambled my direction.

Aaron.

Why was he looking in my restaurant?

Terror bottled in my throat, and I took a step back when he took one toward me.

He smirked, every slimy inch of his arrogant face lit in the lamps. This time, the asshole clearly knew who I was. "Well, Rynna Dayne. Thought you looked familiar before. Just couldn't place you. You look good. Real good."

He grabbed me by the wrist.

Something took me over. The fear gone, replaced by something fierce. I wrenched out of his hold. Disgusted. Anger burst free. "You didn't recognize me? Why's that? Because I wasn't naked, letting you take advantage of me? Because I wasn't following you around like a fool? Because I lost a few pounds? Which is it?"

He let loose a low, amused whistle. "Ah, I see the way you look isn't the only thing that's changed. Feisty. I like that."

He went to touch my hand, and I jerked it back. "Don't touch me. Don't look at me. Don't come around me. In fact, stay off this street. Don't want to see you in front of this diner ever again."

I ducked around him, trying to keep it together, pretending as if I weren't shaking all over the place. I was seconds away from coming unglued. Unhinged.

A chuckle rumbled from his mouth, and he looked back at me, shaking his head. "Always in Janel's way, aren't you? Brave girl. Just wonder who she's going to hurt most this time."

I whipped around. "What did you say?"

He just smirked then he turned and sauntered down the street.

By the time I made it home, I was trembling so hard I could

barely see. I killed the engine and sat in the darkness of the cab. I clutched the steering wheel, sucking in breaths.

What was I supposed to do?

What did any of this mean?

I forced myself out into the night. Wind gusted and worry climbed through every inch of my body. Despite all my efforts, my attention tuned to his house. It was lit, all the windows shining with a soft yellow glow.

Janel's car was in the driveway, but Rex's truck was gone.

At least there was some comfort in knowing they weren't together. It was Friday night, so Rex would be at the bar and Frankie would be spending the night with her grandma, who so obviously had Frankie's best interest at heart.

I forced myself up the steps, across the porch, and fumbled to get the key into the lock. The door swung open.

Dread echoed back from the silence.

God. I was losing it. I had to be.

But everything felt . . . off.

I swore a disorder tumbled through the air, a disturbance ricocheting from my grandmother's walls that hadn't been there when I'd left this morning.

I flicked on the light. Eyes jumping around. Calculating as I took everything in.

Nothing seemed out of place. But my gut? It warned me someone had been there.

Fear slithered beneath the surface of my skin, and I stepped all the way inside and locked the door. I went into the kitchen and flicked on the light.

Empty.

I was alone. Somehow, that didn't make me feel any better. I warmed up some leftover pot pie in the microwave and sat down at the table by the window. It was like sand in my mouth, but I forced it down since I hadn't eaten in days.

Forty minutes later, a loud engine rumbled down the street. Approaching. Coming closer.

A frenzy climbed to the air.

Awareness.

Confusion.

Dread.

Headlights sliced through the darkness before Rex's big truck turned into his driveway, way earlier than I'd have expected him to.

That frenzy roiled.

The breath got locked in my lungs when he finally stepped out, and I couldn't look away as I watched him, his head drooped between his shoulders as he ascended the porch steps and made his way inside.

My eyes squeezed closed, and I pressed my hand over my heart.

God. What was I supposed to do?

thirty-six

Rex

I sat at the bar, tossing back beer after beer. Olive's was packed, same way as it was every Friday night. Hoards of people were out living it up, having the time of their lives, their laughter and voices and conversations ringing out.

It only amplified the hollowness.

The vacancy that wept.

That turmoil I'd stumbled into the day Rynna had pushed me away had only grown with each moment that passed. Janel's presence had gotten harder and harder to bear. Every single time I opened my goddamned door and she was there, it hit me anew.

It made my stomach clutch and my heart wrench, hating that I wasn't coming home to Rynna. Hating that Frankie still didn't know how to act around her mother, uneasy and unsure and a little bit scared. Hated that it made my skin crawl every goddamned time Janel took my baby girl in her arms.

I just fucking . . . hated.

Ollie appeared in front of me, popping the cap off a fresh beer. He slid it across the shiny bar. "Don't know whether to keep feeding you these or cut you off."

I lifted it to my lips and took a long pull before I tipped the neck his direction. "I'm pretty sure the answer to that is to keep them coming. You know what they say, it's all about who you know."

Chuckling beneath his breath, he planted his hands on the bar and stretched his tattooed arms out between us, dropping his voice when he leaned in close. "Yeah, well that might be the case, but that also means I know you. And I know you're fucking miserable, man. This isn't healthy."

I took another sip. "Not much to be done about that now, is there?"

Ollie's face screwed up in concern. "Not sure wasting away at my bar is the solution."

"Just . . . can't go back there, Ollie."

He sighed and wiped a palm over his mouth before he turned his attention back on me. "So, you let your ex-wife back in your house, and now you can't go back to it? You not seeing an issue with that?"

Oh, I was seeing plenty of issues.

Harsh laughter rolled from my tongue. "That's the problem, Ollie. Janel's not my ex. She's still my fucking wife."

A frown pinched between his brows. "Only thing claiming it is a piece of paper. And you know what that piece of paper says? It says the two of you would cherish each other, love each other, respect each other for all of your lives. It says the two of you would stay true through thick and thin. Through the good and the bad. I was there, remember? You really think Janel has been faithful to you since she left? You think her running off on you was fueled by her respect?" Quiet outrage shook Ollie's head. "Pretty sure any contract you two had is expired."

I jumped when a hand clamped down on my shoulder. My head jerked that way. Kale was there, grinning down, sliding into the stool next to me.

"Oh, do tell me I'm just in time for the conversation about the fucked-up situation our boy here has gotten himself into."

Just fucking great.

All I needed was the two of them razzing me. Teasing and

taunting me with what I already knew.

Ollie lifted his chin to Kale. "Yep. Right in time, brother. Pretty sure this asshole thinks he's going to sit here all night and actually manage to drink his cares away." Ollie turned back to me. "But believe me, when you wake up in the morning? They're going to be right there waiting for you."

"Comforting," I grunted, taking a quick swig.

Ollie shrugged. "Just telling you like it is."

"And what the hell do you expect me to do about it? Rynna already made her decision." Didn't mean to come off so pissy and irate, but I couldn't stop it. Because I was.

I was angry.

Hurt.

This raging storm billowing inside of me where I was lost, going down in the middle of the sea, getting swallowed by the waves. No goddamned chance of being saved.

"Yeah?" Kale challenged, angling to the side in his stool so he was fully facing me. "And why's that?"

"Because she knows it's not worth getting involved in my mess."

"Really?"

"Really."

"I call bullshit."

A huff of frustration bled out. "I went to her, Kale, I went to her and I begged her and she sent me away. I betrayed her, man, withholding that truth. She doesn't trust me, which I can't expect her to. I fucked it up, just like I always do."

"Yeah, because she got railroaded by the truth that you're still married. You think that whole thing wouldn't have gone down differently if she would have been prepared? If you would have already been taking the steps to end that bullshit marriage that never should have existed in the first place?"

"Or maybe she should shut me down. I made a vow, and for once in my life, I need to stick to it."

"Once in your life?" he bit out like he couldn't believe his ears.

"Yeah. You think I didn't make the same damned promises

to Sydney—"

I slammed my mouth closed, a fence going down in front of the words that wanted to keep rolling out.

Ollie looked like I'd punched him. "What does Sydney have to do with any of this?"

Fuck. Fuck. Fuck.

I'd slipped.

Just like I'd been saying all along, ever since Rynna had come into my life, things had spun out of control. In the best of ways. In the worst of ways. I had just ripped open the locks to a past I didn't want to unleash. A goddamned train wreck, no consideration to who was going to get in the mix of it.

Last thing I wanted was to hurt Ollie more than I already had. He didn't need this. Fuck, he didn't need any of this. Never had deserved it.

"What did you say?" Ollie's voice was muted and strained.

I hopped up, hands gripping my hair, trying to reel it all in. Tossed out a few more lies. Not like they made any difference anyway. "Nothing . . . just should have stopped her that night."

I drained my beer and slammed it down on the bar. "Gonna get out of here."

Throwing a handful of twenties down, I spun on my heels and wound back through the crowds, shouldering through the bodies packed tight, their laughter and joy grating in my ear. A fucking grinding pad against my consciousness.

Swore I was close to a panic attack by the time I stumbled out into the night. I sucked down the cool breeze, lifting my head to the sky, wishing on any goddamned star that might appear.

I cringed when the door swung open behind me.

Didn't need to turn around to know it was Kale.

"Just go back inside," I told him.

"You really think I'm going to turn my back on you? Now? When you need me most? You might have done a bang-up job of convincing yourself all these years that you didn't need anybody, but I think it's plenty clear by now you're wrong."

He took a step toward me. "Tell me what you want, Rex. Tell me. Who?"

Frankie and Rynna. Frankie and Rynna. Their names spun on a circuit. Nonstop.

I shook my head. "This is all so fucked up, Kale."

Slowly, I turned. "So fucked up, and I don't have a fucking clue what to do."

"Yes, you do. You know exactly what to do."

Air puffed through my nose, and I looked away, raking a hand through my hair. "And what's that?"

"You probably should start by forgiving yourself for Sydney. By finally letting go of what you've been carrying. Tell Ollie. He deserves to know."

Fear clamored through my nerves. "Sydney doesn't have anything to do with this." Could barely force out the defense.

Kale took a step forward, angling his head. "Really? You're really going to stand there and act like it doesn't have everything to do with every damned decision you've made since it happened? Are you really going to act like it didn't have everything to do with Janel in the first place?"

I blanched, attention swinging back to him, anger filling the words. "What? I'm not seeing how the two relate."

"You settled, man. You settled because you thought you didn't deserve to be happy. Because you thought you shouldn't ever get to love again. And then Frankie, that sweet baby girl, came into your life, and you didn't know how *not* to love anymore. So you gave in, opened your heart, loved. You loved, man, and then Janel destroyed it all over again. And now she's back and you're settling again."

He edged forward, voice dropping low. "You really think Rynna's not worth the fight?"

Anguish fisted my heart. "Of course, she's worth the fight."

"Then fight for her, Rex. Fight for her and fight for Frankie, and for goddamned once, fight for yourself."

Every muscle in my body recoiled. "What if I don't deserve it, man?" I swam against all the emotions that came rushing in. "I fuck everything up. Every single time. Lose the people I love. I thought this time . . . I thought this time with Rynna I'd finally outrun it. That I'd gotten a second chance. And the next thing I know, she's gone, too. She doesn't want me, man. She doesn't want me, and I don't know how to stop it. I don't know how to stop it."

The last left me on a wheeze, and I pressed the heels of my hands into my eyes.

Fuck.

I didn't know how to stop it.

I drove back home in a blaze of pain. I'd sat in my truck for two fucking hours, letting the booze run their course, before I forced myself to move. I pulled into my drive, trying not to look behind me to Rynna's place. Maybe if I blocked it all, I wouldn't feel it anymore.

Frankie and Rynna.

Maybe if I managed to go numb, it'd erase all the pain. Maybe then I could float right through the days.

I heaved out a couple of breaths before I forced myself from the cab. Footsteps dragging, I made my way up the porch and to the door.

I was in a daze when I walked through it, and I squinted when I stepped inside and let the door fall shut behind me. Like I was watching the scene through a dream. Everything distorted.

Janel was in the kitchen.

Cooking dinner.

Frankie and Rynna.

The smell of pork chops hung heavy in the air. But it felt all off. A knot formed in my throat, and I tried to swallow.

Her blonde hair swished around her shoulders when she turned to look at me, taken by surprise. She quickly tucked her phone in her back pocket, hands shaking. "Oh, you're here early."

She dipped into the fridge and grabbed a beer. "Here. You look like you could use this."

She was all care and concern when she sauntered over to me, twisting the cap from the beer, leading me to the couch.

"Did you have a bad day?" she asked, sinking to her knees on the floor, staring up at me.

I choked out a laugh. A bad day. She had no clue what her returning had done to me. Had done to Rynna. The toll it was taking on Frankie.

And I still had no idea if this was right, letting her into our lives, giving her a chance to be a mother.

She'd gone to dance with Frankie twice, done everything I'd let her, taking her to the park, playing with her every chance she got, even though every time they were in the same room, I wanted to rip my hair out.

But she was trying.

Shouldn't I?

"You might say that," I told her.

She pressed both her hands on my knees and leaned up, her voice going quiet when she reached for the fly of my jeans. "Then let me take the bad away. Let me take care of you. Please, Rex, let me take care of you."

I groaned, head rocking back on the top of the sofa, breath a hiss on my tongue.

Frankie and Rynna.

thirty-seven

Rynna

I paced my kitchen.

I felt as if I were stuck in limbo.

A path set out ahead of me that I didn't yet know how to take. Stuck in a purgatory of worry and jealousy and loss. A shimmery anger that lit up at the edges where it kept me enclosed.

Helpless.

And helpless was the last thing I wanted to be.

Milo was asleep on his bed in the corner, and I shuffled around in my kitchen, trying to distract myself from it. Maybe baking would give me a little clarity. Insight to the right decision. A calm in the midst of the worst kind of disturbance that still rattled my walls.

I tried to reject the shiver of unease that slipped down my spine, still unable to shake the idea that someone had been in my house when I was away.

Wondering if it was just me being foolish—jealous and petty and needy—or if the foolish part was me ignoring it.

Gramma had told me to always, always trust my gut.

But my guts were tied in one of those impossible knots. The kind where you couldn't tell what was what, where one loop started and another ended.

"Gramma . . . I wish you were here. You would know what to do," I murmured under my breath, pulling the ingredients for an apple pie from the pantry and refrigerator. Night pressed in at the window, the globe light on the ceiling a hazy hue of yellow that lit the dated kitchen.

I had just set everything on the counter when I stilled.

A prickle of awareness flashed up the nape of my neck. Though this was an entirely different kind of fear.

This was hope and excitement and the worst kind of confusion. Sucking in a breath, I took a step backward and craned my head out the arch and into the living room.

Listening.

Silence echoed back. But that silence was thick. Weighted. Heavy.

Like a tether was tied around my waist and anchored in my belly.

Drawing me closer.

I edged across the room, my footsteps subdued, my breaths shallow when I inched toward the door.

One solid knock rattled against it.

It rang out like a call.

A beckoning.

A plea.

My hand was trembling when I reached for the lock. Maybe it made me a fool, but I twisted it, anyway. The scrape of metal pierced the bottled quiet. For a flash, I squeezed my eyes closed before I turned the knob and pulled open the door.

He was there.

Standing on my deck.

A scatter of stars stretched across the heavens above, and gusts of wind whipped up the long pieces of his hair, his expression pained where his face was cast in a haze of milky moonlight.

A perfect picture of hope and despair.

It was instant, the way tears streaked free from my eyes.

"Rex."

His hands were balled into fists, jaw clenched, eyes hard.

Dominant and dangerous and somehow chained by all his doubt.

Energy lashed. Whipping and inciting.

Compelling.

And God, I wanted to fight. Fight with him for lying to me. Fight for him because I wanted him so badly. Fight for what was right. The problem was, I wasn't certain of exactly what that was.

Rex's nostrils flared, and we stood there staring at each other. Captives to all those questions that bounded between us. Coming faster and faster and faster.

I saw the second he finally snapped. He pushed across the threshold, on me in a flash, the heat of his strong body lighting me up like a furnace.

My heart fluttered and drummed.

He wound a big hand in my hair, tugging, forcing me to look up at him.

"Little Thief."

The accusation was gravel, and I sucked in a staggered breath. It only drew him deeper, his presence sinking in, penetrating every cell. Emotion swelled just as the pain of my past went rushing through my veins. A raging river that threatened to drown.

The fact of who Janel was. What she'd done.

I gasped over a cry. Unable to keep it in any longer.

"I married her, Rynna, I married her, and I knew all along, I shouldn't. Maybe I was ashamed to admit it to you or maybe I was just afraid of your reaction when you found out I hadn't severed it. But I promise, I promise you I was going to. When I told you I needed to get some things in my life in order, that's what I was referring to. Ending that marriage like I should have years before."

Another cry wrenched free.

He took my face in his big hands, fingers in my hair. "Rynna . . . baby . . . Rynna. Don't cry." He was kissing me through a tumble of frantic words he mumbled at my mouth. "I'm right here. I'm right here. I'm not going anywhere. I told her to go. I told her I was leaving and would be back in an hour and she and her things needed to be gone when I got back. I told her, Rynna. I told her my heart belongs to you, even if you won't take it. But I want you to. I'm gonna fight for you, Rynna. I'm not giving us up. Not ever. You and me . . . we're what's right."

I choked over a cry, and he kissed me deeper. The only thing I wanted to do was succumb.

Get lost in this man.

In his presence and his power and his overwhelming heart.

Another ripping sob tore from my throat. Unstoppable. Wounds fresh and raw. Too much. "It hurts so bad, Rex. I didn't mean for it to. I thought I was over it. Bigger than it. And it's right there. I don't know how to handle what happened. It's just . . . I think about it and it hurts all over again."

Framing my face in his hands, he edged back, confusion a flash across those striking features. "What are you talking about, baby?"

A car engine churned to life from across the street. A reminder of who we were and what we were battling.

I could hear the car crunch on gravel as it backed up, accelerate when it took to the street.

Janel. I knew it was her. It only made me cry harder.

"Janel," I hiccupped over her name.

He looked over his shoulder. "I've been outside pacing your lot for the last hour. I came home tonight, thinking that was the only thing I could do. Condemn myself. Walk away from you and pretend like this thing we've got doesn't matter. I almost gave in because I thought it might be the right thing to do. But it's not, Rynna. It's not, because you and me? We're what's right. I'm not willing to settle or turn my back or act like I'm not dying for you. I walked out on her and right to you. And this whole time, I've been trying to get up the courage. Trying to find the words to convince you that *we're* what's right. Please, Rynna. Please put me out of this misery. I can't lose you. I can't lose you, too."

"Janel." Another whimper, and I knew I wasn't making any sense, because none of this situation did.

"She doesn't matter to me, Rynna. I promise you. Yes, I was waiting for her all those years. Stayed loyal because I had some messed-up notion that one day she was going to come back, and it was on me to keep our family intact. And then there you were, Rynna. My second chance. You changed everything. You became my loyalty. My heart. You and my Frankie. That's all I need."

"Janel hated me, Rex. She hated me so much. And what she did . . . I don't know how to get past it. Forgive her and move on, because I know she's going to be a part of Frankie's life."

He jerked back, holding my face tighter. "What?"

A ramble of incoherent words slid free. "Janel . . . she was the one who hated me so much. I think I pushed you away, clung to your omission, because of her. Not sure how I could handle the fact that the two of you had been together. So I tried . . . tried to hope that she'd changed. For your sake. For Frankie's sake. But I don't—"

"What did you just say?" Rex's words were a growl, menacing and fierce. His demeanor shifted in a flash. From pleading to completely on edge.

"Janel. Janel's the one who's responsible for what happened to me. She set the whole thing up. She had Aaron pretend like he wanted to date me. I didn't know she was your wife, Frankie's mom. I didn't know until I opened that door."

Rex blew back like he'd been struck by a bomb. "Aaron? Aaron who?"

I blinked at him. Aaron didn't matter in the end. "Aaron Reed."

Shock blanketed his face before it turned into panic. He began to pace, back and forth, ripping at handfuls of hair. "Fuck. I knew it. I fucking knew it. I knew it."

I reached for him, his frenzy breaking into mine. "Calm down, Rex. What's wrong?"

"Aaron Reed used to be my business partner." His head shook through his stupor. "He and Janel . . . they acted like they didn't know each other. But he was at the bar with me across town the night I met her. He was the one who'd suggested that bar to meet up at after work. He was the one who noticed her . . ." Rex whipped around, grabbing me by the arms. I wasn't sure who he was steadying—me or himself. "He pushed me toward her. Told me to go for it. That she looked exactly like my type. And Janel . . . she was instantly all over me. Like . . . she'd been expecting me."

He pulled away, back to gripping fistfuls of hair. "They were together the whole time, weren't they?"

Rex punched an aimless fist into the air. "Fuck. They were together the whole goddamned time, and I didn't have the first clue. Or maybe I did."

His gaze dropped to the floor, his head shaking as if he were adding it all up. "When Aaron was arrested for embezzling from the company, there was something off. I got this feeling . . . this feeling that there was something more to the whole thing. That he couldn't have been acting alone. All those documents that had been tampered with. The money that had gone missing."

"Oh God." I pressed my hand over my mouth.

Rex looked at me. Panic streaked through his expression. "She left the day before he went to jail, Rynna. He got his sentence, and I thought things were finally going to be okay, and then I got home to find Janel leaving me."

"Oh God," I said again. "Aaron . . . he was outside the diner this evening. About a week ago, too. He said something about me getting in Janel's way."

Rex stared at me for a beat before his eyes went wide. Then he was bolting out the door and flying across the street.

thirty-eight

Rex

I sprinted across the street, taking the porch steps in two bounding leaps. I barreled through the front door. I had no clue what I was even searching for, but an overwhelming anxiety pushed me forward.

I'd felt nothing but relief when I'd heard her car taking off ten or fifteen minutes ago. But right then? Nothing made sense. Everything I'd thought I'd known as truth had only been some kind of twisted fabrication. All these years, and I'd fucking thought I'd done something wrong. Neglected Janel. Didn't treat her well enough. Didn't give her enough time. Made her feel less than worthy. Because in truth, in my heart, she'd never been.

Had every second of it been a set up?

My eyes darted around the room, hunting for anything that might be amiss. Dishes littered the kitchen from the dinner Janel had been preparing, the trash bin out in the middle of the floor, pork chops dumped inside. Like she was pissed at me for suddenly sending her away.

That, I understood.

The idea that she might have been an accomplice to the

bullshit Aaron had pulled all those years ago I did not.

I couldn't grasp it. Accept it. But the truth of it rang out in my consciousness. A promise she was guilty. That she'd been using me all along.

Anger spiraled, and I clenched my teeth, turning to head down the hall, going directly for my room.

It was just like I'd expected. It was torn apart. Ransacked. The contents of all the drawers were dumped out onto the floor in a mad search for anything of value.

Blankets pulled from the bed, mattress shoved to the side, the small safe hidden under the bed gone.

"Bitch," I seethed.

I should have known.

I should have known better than to let her back into my damn house. Into our lives so she could just turn around and make another mess of it. But honestly, the only thing that mattered right then was the fact she was gone. I'd gladly accept the loss of the bit of cash in that safe if it meant Janel was eradicated from our lives.

A plague eliminated.

Extinguished.

"Rex!" Rynna's scream flooded my ears. I pushed back out of my room and into the hall.

She was at Frankie's door, her hand pressed to her mouth, the girl staring inside.

For a beat, I froze in terror.

Frankie.

I sprang into action. Rynna stumbled out of my way when I rounded the doorway. I jerked to a stop in my daughter's room.

In a fleeting glance, you'd think nothing was out of order, her bed made and her stuffed animals still lined against her pillows.

But the closet—clothes were pulled from the hangers and some of her shoes were gone. Frantic, I rushed for Frankie's dresser. The drawers . . . they were empty.

The worst kind of terror took hold of me.

All the fears I'd ever had of losing my child rose to the surface.

Rising above.

Pulling me under.

I couldn't fucking breathe.

My hands were shaking when I dug into my pocket for my phone. It was already ringing before I had the chance to dial, my mom's name lit on the screen.

I answered it, and every part of me twisted in two.

My mother . . . she was screaming. Screaming and screaming and screaming. "She's gone. I don't know where she is, Rex. She's not here. Frankie's gone."

thirty-nine

Rynna

Jenny Gunner's cries poured through the phone. Begging and screaming and weeping.

And Rex? Oh God, Rex made an inhuman noise. Wailed this wail that came from his soul.

Agonized.

Devastated.

Crushed.

It reverberated from the walls and pummeled through my senses.

I wound my arm around my stomach as if it might staunch the pain that split me from the inside.

Frankie Leigh.

I could feel my heart shredding at the same second my spirit moaned.

I should have done something, said something earlier.

My fault. All of this was my fault.

Right from the beginning. I should have stayed that first night when Janel had cut me apart. I should have stood my ground and stood up for myself. Exposed Janel for who she really was.

But I'd let her get away with her sins as if they hadn't been committed at all.

Rex spouted a bunch of incoherent words to his mother before he ended that call, quick to dial 9-1-1. I could hear the moment the operator came on.

Rex had made another switch, pulling himself from the spiral of torment. His shoulders rolled back and determination set on his face. Refusing to allow his worst fears to happen. His voice was gritted—direct and hard—as he quickly relayed the information to the operator. Her name. The make and model of her car. Description of both her and Frankie. The last time both of them had been seen.

Then he ended the call and came striding across the room and into the hall, all power and barely contained intensity. He grabbed me by the outside of my shoulders, his voice a plea. "Stay here, Rynna. In case they come back, stay here. Have your phone ready to call 9-1-1." He gave a gentle shake. "Okay?"

"Of course," I told him, but the words were barely a breath. He pressed his lips to my forehead and then he was gone, the only trace of him the sound of him gunning his truck and it roaring down the street.

Silence swooped in like a cold, steely drape. Clamoring against the walls and trembling across the floors.

Ominous and foreboding.

I wrung my fingers, and my feet took the hall. Back and forth. Back and forth. Desperate to do something. Intuition promised there was no chance Janel would come back here.

My mind rolled. I couldn't quiet it, the way images flashed and blipped, the way voices murmured as if someone were right there, whispering them in my ear.

Jenny Gunner's words when she'd come to Pepper's Pies.

"Don't really know a time she lived in this town when she didn't work for your grandma. From what I know, she started out when she was in high school."

My mind flashed to Aaron on the street, the way he'd been peeking in the window.

"Always in Janel's way, aren't you?"

All of it spun and spun. Winding to a sum.

That thread of awareness finally took hold.

It'd hadn't been by chance that Aaron was outside the diner, peering in. It wasn't out of curiosity or the interest of an old restaurant reopening.

He'd been spying. Wondering exactly what was going on inside.

A slow chill trickled down my spine.

Freezing ice.

Cold.

It seeped into every cell. I could barely breathe. Lungs heaving around it, breaking its bindings, I fumbled for my phone. I was already racing out the door and across the street when I put it to my ear.

Rex's phone went straight to voice mail.

"Shit," I mumbled, trying to balance the phone between my ear and shoulder so I could unlock the door. I was jumping into the driver's seat when the message beeped. "Please don't be angry, but I'm going to the diner." The words were a ramble.

I threw my SUV in reverse and backed out, quick to shift into drive. "It's probably just a hunch, and God, the last thing I want to do is distract you, but I can't ignore this. I need to make sure Janel isn't there. I just . . . have this feeling, and I have to act on it. I'll let you know if anything seems off."

I ended the call, tossed my phone to the passenger seat, and flew. Flew through the neighborhood and onto the main street. Streetlamps blurred past, streaked in my eyes and sent my heart into overdrive. I took the three turns required to get me into the middle of town faster than I should, until I finally made the last left onto Fairview.

The entire street was shut down for the night except for the single bar on the end, and only a few exterior lights shined from the awnings of the rest of the businesses that had been closed for hours.

I slowed when I reached Pepper's and swung into a parking spot. My headlights sprayed across the long pane of darkened windows. Glinting, blinding light reflected back.

I killed the engine, cracked the door, and stepped out. The construction site directly across from the restaurant was dark.

Vacant.

The only movement on the whole street was a foreboding breeze that blew through.

I was scared.

Terrified, really. I'd walked in this diner a million times, and never before had it evoked this type of reaction in me. But I couldn't ignore what was screaming out from inside.

I grabbed my phone, 9-1-1 already programmed to dial, my footsteps slow and cautious as I edged around the front of my SUV and along the sidewalk that ran in front of the restaurant. Holding my breath, I slid the key into the lock and quietly nudged open the door.

Silence rained down.

Ominous and thick.

Too thick.

So thick, dread flashed across my flesh. It sent a tumble of goose bumps across my arms and tingling in my hands, awareness a prickle of needles across my neck.

I inched inside, each footstep measured as I tried to keep completely silent. I eased through the dining room, my breaths shallow and panted as I wound around the long counter and pushed open the shiny metal swinging door.

I inched forward, vigilant as I stepped into the kitchen.

A footstep crunched. A reverberation through the dense, dim air.

A footstep that wasn't mine.

Every cell in my body seized in fear. Slowly, I attempted to slide my finger across my phone.

A swish of blonde hair flashed at the corner of my eye. Fear sped and my finger fumbled. I sucked in a breath when I heard the *whoosh*, felt the shift in the air, before something metal cracked against the back of my head.

Pain. So much pain. I tried to hold on to consciousness. I needed to fight. Fight for Frankie. But I could feel darkness pressing in, taking over, and everything went black.

forty

Corinne Dayne – Three Years Ago

Anger burned through my old, brittle bones. Apprehension sank into the pit of my stomach, my veins drumming with sluggish, burdened blood, a shrinking fear that vibrated out to take hold of my already shaky, weathered hands.

I should have realized it a long time ago. There'd always been something off about that girl. But I'd been the fool that'd ignored it, thinking people were different and I didn't have any right to make judgments about them.

But this?

I did.

When her car pulled in across the street, I moved out the door and onto my porch. For the first time in a long time, I wished I were younger. Stronger. That I didn't do it with a limp and my body didn't protest every step.

She pulled that sweet baby girl from the backseat and kissed the side of her head as if she weren't wretched all the way through.

The sky had darkened to a dusky blue, the horizon holding the last vestiges of oranges and pinks as the day fully melted away. Ambling across the street, I held the evidence tight against my chest, voice shaking, no longer able to hold back the accusation. "What did you do?"

Janel's head whipped my way. She huffed out a breath. "Corinne, I don't have time for your nonsense ramblings today. It's been real rough around here, with all that's been going on at Rex's company. Need to make him supper. He'll be home shortly." She turned her back on me, Frankie Leigh hooked to her hip, and started for their porch steps.

"That's awfully convenient, isn't it, fact that Aaron boy you were always so chummy with growing up is getting sent off to prison for doing your husband wrong? Stealing all that money. What a shame. And here you are, playing the innocent card. Guess that's the way it's always been, hasn't it? Playing us for fools while you ran around manipulating everything to get your way?"

Regret slithered through my spirit. Should have known it back then, in the days when my Rynna had run away. Oh, how my girl had pined after that Aaron boy, eyes always dreamy anytime he wandered in for a piece of pie, her whole world made when she'd finally caught his eye.

Wasn't until I was watching this video that I realized those two were to blame for her running.

Janel and Aaron.

Same as they both were to blame for what was happening to Rex.

This time I wasn't about to turn a blind eye.

Janel froze at the door that she was pulling open. Slowly, she edged around to face me, her voice going dim. "What did you just say? Because it sounded to me like you were accusing me of something you shouldn't be."

The videotape felt heavy in my hands. An overbearing weight. "You know . . . all these years the register has been coming up short. So many times that I thought I was goin' crazy or maybe I just couldn't count. But I figured I needed proof that it was time to shut the place down and retire if I couldn't handle running the day-to-day. Imagine my surprise when I sat watching the video from last night."

Janel blanched. White as a ghost.

She knew as well as I did what was on this video. Had considered telling her about the new cameras going in, but thought better of it, figuring I was either going senile or somebody was stealing right from under my nose.

Just had no idea of the enormity of the stealing that'd been going on.

The blip of video had been caught in the middle of the night in the back office, Janel and Aaron arguing about the fact Aaron was going away for embezzling from RG Construction.

"You're the idiot who went and got yourself caught," Janel seethed.

"And you're the one who put me up to it. You're the one who has the money, and I'm the one who's gonna land in jail? I don't think so, Janel. This was all your idea, and you're gonna tell him. You've been controlling things for years. It's about time it stopped."

"The hell I am. Rex doesn't know shit, and it's going to stay that way. You do what you're supposed to do. Follow through, like a man, because from where I'm standing, you don't look like anything but a pussy."

She edged closer to him, slid a hand up his chest. "Besides, it won't do either of us any good if we're both behind bars. We still have all that money they never accounted for. I'll hide it, and when you're out, we'll pick back up right where we left off. Now that you're out of the office, Rex is gonna need someone to take over. Who better than his loving wife?"

Then they'd been kissing—along with other unsavory things that'd made my skin crawl. I'd been flooded with sympathy for that poor man who'd not done anything but work himself to the bone to take care of his family, Rex having no clue he was being betrayed.

Janel set Frankie on her feet. The cute thing toddled forward, barely keeping balance as she blabbered around the two fingers she had stuffed in her mouth. Janel rolled back her shoulders. "Messing with me would be a mistake, old lady."

Probably so, but I couldn't regret it. Not when that little girl squealed, innocent joy. Not when I knew the woman standing over her was nothing but poison. The only thing Janel was good for was destruction, and I wasn't gonna stand aside and watch her ruin anyone else.

"Seems I'm holding all the cards this time, now, doesn't it?"

In a flash, Janel came blazing down the steps and rushing my direction. I rasped out in surprise when her fingernails dug into the skin of my wrist. "Give it to me."

Even though she was hurting me, mocking laughter rolled from my tongue. Anger for my Rynna. Anger for Rex. Anger for any other person she'd done wrong, because I was betting these two weren't her only victims. "Take it. Plenty more where that came from. All set up and ready to go straight to the police."

She stumbled back a step. "I think you're bluffing, Corinne Dayne, because if you had anything on me, you would have already run and snitched to the cops, just like your prissy granddaughter did when she went tattling to my mom. Two of you are just alike. What is it you think you want from me?"

But that was where she was wrong. I wasn't bluffing. I just wasn't taking the chance that the cops would disregard the video or deem it inconclusive. Wasn't taking the chance this schemer might go and convince that trusting man that I'd construed it all wrong. Take her back or give her another chance.

I just wanted her gone.

"What I want is for you to go. Go pack your things before Rex gets home and get out of town. Don't ever come back."

Her blue eyes flamed with hate. Ice cold. "Are you insane? I'm not doing a thing you say."

"Then I'll gladly forward this along. And if something happens to me, who knows where one of these videos is going to pop up."

Steam might as well have been rolling from her ears, her jaw sharp and clenched, hate pouring out. "You bitch, just like your snot of a granddaughter."

"Maybe, but it sure beats being a thief and liar and a cheat. I'm thinking your husband might agree."

She paled, as if she were only just then realizing I was serious. The words were choppy when she released them from her vile mouth.

"You're asking me to leave?"

"Oh, I'm not askin' anything. I'm tellin' you."

"So what . . . I get out of town, don't come back, and that video isn't ever gonna appear? You're saying those are your terms? You aren't angling for anything more?"

Leave it to the thief to think I was aiming to steal from her.

"That's it. Just go."

She laughed a sour, hostile laugh, before she squared up, lifted her chin as if it didn't hurt her none. "Fine."

She spun around and flew back up the steps, door banging as she rushed inside. Rex's dog, Missy, yelped when she slid out the door, door catching her tail before she went to stand guard at Frankie's side. Frankie giggled and pushed her fingers through the dog's hair. I took a couple steps into the driveway, figuring I best be guarding, too.

Ten minutes later, Janel came barreling back out, wrangling a big suitcase in both hands. She fumbled down the steps and heaved them into her trunk before she went running back up the stairs.

She scooped Frankie Leigh off her feet and raced back with her to the car. Missy scrambled down at their sides, whining, sensing that something was wrong.

Panic just about squeezed my heart into a million pieces, and I rushed that direction just as Janel was shoving Frankie into the backseat. She slammed the door shut and rushed to get into the driver's seat before I could get there. Gunning it in reverse, she started to peel out of the drive.

I barely caught onto the back handle and jerked open the door. Hating the idea of putting Frankie in danger, but I couldn't allow her to drive off with her.

The car screeched to a stop as I was hauling Frankie into my arms. Janel's door flew open, fury on her face when she jumped out. "You might want me gone, but I'm not leaving without my daughter."

She tore at my arms, skin breaking under the claw of her nails. Frankie started crying. Crying and crying. A jumble of confusion and fear. A baby who deserved none of this.

I fought her, backing down the driveway and holding Frankie

protectively against my chest. "You're not taking her, Janel. You are the devil and I'm not gonna allow you to taint this child. Leave her or I'll gladly die showing Rex exactly who you are."

Missy jumped around us. Yipping and barking. Not sure who she was supposed to be fighting and who she was supposed to be protecting. Janel continued to try to rip Frankie from my arms, two of us scuffling closer to the road.

And I tried to hold on. Not to let Frankie go. But Janel was stronger than I was. She finally tore her free, a sneer of victory on her face. That was right when we heard the loud rumble of the ever-distinguishable truck, the powerful engine rumbling as it turned onto the far neighborhood street.

For a second, Janel froze. I took the opportunity to lunge for her, grasping for Frankie, arm locking around her waist. I dislodged her from Janel's hold just before Janel shoved me just as hard as she could. Both Frankie and I tumbled to the ground.

A wail of a cry rose from Frankie, and she climbed to her feet, wobbling at the back of the car. I skidded across the gravel, coming to a stop just to the side.

That engine roared in the distance. Coming closer and closer.

Panicked, Janel jumped back into the front seat and threw her car in reverse. Caring about nothing but setting herself free.

I screamed, "No!"

Tires screeched and dust billowed. It was so loud, the engine and my screams and Frankie's cries, and I couldn't make sense of the picture, nothing except her car hitting the street, shifting into drive, and then tearing down the road in the opposite direction of Rex's truck.

No. Frankie Leigh, oh God, no.

It was a prayer from my soul. A cry from my lips.

A strangled sound of relief left my throat when my eyes landed on Frankie. She was crying, sprawled face-down on the dirt where she'd been thrown.

My eyes drifted back, and horror took to my throat.

Missy was dead in her place.

A heap at the side of the road.

Missy had saved her. Pushed her out of the way.

Rex's truck jerked to a stop in the middle of the road, and he stumbled out, the glare of headlights cutting into the descending night. A cry wrenched from his mouth. "Missy. Oh . . . no . . . oh God . . . what . . .Frankie!" Second he saw his daughter, he went rushing her way. Stunned, he looked over his shoulder to the taillights disappearing in the distance, his expression shattered when he turned back to the scene.

But that was the thing. This loyal man had no clue just how much worse it could have been.

forty-one

Rynna

Pain throbbed at the back of my head. Blinding. Excruciating. I fought it, swallowed the nausea and forced myself to climb to my knees. My hands fumbled around, searching the floor for my phone.

Gone.

It was gone.

Mumbled voices echoed from the depths of the kitchen. They were coming from the old break room and office.

Fighting the terror lining my veins, I pushed myself to standing and squinted through the darkness. I pressed my back against the commercial ovens just inside the kitchen. I fought to stay as small and quiet as possible.

Slowly, I edged toward the voices.

Sinks lined the far back wall. A huge dry storage pantry was to the right of them and the old office was down a short hall to the left.

Keeping myself plastered against the metal, I shifted so I could peek into the murky depths.

A flashlight and the flickering flame of a candle cast the small room in leaping shadows. Two people were inside, their silhouettes striking against the wall as they moved.

Where was Frankie?

A cold sweat broke out across my nape, and I squeezed my eyes again, gathering courage, calculating whether I could make it to the phone that rested on the old desk that sat right inside the office.

I eased down the short hall, those voices coming clearer with each step I took. Panicked whispers, frantic as they searched.

"Where is it?"

"The question is, where the fuck did you hide it?"

"It has to be here . . . I . . . it's been a lot of years. I'm not leaving without that money. That money and my daughter and that goddamned tape."

"You think they aren't already going to be looking for you since you took that kid? That was so stupid, Janel. I warned you that was the dumbest thing you could do. Going back to his house. What were you thinking?"

"I'm not leaving my baby behind. Not again. It wasn't supposed to turn out like this."

"Yeah, and what'd you expect? Me just to sit on the sidelines while you cozied up with that arrogant asshole again? Taking what's mine? You're insane if you thought I was going to let you stay there."

"Just shut up and help me find it. None of that matters anymore."

I kept edging closer, footsteps subdued, my heart threatening to pound right out of my chest.

"Yes! Here it is . . . it's here!" Janel suddenly shrieked, coming into view when she jumped to her feet with a box in her hands. A box she had to have found beneath the floorboards.

I knew I didn't have any more time. I rushed for the phone that was four steps away. I grabbed the receiver, fumbling to hit those three simple numbers.

I made it. I made it. One second before the receiver was yanked out of my hand. I started to spin around, caught off guard when I was shoved in the side.

Hard.

My feet flew out from under me.

I slammed against the wall. But this time, I was ready. Ready for this fight. A fight that'd been coming for years. For what felt like forever. I was fighting for Rex. For Frankie. I was fighting for me. "You coward, taking a little girl."

I charged her. Rammed my shoulder into her chest as hard as I could.

Pain splintered through my head, but it was worth it. It was worth it because Janel stumbled back, arms flailing and hair whipping around her. The box she'd had in her hands went sailing through the air and crashed to the floor.

I dove for it. A hand fisted in my hair, yanking it back. "You stupid bitch, always in my way. Not this time. Not this time."

I threw an elbow back and caught her in the ribs.

She heaved out a cry.

I spun around and rushed her just as she was rushing me.

Our bodies collided.

A clash of souls.

I hooked her around the neck, trying to pin her, hold her.

She jerked free, so frenzied that she reeled, her footing gone. She stumbled back until she hit the desk.

I dove on her, and we slid across the slick wood, knocking everything that had been on the top to the floor.

Papers and the phone and the candle.

And we fought. Arms and fists and ripping hair. Fought until a big body was yanking me off. I screeched and kicked and fought. Fought in fury. In hate. In the desperate need to get to Frankie.

Frankie.

Frankie Leigh.

Aaron's cologne filled my nose, the memory of it making me gag. I struggled to break out of his hold, but he was too strong. He tossed me aside. As if I was nothing.

Trash.

Just the same as he'd treated me before.

Aaron grabbed the box from the floor and then snagged Janel

by the wrist. "We have to get out of here. Right now."

My attention caught on the floor across the room. A tiny flame leapt to life. The candle a match to a piece of paper that'd floated to the floor.

Part of me wanted to go for it. Stamp it out. Protect my gramma's legacy. But none of that mattered if they got away with Frankie. I couldn't—wouldn't allow it to happen.

Hand-in-hand, Janel and Aaron ran down the short hall and escaped out the back door. The door they'd most likely broke in through.

Frankie was my only concern. Not a building or its memories or the hopes of what it may be one day.

Only that little girl.

Crying out in pain, I struggled to get to my feet, chasing right after them. By the time I made it out the door, they were sprinting toward a black Durango parked in the back lot. In my periphery, I could see the spark of fire.

And I knew my grandma's restaurant was getting ready to go up in flames.

I didn't slow, only pushed myself harder, desperate to get to Frankie.

Aaron tried to force Janel around to the front passenger seat, but she diverted and wrenched open the back passenger door. "Frankie . . . Frankie?"

Janel started to panic, shouting it again. "Frankie!"

Struggling to jerk out of his hold, she whirled on Aaron. "Where's Frankie?"

I stumbled to a stop halfway across the vacant lot, heart crashing against my ribs.

"Warned you, Janel, but you wouldn't listen. We're not taking that fucking kid. We're getting out of Gingham Lakes and out of this country, and I won't have anything slowing us down. Now, let's go."

"Where is she?" she screamed.

Even though he seemed to avoid it, Aaron's attention darted back to the diner, expression twisting in the briefest flash of guilt.

Guilt aimed at my gramma's diner that was going up in flames.

No.

Oh my God.

Slowly he shook his head. "Didn't expect the fire. That's not on me. Now get in or I'm leaving you behind."

Janel's expression froze in horror. And I thought maybe it was the first time I saw any true humanity in her. Any true care. Just as fast, it was gone, and Janel started around to the front of the SUV.

She was just going to leave her.

I spun around in my own horror. Flames licked out from the back window and glowed through the gaping door.

For a flash, my eyes squeezed closed, my gramma's voice a whisper in my ear. Her presence overwhelming, so much I could feel her belief penetrating to the depths of me.

All moments matter. We just rarely know how important they are until the chance to act on them has already passed.

I'd always known Rex and Frankie were worth the chance. This one might cost me it all. Everything. But they would always, always be worth it.

My feet pounded against the pavement. Adrenaline and fear were a thunder that stampeded through my veins and whooshed in my ears.

I held up my arm as if it might protect me when I barreled through the doorway and into the kitchen.

Smoke swallowed me.

Taking me whole.

Black.

Thick.

Suffocating.

Holding my breath, I tried to get as low as possible as I began to search.

When I couldn't do anything else, I tugged my shirt over my nose and gave in.

Inhaled.

It burned.

Burned so badly that my lungs wept, just the same as my insides.

Heat licked across my skin, so hot I wanted to scream.

Scream for help.

For sanity.

For Frankie.

Most of all, for Frankie.

I groped along the walls. Trying to find my way. To make sense of where I was.

Disoriented, I fumbled, trying to focus.

A wall.

An oven.

The pantry.

Oh God, the pantry.

The door was closed.

When I'd left this evening, it'd been wide open. I was sure of it. I'd been moving things in and out and had propped it open.

I slid my hands over it, feeling, searching. Relief wrenched from me when I found the latch. I managed to drag it open.

Smoke billowed inside. It was at the same second I heard Frankie's cry.

"Frankie!" It was a shout.

Joy.

Solace.

Fear.

Each emotion rushed me. One after another.

Because I couldn't breathe and I couldn't see and everything hurt so bad.

The radiating heat and the asphyxiating smoke.

But there was no chance I was giving up.

Flames bloomed just outside the pantry door, consuming the kitchen, eating away the plaster and wood and memories.

I dropped to my knees and crawled across the floor. My hand came into contact with something that moved. A foot. A leg. A tiny body that I pulled into my arms, holding her against my chest, burying her face in my shirt.

Because I'd do anything to protect her. To save her.

Dizziness swept through my being. Head. Body. Soul. I fought to stay coherent. To stay awake. To fight.

I clutched Frankie to me, rocked back, and screamed.

forty-two

Rex

I rushed through the doors of the police station. I'd been on the phone with my mom the whole way over, trying to get as much information from her as I could and settle her down at the same time. Which was a ridiculous notion in and of itself, considering how close I was to coming unglued. Torn limb from limb. Janel's fist punched right into the center of my chest, the bitch ripping out my still beating, bleeding heart, holding it hostage in her corrupt, vicious hand.

Never in a million years would I have imagined she'd stoop this low. Of course, I'd had no clue how deep her betrayal went, either.

Treason.

Treachery.

It was nothing less.

Lieutenant Seth Long was already coming out of his office when I skidded to a stop in front of it. We'd gone to school together, had been friends for as long as I could remember, the guy devoting his life to the greater good.

"Rex," he wheezed, amped up, whole station already on red

alert. "APB has been issued, and I have every available cruiser already on the streets. We're going to get her back. I promise you, Rex, if it's the last thing I do, I'm going to get your daughter back."

I nodded, though it was choppy, jerky with hatred and fear. The two together were a dangerous combination. They itched my fingers in direction's they shouldn't go. Thoughts of vengeance and retribution skating my skin, a twine that bound my body.

"I just . . . I've got to do something."

He set a hand on my shoulder, head dipping down, eyes meeting mine. Like he was trying to get through to me. To get me to see reason when all I was seeing was red. "I know you do. But I need you to make an official statement first then you can ride with me, okay? I don't want you running off doing something stupid."

Another spastic nod, filled with reluctance, but what the hell else was I going to do? "Okay," I agreed.

"Come on, let's get this moving so we can get out of here."

I started to follow him into his office, when my phone chirped with a message. I pulled it from my pocket, squinting when I realized it'd come in close to fifteen minutes ago, during the time I'd been talking to my mom.

Rynna.

Apprehension pressed against my ribs, and I quickly thumbed into the message, pushing the phone to my ear. Rynna was on the other end, sounding panicked and worried and a little shamed, telling me she was sorry but she was going to Pepper's.

That was at the same second a radio bleeped in the station, a code issued and an address given, an officer asking for backup.

It was to an address I knew all too well.

My gaze locked with Seth's. Time froze while awareness shot between us. Then I was running. Running back out into the night and into my truck. Seth was right on my heels, sliding into the front seat of his cruiser. I floored it, didn't care that I was breaking about fifteen different laws as I sped toward the diner.

Toward Rynna.

Toward Frankie.

Toward my entire life.

The center of my world.

Felt like it took me forever to get there when not more than five minutes could have passed. I skidded around the last corner, taking a sharp left turn, roaring down the road.

All the breath left me when the building came into view.

Pepper's ravaged by fire and smoke.

No.

No. No. No.

I didn't slow. Instead, I accelerated, truck careening, everything lurching and jostling when the tires hit the curb and jumped the sidewalk. Second before I hit the brick wall, I rammed on the breaks and jumped out without bothering to put it in park.

Anguish pulsed through my veins. Spurring me faster and harder.

I went right for the front door and flung it open.

Desperation makes you do desperate things.

And there was no hesitation. No thought except for getting to them. I knew they were in there. Knew it with every part of me.

A thick plume of smoke gushed out when I rushed in.

It felt just like I was stepping into a furnace.

Seth was there, screaming at me to stay. Not to move.

But there was no chance of him stopping me.

Lifting my shirt to cover my mouth and nose, I edged in, following the smoke that was coming from somewhere in the kitchen like a target.

I made it to the swinging door. My eyes burned when I pushed it open, every inch of me swallowed by the heat.

An inferno.

I refused to let it become our hell.

"Rynna!" I shouted. Beside me, an avalanche of metal clattered to the floor, and I jumped back, dodging it two seconds before I became a pile of rubble right along with it.

God. It was so fucking hot. So hot, I swore I could feel my skin melting from my bones. But I pushed forward, adrenalin thrumming through me like a bullet. I screamed again, "Rynna!"

It was faint, barely discernable. But I heard something rise above the thunder. A foreign sound just to my right. Or maybe it was just some kind of sixth sense. An acute kind of awareness. A need inside that became my greatest strength.

Blindly, I fumbled that way, dropping to my knees, teeth gritted against the flames.

My hands, they searched, running over everything like the diner was written in Braille. Each bump and dip telling me to hurry. That every second that passed brought me closer to running out of time.

Then my hand, it ran over something solid but soft. Something sweet.

And I was struck with so much goddamned relief, because it was my girls huddled at the foot of the back door. Rynna was slamming a pot against the floor, guiding me.

I tried to push the heavy metal door open, but it was wedged shut, surely why Rynna hadn't been able to get out.

I felt like my lungs were exploding, but I gathered all of me. All my love. Every devotion. Every hope.

I reared back and kicked it.

When it didn't give, I kicked it again.

It burst open.

I wanted to shout in victory. In hope. I rushed, grasping Rynna from behind, my little girl still in the safety of her arms. I dragged them out onto the pavement of the back lot, as far as I could get them away from the fire, before I collapsed to my knees beside them.

I choked and coughed while around me voices shouted and sirens blared.

Someone was on a radio, calling for help in the back lot, three victims down.

But the only thing I could focus on was their ash-covered faces. Frankie clutched in Rynna's arms. I didn't want to touch them, worried I'd cause more damage, but I was certain my baby girl wasn't breathing.

My already failing heart stalled.

Oh God, please, no.

Rynna dragged in violent, choked breaths, eyes wide, no coherency in their depths.

"Help!" I screamed. "Somebody help."

Footsteps pounded around me, rushing in. Someone pulled me away. I fought to get back to them, but hands were on me, restraining. "Let them take care of them, man. You've got to let them take care of them." Seth's voice was grit in my ear.

I slumped forward, dropping back to my knees.

Fireman and paramedics swarmed. Working. A controlled, frantic storm.

My world spun, and one was in front of me, taking my pulse and asking me questions, if I was in pain or if I was having trouble breathing.

He just had no idea all my breaths were wrapped up in them. That I'd gladly give mine. Every breath. Every heartbeat. Everything. Just as long as they were okay.

I sat hunched over in the hard plastic chair, elbows on my knees, exhaustion in my bones. People hustled on the other side of the door that'd been wedged open a crack. But inside this room? Time had stopped. Nothing less than a mind-altering waiting game.

Dimness floated on the feigned peace, and that steady beeping of the monitor lulled me into a sense of security I was praying wasn't faulty.

"You should go get some rest, man."

I jumped when the muted voice hit me from behind. I scrubbed a hand over my face, trying to clear the daze, and shifted to look over my shoulder.

Kale stood there in his scrubs. Dude looked just about as weary as I felt. Since the second we'd rushed through the emergency room doors, he'd been running nonstop, making sure every test possible had been run on my daughter. Ensuring nothing was missed.

He'd been up all night and all of today.

"Think it's probably you who should be taking a break," I told him.

He let a smirk ridge his mouth. "Nah, I'm basically a super hero. Can't keep me down. "

Cocky asshole.

A light chuckle rumbled from my tongue. "That so?"

"Come on, look at me, you know it is." He was all affable grins.

I turned my attention back to my daughter. Frankie was lost to sleep, tiny body tucked beneath stark white sheets.

Resting.

Whole and right.

According to Kale, things could go south up to two days after prolonged smoke exposure.

Which left me an unwilling player in this waiting game.

But Kale kept insisting I shouldn't worry. That she was going to be fine. That he'd make sure of it.

She'd been dosed with precautionary antibiotics and breathing treatments, and Kale promised not a single base had been missed.

I'd always known it, but it wasn't so clear what a damned good doctor Kale was until then.

"Thank you, man," I muttered quietly. "No way I could ever repay you for what you've done."

He made a sound of rebuttal. "I was just doing my job, Rex. You know she wouldn't be here if it wasn't for you and Rynna."

Rynna.

Beautiful Rynna. This girl who'd become my orbit. My sun. My gravity.

Rynna had saved my daughter's life. She'd put herself on the line. She fought for her. For us. She loved her in a way that was absolute.

"Almost at the cost of her own."

Everything pressed and pulled.

This gratefulness that had taken up residence in every part of me, up against this blistering agony at the thought of almost losing her, too.

"I won't pretend to know Rynna all that well," he said. "But from what I do? I'd bet she doesn't regret rushing into that fire any more than you do. Which is why I'm here. You can see her now."

My body swayed with the harsh heave of my breath. "Can you sit with Frankie for a while?"

"It'd be my honor."

He shuffled in, his own exhaustion making itself known. I stood and then hesitated before I reached for him. I gripped him tight, hugged him hard, hand fisted in the middle of his back. "Couldn't do any of this without you. Thank you, man, thank you so much."

He hugged me back, saying nothing, both of us giving a moment of silence. A moment for grief. For what might have been.

Then he stepped back. "Go. Frankie's in good hands."

I started for the door when Frankie shifted and released a tiny moan. Instantly, I changed directions, going straight for my daughter, who hadn't been awake for more than a total of an hour the entire day. Kale clapped me on the shoulder. "I'll be right outside the door. Let me know when you're ready for me."

"Thanks."

I slowly sank back into the chair, every inch of me glowing when I brushed my fingers through my daughter's hair, staring down at my world.

"Hi, Daddy," she said, so close to managing her precious grin.

I ran my thumb over her squished-up brow, my voice so low. "Hey, Sweet Pea. How are you feeling?"

"My's froat hurts."

Anger pulsed, but I tucked it down.

"I know, baby. Uncle Kale is working on fixing you up so you're good as new. Better than new. You just need to get lots of rest, okay?"

She barely nodded, her brown eyes wide in the muted light. I hated that I saw fear in them. That she'd been subjected to evil and greed. I kept brushing my thumb over her brow, letting her know I was there, that I wasn't going anywhere.

Finally, she broke the silence, her words the barest whisper. "Daddy, I gots a secret."

My heart fisted, threatened to fail, terrified of what she might say. Of what she might have experienced during the short time Janel had her.

Couldn't stomach it, and honestly, I was a little worried about what I might do. What I already wanted to do. But I held all that back, because my daughter was the most important thing, not the rage boiling inside me. "What, baby? You can tell Daddy anything."

She hesitated, like what she was going to say might get her into trouble. "I wants Rynna to be my mommy. Nots Janel."

I choked over a quieted laugh, blinking at my sweet girl and wondering how I'd managed to get so lucky.

Edging forward, I pressed a kiss to her temple before I pulled back to meet those wide, trusting eyes. "How about we don't keep it a secret? I say we tell the whole world."

I'd been terrified of falling in love. Of losing someone else. Knowing there was no place inside me left to lose. Those vacancies went too deep.

But Rynna.

She filled them. Saved my world and gave me back my heart.

Rynna.

Fucking Rynna.

Little Thief.

forty-three

Rynna

The door creaked open. I rolled my head that direction and tried to keep the tears out of my eyes when I found who was standing there. But I couldn't. They escaped, hot rivers streaking down my face.

"Hey . . . you're awake." His voice was a murmur, cautious and low. Still, the magnitude of him hit me like a flashflood. Overpowering. Overwhelming.

"Frankie?" Her name felt like fire where it grated from my raw, blistered throat.

Fear and anxiety and hope.

The second I'd awoken, I'd begged the nurse for an update, for her to tell me that she was okay, for any news.

Because the last thing I remembered was Rex standing over the two of us while I'd held on to Frankie.

Instead of an answer, she'd promised me she would let them know I was awake so someone could come talk to me.

For a beat, he stared at me, his lip trembling while that powerful gaze bore into me. Then he smiled. This slow, amazed, adoring smile. "Because of you, Rynna. Because of you, Frankie's going to be just fine."

More tears fell. But these were pure, unbridled relief. I released them as if I were pouring them into the heavens. Gratitude for the prayers I'd been granted.

Rex angled the rest of the way into the room, footsteps eating up the floor, the bed shifting when he gingerly eased down at my side. He brushed back the matted hair stuck to my forehead, voice cracking when he repeated, "She's okay . . . because of you."

All the turmoil I'd held back suddenly came spilling out.

"I should have told you from the beginning. If I had, this never would have happened. I'm so sorry."

Rex gave a harsh shake of his head, big hand cupping my cheek. "Don't you dare apologize, Rynna. I could accuse myself since I should have known the whole time Janel was no good. That only a fool wouldn't have known she'd been stealing from me from day one. Our relationship, *our daughter*, nothing but a ploy for her to get close to me. To gain access to my accounts so she and Aaron could embed themselves deeper into my life."

His hold tightened on my face. "But all the blame? It's on them. What they did to both of us is on them. They're the ones who are guilty, and they're going to be paying for it for the rest of their lives."

"Did they catch them?" My voice quivered.

He gave a slight nod. "Twenty miles out of town. Cargo area loaded down with cash that most definitely didn't belong to them. Apparently, there was a tape, too, one that implicated Janel in the original embezzlement charges that Aaron went down for."

Tone laced with the significance, Rex continued carefully, "The video was from right before Janel left and was recorded at Pepper's, Rynna . . . in the back office. Both she and Aaron were there."

His statement hovered in the room. Permeating. Seeping into my consciousness.

Realization settled slow. "My gramma knew," I finally said.

He nodded. "Yeah, I think she did. Now that I got a few

more details, everything makes sense. The fact your grandma was right there the day Janel was driving away, shaken up, supporting me with the blow of both Janel leaving and finding Missy on the street. I think your grandma might have scared her away, probably why Janel came back after she heard she passed."

Sorrow bloomed, weaving through that hollow space, the loss of my gramma a wound I was sure would never go away. But in it was something sweet and tender and gentle. Knowing. Just like my gramma had always been.

Rex's jaw ticked. "I just . . . I'm not even sure I want to know what happened that day. Leading up to that moment. And even though it destroyed me at the time, the only thing I'm doing right now is thanking your grandma for everything she did. For protecting my daughter. I might not know exactly what happened, but after Janel tried to take Frankie tonight? Pretty sure I would have lost my daughter a long time ago if it wasn't for your grandma."

Adoration pulled at the corner of his mouth. "All the Dayne women, saving my little girl. Both coming into our lives exactly when we needed you."

And that spot inside? It glowed. Warmth and light.

A soft smile fluttered at my mouth, and I shifted, ignoring the pain that burned hot on my left arm. "Maybe my gramma knew it all along, Rex. Maybe she knew it was supposed to be us. Maybe that's why she was so insistent I come back here. She had a way of seeing things long before they happened."

He smoothed his hand over the side of my head. Comforting. Soothing. I wanted to fall into his touch. Forever disappear. "You think she knew you were meant for me?"

My smile was timid, and I gave a slight nod. "Gramma always said we'd just know. That it'd be magic when it happened. Maybe she felt that magic long before either of us could."

"It is magic, Rynna. Frankie's here. You're here. We're together. And that's all that matters."

As soon as he said it, he winced, and a hard gush of air left his lungs. "I'm so sorry, Rynna. About the restaurant. So goddamned sorry."

Reaching up, I wrapped a hand around his wrist, brought his palm to my mouth and kissed him there before I tugged it flat against my beating heart. "I would have given up anything to save her, Rex. Anything. The restaurant. My heart. My life."

I clutched him a little tighter. "And I thought I was going to. I thought both of our lives were slipping away. And then you were there. Saving me. Saving Frankie."

His expression tightened, almost grim in its emphasis. "Maybe that's what being a family is all about. I've always been terrified of losing Frankie. Knowing I would never survive that kind of loss. When it became a possibility—losing either of you—I would have sacrificed everything. Anything. Sold my soul. Lost my life. And you . . . you, Little Thief . . ."

Thumb brushing across my cheek, his head angled to the side. Those sage eyes speared me, finding their way to my soul.

"You saved my daughter, Rynna." He blinked at me, as if he were struggling for the right thing to say. "I knew the moment I met you that you were different. I fought it and fought it while you just continued to fight for me. To fight for us. But every time our paths crossed, I knew my life changed a little more. Truth is, I was terrified to take the chance. But like you said, it's all about taking the *right* ones."

He edged in, so close that our noses brushed and his breaths became mine. "You and Frankie? You were the best chances I ever took. And I was terrified both times. But if something doesn't scare you? Maybe it's not important enough. You are my life. You and Frankie are what it means to be a family. Do you understand what I'm telling you?"

My heart went wild, flailing against its boundaries.

He dipped in and pressed his lips to mine. So sweet. Before he pulled back, pinning me with that mesmerizing stare. "I love you, Rynna Dayne. I love you so much, and I'm not ever going to let you go."

Love. Love. Love.

It surged and spread and flowed. Filling every crevice. Every void. And my heart. I think maybe it did manage to split in two. Held in the hands of two people. Two people who'd become my center. My focus. Etching themselves into my being.

Mounting Rex Gunner's walls had seemed impossible. Those towering obstacles insurmountable.

Impenetrable and impossible.

But my gramma had always told me that life was just one long string of possibilities.

That chances were worth taking.

And this man and his baby girl? They were worth every single one.

the epilogues

Epilogue One – Rex Gunner

"Are your eyes closed?" I asked, unable to keep from peeking over at her. At the incredible woman who rode in the front seat of my truck.

Just looking at her had every inch of me tightening.

In need.

In want.

In this mad kind of love.

She was beautiful.

So damned beautiful she was hard to look at. Rynna was the kind of beauty that shined and blinded and radiated. Inside and out. Flush with goodness and grace. That body still my greatest temptation.

Though, I had zero qualms about giving in.

"Yes. And you put this blindfold on me." Rynna pointed at the strip of purple fabric, like I wasn't already well aware it was there.

I suppressed a chuckle while she continued her little rant.

"Seriously, I'm not sure what you think I'm going to see because it's pitch black in here." Rynna almost whined, all of it done behind the most brilliant smile, the girl biting at her lip, totally failing at trying to keep her excitement contained. "And I'm pretty sure you've been driving in circles, trying to throw me off. Or get me sick. There's that."

But she was grinning so wide that I knew she was loving this every bit as much as me.

"Hold tight, baby. Your surprise is right around the corner."

I eased the truck into a parking spot and killed the engine. I leaned across the cab, enjoying the way she inhaled sharply when I got close to her face, the way a shiver rolled down her spine when I leaned around her and gently untied the purple silk fabric from her eyes.

Slowly, I eased it back. The girl blinked, reoriented herself, needing time to grab on to her senses. Nothing made me happier than the fact when she did, she was looking directly at me.

I'd become her focal point. Just the same as she'd become mine.

"Hey," she murmured, her expression soft.

"Hi, beautiful." For a few seconds, we floated on the moment, just loving being together. Then I grinned and angled my head, urging her attention out the windshield.

She laughed. Laughed loud before she looked back at me like I'd lost my mind.

Truth was, the only thing I'd lost was my heart.

"You brought me to Pepper's? After I was here all day, slaving away? Tell me we aren't here for me to bake you a pie." Every word that fell from her mouth was playful, filled with a tease.

A chuckle rumbled free. "Wouldn't dream of it, baby. Come on." I unlatched the door, hopped out, and jogged around to her side. I was already there, helping her down when she opened her door. I threaded our fingers, brought her hand to my lips, brushed them across her knuckles. "Tonight's all about me taking care of you."

Six months had passed since the fire.

This day could have been somber.

But no.

Rynna and I? We were celebrating.

I led her across the sidewalk to the door, and she giggled, struggling to keep up with my long strides in her heels. I was quick to insert my key, unlock it. I pulled it open a fraction and stood in the middle of it, turning around to face the girl who'd changed everything.

The one who'd knocked free all the bitter, broken pieces of my heart and found what was hiding underneath.

"This building, Rynna . . . this building has come to mean so much. That fire—" My throat grew thick and moisture gathered in Rynna's eyes, her gaze so intent as she stared back at me. "You and I, we almost lost everything in that fire. This building. Your dreams. *Frankie. Each other.*" Each word that fell from my mouth came more intense with each one that passed.

That energy lapped, blazing to life. Inciting that never-ending desire.

"But from those ashes rose the greatest hope. My greatest joy."

I'd never thought I'd truly love a woman again after I'd lost Sydney. But Rynna changed all of that. Rekindled places in me I'd thought had gone forever dormant. Even though I hadn't told Ollie yet, I would. I was no longer afraid of him hating me, I was just worried that I'd bring him more pain.

But Rynna and I had also learned that keeping those kind of secrets only hurt us more in the end.

I gathered both her hands in mine, pulling her inside, quick to lock the door behind us.

It was dark, all except for the hurricane lamp I'd placed on a blanket on the floor in the middle of the room. Beside it was a bucket, chilling our champagne. It was all set up right where all the new booths would be installed next week. This afternoon, me and my crew had raced in after Rynna left and hung pictures on the walls.

They were pictures I'd had enlarged, all in black and white, and set in giant frames.

They were images of Rynna's grandmother in this place, serving her pies, baking in the back, working the register, and making customers smile where they sat at the counter. The old pictures had been in a box in Rynna's bedroom closet, waiting to be reclaimed. To be given a voice.

Overwhelmed, Rynna looked around. Tears glided down her cheeks, glistening in the faint electric light that danced in the lamp.

"Rex," she whispered, biting down on her lip, trying not to cry. "This is amazing."

I pulled her a little farther into the room. "Nothing has made me happier than giving this building back to you, Rynna. There's been no greater honor than resurrecting each brick. And I've never been prouder than being at your side while you've brought this place back to life."

Another two steps, and her chest was heaving while my heart was running wild, blood a thunder in my veins. "Six months ago, we could have lost it all, and instead, we were given everything. We were given another *chance*."

I blinked at her. Overcome by emotion. By feeling. "You came into our lives, Rynna, and you made everything better. I was filled with so much fear and hate, and you taught me how to love again. You showed my daughter what it is really like to be loved by a mother. You gave us a joy unlike anything we've ever known. I see you with her—"

I gulped around immensity of it. Rynna and my little girl. The way it felt when Frankie called her Mommy. The way Rynna adored her with all her soul.

I squeezed Rynna's hands. "I see you with her, and every single thing in my world is right. Because you and Frankie, the two of you are my world. My entire world, and I don't ever want to be without you."

I dropped to a knee and shock jetted from Rynna's mouth.

Tears came in a free fall, the wet streaks doing nothing but illuminating that gorgeous face.

I pulled the ring from my pocket and held it up between us, my hand trembling while I offered this girl all of me. "Marry me, Rynna Dayne. I want to give you all my days. My heart and my life. Tell me, you're always going to be mine."

A tiny cry erupted from her, and she stood there staring down at me for the longest time, the smile lighting her mouth soft and soggy and so goddamned sweet. "And you . . . you gave me everything, Rex Gunner. My dreams. My hopes. A little girl to call my own. You and Frankie, you are the parts of me I hadn't known I was missing. Both of you, you are my heart and my life. And I promise you, I will always be yours."

Overcome by emotion, blinking back my own tears, I slid that ring on her finger, and Rynna dropped to her knees on the blanket in front of me. Those eyes searched me, flitting all over my face. "I knew today was a special day, and I've been saving you a surprise of my own."

I cupped her face, tracing my thumb along the curve of her jaw. Just needing to touch her. "You've got a surprise for me, huh? Not sure I need anything but what you've already given me."

Her eyes fluttered, and her head dropped, and she set both her hands on her belly. Then she peeked up at me with a timid smile, wearing eternity on her face.

My eternity.

My forever.

My second chance.

I pressed my hands over hers, hardly able to speak. "You telling me I'm lucky enough that you're going to make me a daddy again, too?"

Quickly, she nodded. "I know, I know it's soon, but you and I, we haven't exactly been careful all this time . . . and . . . and . . . oh God, Rex, I'm so happy. This baby makes me so happy."

She was rambling. Nervous. Excited.

Wondering how I'd react.

Crazy thing was, we'd never had this conversation, but all along I'd been taking that chance with her.

I dropped my forehead to hers, her hair wound through my fingers, our noses touching as I murmured, "Nothing could make me happier than growing this family with you. I'm so happy, Rynna. So goddamned happy. You're my second chance, Rynna, and I'm not afraid of what this life will bring."

Little Thief.

She'd stolen my heart.

And I was going to give her everything.

Epilogue Two – Rynna

I paused just outside the swinging kitchen door—a fresh cherry pie in my hands—staring out into the dining room.

Every person I loved was there for the grand re-opening of Pepper's Pies.

There for me. Because of this legacy. A private party just for my family and friends.

My husband.

My sweet daughter, Frankie Leigh.

The woman I'd come to adore, to claim as my own, Rex's mother, Jenny. She was such an important fixture in our lives, there to give me advice and an encouraging word when I needed one, or simply being a friend at other times. Fun and caring with that wild streak I was sure she'd never outgrow. Loving us unconditionally, in her own perfect way.

Ollie and Kale, Nikki and Lillith and Brody were all there, laughing where they stood by a few tables we'd pushed together in the middle. Seth Long, the officer who'd worked to put Janel and Aaron away, and a few of the guys from RG Construction I'd gotten to know were there, too.

Macy had flown out just for the celebration, and she mixed in just fine, laughing at something Kale had to say, which was probably something entirely inappropriate.

And I swore, as I looked around, my gramma was there, too. Her spirit always so strong. Her presence so profound.

Forever guiding me with the whisper of her encouraging words. Comfort covered me, a warmth that lit me from head to toe, her voice a murmur in my ear.

"Someday you'll understand what I'm talkin' about. Someday you'll know what it's like to be in love . . . You know you're in love when their happiness counts more than yours. The key is your happiness meaning most to them, too. Put those two together? That's magic, Rynna. That's what real love is. It's two people giving all they have."

Magic.

That's what Rex and I were. Two people giving it all we had.

We both loved the other first, their happiness before our own. Approaching our relationship that way? That happiness could only grow as it was poured out in the day to day, amplified in the little things and strengthened when life threw obstacles in our way.

Frankie suddenly looked my direction, wearing that grin on her face that always managed to touch my soul, the word falling from her mouth making my spirit thrum with joy. "Mommy!"

"Yes, baby?"

"Is that a Pepper's Pie?"

"Of course it's a Pepper's Pie. I made your favorite kind."

"Dids you know my Gramma C'rine used to make me all the Pepper's Pies?" she turned and continued to ramble at Macy, who seemed to be her new best friend. "She used to works here, too, but now my mommy does and she makes me pies and they're soes good, and my daddy eats them all, all, all gone and I have to race him to even get a piece."

"No!" Macy said in mock horror.

Heart so full, I wound around the counter, heading their direction. My man shifted, like he felt me approaching.

Those sage eyes pinning me.

Capturing me.

So beautiful.

That coarse, rough exterior with the most beautiful, giving heart underneath.

He no longer kept it hidden.

He'd welcomed me into it.

Wholly.

No questions blocking our path.

Rex took the pie from my hands and placed it on the table, turning to me wearing that sexy smile riding the edge of his full, full lips. The one that tipped my tummy and sent that attraction rushing free. Then his hands were on my stomach, over our son, his love pouring from him in shattering waves. "I love you, Rynna Gunner," he murmured.

"I love you so much," I told him.

Our gazes tangled for a moment, before he swiveled me, tucked me to his side. He lifted his glass just the same as he lifted his voice over the perfect clatter of voices. "I think a toast is in order."

Everyone turned their attention to us. Their smiles so bright, brimming with the bonds of friendship and family.

Rex glanced at me, then back to them. "To Gramma Dayne. For the woman who loved this restaurant, but loved the people of Gingham Lakes so much more. To her courageous, gracious heart. I'm not sure where I'd be right now if it wasn't for her."

He lifted his glass higher.

Toward the heavens.

"You'll always be a part of Pepper's Pies. More so, you'll always be a part of our lives."

It was a chorus of cheers.

Cheers to Gramma Corinne.

To the woman who'd given us her all.

For her love and her inspiration.

All moments matter. We just rarely know how important they are until the chance to act on them has already passed.

Because of her I'd acted. I'd taken the chance.

The chance on love.

The chance of forever.

And I was never looking back.

the end

Thank you for reading *Show Me the Way*! Did you love getting to know Rex and Rynna? Please consider leaving a review!

I invite you to sign up for mobile updates to receive short, but sweet updates on all my latest releases.
Text "aljackson" to 24587
(US Only)
or
Sign up for my newsletter
http://smarturl.it./NewsFromALJackson

Watch for *Follow Me Back*, coming early 2018!

Want to know when it's live?
Sign up here: http://smarturl.it/liveonamzn

More From A.L. Jackson

Bleeding Stars
A Stone in the Sea
Drowning to Breathe
Where Lightning Strikes
Wait
Stay
Stand

The Regret Series
Lost to You
Take This Regret
If Forever Comes

The Closer to You Series
Come to Me Quietly
Come to Me Softly
Come to Me Recklessly

Stand-Alone Novels
Pulled
When We Collide

Coming Soon from A.L. Jackson
More sexy, heartwarming romance in the new Fight for Me series

Follow Me Back – Early 2018
Lead Me Home – Spring 2018

Hollywood Chronicles
A collaboration with USA Today Bestselling Author, Rebecca Shea

ABOUT THE AUTHOR

A.L. Jackson is the New York Times & USA Today Bestselling author of contemporary romance. She writes emotional, sexy, heart-filled stories about boys who usually like to be a little bit bad.

Her bestselling series include THE REGRET SERIES, CLOSER TO YOU, as well as the newest BLEEDING STARS novels.

Watch for FOLLOW ME BACK, the second sexy, heart-warming romance in the new Fight For Me series, coming mid-2017

If she's not writing, you can find her hanging out by the pool with her family, sipping cocktails with her friends, or of course with her nose buried in a book.

Be sure not to miss new releases and sales from A.L. Jackson - Sign up to receive her newsletter http://smarturl.it/NewsFromALJackson or text "aljackson" to 24587 to receive short but sweet updates on all the important news.

Connect with A.L. Jackson online:

Page **http://smarturl.it/ALJacksonPage**
Newsletter **http://smarturl.it/NewsFromALJackson**
Angels **http://smarturl.it/AmysAngelsRock**
Amazon **http://smarturl.it/ALJacksonAmzn**
Book Bub **http://smarturl.it/ALJacksonBookbub**
Text "aljackson" to 24587 to receive short but sweet updates on all the important news.